T0114983

# IN BETWEEN
# THE RAILS

## CHARLES F. MORI

iUniverse, Inc.
Bloomington

# In Between the Rails

iUniverse books may be ordered through booksellers or by contacting:

iUniverse
1663 Liberty Drive
Bloomington, IN 47403
www.iuniverse.com
1-800-Authors (1-800-288-4677)

ISBN: 978-1-4502-8180-5 (sc)
ISBN: 978-1-4502-8181-2 (ebook)
ISBN: 978-1-4502-8182-9 (dj)

Printed in the United States of America

iUniverse rev. date: 10/12/2011

# ACKNOWLEDGEMENTS

Baker, Mike - for giving me the opportunity to learn, and instruct railroading

Bannister, Scott - for having the faith in me to promote me into management

Hardesty, Merlyn - for being my great mentor in the Federal Railroad Administration

Hassler, Al - for breaking me in as Nebraska Division Personnel Officer

Hoogeveen, Alison - for being one of my angels when I really needed it

Jacobson, Jake - for being the World's Greatest Railroader, and a great friend

Johnson, Bev - for being one of my angels when I really needed it

Krider, Vern - for having the faith in me to promote me into management

McCall, Donna - for keeping me in floppies for this book

McCall, Terry - for being the World's Greatest Friend, and having a razor wit

McShane, Tom - for hiring me initially in 1974, and directing me to management

Mori, Geraldine - for being the World's Greatest Mother, and one of my angels

Mori, William A. - for being a great brother, and sidekick, with a great mind

Mundorff, Norma - for being a great mother, whose generosity knew no bounds

Pringle, Fred - for being a great, gifted friend, a great Christian, and a great man

Ridge, William Allen - for being a tough, exceptional railroader, who taught me much

Weatherford, Dale - for having a great wit, and keeping us all smiling

Wyker, John - for hiring me as an Operating Practices Inspector in the Federal Railroad Administration, and being a great mentor, and friend.

Younghanz, Terry - for being a tremendous friend, and an unequaled strategist

# CHAPTER 1
# SAFETY IS OF FIRST IMPORTANCE
# IN THE DISCHARGE OF DUTY

Dead dogs, cats, skunks, raccoons, deer ... A blood-and-guts-smeared panorama of animal remains, painted on the highways. In the seventies, Loudon Wainwright III sang of a "Dead Skunk in the Middle of the Road." Jonathan Winters, with professor-like timing and delivery, once described a "Sail-Cat." This was a cat that had been run over so many times and dried by the sun that you could just pick it up and sail it off the road, Frisbee-like. Everyone sees the mutilated roadway matter in living-dead color and is more or less unaffected. It's normal. It's accepted. Animal death is part of life.

But a dead human is a sight rarely seen by another human. Humans are supposed to be mobile, kinetic, animated beings, with drive, purpose, emotion. They're not supposed to be dead like animals in the road.

But "dead" was what Ralph Dunne was. Some switchman would later remark that Ralph was finally "done" for good. Ralph had departed the third dimension awaiting his next conversation, which ideally would be with St. Peter, if he made the final cut. Because considering what was left of Ralph back at the earthbound railroad yard, habitation by a soul would have been pointless. He had been rolled up under a grain hopper car. Contact with the knuckle of the car had initially knocked Ralph to the ground. Then, while he was disoriented and on all fours, the car body sheared off the left side of his head, tearing away his cheek and ear. The monumental pain Ralph experienced at this instant was overwhelmed by two instinctually known potentials: this horrible life-changing event may worsen, and it might even be what people in the forties referred to as "curtains."

The grain hopper, which had four huge, vertically extended dump bins underneath the car, continued rolling Ralph's further-to-be-bludgeoned body. In the next two seconds, Ralph's spine was shattered in three places, rendering him a bloody, uncontrolled flesh-puppet. Ralph's roll stopped with his left foot over one rail, which was immediately sheared off by a huge steel wheel. A mindless, panicked reflex to "get away" stimulated his leg muscles to flex and extend in unison. The now bloody stump of his left leg slipped off the top of the rail. But his remaining right foot pushed inside the rail, thrusting him back across the inside gauge of the track, which was 4 feet 8½ inches. This caused Ralph's bloody, disoriented head, and his left shoulder, to be positioned over the opposite rail. At this point, Ralph's body was experiencing uncontrolled muscle spasms. The horrific scene was reminiscent of an animal that's hit by a car and exhibits random muscle-twitching movements until it finally dies.

A following wheel immediately severed Ralph's extreme upper torso and head from the rest of his body. The pulverized, severed upper torso dropped to the outside of the rail. Ralph's inconceivable pain had ceased at this instant, as his life also ceased. His early-seventies-style, lengthy, graying hair was splotched red with blood from the horrible ordeal that was now over. It all happened in a few quick seconds.

The best forensic doctor could only speculate exactly what time Ralph's soul bailed out, ideally headed for the High Country. An estimate was all that was needed by the coroner anyway. But there was no speculation as to Ralph's status on this earth. Blood-red, scattered body pieces and a mangled, fleshy ball were now all that remained of Ralph. The shoving movement finally stopped.

Ralph had been standing in between the rails, a cardinal sin in railroading. This is where the damage is done, as proven *en finale* by Ralph Dunne. Cars could be extremely silent when rolling down tracks singly, or in a "cut," as a group of cars is called. Even if being shoved, as was the case when Ralph was killed, car movements could be very silent. Roller bearings, which replaced friction bearings in the late sixties and early seventies, allowed rolling cars, or "stock," as they were sometimes termed, to approach imperceptibly, compared with their squeakier forerunners. The cars were Silent Death, just like *Jaws,* and they could mangle you just as professionally as a great white. And you would be just as dead, as Ralph's grotesque remains substantiated.

Ralph had been standing right in the middle of 16 Track when he gave the engineer the command to shove his direction: "Okay, Mel, shove this way." Signs on the railroad, whether they were verbal, over the radio like Ralph's, or hand signals or lantern signals, dealt with direction by telling the recipient of the command to come forward or move backward. Verbally, this could be accomplished by saying, "A-head," with the accent on the *a* (pronounced "eh") for "come forward." "Back 'em up, Harry" would be used for a backward move. Forward and backward commands referred to the direction the locomotive was facing. Or a trainman might say, "Bring 'em my way" or "Take 'em your way" without regard to locomotive direction. In the future, there would be rule arguments about whether or not "my way" and "your way" were considered directions.

These commands were almost as varied as the trainmen who gave the commands, not unlike CB radio chatter. So engineers had to be constantly on their toes. It was a *must* that engineers be *absolutely* sure they were not taking someone else's verbal command from another crew working on the same radio frequency. Technically, federal regulations required the locomotive number to be used, so there would be no question which job was to get the command. But the "good ol' boy" network was always invoked, and radio commands were diminished to "Shove ahead, Bob" when two Bobs could be working as engineers on the same radio channel, or "Shove ahead, double-header" when several crews were working with two locomotives coupled together, each being termed a double-header. More than one individual had shared Ralph's fate as a result of lax radio communications.

When Ralph gave the "Shove a-head" command to Engineer Mel Landers, he had miscalculated the cars' distance from him. He knew they were "back there somewhere," and he would get out from in between the rails when he felt like it. He'd done it successfully thousands of times before. Mel was shoving around a large curve and relying totally on Ralph for commands. It wasn't a "blind shove," another cardinal sin in railroad safety rules, because Mel knew Ralph was watching the point, protecting the shove. After all, Ralph did give Mel the command to shove a-head.

Ralph moved a lot of cars for the yardmasters. That was the idea. He had a good work ethic, except for one very unacceptable thing: a switchman should move the cars *safely*, first and foremost. Ralph took chances. For those who took chances on the railroad, it was only a matter of time, not unlike Christopher Walken's character in *The Deer Hunter*. A person's good fortune playing Russian roulette with safety ultimately became bad fortune.

It was a pleasantly warm, drizzly night, about 10:00 p.m., on June 5, 1999. Ralph had been railroading for twenty-eight years, hiring out in the spring of 1971. He had, not uncommonly, become too comfortable with his craft to worry about safety, and now, it was too late.

Several tracks over, Phillip Barnes, Central Pacific (CP) engineer, and his crew were getting 9 Track together for doubling it to 4 Track, and then to 16 Track, where Mel's crew had been getting 16 together. The final double was to become the SKBC Train. When cars are switched into tracks for classification and routing, they do not always make the coupling, so crews with a locomotive go into these tracks and couple them up, which is known as getting the track together, or in some yards, "trimming." One crew will then be directed by the yardmaster to "double" all these tracks together, after they are all coupled. After the final double, the crew will take the newly made-up train to the "outbound," or departure, yard. There, carmen will couple the brake pipe between the cars by hand, allowing the cars to receive train-line air from the locomotive compressors and air reservoirs, after the locomotives are attached to the train. This allows the engineer to set and release brakes on the train when performing required air tests. Local jargon for connecting the brake pipe is known as "lacing up the track." Carmen or trainmen could have this duty. Ralph Dunne wouldn't be having this duty, or any others, ever again.

For Phillip Barnes, the night had been quiet and normal. In the cab of the locomotive, he was subconsciously listening to the rhythmic *sh-sh-sh* of the vacuum-powered windshield wipers. He'd previously adjusted their speed, using the grooved brass knob in front of him under the engineer's window. The wiper speed adjustment was hair-trigger. If you didn't get it adjusted just right, it would *SH-SH-SH!* in a frantic, slamming motion, back and forth. But tonight, Phillip had it adjusted perfectly to wipe the buildup of drizzle away in a quiet metronome of sound. The rhythm of the wipers was somehow peaceful. The faint smell of diesel fuel was in the air, to which Phillip's olfactory senses had long since, like all railroaders, become immune. Railroaders' wives and girlfriends often commented to their men, "You smell like the railroad." The railroaders smelled nothing.

Phillip had been listening to the conversation between Ralph and Mel on the radio, as a good engineer does. An engineer needs to know where everyone is working in his vicinity *all* the time. Right now he was listening to Mel's excited voice asking, "Ralph, do you read this radio? Hello, Ralph?" It was every engineer's worst nightmare: no response from crew members. But it happened quite often. Almost 100 percent of the time, there was a logical explanation for a communication lapse. The most common was crew members taking a "spot," what railroaders called a break. The term came from the placement of cars at an industry for loading or unloading. A car might need to be placed in Track 3, Spot 2. A spot could be for a smoke, or to take a leak, or maybe to just ensure the crew didn't do "too much work," thereby implying to the officials that they should be doing that much work all the time. Engineers would call and crew members wouldn't answer, leaving the engineers to run the mental gamut of possibilities, the last—and worst—being Ralph Dunne's fate.

There could also be radio failure, although over the years, radio communication had evolved into adequacy, especially when compared with the radio communication of the late sixties and early seventies. But radios still tended to cut out near large objects such as towers or buildings, batteries still became weak, and trainmen still dropped them or left them at the last location. Mel Landers was hoping for any of these explanations, and not for what had actually occurred.

"Are you hearing that, Casey?" Phillip said to Herman Jones, his assigned yard foreman, who was nicknamed Casey because of the railroad affiliation with his name. It was a natural. There had to be hundreds of Casey Joneses in the railroad industry.

"Yeah, I do, Phil. Hello, Ralph, you read this?" No answer. "I think I'll go have a look, Phil."

"Let me know as soon as you find out something, Casey," Phil replied, for some reason sensing the worst.

A few minutes later Casey's voice came back on the radio, extremely anxious, but attempting to sound official. Casey was breathing loudly and heavily, but it wasn't from being out of breath. It was because he had just received a shot of adrenaline from seeing what most humans never see, unless at an open-casket funeral service. And this dead human wasn't in one piece, dressed in a suit, "never looking so good." Casey was viewing a horribly mangled, headless, armless, and footless dead human, a scene that would provoke many to spew. Blood was everywhere. Entrails were everywhere. Pieces of Ralph were scattered for about seven car lengths, about 385 feet, since a standard boxcar's average length is 55 feet. Subconsciously, Casey smelled an odor reminiscent of the one when his grandmother would cut up chickens on newspapers, on her red linoleum countertop. The drizzle seemed to trap the smell at ground level. When Casey found the Ralph-part that was the sheared-off upper torso and head, the visual did not equate to logic. The eyes were half open and bulging in a mindless stare like those of a gigged bullfrog.

"Wuh-we have a f-fatality on Track 16," Casey managed in a shaky and breathless but official-sounding voice. "Phil, you might try to get a trainmaster. Ralph didn't make it." Casey knew the locomotive radios were generally stronger than the walkie-talkies used by the trainmen. Monitoring the conversation, a concerned Mel Landers swallowed hard and felt a dizzying sickness overwhelm him.

"Got it, Casey." Phil switched his radio to a different channel. "Engineer Barnes to Trainmaster Simon. Come in. Over."

"Yeah, Barnes, this is Simon. Over." Trainmaster Simon had been having coffee at the local Dunkin' Donuts. Things were quiet. Trains were going to make schedule. Simon had played the evening chess game of train makeup, transfers, industry switching, and run-through expediting well. He was taking a well-deserved "spot." All was well—that is, until this radio message.

Phil continued, "Trainmaster Simon, we have a man down, possibly deceased, here at the North Yard, on 16 Track. It's Ralph Dunne. Better call an ambulance, and we may need the coroner." Phil shook his head, pondering the thought of not seeing Ralph around anymore. Phil was pretty sure from Casey's initial communication that Ralph was dead.

But somehow he couldn't bring himself to express the obvious finality. He was thinking, *There might still be a chance,* not having seen what Casey saw: that Ralph was now in pieces. Phillip didn't deal with death well.

Trainmaster Simon choked on his Dunkin' Donuts coffee after Phil's transmission, swallowing as much air as coffee. "Stand by, Phil," Simon said with a slight cough, further clearing his throat. Then he sighed a deep sigh. Simon had known Ralph Dunne for years. On the railroad, everybody knew everybody. All railroaders knew in the back of their minds that at any time, they too might share Ralph's fate. Simon was glad he was an official. There was a whole lot less chance he would ever be in potential life-threatening jeopardy in between the rails. He'd already paid his dues there, working as a switchman when he was younger. He was in between the rails thousands of times then. But as an official, there would rarely, if ever, be any reason for him to be "in there." That was a common duty for the carmen and trainmen. He called the emergency responders.

Engineer Mel Landers had proceeded exactly as he was supposed to. He had taken the command from Ralph, repeated it, and began shoving ahead. When he hadn't heard additional commands from Ralph, he had stopped. A time-proven safety rule in railroading is that if an engineer is in doubt, he doesn't move the locomotive. Mel had never even been "on the ground," what railroaders referred to when they were no longer on the rails, or "derailed." Usually, there was a time when everyone was on the ground, often through no fault of his own. A job could have run through a switch right before another job moved over the switch from the opposite direction. The following job through the switch would split it, with the left wheels taking one route and the right wheels taking the other, and the locomotive would derail. Enginemen and trainmen were taught to look at the switch points, rather than rely on the switch target for direction, for this very reason. A car might simply be defective and jump the track. Or, some kids could have deliberately placed iron or wood on the rails that would derail a car or locomotive. Once, a heavy ice buildup on the rails actually caused a car to "take the ice" rather than the rail. There were literally dozens of reasons a crew could wind up on the ground. But Mel had worked 3:00 p.m. North Yards for years and had been very careful, as were his crews. At times, some of the cars

Mel's crews had been switching had wound up on the ground, but his locomotive had never been on the ground. He was a safe, conscientious engineer.

Years later, operating rules would add distance to the direction command, increasing safety. "CP 628, shove west twenty car lengths." If the engineer did not hear another command, he was to stop in half the distance stated—in this case, ten car lengths. But the rule wasn't in effect yet for Mel Landers and Ralph Dunne. It could have made a difference.

Mel had never even had any "brownie points," which were negative points, usually accrued in fifteens or thirties and assessed for various perceived or actual infractions of railroad operating, or safety rules. When one had built up a total of ninety points, a "fair and impartial" hearing, known as an "investigation," was convened, after which the railroader might be "fairly and impartially" fired. He would later return after union labor and management negotiations determined total time off. A person could also achieve "brownies" by missing calls. If the railroad hired you, they expected you to be available to work. Being dependable was everything in railroading.

And Mel Landers had been as dependable as an atomic clock over the years, and as dependable as any employed by the Central Pacific. The North Yard yardmaster loved seeing Mel on the job, because he knew he would get extremely conscientious, safety-oriented work performances out of him. That's the way Mel Landers always worked. But tonight, the performance, even though still conscientious, resulted in tragedy. It was a tragedy that all who viewed Ralph's remains would have sealed in their memories forever like some grotesque mental tattoo.

The ambulance siren began after only a couple of minutes, since St. Mary's Hospital was very close to the Central Pacific Railroad's North Yard. Over the years, the CP had not had to call on the emergency services of St. Mary's very many times, thankfully.

"Phil, you still with me?" Trainmaster Simon disregarded the radio rules in his excitement.

"Yeah, I read you, Bob," Phillip replied, still on Simon's channel and neglecting to say "Over," the correct verbal procedure.

"Phil, I'm about there. I'll let you know about all this. We'll probably need you to come in and make some statements ... what you heard on the radio, weather conditions, visibility, and so forth … Casey and Jamey too." Trainmaster Bob Simon was referring to Yard Foreman Jones and Field Man Albright, who had been "taking a tab," writing down car numbers in the hold yard for comparison with the yardmaster's computer printout. Jamey Albright had been listening on the radio also, but he was too far away to be directly involved. He was on the way back to Phillip's locomotive.

Phil switched his radio back to the standard yard channel. "Engineer Barnes to Field Man Albright. Over."

"Yeah, I'm headin' that way, Phil. I heard it." Both Casey and Jamey had been switching channels on their walkie-talkies, listening to the conversation. Jamey Albright had stopped for a couple of beers after work many times with the likable Ralph Dunne. Ralph was the "lovable rogue" type, always joking, laughing, and teasing. Jamey didn't know how he felt about anything right now.

Phil again changed to Simon's channel. "Bob, we'll wait till we hear from you. Casey and Jamey both heard. They're both on their way. Over and out," Phillip said, correctly applying the radio rules.

"Thanks, Phil," Trainmaster Simon replied with regret and sadness in his voice, again too distraught to correctly apply the radio rules.

For many years, the majority of railroad operating and safety rulebooks listed as the first rule, "Safety is of first importance in the discharge of duty." It was, is, and will always be absolutely true. Ralph Dunne had violated the rule, and it had cost him his life.

The minutes of waiting for Simon seemed like hours. Phillip Barnes thought about the last twenty-five years and wondered how he, his younger and much beloved brother, Paul, and his best friend, Barry McAlister, had gotten stuck down here at the railroad. He remembered April 1974. It was April 15, to be exact. He, Paul, and Barry had gotten out of their various branches of service in the early seventies. All three had lucked out, losing neither their lives nor any body parts, as thousands of other Americans did during the Vietnam years. Phil and Paul met Barry in grade school, and they all went through junior high and high school together. Phil and Paul finished college together. All three had attained degrees. And all three had merely been "existing" at the railroad for twenty-five years. Well, two of the three had been.

After finally finishing college and completing their military obligations, a very good friend of theirs, Ned Lingle, had told them the Central Pacific was hiring. Ned had been the proverbial "wild child" in high school, playing sports with Phil, Paul, and Barry, and playing chicken with his young life, overindulging with every known and senselessly cherished vice of the young. Ned had perfected an ingenious way to serve rum and Coke in the car, without the visual "whistle-blow" of a partial fifth in the car seat. He simply poured out the window cleaner from the water reservoir under the hood, cleaned it, and then added rum. Then he pulled the connecting tube from the wiper squirters and pushed it inside the car, under the dash. The gang would go through a drive-in, get Cokes, and then push the wiper squirter button. Voila: a perfect shot of rum for the Coke with no evidence of a bottle. But after a stint in Vietnam himself, Ned had experienced the proverbial "one-eighty." He had joined the Marines already a "killer," but he returned as a godly flower child. Ned had correctly attributed his literally miraculous escapes from sure death in Vietnam to the Lord's will. As a result, he had decided that everything he did in life would be for the Lord, in reciprocal thankfulness. He was now working for the CP and earning money to help him finish seminary, where he was currently enrolled. Ned had heard Phil, Paul, and Barry were looking for work.

"You don't have to stay," Ned told them, "but while you're making your minds up about what you really want to do, it's a decent existence and excellent money. God bless all three of you. Hope it works out." Ned had used God's name in high school, but *bless* had not followed the name.

None of the three were specifically long-term goal-oriented at this point in their lives. In the mid-sixties, the government chose a goal for them in the form of the draft. Aside from this forced goal, eventually Phil, Paul, and Barry had all met their college goals also. It was both a societal and a family expectation for many in the boomer generation. But none of the three had set long-term goals. What would have been the use if they hadn't made it through the military alive? The mid-to-late sixties were so intense and convoluted that survival and delirium seemed the best approach. Who cared about a future that might not happen? Some boomers *were* goal-oriented. But Phil, Paul, and Barry were not. They were degreed and nonmotivated for the most part, in a "now what?" mode. They had successfully stayed alive through the war years, but none of the three had focused on any life plan. The words *with no direction home* from the Dylan song "Like a Rolling Stone" was a bull's-eye.

So after Ned's call, all three went to CP headquarters in Kansas City, Kansas, to fill out applications at the personnel office. Tom Moffat, the division personnel officer, had asked them before looking at their applications if they had finished school.

"High school, or college?" Barry had asked.

"You guys went to college?" Tom asked, misjudging their ages.

"Yeah," Phil said, smiling. "We're all degreed." It sounded like a disease requiring quarantine when Phil said it.

"What in?" Tom asked excitedly, knowing that hiring degreed individuals would be a feather in his CP cap.

All three young men answered at the same time. Phil said, "Philosophy." Paul mumbled, "Psychology." Barry said, "Business."

"You have a degree in psychology?" Tom asked, double-checking with Paul.

"Yeah," Paul replied, almost sounding bored. Although Phil and Barry were sort of excited about the prospect of railroad employment, Paul basically didn't care that much.

"No wonder you don't have a job," Tom quipped while smiling, and then added, "That's what my degree is in, too. And you, Phil ... lots of potential for philosophy majors, huh? Big-time bucks."

Phil, Paul, and Barry liked Tom. He was a no-BS type, who called it like he saw it but was still diplomatic in doing so. And, Tom Moffat was not averse to adding humor to the conversation at any time, something all three young men enjoyed.

"Barry ... looks like you're the only one we can use, with a sensible degree. Seriously, if you guys pass your physicals, we'd like to have you all. We don't get many degreed people down here, and CP likes to pull from the ranks when they hire management people." Tom winked and nodded as he said this. Phil and Barry nodded back. Paul was expressionless. "Trains are *the* most efficient way to move *anything*! CP is the biggest and best railroad! You're going to like it!" Tom was feeling the CP Loyalty Gremlin beginning to surface. "I'm setting up some appointments for physicals. If you pass, switchman's class starts Monday. I should have the results later today. Give me a call first thing in the morning."

That was twenty-five years ago.

# CHAPTER 2
# THE NEW RAILS

On April 15, 1974, switchman's class convened with some disinterest, yet still coupled with the minor anxiety that accompanies any brush with the unknown, in any situation. Inane conversations transpired between some of the prospective railroaders. Others thumbed nervously through the handouts and rule books already on the desks where they sat.

Enter Peter Steinman, switchman-brakeman extraordinaire and resident yard snitch, as the new trainees would find out later when they began regular yard assignments. He was the kind who could tell nonstop jokes and smile all the time, but would turn your posterior in for a nickel ... even less. Peter viewed this "ratting-out" behavior as a tremendous asset for management potential, a status for which he dearly longed and for which he would have sold his mother and anyone else he deemed marketable. Oh, to be *someone*.

As he walked in and faced the class at this moment, however, he *was* someone. He was the CP authority figure for the new trainees, and they were relegated to listening to his instruction, taking his tests, and laughing at his semi-sorry jokes for the next ten days. Then they would ideally be considered trainee switchmen-brakemen. Peter had about thirty-five years' seniority, and like him or not, people had to admit Pete was "by the book." He had the "whiskers," which meant enough seniority, to hold "bum" jobs, which referred to the overtime jobs that delivered a "drag" to a foreign yard. A drag was another name for a cut of cars when they were pulled for delivery. These jobs would switch in the yards for a few hours, go to dinner, or "beans," as was the railroad term, and then deliver the drag, passing the bums in their bum dwellings, under certain choice bridges, hence the name. "Beans" was the operative term, because railroaders on different jobs ate around the clock and never really knew if they should still call their second meal of the day "lunch" if it occurred at 3:30 a.m. "Beans" sufficed for any time railroaders were directed to eat, and no doubt also referred to the actual cuisine consumed during the Depression years.

In fact, these bum jobs were extremely sought-after by Depression-baby railroaders who were still around in the early seventies. They wanted to make all they could, as long as they could, never wanting to be without, ever again. The reward for holding a bum job was time and a half after eight hours, with at least four hours overtime, and usually much more, on a daily basis. The excessive overtime occurred for several reasons. When crews delivered to other railroad yards, a crew wagon, or "jitney," as it was called on the Central Pacific, was dispatched to pick up the crews. They were usually Chevrolet Suburbans. Sometimes the jitney would be waiting as the crews arrived. But most often it would not show up till much later. This could be because of other assignments or the driver being blocked by a train, or simply because the driver got lost. The crews were on the clock this entire time, at time and a half. Sometimes dispatchers and control operators could not move the crews because of other higher-prioritized rail traffic, and the crews would "die" behind a red block signal. This referred to exhausting their time on duty at twelve hours. After twelve, they could no longer perform "covered service," as it was termed. And sometimes the local yardmasters at the foreign yards would literally forget about the crew, after having placed them in a track for yarding their drag at a later time. The crews would deliberately keep silent, making that good time-and-a-half money until someone finally checked on their whereabouts.

By government directive—the Hours of Service Act of 1907—it was unlawful, after 1970, to work crews longer than twelve hours. After twelve hours, crews claimed what was called "tow-in time." This tow-in time was also time and a half. The crews didn't do any more physical work after twelve hours, but they were still on the clock till they "tied up," rail-speak for ending their shift, like cowboys ending their day tying up their horses. Locomotives were sometimes called "horses," referring to the horsepower and pulling ability, and they too had to be "tied up." Phil had always thought draft horses were called that because they pulled draft beer, given the St. Louis Anheuser-Busch Draft Horses Team. Budweiser was the beer of choice in high school for Phil, Paul, and Barry. But the word *draft* referred to a pulling force, opposing a "buff," or bunching force, both of which were common in-train forces to every train operation. The diesel shop was appropriately referred to as "the barn."

It was not uncommon for crews to claim six hours of overtime, which amounted to more than another day's pay. Five hours and forty minutes of overtime equated to another eight hours' pay of straight time and was referred to as "double-bubble." So the bum jobs were quite lucrative. But a person could give up his entire life for a bum job—and usually did. Engineer Sam Harker worked all his rest days at time and a half, and holidays at double time and a half on his bum job assignment, and made more than the division superintendent.

Peter Steinman could hold a bum job but preferred to make much less money as a trainer, because the trainer job had a certain amount of prestige associated with it. At least that's how Peter perceived it. It also allowed him to rub elbows with the local officials. The Central Pacific operating rule book had a line that read, "To obtain promotion, ability must be shown to accept greater responsibility." Peter viewed the training classes as just that, and so did local management. The only problem was that Peter, at sixty-four, was about ready to retire. His hope was that he could grab an eleventh-hour promotion and "up" his retirement. Although Peter had developed his apple-buffing abilities at an early age, the Central Pacific local managers would never promote him because he was too valuable as a yard snitch. Why promote him and bring him into an office, when he was more effective working among the crews, reporting information back to the bosses?

Peter was immaculately dressed, with a white shirt, a CP officer trademark at the time, and pressed black pants. His hair was gray white and slicked back with too much tonic, and his nose was bulbous from endless happy hours. His eyes were squinty from working daylights in the sun. He began his instruction after a brief introduction by pointing out the fact that his shoes were shined and always *were* shined. He then snorted, inhaling through his nose in a semi-laugh and further squinting his eyes, as if he'd said something amusing. Barry nudged Phil, and they glanced at each other and rolled their eyes … eye contact that said, "This guy is a frickin' genius."

Phillip Anthony Barnes was the eldest son of Harold and Rose Barnes. He was named after his uncle Phil DeSimone. He and his brother, Paul Joseph, were half Italian, as their mother, Rose, was a second-generation Italian from the old country. Rose could speak excellent English, but when she became excited, she would begin to stick an -*a* on the end of a word or two, and sometimes lapse into full Italian. And she usually *was* excited. Phil had often wondered, when people asked him his heritage and he said "half Italian," why he wasn't accepted as simply "Italian," the way African-Americans are accepted as African-American, no matter how many other bloodlines they had other than African. A little was enough. Rose was as dark as Harold was fair-skinned. Her eyes were very dark brown, almost black, and Harold had milky blue eyes to go along with his relatively pale complexion, which the sun blitzed to crimson every summer when he accomplished his perpetual yard work. Harold was tall. Rose was short. Phil had often wondered if their parents were attracted to each other because of their opposite looks and personalities. But then, being a philosophy major with almost enough hours for a minor in psychology, Phil would *always* wonder about things like this. Phil tended to be like his father, laid-back, classy, thoughtful, and extremely easygoing. Paul tended to be more like his mama, with a penchant for excitability. Unlike Rose, it took Paul a while to get there. But once there, it was a sure thing there was an "ow-ee" in someone's or something's future.

One time Rose, who was an excellent cook, caught a mixture of olive oil, butter, and bacon grease on fire in a pan on the kitchen stove. The resultant flash lit up the kitchen, and Rose was screaming, "Oh my God, oh my God" in terror, holding on to her substantial breasts with one hand in the middle and fanning the air in front of her face with the other. The boys had witnessed Harold calmly put his newspaper down, walk toward the kitchen, and soak a large dish towel, laying it across the flaming skillet. The flames were immediately doused. Harold, without saying a word, returned to his chair and his newspaper. Phil remembered the whole scene looking almost as if it were in slow motion.

It was Harold's home version of Batman ... just as efficient, without the bravado. That was Harold.

At the opposite end of the spectrum, Rose, although a very good Catholic woman, tended to be high-strung, volatile, and seemingly always dealing with some supposed crisis. Phil thought it took a personality like his father's to handle one like his mother's. Anyone else would probably have killed her after twenty-eight years of crisis-oriented marriage. But Rose had virtues most other women couldn't even begin to claim.

Every night at dinner, or "supper," as Harold called it, was like a night with Julia Child. Rose was that good. It was "bon appetit" nightly for the Barnes family during their family years. For Italians, life in general was a celebration. This celebration was never more evident than in an Italian kitchen. For Rose, great cooking was a way of life, how she'd been brought up. To her, her abilities were nothing special. Indeed, Phil and Paul, as kids, took Rose's substantial culinary ability for granted. But Harold never did. He, like Rose, had been through the Depression as a child, and he had had to eat delicious navy cuisine during World War II. So Harold never, ever tired of Rose's wonderful meals, and considered himself extremely lucky.

More important, Rose also possessed that greatest of traits, *loyalty.* In twenty-eight years, Rose had never even fantasized about another man. She was a striking woman, still with a great figure even though crowding fifty rather closely in 1974. Her beautiful Sicilian complexion was absent the lines of most women in their midyears, belying her age. Over the years, many men had served notice to Rose—some of them Harold's "friends"—that if she were "willin'," so might they be. But Rose had always dealt with these uncomfortable situations with a smile and a shake of her pretty head, her black eyes smiling a "thanks for the compliment," never returning the interest and *definitely* never telling Harold.

It was a very good thing Rose had never told Harold of these times, because Harold, although basically quiet, had been a heavyweight boxer in the navy during World War II. He had been stationed on a carrier in the South Pacific as an aviation mechanic. When he wasn't turning aircraft wrenches, he was turning jaws. Harold would box, and box, and box. Harold was awesome. No one could touch him. The few times he did get hit solidly, he never even moved. For his opponents, it was like hitting a tank. Then Harold would keep coming, throwing jackhammer rights and lefts. The result was usually a cold bucket of water on Harold's opponents' knocked-out heads. Everyone on the carrier was glad Harold was quiet and religious. Some even said he could have been ranked nationally, had it not been for the war.

Harold, with much complaining from Rose, had taught the boys to box at an early age, and directed that they go a couple of two-minute rounds every day before school. This led to embarrassing biff marks and scratches, and sometimes blood, even though the boys used sixteen-ounce gloves. Had schools been as aware of child abuse in the fifties and sixties as they are today, Harold and Rose would probably have been called by school authorities for an explanation.

The daily boxing had made Phil and Paul extremely tough, self-controlled, and self-assured. Along with the boxing lessons, Harold, as well as Rose, had instilled a keen sense of fair play in their sons, stressing the Golden Rule. The boys had grown up with both a Catholic and a Protestant background. It was the same God, after all. Rose and Harold had wanted to get married immediately after the war. They didn't want to forgo the physical with each other while experiencing the arduous though beneficial weeks of premarital requirements dictated by the Catholic Church, Rose's religion. People worried about sin back then. Harold was Methodist, and they were married in a Baptist church, on neutral ground, considering their differing religious backgrounds, but nonetheless holy ground. Phil had been born nine months and four days after his parents were married, putting an exclamation point on the obvious reason Harold and Rose were in a hurry to be married. Paul was born a year after Phil. Phil and Paul were comfortable with both forms of worship—Phil more than Paul, since Paul basically didn't care that much. Both boys were taught to be tough, but at the same time, to have compassion and respect for the dignity of others.

One time in high school, Paul was getting shoved around and called names by a guy who had accused him of "looking" at his girlfriend. The guy was a known tough guy and struck fear in most students. After unsuccessfully trying to coax the guy out of the fight, Paul worked him over in about twenty-five seconds. Students who had gathered around, hearing the tough guy's yelling and taunting, were so impressed with Paul's ability and quickness that they nicknamed him Taz, after Warner Brothers' famous cartoon character the Tasmanian Devil. The name stuck, and Paul became simply Taz to many of his classmates. Paul had enjoyed the fight. Harold had taught him and Phil to always attempt to avoid a fight, if possible. But if they were cornered, he told them, they should never get mad but get serious, think through their strategies, and win.

To the Barnes males, Jack Dempsey was a role model, who at only 187 pounds or so was as tough as they'd ever come. They enjoyed the alleged story of the time when Dempsey, in his mid-seventies, was riding in the backseat of a cab at night in a bad part of town. When the cab pulled up to a stop sign, two punks on opposite sides of the street ran to the cab to rob "the old man" in the backseat. As the punks opened the rear taxi doors, each reaching in to subdue the old man, Dempsey beat them both senseless—a little good news and a little bad news. The good news headlines on the *Punk Daily Register*: "An ol' man's in the backseat of the cab just right for robbing." The bad news: "It's Jack Dempsey."

At any rate, even though he was quiet at 6 feet 4 inches and 250 pounds, when it came to Rose, Harold would have killed these would-be romancers with two left jabs, a head fake, and a home-run right cross. Rose too was tough, maybe even tougher, pound for pound, than Harold, and tolerated no whining from Phil or Paul when they were youngsters. If either one would get a scrape or a scratch and begin to whimper, she would say, "You're-a no-a Spartan-a, Phil," or, "Some-a Roman-a soldier, you'd-a make-a, Paul."

One time in the fifties, Rose took Phil and Paul to their favorite entertainment at the time, a horror show. She took them to see *The Fly*, with Vincent Price. The boys were eight and nine years old. They were only minimally terror stricken, until the wife pulled off the cloth cover that was draped over her husband's fly-head. Paul immediately hit the aisle, attempting to sprint for the lobby. But in a move that would have made Mike Singletary proud, diminutive Rose instantly nabbed the back of Paul's T-shirt. At eight years old, Paul was nowhere close to the mountain of a man he would become, but he was still a pretty stout eight-year-old. However, he was no match for his little mama ... not even close. Paul just ran in place, his juvenile legs churning on the well-worn paisley-patterned aisle carpet. Rose had a vise grip on the middle of the back of his T-shirt, forming a horizontal cone. Paul eventually slipped and fell forward, catching himself with his hands, and finally stopped struggling. Phil remembered witnessing the whole incident as a "side show," sitting on the other side of his mother. It was the only way Rose would take them to the movies. If he and Paul sat together, it would be a continual slap-fight through the whole production, and Rose wasn't having that. The commotion was embarrassing for Paul, with Rose calling him "a big-a baby" while he ran to nowhere. The embarrassment was worse than the fear, and Paul finally settled back in his seat next to the aisle for more fly terror. Phil was just as scared, but couldn't get to the aisle over his mother, who wouldn't have let him out anyway. Besides, Rose was meaner than an old fly-head any day. Still, for months afterward, the boys could hear that nasty little voice from the miniature, flying version of the fly with the human head, screaming, "He-e-e-lp m-e-e! Please, he-e-e-lp me-e-e!"

Phil, like his father, was 6 feet 4 inches and had been quite a basketball star in high school, being awarded a partial scholarship to Missouri University. Paul, at 6 feet 3 inches, was shorter than his brother but broader, and like Phil, received a partial scholarship to MU, although his was for football. Neither of the boys, as is often the case with young people, was ready for more school after twelve years. Phil began attending MU in the fall of 1964. He managed to squeeze out three semesters before rendering himself a total buffoon, scholastically. He didn't take any of his finals at the end of the first semester of his sophomore year, a decision frowned upon by most university professors. He stroked a .75 on Missouri's four-point system, 4.0 being an A and so forth down the line. A .75 was so low, it was almost as if Phil wasn't even there.

As a sophomore, Phil pledged a prestigious fraternity that was basically Catholic. Unlike other fraternities, this one designated the cross as the symbol for their rings, something Phil held as very much hallowed. At the time he pledged, Phil thought he would follow his father's lead and major in engineering. He had taken calculus, college trig, German 103 (German reading, i.e., third-semester German), physics, and history. This curriculum proved to be more than enough to temporarily annihilate him when coupled with the extremes of pledging and some very serious drinking. As the semester progressed, complete with fraternity insanity, he fell behind and just gave up. After his splendid .75, he received a letter from Dean Myers, the dean of arts and sciences, which said, "Failure in one aspect of life does not necessarily denote failure in another." The words *does not necessarily* would echo in Phil's mind forever. To him, those words meant, "does not necessarily mean you're a dumbass, but we're relatively assured you *are*." Phil joined the air force and was drafted by the army while he was in basic training. "Greetings, Beloved." "Nowhere Man" by The Beatles was the number one song at the time Phil pledged and then flunked out. Phil was sure the song was about him.

Paul, who was a year behind Phil, was suspended the same semester Phil bombed his grades. Although Phil had tried to coax him, Paul didn't pledge, because basically, he didn't care that much. In Paul's freshman year, he made a 1.25. Both boys had majored in women, booze, and general jacking around, the pastimes that take out the majority of the freshman and sophomore classes. Drugs were not prevalent on midwestern college campuses in 1964–65, and were not yet in the mix of flunking devices. Phil and Paul were very bright and had made good grades in high school. But neither was ready for the discipline needed to succeed in college. The professors didn't care if you came to class or not. There were too many students for them to care. So because *they* didn't care, Phil and Paul didn't either. It wasn't the same as having their mom's terrific breakfasts and her constant prodding to get to school on time. At college, if the weather was snowy or rainy, Paul would roll over and go back to sleep rather than go to class. Sometimes he would sleep when it was sunny. Discipline at college was a different kind of discipline, without outside commands. It was personal discipline. Almost everything in college was self-imposed, especially success or failure. At this point in their lives, both Phil and Paul decided to impose failure on their futures.

Paul met a very beautiful, very interesting girl he became close with, in a freshman English class. Her name was Crystal Matthias. It took only one look for Paul to know she was different. In an era when the gloves were about to come off sexually and socially, Crystal had a definite aura of goodness about her, and one could tell there was no compromise in Crystal. She was a devout Christian and reminded Paul of Rose: tough and strong, but beautiful and loving. Crystal talked with Paul the entire semester about the Lord. Paul listened, and he enjoyed Crystal, but he really didn't seem to care about it all that much. He didn't understand. The two would remain friends throughout life, occasionally calling or writing each other. Communication with each other was always a nice experience for both of them. Paul would think often about Crystal over the years and wonder if she was supposed to be "the one." But during that semester, although he was attracted to Crystal, as was the norm for Paul, he really didn't care that much.

College was the first time Phil had ever experienced failure, and he hated it. He had never felt so inadequate. Most of his pledge brothers made their grades to be initiated, and he failed. It was true that most were freshmen and had easier courses, but Phil didn't view it other than he just didn't measure up. He really enjoyed his pledge brothers and became very close with several of them. He was amazed by their quick minds, their outstanding traits, and their ridiculously good looks. Every one of them was superbly exceptional. And Phil didn't remember any of them being cocky. He would never see them again.

Paul basically didn't care that much about his grades or college. He had no one to impress, so he didn't care about appearing unimpressive. When he found out Phil had flunked out the same semester he was suspended, he popped a couple of beers he had iced down in the back of the '55 Chevy Harold had bought him, handed one to Phil, and said, "Looks like we're just a couple of nitwits, huh, Philsy."

Paul was a linebacker in high school football and loved to screw up quarterbacks. His favorite pro was Tim Rossovich of the New York Jets, who, it was rumored, used to pour alcohol on his upper torso, set himself on fire, and then ring a doorbell somewhere. Rossovich also allegedly used to drink quarts of motor oil. Paul thought that stuff was great, and in his own ways, attempted to emulate Mr. Rossovich. At 225 pounds, Paul loved to blitz, and he believed the coaches when they said, "The quarterbacks get all the girls. Make them pay!" Paul enjoyed humiliating quarterbacks, and sometimes, if a guy was rumored to be a real "Oscar Meyer," Paul, after a Dick Butkus tackle, would make kissing sounds through his helmet at the quarterback and say, "My, aren't you pretty, today, Alice. See you next play."

At the end of his first semester, Paul received a letter from Dean Myers that was as degrading as Phil's. In true maniacal Taz style, Paul joined the marines, volunteering for Vietnam and adding whitening to both Rose's and Harold's hair color.

# CHAPTER 3
## MORE OF THE NEW RAILS

Barry McAlister had been Phil and Paul's close friend since grade school. They met one another for the first time in the third grade. Fran McAlister, Barry's mother, had moved to the Kansas City, Missouri, area from Los Angeles with her eight-year-old son in 1954. She had grown up on a small dairy farm near Vinton, Iowa, the middle child of seven children. She had driven to Kansas City after graduating from high school to seek employment, which she gratefully finally found with Trans World Airlines (TWA). A year later, she was offered a transfer to California, because Fran was not only exceptionally bright but also had a fine work ethic. She was one of the first women in business to be afforded an inter-company transfer. While in Los Angeles, she met and married Bill McAlister, Barry's dad, who played Pacific Coast League baseball and also grew up in the Midwest. While attending a minor-league ball game with her girlfriends from TWA, Fran was walking with them behind the backstop looking for good seats. She noticed that the catcher for the Oakland Hornets looked great as he bent over to retrieve a wild pitch. He *was* an Oak. Fran made it a point to sit behind the backstop while watching the rest of the game. Minutes later, Bill turned and ran toward the backstop again, this time catching a foul ball. When he braced himself against the fence after making the catch, there was beautiful Fran saying, "Nice catch!" The outside curve ball got him. Bill was hooked. Bill, like Fran, had grown up on a midwestern dairy farm, near Cameron, Missouri, where his parents raised Holsteins. They were married in three months, and a year from that first conversation, big little ten-pound Barry came into the world. When she learned she was pregnant, Fran went to one of the TWA business managers, Dennis Slater, informing him of her condition, and told him she intended to resign. Slater, who had been attracted to Fran ever since she'd first transferred to California and was aware of her extremely keen mind, told her that TWA hated to lose her, but that he truly understood. He further told her she could have her job back anytime she chose.

Bill McAlister had been assigned to oversee German prisoners during the war, and was still a little crazy from his war experience. He was a young, handsome, wild man, and dated many women before marrying Fran. He had always loved baseball, and after the war, he became a minor-league catcher. He dragged Fran and Barry all over the West Coast and elsewhere, even up to Calgary, Canada, playing baseball and hoping for an eventual major-league contract. With Barry only a baby at the time, it was too much for Fran, staying in shabby dwellings and feeling like she and her son were no more than vagabonds. After three years of this unwanted lifestyle, she told Bill, "You are going by yourself this season." After some screaming from both of them, Bill *did* go by himself to play ball. Fran returned to TWA, leaving Barry at the babysitter's. The following months saw the letters to each other dwindle. Fran eventually succumbed to the charms of Dennis Slater, who had pulled some strings to have Fran transferred to work under him, literally as well as figuratively. Dennis had immediately told Fran, referring to her life with Bill, "You deserve more than this." It was a very tired but standard and effective line that worked almost 100 percent of the time on a woman unhappy with her husband. It was a surefire score. It was one of the devil's best utterances. When Bill returned home from playing ball in the fall of 1950, Fran informed him she was leaving him for Dennis. After realizing killing Dennis wouldn't be the thing to do, Bill agreed to a divorce. Three months later, Fran became Mrs. Slater for four stressful and tedious years. Although Fran tried very hard with the marriage, she was never able to conform to the bartending position Slater had arranged for her at home. Barry recalled from his young childhood, "Mix me up one, Frannie, will ya?" Fran realized from the beginning she was married to a selfish drunk, but tried to make it work. Slater used to think of Barry as "that little bastard," but knew better than to voice that opinion around Fran. Like so many other miserable stepfathers, he wanted the woman but not the kid.

During this time period, Barry was lost. He longed for his daddy, Bill, and was reduced to being an occasional orphan. Barry hated being babysat. During the week, his babysitter was an old woman who smelled and from whom Barry felt zero compassion. The kid up the street who babysat Barry on the weekends used to torture Barry with sadistic games while Fran and Slater went out for drinks and dancing. He would get on top of Barry and slap him and laugh. He would hide from Barry, scaring him into thinking that he was totally alone. Then he would run at him and knock him over. Barry never told Fran. If she had just checked him, she would have noticed the bruises, the redness. But when she arrived home with Slater, the "party" continued. "Mix me up one, will ya, Frannie." And Fran swilled, too. So Barry was a lost, lonely little boy. TV was Barry's solace. He loved all the kid shows of the time, and when the *Mickey Mouse Club* hit the airways, Barry had his escape. He loved every aspect of that show.

Fran divorced Slater in 1954. After that, she decided she would continue working, raising Barry herself, without a "lousy man" to make her life miserable. She and Barry moved to North Kansas City, Missouri, for a new start, two doors down from the Barneses. As a result, Barry grew up accustomed to having them as *his* family, ever since he was eight years old. Phil and Paul were much more like Barry's brothers than his close friends. And Rose and Harold were like parents, correcting Barry when he needed it, as well as teaching him and yes, *loving* him. Harold and Rose were the *best*. They *were* Ozzie and Harriet.

And Fran was a second mother to Phillip and Paul, treating them as second sons. As pretty as Fran was, Harold Barnes never even looked at Fran with lust. He couldn't have cared less. He was an ideal husband for Rose, totally satisfied with her and her stable but sometimes high-strung ways. About all Harold ever did over the years was notice when Fran was dressed inappropriately for her age, which she was, quite often.

Fran really wasn't cut out for motherhood, caught up in the subconscious, flaky pursuit of emulating la-de-da Hollywood and all its unrealistic portrayals. The idea had rubbed off on her when she first moved to L.A. It was the "Iowa Farm Girl Goes to Hollywood" story. Although she never tried, Fran always thought she could have been an actress, and sometimes it was hard to tell she wasn't. As well as being attractive, she was always smiling or laughing, which she perceived correctly as enhancing her attractiveness. She emulated being full of life, like Loretta Young bursting glamorously into the room before prefacing the content of her TV show in the fifties. Fran was always attending a cocktail party somewhere, where she would be dressed immaculately yet somewhat inappropriately, exposing too much leg or too much breast, or both. She was always smoking, holding her cigarette between her index and middle fingers, palm up, fingers back, with supposed sophistication. An air of nonreality emanated from Fran, as though life were a screen test. Modern-day girls would have called her a "poser." Fran was bright, tough, and beautiful. But Fran was inherently mentally unbalanced. She was very good at concealing her sometimes almost insane inner feelings, realizing the inappropriateness of her thoughts ... just not her dress code. Occasionally, Fran's eyes would represent resident evil, but since she was always smiling, no one ever noticed. And usually, they weren't looking at her eyes. "Oh you never turned around to see the frowns on the jugglers and the clowns when they all did tricks for you," as Mr. Dylan wrote and sang in "Like a Rolling Stone."

Even though Fran appeared like Superficial Suzy, her big, wide, "flash-thirty-two" smile getting her through many a social situation, Rose liked her as soon as she met her. To Rose, Fran represented the tough, successful female she had envisioned herself as being. But unlike Fran, Rose never had the chance to prove as much, at least in the business world as Fran was doing. In a way, Rose and Fran lived vicariously through each other. Rose liked to listen to Fran's accounts of office shenanigans, since Fran landed a job with a local car dealership where she would work twenty years, achieving a small retirement. Fran, on the other hand, enjoyed Rose's commentary on the boys' behavior over the years, and actually learned some things about her own son through Rose's recollections of days with them. Fran had mistakenly assigned a mothering instinct to herself she actually did not possess, falsely assuming an attitude of "If only I could have been home with Barry." In actuality, she would not have been able to stand it. It wasn't that she didn't love Barry in her own way. She just needed to "go to work" to feel fulfilled. This trait also contributed to the failure of her marriage to Barry's father. She just needed to be going in general. Fran was totally opposed to housekeeping, and in her later years would develop a horrible hoarding obsession, bringing home piles and piles of stuff to surround herself with and gather dust. And yet, she still never stayed home to clean.

Barry's father, Bill, after five years in the minors, realized it probably wasn't going to happen for him and moved back to Cameron, Missouri, to be close to Barry. He joined the Cameron Police Department and married a wonderful woman, Martha, who, like Rose, had enough love in her heart for Barry as well as her own children with Bill. Eventually, Bill and Martha had four children and many years of a good marriage. Barry loved his younger brothers and sisters and did not consider them as "half," but whole, like the positive view of the half-full or half-empty water glass. It was a kick for Barry to look like them and have them look up to him. They didn't realize it, but Barry looked "up" to them, too. He didn't see as much of them as he would have liked while growing up, but Phil and Paul filled the sibling void very nicely.

Another positive for Barry besides his father moving back close to him was that Bill McAlister's parents still lived on their Holstein farm near Cameron. There were no Holsteins left since Grandpa and Grandma McAlister were now retired, but they still rented out pastureland to the locals. The locals raised Angus cattle. The McAlisters had always liked Fran when she and Bill had visited from California. They thought their son was too much of a philanderer to ever be successfully married. They also mistakenly perceived that it was Bill's negative treatment of Fran that drove her into Slater's arms. So Fran was always welcome on their farm. Fran wanted Barry to be near his grandparents, both sets, as much as possible. It was the main reason she moved back from California. She thought it was "right," but also wanted the grandparents to take some of the responsibility for raising Barry from her. On many Fridays after school, Fran would drive young Barry up to Cameron to spend the weekends at the McAlisters' farm. Barry, as well as his grandparents, loved it, and it gave Fran weekends free to enjoy her cocktail parties without worrying about Barry. Fran's own parents had retired early and moved from Iowa to the Ozarks in southwest Missouri.

As a child, Barry especially liked the pond on Grandma and Grandpa McAlister's property. He would sit and watch the pond denizens for hours. It was incredibly peaceful. When he first sat down on the bank, there was no evidence of movement anywhere around the pond. Then a red-winged blackbird would sing out, fly in, and land in the cattails to feed her babies. Dragonflies would glance off the surface of the water, hover a bit, and eventually land on a weed or shrub. Barry would try unsuccessfully to catch them. They had to be some of the fastest, most maneuverable creatures on earth.

A snake would slither into the water and swim across the pond looking for a frog-burger. At the water's edge Barry would see whirligig beetles swimming in wild, sporadic semicircles, and water striders that somehow miraculously could "walk" on the water. Under the shallow water, Barry would see dragonfly larvae looking for something to spear. They had an eating device very reminiscent of the alien in the *Alien* films with Sigourney Weaver. It would shoot out from under their larval heads and spear food, even fingerling fish. Barry saw what looked like a walking stick insect under the water but was actually a water scorpion, as the nature books Fran bought him would reveal. Catching and observing all these creatures gave Barry great satisfaction.

Sometimes Barry would walk around the pond at first, rather than sit. Many frogs would jump in and scoot left and right, deliberately kicking up a mud screen of protection. Barry would wade in and feel around on the muddy bottom and grab them. It made him fast. Eventually, the frogs Barry didn't hassle would pop their heads up, needing oxygen, and swim back to shore, again positioning themselves for some afternoon sun and food. Sometimes Phil and Paul would go visit the farm with Barry, and they'd all carry rocks down to the pond and paste frogs. They would also unscrew the handle from Grandpa McAlister's barn broom, wade out in the middle of the pond, and swing at dragonflies, occasionally actually hitting one. Barry remembered seeing the dragonflies actually "hop" over the broom handle as he swung, returning to the same position before darting off. Not even Hoyt Wilhelm could make a knuckleball do that. Both of these questionable endeavors added greatly to the boys' quickness and coordination for serious sports in later years.

But most of the time Barry was by himself when he was at Grandpa McAlister's pond. It was the most peaceful place he ever knew. Sometimes on the way to the pond through the beautiful pasture that the locals' cows kept well cropped, Barry would lie down on his back and watch the clouds change shape. The turquoise-blue sky looked huge and beautiful. When he would attend Mass or church with the Barneses, Barry would hear Psalm 23 and identify. When the psalm was read, "He maketh me to lie down in green pastures. He leadeth me beside still waters. He restoreth my soul," Barry thought of the peace of Grandpa McAlister's pasture and pond, and how he'd experienced exactly that. As a child, Barry understood why God wanted each of us to experience "green pastures" and "still waters." At the pond, he never once thought of the confusion of growing up without his own father in his house in an era that listed only 7 percent of homes in America as "broken." On Grandpa McAlister's farm, Barry didn't feel broken. He felt whole. It was *his* private paradise.

In the summertime, Grandma McAlister always had a wonderful garden growing, and Barry loved to wander through it, looking to see which bugs liked what plants. The tomato garden smelled good, and Barry thought it great to be able to pick and choose which variety of tomato he wanted. Grandma McAlister planted many types, but Barry's favorites were the Big Reds and the Ox Hearts, which Barry called "Ox Carts" when he was a child.

In the evenings, sometimes, Grandma and Grandpa McAlister would have some of Barry's relatives over to sit around in the yard and drink iced tea and fight mosquitoes. Barry never knew any of them very well, but he enjoyed, as usual, watching nature continue its amazing transition into the evening. Barry's favorite time was on the Fourth of July, when Fran too would attend, as would Bill and Martha and their kids. When it became evening, lightning bugs were always lighting. The smell of honeysuckle was strong and sweet, and Barry noticed these quick large moths, hovering at the honeysuckle blossoms and drinking the sweet nectar. Barry called them "hummingbird moths," because of their size, shape, and movement. But he later learned from the nature books that they were called sphinx moths or hawk moths. Further, Barry learned that the large, pretty green caterpillars he found on the tomato plants were the larvae of these beautiful, large moths. The caterpillars were called tomato hornworms, from the horn that extended from their rear quarters, probably to deter predators. Barry supposed the name *sphinx* came from the caterpillars' penchant to raise the front third of their bodies while resting, in a still, sphinxlike posture.

One day Barry was examining one of these caterpillars and saw that it was covered with dozens of miniature white vertically situated egglike things. The body of the caterpillar was not plump like the rest of the caterpillars, but was thin and emaciated. Back to the nature books: Barry read that there was a wasp that laid its eggs *in* the caterpillar, so that the wasp larvae could feed on fresh meat. The egglike things were wasp cocoons. The caterpillar was going to die. It had literally been eaten alive. Young Barry thought this extremely unfair, and mumbled to himself, "What a slow, horrible death." Barry was born a gentle soul, perhaps too gentle for his own good. But he didn't know any other way to be. Throughout his life, Barry would remain gentle and caring.

As a young adult, Barry was athletic and large, like Phil and Paul, and also stood about 6 feet 4 inches. Phil and Paul thought he was the best athlete they'd ever seen. Like Paul in football, Barry was a defensive wizard, and at defensive end, crashed through offensive blockers to hammer quarterbacks and tackle running backs, just like Paul. When Paul and Barry were involved together on a good tackle in high school, they really enjoyed it. One time when they had just sacked the quarterback together, Paul had said, "Nice goin', Bare." The offensive lineman they smashed through together thought Paul had called Barry "Bear," as in Bear Bryant of Alabama fame. Later that evening at the local Griff's, the lineman recognized Paul and Barry and said to Barry, "I can see why they call you Bear." From that point forward, it was "Bear McAlister." It also fit because Barry was the first to become hairy in junior high, and had a pretty good crop in the field as a man. So even though Barry was Phil's age, he and Paul, too, had a good brotherly rapport in the Bear and Taz years.

Barry had gone two years to William Jewel College while Phil and Paul were at MU, and had joined the army as an officer. But instead of going to Vietnam, almost a sure bet, he was stationed stateside, at Fort Leonard Wood, Missouri. It was there that he met Susan, his wife. She was a local service brat who grew up in St. Robert, Missouri. Her father was a master sergeant instructor at Fort Leonard Wood. Susan had been enamored of Barry from the minute she laid eyes on him, as he was with her. There was a seven-year age difference, and Barry, who like Phil and unlike Paul, tended to feel God in his life, thought God had "saved back" Susan for him. Barry viewed her as awesomely beautiful, and he treated her like a young lady.

Also at the time, Susan, who was only sixteen, lost her mother to cancer. Although the cancer had been correctly diagnosed as terminal, it was extremely devastating for Susan and her father when her mother's death finally occurred. Barry was there for them both at the time, and thereafter. As is often the case, the tragedy bonded all three of them even more closely together.

While stationed at Fort Leonard Wood, Barry took courses offered on base from the University of Missouri–Rolla, and graduated with a degree in business. Barry and Susan were married in 1973. A year later a miniature McAlister was born, Erin Estelle.

Paul returned from overseas, having served in combat close to the Mekong Delta. He was even tougher, and basically, cared even less about anything than he had before. In a semi-drunken stupor in 1972, he had sexual relations with a young, beautiful Spanish woman, Ramona, and unintentionally conceived a child, a beautiful little girl, whom Ramona named Rosalinda, or "Beautiful Rose." Ramona did not want to get married when she discovered she was pregnant, but Paul, though wild, still held close the parental values and virtues Harold and Rose had instilled throughout his life, and loved his child before she was born. After some reasoning, he convinced Ramona that they should try to accept each other, since physically they already had, and dedicate themselves for the sake of the baby. They got married without ceremony, a justice of the peace doing the honors, much to the dismay of Harold, and especially, Rose. Four months after they were married, Ramona gave birth to Rosalinda, who was very aptly named. She *was* a beautiful rose. Six years later, Rosalinda would giggle with delight when she heard Billy Joel's great song with her name in the title, "Rosalinda's Eyes."

But Ramona never even tried, and one time Paul returned to their home to find someone else's cigarettes in Ramona's ashtray. The normally psychology-minded Paul ignored the Freudian implications. Shakespeare said something to the effect of "To those that feel, life is a tragedy. To those that think, life is a comedy." This was one of those times that feelings won out over intellect. Paul had never had much faith that the marriage would survive, basically because Ramona just didn't have the character to be loyal. Ramona didn't even bother to cover up the situation. When Paul asked her about it, she just said, "We might as well get divorced, Paul." Paul left that day by going through the door without bothering to open it. After Paul had beaten his way through the closed door, which took one right linebacker forearm shiver and one left palm push, he pitched two twenties back through the Paul-sized hole. "Fix it," he said disgustedly to Ramona. Taz had a flashback. After Paul and Ramona parted, either Phil or Barry (Paul couldn't remember which) commented that it was better for Paul to depart from "Open Kimono Ramona." That talk ceased when Rosalinda began to understand English.

Phil was stationed overseas at Cigli Air Force Base, in Turkey, after graduating first in his class of barracks personnel in Weather School, at Chanute AFB, Illinois. Rose had bought the *Little Golden Book of Weather* for Phillip when he was a child, and he always enjoyed storms. The air base was about fifteen kilometers from Izmir, Turkey, which was south of Istanbul on Turkey's western coast. He was there for a year and a half, the standard tour for single airmen. Marsha Langley, his high school sweetheart, wrote him the entire time. Phil was the only one of their group who didn't receive a "Dear John" while overseas. He came close, though, he thought. He didn't hear from Marsha, who was attending the University of Missouri in Columbia, for about three weeks. She was an extremely beautiful sorority girl, having been elected queen of something (Phil hadn't paid attention), and was also an MU pom-pom girl. Since she had neglected to write him for three weeks, Phil wrote her a "see you around the campus" letter. He received an immediate reply from Marsha after she received his uncharacteristically indifferent letter.

The letter from Marsha began in one color ink and ended in another, with the explanation that she had been "busy" with tests and studying. This meant either of two things to Phil: one, it *was* the truth, and was understandable; or two, it wasn't the truth, but Marsha cared enough about him to represent it to him like it *was,* changing ink colors, as though she had indeed gotten busy in the interim between starting and finishing the letter. Either was fine with Phil. Both meant she cared.

Marsha was there at the airport with Harold and Rose when Phil returned stateside, and she looked incredibly beautiful to Phil, more beautiful than he'd ever seen her, all tanned and miniskirted. They had a wonderful, vivid time together during Phil's thirty days of leave before he was to report to Forbes AFB, in Topeka, Kansas. Marsha and Phil might have made it as man and wife, except for the constant separations. It was now only a couple of hundred miles instead of thousands, but it was a separation just the same. Separations are tough on youthful lives, when immediacy is always preferred.

Three months after Phil returned stateside, he and Marsha sort of gave up on each other. It was the hardest thing Phil had ever faced. He'd flunked out of Mizzou, and now he'd lost the love of his life. Couldn't he do anything right? Could anything go as he hoped?

# CHAPTER 4
## PHIL'S DESTINY

But that all changed one beautiful, warm Topeka summer evening. He and some of his service buddies were at the College Hill Inn, enjoying some burgers and brews. Very uncharacteristically for the Washburn University crowd, they actually spoke to the airmen from Forbes. "Hey, you guys want to go to a wild party?" That question had both the operative words associated with a great evening. *Wild* and *party,* when separate, were wonderful enough, but together, they were dynamite. The strictness of service discipline was beginning to melt away. After receiving directions, and grabbing three six-packs, Phil and his buddies were on their way.

It was the summer of 1968, and The Beatles were singing "Hey, Jude" on the local rock-and-roll station, on Phil's buddy's Camaro car stereo. All the young airmen were finishing off the song with the "Da-a-a da-a da-a da-da-da-da's" and laughing at nothing. When they got to the address, it was an old, large, white, turn-of-the-century house. Cars were parked everywhere, including several up on the lawn. Young people, also, were "parked" everywhere, sitting on the steps outside, on the porch, and obviously, situated throughout the house. "Jumpin' Jack Flash" by the Stones, one of Phil's favorites, was blasting from a rather respectable-sounding stereo system inside. "I was born in a crossfire hurricane … And I howled at the foggy, drivin' rain." There was a faint scent of marijuana in the air, combined with a strong scent of blooming honeysuckle growing on the latticework of the house.

As the young men walked around the step dwellers and porch dwellers, they were greeted with smiles and nods. It was almost *Twilight Zone* stuff for a day and age when long hair and facial hair were such a part of acceptance, so important to young people. Phil and his friends had shorter hair, and mustaches that could not fall below the corners of the mouth, á la air force directives. They *could* wear tie-dye jeans and flowered shirts when not doing service work, and did, but their facial appearances said "service clowns" to the local college kids. Amazingly, though, this strangely decent night in a town where it wasn't uncommon for college jocks to square off against service jocks (even though some of the service jocks had been college jocks, and some of the college jocks would become service jocks), everyone was in a wonderfully accepting mood. It was Topeka's version of a Haight-Ashbury love-in.

As they entered the house with their six-packs, a guy with long hair smiled and said, "You can put 'em in the kitchen, man. There's big tubs 'a ice and a coupla kegs. Don't worry. Everyone's drinking everybody else's beer anyway. Someone even mixed up some Purple Passion in that plastic wastebasket over there ... Six quarts of straight grain alcohol and several gallons of Welch's grape juice." This was going to be good.

Phil pulled off one of the four remaining beers from his six-pack and dropped the other three, still in the plastic sheath, in one of the four iced-down tubs in the kitchen. He walked back into the main room and found a spot on the floor just barely big enough for him to occupy in a sitting position, leaning over his knees pulled toward his chest, Budweiser in hand. Over in the corner, some freaks had tied several plastic six-pack sheaths together, hanging them from a light cord. They had lit the bottom sheath on fire, and the burning plastic structure was firing miniature air-to-surface missiles, complete with lifelike sound, at all those underneath. "Sonofabitch," someone yelled as the mini-missiles landed in their hair. Some of the freaks were too stoned to notice. Phil, although he thought there was too much furor over it, as depicted at the time in "Don't Step on the Grass, Sam," by Steppenwolf, did not partake in the smoking of cannabis. He was what his former fraternity brothers referred to as a "juice freak." Beer, and rum and Coke were just fine with him, and they were legal, and Phil reasoned they didn't screw up your lungs or brains, at least not as much.

So Phil was enjoying his juice at the great party when something happened he would never have thought possible. The thunderbolt got him. Right in front of him appeared the most beautiful pair of eyes Phil had ever seen. The girl had knelt down, facing Phil, in the very limited floor space, rested her forearms on Phil's knees, and gazed into his green Sicilian eyes. Her eyes were almost orange, they were so exquisitely light brown. Below the eyes was a beautifully symmetrical miniature Italian nose, not unlike Phil's larger version. Below the nose were two lovely, red Sophia Loren lips. The lips spoke to Phil.

"Hi," they said, smiling and parted to show beautiful white teeth.

Phil couldn't believe it. When he was nine years old, his uncle Phil DeSimone, Rose's much older brother, had said to him, "C'mere, Phillip," his voice raspy from smoking too many Petri cigars. He had pulled young Phil close to him with his arm around Phil's waist. Uncle Phil, a short, stocky Sicilian, smelled like smoke and Old Spice. "I gonna tella you somp-a-ting, Phil," he began. When Uncle Phil spoke the words, "I gonna tella you somp-a-ting," young Phil always enjoyed it. Old-country wisdom was about to be spoken. Uncle Phil's dark, thick eyelashes blinked, momentarily covering his large, always-expressive black Sicilian eyes. Then, his eyes slowly opened and stared into a private space known only to Uncle Phil. "Phillip ... Da tunderbolt-a. It-a will-a getta you some-a day. It gotta me. You aunt-a Josephine-a. One-a look-a. Dat-a was-a *it*. She gotta me. *It* gotta me. *It* will-a getta you, too, son. Some-a day ... *it* will-a getta you." Phil loved his uncle Phil, his godfather for whom he was named, and always remembered about the thunderbolt, but he didn't think Uncle Phil was right. He thought it was a combination of old-country romanticism and self-fulfilling prophecy. If you believe it will happen, it will. But Phil didn't believe, and it *was* happening anyway.

"Hi," Phil returned the greeting. "You Italian?"

"Half," the Loren lips replied. "How 'bout you?"

"Half," Phil also said. "My mom is an FBI."

"Which half is the best?" the Loren lips teased. "And what do you mean, *FBI*?"

"I think both halves are okay," Phil thought he said rather lamely, "and *FBI* is 'full-blooded Italian.'"

Again, for some reason, Uncle Phil came to mind. "C'mere, Phillip. I gonna tella you somp-a-ting. Deys-a only a-two kind-a people inna da world, son. Dose-a dat are Italian, and dose-a dat wish-a dey were. Ha!"

"Both halves look okay to me, too," the young beauty answered, still smiling the cover girl smile. "Dance?" she asked as she stood up, knowing Phil's answer.

"Sure," he said, emphasizing it more than he wanted to, because of the strain of getting up and a foot that had somehow gone to sleep. Usually calm, Phil was feeling a slight nervousness he wasn't used to feeling. His immediate and strong attraction to this young woman lacked logic, and Phil was normally very logical. Mr. Spock was his favorite *Star Trek* character. His always-lingering thoughts of Marsha completely vanished. A fast song Phil hadn't recognized had just ended, and "You're All I Need to Get By" by Marvin Gaye and Tammy Terrell was just beginning. It was right on. Ashford and Simpson's "Stand by you like a tree, and dare anybody to try and move me" described exactly how Phil felt about this young, vibrant woman, whose name he didn't even know yet. All the words to that song were romantically pertinent for Phillip, and he hoped they would prove to be the future. The thunderbolt was the Italian explanation of the Peckerwood experience, "Love at first sight," only with much magnification.

"May I ask your name, please? I'm Phillip Barnes." Phil felt some composure returning.

"I'm Carla De Capo, and I'm *really* glad I met you this evening," she said, appreciating Phil's manners.

Phillip slipped his big arms around Carla's waist. His hands had been resting on her shapely hips, holding her waist. Her hands had been gently pressed to Phil's large muscular chest. As he pulled her closer, she moved her hands behind Phil's neck and began gently rubbing the back of his head and neck with the ends of her fingers. It felt wonderful as Marvin and Tammy sang, "There's no ... no lookin' back for us ..." And there was no lookin' back for Phil and Carla. They went to breakfast together and thought about no one else but each other from that point forward. Before meeting Carla, all Phil could see was Marsha. Carla had now broken that chain. She and Phil were married eight months later in Topeka. It was a beautiful, large Italian wedding that lasted the entire weekend. There were only a few fights. Rose was delighted with Phil's choice, as was Harold. She would share with Carla her recipe for *sugo*, or sauce, which came from the old country. Harold, Phil, and Paul had no clue about what Rose did to the sauce to make it so good, and they never would. Carla would continue the traditional mystery and pass it on to her girls. There would soon be someone to pass it to. A lovely little girl was born to Phil and Carla a year and a half later. Her name was Angela.

After Phil's honorable discharge from the air force, he and Carla moved back to Kansas City so he could finish his degree at the University of Missouri–Kansas City, or UMKC. It was only sixty miles away from Carla's parents, so it was fine with her. Besides, she liked Rose and Harold very much. Also at this time, Paul finished college at UMKC, and he and Phil actually had some classes together. They both graduated, Phil with a degree in philosophy, and Paul with a BS in psychology, something Paul always felt was very apropos and went together like bread and butter—BS and psychology. Phil was extremely happy after finally getting a degree, but Paul basically didn't care that much. Paul had completed college because Rose and Harold expected it, and the GI Bill finished paying for it. And Paul enjoyed the beautiful babes at college. Barry and Susan had also returned to the Kansas City area from St. Robert when Barry was honorably discharged from the army.

Uncle Phil had started selling fruit from a cart when he was a boy in Kansas City's North End. As a result of his sixteen-hour days of very hard work, and his frugality and saving, he had turned his business into a fruit stand, then a small grocery store, and then a large grocery store. Then he sold it. He was fifteen years older than Rose and very well off in his retirement, though he still lived simply and, as a result, happily. When he heard Phil and Paul were graduating from college, he made a special effort to talk with the young men: "C'mere, Phillip and-a Paul. I gonna tella you somp-a-ting. I know-a you gonna graduate-a from-a college-a now. You two-a are bigga men-a on-a campus. Well, letta me tella you. We gotta no room-a for bigga shots-a in-a dis-a family. If I hear-a you-a two-a becomin'-a bigga shots-a, I gonna getta my fruit-a cart-a, and say, 'Hey-a, getta you'-a peaches and-a you'-a bananas! Dose-a two-a are my nephews-a Phil-a and-a Paul-a! Dey're-a bigga shots-a!'"

So now Phillip, Paul, and Barry were about to become railroaders. Phil and Paul figured it would be a good job for earning good money until something better came along. Paul also considered the Central Pacific a good source for child support money for Rosalinda, which it was. Barry figured it was a good way to earn money for dental school, something he'd always thought he'd like to do ever since he was a young child. Barry had planned to use his business degree as a stepping-stone for entering dental college. Although he hadn't experienced it yet, he had supposed that life in business was rather mundane, dog-eat-dog, and in general, quite uninspiring. Barry viewed it as a forum where mediocre people could work exceptionally hard, buff a few shoes, stab a few backs, develop a relatively respectable position and portfolio, and ultimately die in semi-opulence, telling themselves throughout the journey that they'd "made it."

As a child, Barry's dentist was Jewish, Dr. Finkelstein. Some of the kid patients had called him Dr. Frankenstein, because he was a large, hulking man, with a large jaw and big, hairy hands. But in reality, he was the nicest, most sincere, gentle dentist ever. Fran and Barry had gone to him ever since they'd moved to Missouri. When Barry was a younger patient, Dr. Finkelstein used to give him a capsule of mercury to play with, which Barry would lose almost immediately, usually in the car before he and Fran got home. Fran, in typical tough-gal style, had never used an anesthetic, so Barry did not use it either. To both Fran and Barry, the needle for the anesthetic was worse than the minor grinding, and you weren't left with "mouth numb" afterward.

One time in particular, Barry was to have some extra-sensitive work done. He needed three cavities drilled and filled, and one was between two teeth, necessitating use of the hardware clamp. Dr. Finkelstein had hypnotized Barry by first placing the overhead lamp light directly in his eyes, telling him how relaxed he felt. Then he proceeded to take young Barry, by suggestion, through a series of beautiful rooms.

Dr. Finkelstein began by having Barry mentally enter through a door, leading into a beautiful yellow room that had a nice, plush, comfortable carpet to lie down on, which the good doctor suggested that Barry do. He further suggested to Barry that this was the most beautiful room Barry had ever seen. He took Barry through red and blue rooms, in that order, each more beautiful than the last, ending

Barry's mental trip with the most beautiful room of all: the rainbow room. Much later in life, when Barry began feeling the Lord calling him, he would read that the colors in the temple were yellow, red, and blue, and wondered if Dr. Finkelstein chose those particular colors for the rugs because he was Jewish or because God was talking to him. Probably both, Barry thought. The rainbow room was also the most mentally comfortable, and Barry "fell asleep" on the beautiful rainbow-colored carpet. It was the most wonderfully comfortable feeling he ever remembered, aside from Grandpa McAlister's farm. He had not felt like he'd been hypnotized, but the procedure had taken two and a half hours, and it seemed like only fifteen minutes to Barry. Dr. Finkelstein was Barry's dentist for the majority of Barry's childhood, and Barry wanted to be a dentist basically because of him. Besides being nice, Dr. Finkelstein was always going on cool trips all over the world. Being a dentist seemed like a nice gig to Barry.

However, when Barry was about twelve, he informed Dr. Finkelstein that he too wanted to be a dentist. Dr. Finkelstein honestly remarked to Barry, while he contorted his face in a frown-smile-squint, "Barry, why on earth do you want to do this ... sticking your hands in people's mouths all day, smelling their bad breath? Why, Barry?" It was the first time Barry was aware of an "all that glitters" side to life. But regardless of Dr. Finkelstein's negative reinforcement, Barry still imagined himself with a white coat on (not realizing some modern dentists would dispense with that tradition), taking care of people's teeth, and making fine money. Now Peter Steinman's monotonous voice was pulling Barry slowly down on the plush, luxurious carpet of the rainbow room.

As Tom Moffat alluded to, neither Phillip's degree in philosophy nor Paul's degree in psychology prepared them for career fields with a high-reward potential, meaning monetary reimbursement. It looked like they were doomed to be poor and bright if they stayed with their respective degree career fields. They had been to job placement businesses and found the people there were more interested in making their commissions than they were in aligning their clients with beneficial and logical career choices. For the time being, the railroad seemed like a sensible solution for all three. It was extremely good money, but Phil and Barry would find later that this too was classified under the "all that glitters" category.

Tom Moffat was amazed that he was able to hire three degreed individuals. The Central Pacific liked to take their management potentials from the ranks, the logic being that to learn the craft from the ground up was ideal for management comprehension. Directives to be given at a later date would have greater impact if the officers issuing them conceptualized the work involved. And again, anyone the personnel officers could hire who looked like management potential also represented the potential for them to have a feather in their CP caps later. "Yeah, I hired him. I'm a good judge of horseflesh." And although no one bothered to tell Peter Steinman, the Central Pacific (like all railroads in the 1970s) was beginning to see the relationship between progress, black ink, and hiring degreed individuals for railroad management. Before this time, degrees were not considered that necessary. Twenty-five years of railroad experience trumped a degree anytime. But as Dylan had sung a decade earlier, "And the times, they are a-changin'."

Having a personnel officer was a relatively new concept for the Central Pacific. Previously, the railroad workforce was made up of family and friends of current railroaders. This worked, because these new hires were already acquainted with the odd hours, time demands, and generally dislocated lives of railroaders. It increased the odds of them staying around for additional abuse in the future. They knew what to expect. The prevailing sentiment, "If it was good enough for Dad, it's good enough for me," added to the potential for a new hire staying on board. It was traditionally, "The sons of old men porters and the sons of engineers," as Arlo Guthrie reminded us in "The City of New Orleans" in the early seventies. Porters' sons usually became porters, and engineers' sons usually became engineers at that time in history. But when the passenger era ended, the need for subservient crafts also ended, with the exception of Amtrak. So the result was an employee workforce in the transportation crafts that was made up predominantly of white males. And engineers' sons still became engineers.

But the civil rights legislation of 1964 was coming into fruition in the seventies, and to keep Uncle Sam off their backs, the railroads all hired massive personnel departments, sometimes called human resources, to ensure government social stipulations were met. Central Pacific's approach was to study the local demographics on the various minority populations at certain points in their system and ensure that their workforce reflected the same percentages at these locations. Although it was a fair approach, it did not bode well for the railroad traditionalists. These were the superintendents, switchmen, conductors, and engineers who wanted the railroad to hire their sons, nephews, friend's children, and so on, as had been the norm since the railroads began. They just didn't get it. So in the early seventies, it was a constant piss fight between the personnel and operating departments about just who was hired. Phil, Paul, and Barry happened to be white males, but because they had degrees and were veterans, Tom Moffat could easily justify hiring them.

The young men were no less than perfect in their pre-switchman evaluations and tests. Although Peter Steinman viewed them with a degree of wariness (What were three degreed individuals doing, applying for a switchman's position?), he could not help but like their conscientiousness and good attitudes. Because they were all jocks, they all three could maneuver around the railroad cars with ease, climbing, tying hand brakes, and getting on and off moving equipment. Peter actually told some semi-worthwhile jokes during the week, surprising them all, and the class semi-laughed at them. He also tended to snort less, and just smiled after one of his jokes. Peter's snorting could have been a subconscious effect during minor times of stress, like the first day of switchman's class, Phil thought. When Phillip, Paul, and Barry all easily aced their tests on the last Friday of class, Peter was genuinely happy for them. To those who passed their tests, Peter said, "Congratulations. Now we'll see if you can become rails." This was the term defining all railroaders in all crafts, but mostly referring to transportation folks who actually traversed the rails. Phil, Paul, and Barry all noticed the reverence in Peter's voice as he said *rails*. There was definitely a subculture here. Whether the young men would view their railroad careers as hallowed as Peter viewed his own would remain to be seen. For now, it suited them all to become rails. There would be a ninety-day break-in period, after which they would join the United Transportation Union.

# CHAPTER 5
# THE OLD RAILS

After class, the new trainees received a schedule for the next two weeks to work certain jobs already assigned a full complement of crew members. It was the job of these experienced railroaders to see to it that the trainees were properly indoctrinated on that particular job. Phil remembered seeing the huge area of tracks called the South Yards for the first time, and thought, How do these guys *know* every track down here? His answer would be "Just hang around long enough." It was "railroad osmosis." After working different jobs in different locations, with different tracks, day in and day out for about three years, a person learned most of the trackage. It would eventually all sink in. Some jobs switched out industries. One local switched out a cold storage facility in underground caves. Another job switched out an auto assembly plant. Still another switched out a livestock yard. Many jobs switched in the yards, classifying cars for further shipment, like Ralph Dunne's crew was doing when he "bought it." Just about everything imaginable was switched out by the Central Pacific in the Kansas City, Kansas, area.

Some of the crews were very helpful to the new hires, wisely realizing that these new folks would have *their* lives in their hands someday. The more they could teach these new railroaders, the safer everyone would be in the future. Still others wouldn't even talk to the new hires for various reasons. Some saw the company as the enemy: why should they help break in new hires for nothing? In the future, the railroads would pay crew members to break in new hires. But at this time, 1974, there was no pay for this service. Indeed, Phil, Paul, and Barry were among the first new-hire railroaders to even be paid student pay to break in. Before this, new railroaders broke in for nothing. That was another reason for some of the "old heads" not wanting anything to do with the new hires. But the main reason some of the veteran railroaders didn't want to tell the new hires anything was that when they had broken in twenty-five to thirty-five years before, nobody had wanted to help them, either. They were passing it along, yet another example of how gravity affects the direction poop rolls.

There was a lot of yelling in the railroad yards. It was a necessity. The yards were noisy, with cars banging constantly and the roar of diesel engines as a constant background serenade. Sometimes the yelling was an attempt to communicate above the noise. Other times it was to scream at each other, berating a stupid move by some mindless railroader, or to keep him from making one. And rarely (but it happened), the yelling was to keep someone from sharing the same fate as Ralph Dunne. Sometimes the perpetual inventory car location (PICL) list would be incorrectly interpreted by a switchman. At some jobs, the lists were read from the bottom up; at others, from the top down. Once in a while, a switchman would read his list the opposite of what it was supposed to be and switch all the cars into the wrong tracks, not comparing the car numbers with the switch list. Then the foreman would usually holler and scream, complete with industrial-strength cussing. It was either, "You dumb ..." or "You stupid ..." followed by the next descriptive cuss words the foreman chose. This was because now the locomotive had to "reach into" all the tracks where the incorrect cars were switched, pull them up the lead, and re-switch them. Sometimes it could take more than an hour. The PICL lists had the car numbers listed, so when the complacent switchman saw the number of the first car coming down the lead, he should have known which way to read the list. The yelling was well deserved.

The most impressive and constantly obvious perception of the railroad by the new hires was that it was *big! Everything* was *big!* The railroads yards were big, the locomotives were big, the different types of railcars were big, the railroad bridges were big, the yardmaster's towers were big, diesel shops were big, and so on. And things were *long!* Trains were long, railroad tracks were long, the runs to other towns were long, and to many railroaders, their duty hours were long, too. Everything was king-sized. There was an unspoken but felt "This is where the real men are" perception. It takes real big men to move this big stuff around.

And railroaders were *everywhere*. They were up in towers, on the ground, on the cars, in the diesel shops, up on locomotives, at the car department, at the water department, at the caboose track, at the maintenance department, in the shanties, in the jitneys, on the trains, at the offices, and so on. To Barry and Phil, the railroaders in the yard reminded him of ants on the anthills on Grandpa McAlister's farm. In 1974, much of the switchman work was done "up in the air." Switchmen jumped from car to car dozens of times every shift. They passed hand signs from up there. They checked cars from up there. Railroaders were constantly checking, switching, climbing, and walking. The railroad yard was a place of nonstop movement.

Phil, Paul, and Barry would now begin to learn all the jobs, starting with a chronological list of "student trips," as they were termed. Peter Steinman had worked out these first trips for all the trainees. They consisted of road turns, yard jobs, transfers, and locals, and were scheduled over the remaining two weeks of training. The road turns were the last student trips before Phil, Paul, and Barry began their ninety-day break-in period. They ran to Ellisville, Kansas, from Kansas City, Kansas, and to Montauk, Kansas, from "KCK." But the three young men made it only as far as Topeka, or Malfunction Junction, as it was affectionately termed by the railroaders. The reason for this term was that Topeka was considered the halfway point, when actually it was less than half on both runs. Hundreds of cars were set out and picked up by trains daily at Topeka. Besides the many daily run-throughs and work trains, the Topeka yard had its own switch crews assigned to every shift. Topeka was also an interchange with other railroads. It was always busy. Railroaders hoped to catch (or be assigned) run-through trains that didn't stop. But most trains did have a pickup or set-out at Topeka, or both. The increased activity was the reason for the name. Quite often, all the trains and jobs blocked each other, and one job couldn't move until another moved, and so forth, earning Topeka the Malfunction Junction title.

It was at Topeka that either the engineer or the conductor would ask the new trainees if they wanted off to catch the next train home rather than have to go all the way to either Ellisville or Montauk. Of course, the trainees always wanted to go back home. And since they didn't have to turn in time slips, only signed training slips, the conductor signed the slips at Topeka, both for the trip up and the trip back, and no one was the wiser. The trainees then caught the next eastbound train into Kansas City. They were not due to mark up for additional training until their training turn tied up in Kansas City, back from either Ellisville or Montauk. The young men naturally chose to head back home the same day they left for their last training trips. It looked like they would like railroading. It was outdoors. It felt easy, and it felt free.

They would learn flat switching and hump operations, whereby the locomotive would push cars up a hill or "hump," where a switchman would pull the pin, separating the car or cars, and gravity would cause them to roll down the other side of the hump into a bowl yard of classification tracks. Every day was a learning experience. No two days were ever alike, nor would they ever be. They would walk miles. They would make up trains. They would switch out trains. They would cut up (cars in) tracks and switch them. They would get tracks together. And they would be amazed at what the next few weeks would reveal as one cross section of America.

Phil, Paul, and Barry had all experienced much life at this point in their lives with high school, college, and the military. But none of those experiences prepared them for the characters or situations they found at the railroad. The first thing they found different, but enjoyable, was a "quit." The majority of the yard jobs were eight-hour jobs that demanded only so much switching per shift. Those jobs in the yard that switched tracks for classification usually had two jobs working the same lead track. The result was that one job had to stay in the clear while the other switched their respective track. As Mike Bromley put it, "Grab a beer, and stay in the clear." So even when you were at work, conditions always dictated whether you were actually moving or not. "They also serve, who only stand and wait" was always on Phil's mind throughout his railroad career. But the bottom line was, when the necessary tracks were switched, or the designated industries were pulled and set, the switchmen could go home early. This "quit" could be anywhere from thirty minutes to sometimes three or four hours, but the railroaders were paid for eight. It was a great perk.

The yardmaster would hand (or send through the vacuum tubes) the switch lists to the switch foreman. The yardmaster had previously marked all the cars on the list with their destination in the appropriate tracks. Then the foreman would discuss the move with the rest of the crew. This would be called a job briefing in the future. At certain industries, such as the auto assembly plants, the railroad's job was to assist them by being "on call." The plant would call the yardmaster, requesting a switch inside the plant. The yardmaster, in turn, directed the crews. When the plant didn't need further railroad assistance for that shift, the railroaders could go home, or at least play cards or read until the time the yardmaster felt he could let the crews go.

One time after his training regimen, Phil was called to work the Buick, Oldsmobile, Pontiac (BOP) Assembly Plant job in the Fairfax district of Kansas City. It was after evening call hours for the switchman's extra board, which were 9:00 p.m. to 10:30 p.m. If you didn't get called during the call hours, you were normally "free," temporarily. But it was midnight, and Phil and Carla were in the middle of a fine husband-and-wife endeavor when the phone rang. "Barnes? 11:30 BOP," said the expressionless voice of the crew caller on the other end. Phil and Carla needed the money. Young people always do. A man hadn't shown up at BOP, so Phil took his hour and a half to get there, the time designated by union agreement when called after call hours. When he arrived at 1:30 a.m., the crew was shoving their last track for the shift. Phil went to beans with the crew, stamped up on the conductor's time slip, and went home and crawled back in bed with Carla. He couldn't believe it, pleased with the eight hours' pay and minimal time away from Carla.

But unsuspectingly, a dangerous precedent was being set: "To be paid the most for the least amount of work" was the message. It was a common railroad thought process. There were to be a lot of those railroad-associated approaches to life, such as "The engineer's seat is the warmest seat on the property." But probably the biggest trap of all that many fell into was the one that *wasn't* spoken: "The railroad is the world." In other words, all values, desires, living conditions, friendships, jobs, promotions, and so on occur under the umbrella of the railroad.

The outside world disappeared. It could be a good thought process for some, a bear trap for others.

Proof positive of this culture were the "bum" or "tramp" jobs that Peter Steinman could have held had he not wanted prestige so badly. Prestige was hard to eat. These bum jobs were known for their lucrative paychecks, but you had to put your time in, and a lot of it at that. Because the crews switched in the yards till beans, and then delivered, it literally took hours, as a result of the railroad traffic, both in the yards and at interchanges. There was a lot of waiting. Again, this was looked upon as "I'm gettin' paid for doin' nothin'. Aren't I clever?" It was a far cry from research science, or dentistry. Railroaders did this same thing for years. They made a lot of money, but they gave up everything to do so, including their families. It wasn't intentional. They were doing their best.

But quite often, the money zealots would end up working for alimony and child support on these same jobs they had originally marked up on to take care of their families. Their wives divorced them because they were never home. The wives lived separate lives. Less time at work meant less money but *more* family. And, because of the outside world disappearing in favor of the railroad world, these bum jobs were looked upon as very desirable jobs. They went "high," as it was termed, referring to the top tier on the seniority roster. It took a lot of "whiskers" to hold the bum jobs.

The switchmen were all in pretty good shape, having to constantly walk, climb, hang off the sides of cars, and use their arm muscles to tie hand brakes and pass signs. Phil noticed some of the older switchmen ready to retire had trim waists and well-muscled arms from walking, climbing, and tying hand brakes all their lives. But there were still some switchmen who managed to take in more calories than they could burn off. And, unless engineers had a personal regimen, the lack of exercise inherent in their jobs usually led to potbellies in later years. Some engineers looked like baked potatoes with toothpicks sticking out for arms and legs. All they ever did was eat, which earned them the title "hogheads.) This undoubtedly came from the steam era. When the small, vertical locomotive window in front of the engineers on the old steamers became opaque from the coal-burning locomotive smoke, they would have to stick their big ol' heads outside the window to see.

Lack of exercise, beer, and fatty foods enlarged the engineers' heads and necks, earning them the label. It looked like a big ol' hog was runnin' the train.

Some engineers were actually misshapen from hanging out their right-side locomotive windows for twelve hours or more, daily, for years. Hank Evans actually walked bent to the right from the waist up, wearing his old, worn-out baseball cap that said "K.C. Royals," now severely flattened from years of gravity and discolored from Hank's head sweat. The cap was tilted to the left, which matched Hank's lower portion. He looked like a walking Z. The only time and place he walked was to his car or his locomotive. One of the local trainmasters said you had to drive a stake beside Hank's locomotive to see if it was moving when Hank's crew was on overtime. There were definitely different gaits, whether one was working overtime or "running for a quit."

One of the most enjoyable aspects of railroading was the variety of characters the young men met, both in the yards and on the road. There were many young men like themselves, ex-military, which the Central Pacific loved seeing on an application. Not only could the CP reward their veterans with good jobs, but CP supervisors also knew that veterans would generally give them a good job performance. They started something and finished it, something Phil thought was as important an aspect of a college degree as the subjects learned. Most of what he learned in college he considered "MUD," mindless, useless data. But what was significant to Phil was that he knew the material at the time and completed it. He believed college was a record of successful completion more than a reflection of intelligence. Many intelligent people never had the chance to attend college, and Phil would meet them at the railroad. Conversely, many who finished college couldn't find their rear ends with both hands and a switchman's lantern on a sunny day. But completion was everything. "Finish what you start" was the key to success. Phil thought he had read that Woody Allen once said, "Showing up is 95 percent of life." No doubt.

Some of these new, young railroad men were radical and rebellious, aligning with the times of the late-sixties insanity, when protesting the Vietnam War, women (and probably some men) burning bras, and Black Power were in vogue. The young had a high tolerance for everyone, as long as they didn't soak down their respective parades, which they thought some of the World War II railroad jocks were doing. Indeed, there were some verbal comments heaved, as well as written. Since long hair was "in" in the early seventies, many of the new railroaders who were returning veterans grew their hair long and let their beards grow. It was not only a symbol of the times and music, but represented an anti-establishment freedom that the young men had been unable to display in the military. The military was about as diametrically opposed to individual freedom as any lifestyle known, yet ironically, that was the very thing the American military protected. It took discipline to protect the freedom to be undisciplined. The new young railroaders had survived the war and paid their dues, and they were going to "let it all hang out," the current approach to life—like "do your own thing." "Let It All Hang Out" was even a song at the time. Some of these young men were classified as "Jesus freaks," who had, after much drug experimentation, found the Lord. They had chosen to keep their long hair and beards, but were now Christian in lifestyle.

These youthful new employees wore their respective service's fatigue jackets and pea coats as badges of honor. They also discovered the most comfortable of clothing designs, bib overalls. They were perfect for carrying time books, railroad pocket watches, rule books, and so on. And, they aligned nicely with the prevalent anti-nearly-everything culture of the post-Vietnam era. Quite a few younger railroaders wore their bibs on their off-duty time, too.

The World War II jocks, on the other hand, were clean-cut and serious minded. They did not understand the grass smoking, and the increased facial and head hair. To them, it was degenerate, although they themselves were known to take a whiskey-snort once in a while. It became the "rednecks versus the hippies" at the railroad. As Phil supposed it was in all of the industries in the post-Vietnam era, it was "Archie versus the Meathead." On the shanty walls were written phrases like "These young clowns are proof that buffalos mate with human beings" and "These inbred, scroungey bastards need to go back to the jungle." But for the most part, actual confrontations were rare. Everyone got along as much as necessary. For one thing, their lives literally depended upon each other. And everyone was different. There were Christians, devil worshippers, bikers, farmers, and at least one admitted homosexual, Stewart Rosebury, whom the railroaders had nicknamed Rosemary. Stewart was a three-hundred-pound railroad clerk who lifted weights, happened to like other males, and made no bones about it, or at least none that were evident. Some of the crazy biker-railroaders would hug Rosemary, which he loved, and then would hunch him just to be bizarre. The first time Phil witnessed this odd act, he wondered what kind of place he'd found to call his work.

The World War II men were to be respected, for sure. All three, Phil, Paul, and Barry, realized that if the World War II folks hadn't kicked the Bad Guys of the World's collective asses, they might be goose-stepping to work. There were former fighter pilots, bomber pilots, tail gunners, navigators, and infantrymen sprinkled throughout the railroad ranks. Our world was unquestionably better because of the men and women of that era. Tom Brokaw would write about them in the late nineties in his book *The Greatest Generation*. Phil thought Tom was right on it.

One of these World War II jocks was a switchman named Chisel-head Elliot, because his cranium was elongated from his ear-line to the top, and bent slightly to the right. Also, he was bald, heightening the effect. He was very clean-cut in appearance. Chisel-head really disliked the long hair, facial hair, tie-dye shirts, and bell-bottom jeans of the post-Vietnam-era switchmen. He considered it "un-American" rather than Americans who looked different. "Chiz," as some of the switchmen referred to him, incorrectly associated these looks with performance. He was heard to say on many occasions, "These young hoodlums couldn't switch a boxcar of perfume out of a trainload of shit."

# CHAPTER 6
## MORE OLD RAILS

When Phil broke in on his student trip with the Muncie Local, there was an amazingly unusual and likeable character working as the conductor on the job: "Tabacca" Joe Alexander. He was known by this nickname because he always had a chaw in his mouth too large to control, and the tobacco juice was always dribbling. Tabacca always wore a white T-shirt in the summer, a four- to six-inch gap appearing between the bottom of the shirt and his well-worn, ripped black pants. The gap exposed a tan, black-hairy beer belly, and the T-shirt was always stained with brown streaks. Engineers recalled working with Joe when he was a head brakeman. They said that when they were zooming down the tracks in the summertime with the windows open in the locomotive cab, they too would finish the trip with brown tobacco stains on their clothes. The vortex, formed in the cab when both the engineer's and brakeman's windows were open, sucked in Joe's attempted window spits, and distributed brown saliva droplets equally throughout the cab. Joe always wore a fisherman's hat, usually with loud colors on both the brim and top, with a couple of fishing lures hooked on it.

Joe was extremely nice, and like many railroaders, lacked a formal education, but he was amazingly bright. Phil had thought many times how a degree was only a piece of paper that allegedly proved someone was bright. But always being an observer of the human condition, he knew there were many, especially men and women from the Great Depression and World War II era, who were too busy trying to survive to go to college or even finish high school. That didn't mean they were stupid. Far from it. They just didn't have the chance to get a formal education. Tabacca Joe was unable to go after a formal education, having had to start work at eight years old to help his mother and younger brothers and sisters.

When Phil first arrived at Muncie for his student trip, he was greeted by a brown, toothy smile with tobacco juice streaming out the sides. "Hey, kid," Tabacca yelled, obviously happy to meet Phil. "Just do what I do, and we won't get in trouble today, all right?" Tabacca was smiling, referring to passing signs. "How 'bout some coffee?"

"Sure," Phil said, shaking a dirty hand.

"I'm Joe Alexander. You can call me Tabacca. That's what they call me around here, because I chew a lot. We'll git goin' here in jes' a minute. I gotta check the switch lists. Got some extra cars on here, it looks like."

"Nice to meet you, Joe. I'm Phil Barnes."

When the Muncie crew began working the cold-storage facility, Tabacca placed Phil in the pinner's position at a strategic point where Phil could see both him and the engineer, who was about twenty cars away and around a curve. As Tabacca walked toward the opening of the cave, he yelled back to Phil, repeating his original directions. "Okay, Phil, now just do what I do." After Phil passed "come ahead," "easy," "that'll do," and "back up" signs from Tabacca to the engineer for about fifteen minutes, Tabacca scratched his crotch. Phil immediately did the same thing, exaggerating the procedure for Tabacca's enjoyment. It wasn't wasted effort, and Phil watched Tabacca laugh and slap his knee as he realized the "do what I do" command was being obeyed to the ridiculous. Tabacca loved it, and would repeat the incident to other railroaders for years, until he retired, referring to Phil as his "best student."

At beans, Phil and Tabacca had some decent discussions. As Phil bit into a corned-beef sandwich Carla had made him, he made a puzzled face. There was a piece of paper in the sandwich. Phil pulled it out and discovered Carla had written "Ha ha" on it. Phil showed the meat-stained note to Tabacca, and both men smiled.

"She must be quite a gal," Tabacca said as he laughed, enjoying the joke.

"The best," Phil said as he pulled out his billfold, showing him a picture of his gorgeous wife and his daughter, Angela. "She used to do some modeling," he told Tabacca, proudly pointing to Carla's picture.

"Man," Tabacca responded, referring to Carla's beauty, "I'll bet you're in a hurry to get home."

"I'm ALWAYS in a hurry to get home," Phil said, smiling as he tucked his billfold back in his pocket.

"Well, that's something you can't always do around here, Phil. The money's good, but you gotta put your time in to make it. Take this job, for instance. It goes to work at 7:30 a.m. Usually, we finish at 7:30 p.m. That's why I'm on it. I need to earn the money to play the stock options." Tabacca nodded and smiled, slipping the comment in to watch Phil's reaction. Tabacca was the proverbial "dumb like a fox" individual.

"What are stock options?" Phil asked genuinely, at the same time showing Tabacca that the college boy wasn't afraid to show his lack of knowledge about a subject.

"Well, Phil, it's kinda like bettin'. Well, it IS bettin'. You bet on what you think a stock is gonna do. There are 'puts' and 'calls.' You put 'down' and call 'up.' It's whatever way you think the stock is goin'. I've made some decent money doing it." It was rumored that Tabacca had thousands of shares of CP stock and had made thousands of dollars over the years with stock options.

It was further rumored that Tabacca had gamecocks he took to fight on the weekends at secret barns in Condaleo, Kansas. He told a story about his wife, who some said could out-cuss any man. And unlike Carla, she was definitely not candy for the eyes. According to Tabacca, he was in Oklahoma one time fighting roosters and ran out of money. He called his wife to have her wire him some, and she said, "Joe, where in the hell are you?"

"I'm down here in Oklahoma fightin' cocks, honey," he told her.

Tabacca's wife evidently replied, "Well, you better get your ass back up here. I got one up here waitin' on ya that ya haven't been able to whip in thirty years."

It was also rumored that Tabacca had several moonshine stills going at once, and that he knew about thirty different ways to catch catfish on the Caw River, all of them illegal. Tabacca had also, evidently, successfully trapped and skinned several varieties of varmints along the Caw. After one meeting with Tabacca, Phil knew that if there ever came a time he had to live off the land, he didn't want to be too far away from Tabacca Joe.

"Tell you what, kid," Tabacca said, smiling as usual. "Gimme that student slip and I'll sign it, and you can get outta here, an' go home to that sweet little thing you got back at your place. You don't want to leave her by herself too much. Someone'll be tappin' that for sure." Tabacca was subconsciously thinking of the many times he'd heard of one railroader leaving for work as another railroader was leaving work to head for the first railroader's house and wife.

"Thanks, Joe. Pleasure meeting you, and thanks for the OJT," Phil said, as he did indeed intend to do some "tapping" with Carla when he got home. Life was good, he thought.

"Come back anytime," Tabacca yelled at Phil as he walked to his car, which was rail-speak for "You did a good job." Phil would hear that statement everywhere he went while breaking in, as would Paul and Barry. As he drove off, Phil heard Tabacca yell, "Ya pass good signs, kid," and he saw him through the dust in the rearview mirror, laughing, scratching his crotch, and slapping his knee.

In the seventies, there was plenty of tobacco use on the railroad besides chewing. Quite a few railroaders smoked cigars, and many also smoked cigarettes, a word obviously meaning the junior version of cigars. Smoking was the ideal pastime when taking a spot. All three of the young men, Phil, Paul, and Barry, would occasionally have a cigar, but none of them smoked cigarettes. Every time a railroader had a cigar in his mouth, another railroader invariably remarked, "It must be going to rain. The hogs are carrying sticks around in their mouths."

One railroader was called Grasshopper because he constantly spit his tobacco saliva into one of the paper cups the CP supplied for drinking the water in the large, inverted five-gallon glass bottles. Water and ice were of major importance before a trip or yard shift. Years later, the railroads would supply bottled water. But at the time, these cups would suffice for many uses, including covering a light in the locomotive cab that was too bright, serving as an ad hoc coffee cup, or holding Grasshopper's spittle. One famous time, Grasshopper pitched the nasty contents of his cup out the locomotive window just as Burton Crownover, his engineer for the shift, was walking below. Crownover was the type who wanted to look good all the time. He always wore a white belt and white shoes, even though he should have worn boots by directive. He set a record for climbing up the locomotive steps in a split second. "Grasshopper, if you ever do that again, I'm gonna shove that chaw so far down your throat, you'll be spittin' from the other end."

Paul met a guy at the Quindaro Yards he liked instantly, because he had the same "I don't care" attitude he had. His name was Pat Anderson. Pat's nickname was New Man Anderson. They said that even though he'd been at the railroad for four years, every time you worked with him was like working with a new man. Pat, like Paul, was a Vietnam vet who didn't care that much about anything. Pat got blasted every night on copious amounts of beer, but never missed work. Being hung over was a way of life for Pat. His eyes were always bloodshot, and he would carry Alka-Seltzer tablets around with him and eat them like candy. Pat was always mentally in the trees. But everyone liked him and didn't mind the "rawhide" they got, the extra work involved, when working with mindless Pat. When they worked together, Paul and Pat always got barbecue at lunch and downed a couple of beers. Sometimes they would go out after their shift, enjoying a few more beers, looking for pretty representatives of the fairer sex, and not really caring too much about anything. It wasn't a bad life for Paul, either, but he couldn't hold any jobs "regular" at Quindaro yet. Later, he would.

Paul had been amazed at the conditions he saw, working some of the local industries in the Quindaro area. Paul and his crew would go to beans in the cafeteria of a fiberglass company they switched that produced insulation. They had to walk through the main working area to get to the cafeteria. The fiberglass company employees had developed some form of personal lung protection with clothing, plastic, and so on to protect their lungs from the horrible air, or lack thereof. Paul could not believe it. The air was literally yellow from the fiberglass floating around. You could feel it in your mouth and "crunch" it with your teeth. Paul wondered if there might be a "yellow lung disease" that these people could develop, similar to coal miners' black lung disease. Paul's crew would cover their mouths and noses with their hands, and Paul pulled the neck of his T-shirt up over his nose, leaving only his eyes exposed as they walked to and from the cafeteria. Paul could not imagine working in the stuff all day. It reminded him of *The Jungle*, by Upton Sinclair, and the horrid conditions experienced by the meatpacking employees at the turn of the century. But that was the late nineteenth century. Why were these conditions allowed to exist in 1974?

And all three, Phil, Paul, and Barry, could not believe how dangerous railroading was. Again, switchmen climbed on top of the cars to pass signs. If cars were kicked in on them while doing this, they had a great chance of being knocked off and dying, if not crippled for life, at the very least. It happened. Covered hoppers, boxcars, and tankers actually had walkways for this purpose in 1974, and switchmen would jump from car to car quite often during a shift. Also, it was normal for switchmen to climb through what were called "movements." A movement could be a cut of cars, a drag, or a train moving through the yards—basically, any cars coupled together and moving. As a movement passed, railroaders boarded a car, climbed the ladder, walked across the walkway welded on the end of the car while holding on to the grab iron above as they did, and then descended on the other side, stepping off the ladder. If you slipped during this common maneuver, you were hamburger. The yard locomotives, or "switchers," had walkways, or "footboards," as they were termed, on both front and rear ends. In 1974, switchmen would actually stand in the *middle* of the track, *in between the rails*, and the engineer would pick them up with a forward-moving locomotive as they stepped up to these walkways to get on. More than one switchman was maimed for life, or "cashed in his chips," with this absurd maneuver. All it took was a slight misjudgment from the engineer ... "Oops!"

Eventually, all of these dangerous practices would cease, with the exception of climbing through movements. This almost always had to be done by switchmen performing their normal duties. But some railroads eventually required movements to be completely stopped before allowing workers to climb on or off the equipment. There were stirrups, or sill steps, the first rung of the ladders that were pretty safe to step up into. Grab irons on cars for holding on to were normally welded very well, although rarely a grab iron might be defective and loose. And if you slipped in between the rails, even while stopped, you still had a chance to be a cheeseburger with ketchup, since the movement could start at any time. Most railroads have an operating rule that alerts railroaders to always expect movement at any time, anywhere, and in any direction. It's a good rule.

After the bodies continued to pile up, railroads took the walkways off the tops of the boxcars and made it a violation of the rules for their employees to be "up there," except for maintenance reasons. However, hoppers and tank cars still had walkways on top for assisting in loading operations. To enhance switching safety, the CP ordered the footboards taken off the front of the locomotives, still allowing switchmen to ride the back, assuming the safety of the trailing location. Then, someone realized locomotives go both directions on a track. "Duh!" and again, "oops." So after a few more reverse movement mishaps, the CP took *all* the footboards off. And although, eventually, railroading became a lot safer in the years after 1974, there was plenty of room for safety improvement at the time.

Basically, each crew in the yard was made up of an engineer, a switch foreman, a field man, and a pinner. The pinner usually stayed with the locomotive, lining the nearby switches and "pulling the pin," or uncoupling cars, either in the cut or next to the locomotive. "Pulling the pin" was also rail-speak for a railroader retiring. "Moore finally pulled the pin." The field man would go down into the yard and make a cut, or uncouple cars to be switched, and line switches farther down the lead. The foreman would run the job, and also line switches, usually in the middle of the lead, between the pinner and the field man. Sometimes a "rider" would make cuts on higher numbered tracks farther on down from the field man, and ride cars into "alleys," or clear tracks, tying a hand brake. This was done so that other cars switched into that track would stack up against it and not roll out the other end. Riders usually worked with several crews. Modern-day riders would be termed "utility brakemen."

One time Phil was given a wake-up call, given the inherent danger of railroading. He had walked deep into the Valley Yards on 17 Track to make a cut on thirty cars, which the crew would pull up the Mill Street lead to switch. He made the cut, pulling the pin, and then climbed up to the top of the grain hopper. Then he popped a red fusee, a railroad flare, since it was dark, and gave a "take 'em ahead" sign to the engineer, an up-and-down movement with the fusee since he didn't have a radio. The engineer gave Phil "two shorts" on the horn, telling him by whistle signal that he'd gotten the message. Then the engineer began pulling on the cars. The heavy *tink-tink-tink* sound made by the couplers as the slack was stretched grew increasingly loud until Phil's car, the last one, began to move up the Valley lead toward the Mill Street lead. Phil had climbed to the top of the ladder so he could see better, riding the rear of the car.

He slapped the burning fusee against the side of the grain hopper car, putting it out, and then pitched it. As he rode the cars under the 10th Street Bridge, he happened to look around the side of the hopper and almost literally lost his head. Another crew, which was switching down the Valley Yard lead, parallel with the Mill Street lead, had begun shoving toward the Valley before Phil's crew was totally in the clear. The boxcar missed the hopper Phil was riding, and Phil, by less than one inch. It could have been very bad. The car could have literally taken Phil's head off, or a second earlier would have knocked over the hopper car Phil was riding. Phil knew his angels were on the lookout for that one. He knew he had just missed death or crippling literally by an inch and a second.

At Quindaro, Paul and Pat worked with a backwoods-type individual everyone called Jethro, after the character on *The Beverly Hillbillies*, whom Max Baer portrayed wonderfully. He was the epitome of a character from *Deliverance*, complete with small, too-close-together, pale blue, inbred eyes and a horrific speech impediment. The "wailwoaders" called him "Jef-wo, Wef-wo, Jet-wo, Wet-wo," and so on. The first time Paul saw him, he was sitting, peeling an apple. Jethro looked up, attempted to form a visual, and began to speak.

"I wad hunt-in t'oder day. Saw iss doe wunnin' about fowty mial pa 'owa. Heah com-a buck, an' mounted hur, and day jus' kep wunnin' about fowty mial pa 'owa, still hooked up." Then Jethro looked back at his apple and began peeling again. Paul couldn't help but smile. Jethro was known for scaring the new guys by giving them a pale blue stare, and mumbling, "C'mere bo-oy. Le' me show you what we do wif boys wike you in 'a woods."

Paul worked a job at the Buick, Oldsmobile, Pontiac plant with an engineer the switchmen referred to as "Sweet Al, the switchman's pal." Al Hollingsworth worked another job besides working for CP as an engineer. As a result, he was always short-rested, and therefore, short-tempered. He had no care whatsoever for the lives and limbs of the switchmen. When Paul worked with him this particular afternoon, it was raining hard. As the pinner, Paul was to "drop off" the locomotive, to pass signs around a corner. Usually, an engineer will slow down to let off crewmembers, but not Sweet Al, the switchman's pal. He roared around the curve at 25 mph, and Paul jumped off, "surfing" as he hit the slick mud and grass, finally coming to a stop about eighteen feet from where he got off. Actually, Paul thought it was fun, and he knew any time he wanted, he could "explain" to Al in marine terms, such that Al probably wouldn't let him off like that again. From Paul's point of view, compared with the sniping and booby traps of the Mekong Delta area, it *was* fun. But Sweet Al could have killed him, and Sweet Al didn't care.

The footboards were still on the locomotives at this time. Stu Whitehead, who talked with a lisp and was in Phil, Paul, and Barry's switchman's class, quit the railroad because of Sweet Al. Stu was on the front footboard when Sweet Al coupled into some cars, called "making a joint." Some of the young switchmen at the time were aware of another pastime called by the same term, only that joint was rolled. Most engineers were very gentle when they coupled into cars, especially if switchmen were riding on the footboards. But as Sweet Al approached the cars with Stu on the front footboard, rather than slow down for a gentle coupling, Al throttled back and slammed into the cars. Stu, who had been giving Sweet Al frantic easy signs that Al deliberately ignored, was almost knocked off. He immediately jumped off the footboard of the locomotive and began walking off the property, yelling at Sweet Al as he went, "You thunofabith! Thath's the lath thime you ever do that thu me!" That was the last day Stu worked for the railroad. During his short employment with CP, Stu always informed the other railroaders how he was going to get a "peeth 'a puthy." Some of the "old heads," as they were called, nicknamed him that.

During the ninety-day probationary period, and after student trips, Barry worked with a nice but eccentric older switchman, John Burdeau. The other switchmen called him Deacon Burdeau, or Streakin' Deacon. "Streakin'" because John never wanted a quit and moved excruciatingly slowly. He worked daylights, at 7:59 a.m. at Quindaro, and moved like that because he wanted to "split the whistle" at 3:59 p.m. He would overemphasize his hand signs, looking more like an orchestra conductor than a switchman. He would wander off like he was staring at something in the weeds. He would stare holes in his switch lists, anything to slow things down. "Deacon" was given to him because John was a good Christian man, and was always quoting the Bible. He drove the young guys crazy who were basically impatient, wanting to work fast and get off earlier with a quit. Given the option, they had better things to do than railroad. They could have gotten a two-hour quit easily, and did, when Deacon wasn't running the job.

There was a method to Deacon's madness, however. Deacon had recently married a much younger woman who was a schoolteacher, or "schoolmarm," as the guys referred to her. She was finished for the day at 4:30 p.m., so Deacon could pick her up at the school with perfect timing if he got off at 4:00 p.m. Why Deacon couldn't just have "cut in" a little more, as a favor to the rest of the crew, gotten a quit, and then killed time having coffee or something, somewhere, while waiting for his wife, was beyond anyone's conception. But he didn't. So the switchmen were not lax in their teasing of Deacon. At fifty-three years old, Deacon had married this little "schoolmarm," who was only twenty-four. The switchmen used to say, "Hey, Deacon. How many times will fifty-three go into twenty-four? It *won't* go."

Yes, there were some real characters at the railroad, and Phil, Paul, and Barry were amazed for a while, until they realized it was the norm. Ben Davis, a crusty old bloody-eyed engineer, always refused to use a radio. In the early seventies, the transition was beginning to what would eventually be almost 100 percent use of the radio. But for now, hand signs and lantern signs were used more often. Davis refused to work with a radio at all, maintaining they were unsafe and would eventually put people out of work. He was right. Switch foremen would say on the radio, "Shove ahead, 244," Ben's engine number, and he would just sit. His locomotive wouldn't move. "I said, *shove ahead*, 244!" Nothing. Finally, in frustration, the foreman would give Ben a hand signal, and he would finally move. Occasionally, Ben would receive a "finger" signal also, and usually returned it.

The Quindaro Yards had an enormous rat population. Thousands of grain hoppers were switched there each week. Quite often, the dumps for unloading, like the one that massacred Ralph Dunne, would be stuck slightly open, and the contents would leak down the middle of the tracks as the cars rolled. Corn, wheat, barley, soybeans, and so on would pile up down the center of the tracks, some of it actually taking root and sprouting. Of course, this was gourmet cuisine for the rat population. Some of the rats were huge. As the locomotives moved down the tracks, the headlights would spotlight literally hundreds of rats dining on the feast between the rails. The huge rodents would jump to either side of the rails in desperation as the switch engine passed, some not making it. The sight reminded Barry of walking around the pond on his grandparents' farm and watching the plentiful frog population jump in. Half rats would be everywhere. These carcasses, heating up in the sunlight of day, combined with the smell of the rotting grain, gave the Quindaro Yards a mega-stench aroma all their own. Other yards were more olfactory-friendly than Quindaro. One such yard was near a large deodorant-soap factory, and the smell was constantly great. Another yard was near the Kansas City Stockyards … So much for that smell.

# CHAPTER 7
## ALWAYS LEARNING FROM THE OLD RAILS

Phil always enjoyed working nights on Friday or Saturday, because the jobs always went to beans at the local Champlain truck stop. "We goin' to Champlain for beans?" was a standard question. The Champlain waitresses were fairly pretty, and flirtatious. The food was decent, and Kansas's private clubs, which stayed open till 3:00 a.m., would be closing about beans time, and the patrons would come to the truck stop to sober up and eat. Because human behavior was always of interest to Phil, he really enjoyed viewing the wonderful zoo. It was the unintentional "grunge look" in the seventies, before the actual style that would be in vogue in the late eighties and early nineties. The female bar denizens displayed accidentally torn stockings, smeared makeup, tousled hair, and exposed shirttails from wild dancing. It was style serendipity. Some of the girls were actually nice looking, but Phil always wondered how many times their odometers, like the girls themselves, had rolled over. Some of the more senseless switchmen actually began affairs with these high-mileage, high-maintenance honeys.

One time Phil, who was called to break in on a daylight job, marked up with an extra-board engineer who would remain his friend the entire time he worked for the Central Pacific. His name was Alex Hollander. Alex was extremely intelligent and had a keen insight on life. With Phil's interest in human behavior, he very much enjoyed hearing Alex's unique viewpoints. Alex's insights into the human condition were not soiled by any formal education and had been developed by years of observance. He was in his fifties.

The crew had again gone for beans to Champlain, which in the daytime lacked the enjoyable observations of booze-induced behavior and bizarre clothing. The waitresses were still pretty, though, and their old yard foreman today, Chance Armstrong, had been studying one waitress in particular. She was a cute bottle redhead with nice dimples and a sparkling, vibrant, flirtatious personality who appeared to be very much enjoying Armstrong's, and everyone else's, stares. Her dress was short, to show off her extremely curvy legs. Chance had a nasty, gravelly voice: "Man, will you look at that!" Armstrong drooled. Alex, as did Phil, noticed the vivacious redheaded waitress. But rather than drool, Alex quietly studied the waitress and eventually commented quietly, without expression, "She sure looks like she could make your life miserable."

Phil was impressed. It was the first time he had ever witnessed anyone vaulting over the initial attraction phase when first encountering an attractive woman. It was wisdom. Most people never considered the morals, decency, or life habits, in general, of the person they initially found attractive, setting themselves up for potential misery. The visual-physical always seemed to overwhelm the more solid, important characteristics a person could possess, such as loyalty, trustworthiness, integrity, and class. Phil wouldn't have attributed any of these to this redhead. Phil, from this point forward, would engage the "other" part of his brain, too, if an attractive woman came into his line of vision. He would (maybe not immediately) think of these more important characteristics, the *real* woman behind the visual facade, because of Alex's comment with forethought. And although Phil was definitely a people-watcher, on those occasions when he saw an attractive female, such as the bottle-redheaded Champlain waitress, an image of Carla immediately welled up in his brain. He just wasn't interested in anyone else, the same way his father Harold felt about his mother Rose. But Armstrong, unlike Phil, wasn't interested in the real woman. He, like most, observed females in general with a purely id-spawned desire. As Mike McGregor, a yard engineer who loved to fish, always said, referring to the female of the species, "Most powerful bait in the world."

Chance Armstrong temporarily released his gaze on "Red" to tell Phil a tired ol' joke he told to every new hire who would listen: "A big ol' snake crawled across the railroad track one day. He had almost made it across when this train come along and cut off the very tip of his tail. That ol' snake turned around to look at his tail in between the rails, and the train cut off his damn head. The moral to this story is, 'Don't lose your head over a piece 'a tail.'" Chance then smiled a wicked half smile, with self-attributed wisdom, like a railroad Zen master. Phil politely smiled and shook his head.

A couple of weeks later, Phil caught another job with Alex and Chance. The common railroad subject of females was again the topic. Chance, as usual, had been "educating" Alex and Phil about certain "moves" he had that he alleged always led to a score. Alex had listened with quiet disdain to everything Chance was blabbing about. After a few minutes, Alex had endured all the verbal braggadocio he could stand, and felt the need to comment. "Chance," he said, "men don't turn women on. Women turn themselves on." Like with Alex's observation on the physical, Phil had never heard that one before, but he mentally agreed almost instantly. "Look at nature, Chance," Alex continued. "Some of the males of a species go completely nuts, displaying their plumage, or some type of antics, and the females could care less. *The females* have to be in the mood, or in the case of the ones you find, Chance, drunk. It works for birds, mammals, and us. It's estrous, man."

"And I'm tellin' ya, I can get them there to es-ter-ust, or whatever you said, Alex," Chance quickly and defensively responded.

"But only if they're already *ready*," Alex added.

"Are you married?" Phil asked Chance with genuine inquisitiveness. Chance looked offended, as though Phil were insinuating that he ought not to be in such perpetual lust if he were.

"Look at it this way," Chance answered. "My ol' lady's married ... I ain't." Then he winked at Phil and smiled a wretched half smile, almost a smirk.

Chance was often heard quoting simple-minded gems such as "Treat a whore like a queen and a queen like a whore," "One man's meat is another man's poison," and so on. Chance also bragged about seducing the wives of other railroaders. His comment was always, "If it hadn't've been me, it would've been somebody else." Yeah, Chance, it's all the woman's fault … She was just a dirty leg and you were doin' your duty.

Over the years, though, Phil would think about Chance's "Treat a whore like a queen and a queen like a whore." He'd think about it a lot, because he'd observed the behavior often, and it seemed to work. If a guy had a trophy wife and treated her well, she raised hell with him often, bossed him, took him for granted, and often took him for everything he had. If good wives were treated badly, they seemed to stick around, semi-happy, and endure it. Conversely, if a dirty leg were treated badly, she accepted it … business as usual. If she was treated well, she became the best wife and mother imaginable. As one railroader put it, "You never know if your great-great-grandmother started out as a dance hall queen or not." But it did seem to Phil that guys who treated their wives badly had wives who tended to respect their husbands and remain loyal. And conversely, guys who treated their wives with respect tended to have wives who disrespected them. It wasn't true in all cases, but in many cases, it was. It gave some credibility to Chance's crass statement, which Phil did not like. It was illogical. Mr. Spock wouldn't have liked it.

Barry also worked with Chance Armstrong one day of that life-changing summer of '74. Barry noticed that Chance, who was pushing sixty years old, had skin that was almost mummylike from years of sun rays, one of the imperceptible detriments of working a daylight job, which was commonly sought after. To have enough seniority "whiskers" to work daylights was a goal to be achieved. Chance had been around forty years. It didn't take much conversation for Barry to discover what Phil already had learned about Armstrong. He was a "get-what-he-could" individual in constant pursuit of pleasure, irrespective of anyone else's life. He wanted to feel good all the time. Barry seemed to remember reading something he thought George Jones had said. It was something like, when he found something he liked, he tried to get all he could of it. It was extremely well put. Most everyone could understand that. Everyone wanted to feel good all the time.

In short, Chance was what the Bible referred to as a "natural man." His pleasure came first. If someone got hurt in Chance's pursuit of pleasure, it wasn't an issue. It wasn't long before Chance was recalling stories about his extramarital sexcapades with Barry, as he'd done with Phil, even though he had been married thirty-four years to the same woman. Some women try desperately *not* to know. Chance's wife was a queen he successfully treated like a whore. Barry, who deeply loved Susan and Erin, said to Chance defiantly, "I'll *never* run around on my wife." Then Chance said something that stuck with Barry forever, like a smallpox vaccination scar. The old, scaly switchman rolled, and licked to seal, a Prince Albert cigarette and said simply, "Talk to me in twenty years, kid." Chance's comment made Barry think hard about the job, the future, and the undoubtedly many times he'd have to be away from Susan.

Paul also worked with Chance while breaking-in in the yards. Chance had shared his philosophies with Paul, and Paul understood. Chance very much liked Paul, because Paul was somewhat like Chance. Paul, like Chance, operated on the pleasure principle. The difference between the two was that Paul would not do something that would hurt another to achieve pleasure.

Phil noticed that in working all hours in all kinds of weather, he gained a perspective on the beauty of life he hadn't been aware of before. First, he saw for himself that the world never slept. He saw sunrises, and the gradual increase in human activity as the sun rose higher. He saw the incredibly beautiful, always different sunsets. God's paintbrush, Phil thought. He switched in a thunderstorm so heavy one night that his switch foreman was giving him lantern signs to pass, and the light just reflected off the millions of raindrops like a giant all-white kaleidoscope. All Phil could see were thousands of prisms of light. Phil and all the crew members were laughing, it was so absurd to work in the deluge. Most of the time, it felt very good to be outside, although at this point, Phil, Paul, and Barry had not yet experienced winter in the rail yards. But there definitely was a freedom involved in working outside. "Blue Collar," by Bachman-Turner Overdrive, was popular at this time, and Phil could easily identify. It would sometimes be playing on the local rock station on his way in to work a midnight shift: "You walk your streets ... ba-da ba-a-a, and I walk mine ... ba-da ba-a-a."

Phil met another friend while working the stockyard job one night. He had the same keen insights as Alex Hollander. His name was McGee Brown. Brownie, as the railroaders called him, was extremely literate, had a master's degree, and was quiet, yet still very personable. When you talked to Brownie, you knew he genuinely listened. He cared. He was intent on the subject. He looked into your eyes once in a while. He was never guilty of "talk, talk, talk," as many railroaders were; they had no desire to hear any comment from the person to whom they were talking. "Just talkin' loud and sayin' nothin' ... and sayin' nothin'," as James Brown wrote and sang in the sixties. McGee Brown would always listen carefully, and then comment quietly and wisely. He did not tell the other railroaders what they wanted to hear. He told them what he thought. He never beat anyone down with overly eloquent words. The only reason anyone knew he had a master's degree was that another railroader had gone to Missouri Eastern College, where Brownie had been a football star. It was said that he would have been drafted into the pros, but they didn't consider him because of his weight. He was an amazingly quick and deceptive running back, but the pros thought he would not last physically at only 165 pounds. So this railroader, knowing McGee hadn't been drafted, asked him what he'd done after graduation. Brownie had told him, "Got a master's from MU." It was soon common knowledge on the railroad. Word got around. Some ornery railroaders would deliberately start rumors just to see how long it took for the rumor to get back to them.

Brownie was of African descent in an era when very few African-Americans held switchman or engineer jobs. The only other switchman on the property of African heritage was Walt Morehouse, who would become good friends with Barry in the future. Brownie had zero prejudice in his cut body. He thought very strongly that it was "men and women" *period*, enough said. That skin color would make a difference was so asinine to Brownie that he literally couldn't conceive of it. The general population was driven by the physical, not unlike Chance Armstrong's modus operandi. Most folks did not care about the "inside." But that was *all* Brownie cared about. Brownie got his nickname from one of Peter Steinman's faux pas. When Brownie was attending switchman's class, the class roster had the last names first, as usual. At roll call, Peter's first instructing duty was calling out attendee names, first and last, in that order, and expecting a hearty "Here!" in return. When he quickly came to Brownie's name in the roster, he called "Brown McGee," rather than McGee Brown. It was actually because there was already a switchman whose last name was McGee, a Howard McGee. Peter Steinman had known him for years. So in his subconscious, Peter "wanted" McGee to be a last name. In typical quiet and humble fashion, Brownie never corrected Peter, who had called him Brown for the entire class, thinking it was his first name. The result was that his classmates did as well, and the name stuck for life. Brownie actually kind of liked it.

He was what the railroaders referred to as a "high yellow" referring to his skin tone and to the calling out of an approach signal aspect—how a signal appears. Brownie was light-skinned and remarkably handsome. He was cut like a marine because he *was* a marine, having served in Vietnam, as many railroaders hired on in the early seventies did. He always wore an extremely short beard, about a five-day growth, that could not hide his handsome sunken cheeks, the result of a fat-free body. But Brownie was not in the least cocky about it. He was married to a beautiful woman of Caucasian extraction, and as a result, their children were exceptionally beautiful. He had a boy and a girl, and the girl had his beautiful skin and his wife's deep blue eyes. It was a strikingly beautiful color combination.

When Phil approached Brownie to shake his hand for the first time, Brownie said, "Hi, I'm Brownie." Seeing the look in Phil's eyes, Brownie, who was already smiling a genuine smile, said, "No, it's not some railroad prejudice ... Just a nickname." Brownie then explained to Phil how they would spot the loaded stock cars for unloading on this job.

"If you're not used to it, this can be pretty rough," Brownie said, shaking his head. "The stockyard workers can be brutal with the animals. They have these shocking prods that deliver quite a jolt to 'encourage' the animals to move quickly. It's a hell of a sound when they zap the cattle. They're always yellin', hollerin' and screamin', and whistlin', too. Some of the workers seem to enjoy their jobs a little too much. But I try not to let it bother me. The animals are going to be slaughtered soon anyway."

Phil gulped a bit. He had a strong stomach, but he loved all animals. What he would see tonight would change his views of a cheeseburger for a while, but only for a while. Shortly, thinking about a cheeseburger would change back to only what he wanted on it. The night went by quickly, and ended with Brownie and Phil having developed a great trusting friendship in a short period of time. Sometimes it worked like that. Both of them felt inherent honesty from the other. They would work together once in a while, and remain friends for life. Later on, Brownie and Phil would find another reason they felt the bond they did: They were both Christian young men.

Another rail-speak term the young men learned was "setting out a bad order." Again, railroaders constantly checked cars. It was an extremely important part of their job description. Before a train ever left town, the entire train was checked for bad order cars. If found, by either the car department employees, or transportation employees, a Day-Glo red-orange bad order tag was stapled to the car, and it was switched out to eventually be repaired at a "one spot facility." This was where light repair work was done on railcars. A car might be bad ordered during a run, whereby it would be set out in a siding for mobile car department employees to repair it. Then the dispatchers would direct a following train to pick it up and take it to the final destination. The most common use for the term, however, was when a railroader was about to eliminate excrement: "I'm going to set out a bad order."

Phil, Paul, and Barry all discovered that all the various yards to be learned were different, yet similar. They all had lead tracks on which switchmen would switch cars that led into numbered tracks. Most had light towers that illuminated the tracks at night, but there were always dark areas. And of course these yards varied greatly in length. Each track held only a certain number of cars. A car count misjudgment would net you a derailment by shoving cars off the end of the track. Also the new switchmen had to learn if cars tended to roll "into" or "out of" a track. In other words, they had to find out where and in what direction the gradient was in all the tracks.

Most of these yards had yardmasters in control. They could be decent or rotten. Most were decent. Some yardmasters were perched up in yard towers, communicating with the troops below through speakers and sending switch lists through vacuum tubes. But some yardmasters were stationed in shanties: small, very old, wooden buildings, where they would assign switching moves and hand out switch lists. Each tower and shanty were the yardmasters' headquarters to their own mini-fiefdoms. Each yardmaster projected his individual railroad management style. Earl Miller in the North Yards was very fair. Lane Weible, known as

Weible the Weasel, or simply the Weasel, would get in a crew wagon and sneak around trying to catch crews hiding out. He never gave anyone a quit. Gearshond was a decent guy who was so cool that he could carry on a chess game and still keep the yard switched in top condition. He would later have a fatal heart attack on duty, his cool exterior belying the inner trauma associated with meeting switching demands and time frames. Elliot West, whom everyone called Elliot Ness, was a great guy, and a fair yardmaster. He received the same fate as Gearshond. Elliot could be heard huffing and, literally, puffing his end-to-end cigarettes as he thought out moves to give the switchmen over the speaker. Elliot was a 5-foot 9-inch three-hundred-pounder who lived on unfiltered Camels, biscuits and gravy, and endless cups of black coffee. He drank whiskey daily, to "come down" from the inherent tension of yardmastering and the "high wiring" he got from the Camels and coffee. This unhealthy lifestyle, coupled with increased daily job stress, led to Elliot's ultimate death. When he suffered his fatal heart attack, none of the switchmen were surprised.

In 1974, each yardmaster had a clerk assigned to him to assist in the paper shuffling, and to check to see if certain cars that were supposed to be in certain tracks were, indeed, there. Like the yardmasters, they had their own individual approaches to railroading. One clerk, Jack Mooney, was a very large black man who was as gentle as he was big and strong. Mooney would make a huge pot of ham hock and beans, and bring it to work to share with everyone. It was always fantastic. Mooney, who, like Streakin' Deacon, was a good Christian man, would also bring enough cornbread to feed an army when he served his famous delicacy. All that ever remained was an empty pot and crumbs of cornbread, which Mooney would toss on the floor of the shanty next to a mouse hole. Mooney's ham hock and beans and cornbread were famous. Phil, Paul, and Barry all tasted the delicious meal in the summer of '74. Mooney would retire in '75. But needless to say, everyone loved working with Mooney, and no one ever forgot his kindness and generosity, or the mouthwatering, stomach-satisfying food. Everyone would miss Mooney and his ham hock and beans and cornbread. It was yum-yum!

It was in these shanties that the main ingredient for good railroading was found: coffee! It didn't take Phil, Paul, and Barry long to find out that the railroad didn't run on diesel fuel; it ran on caffeine. Copious amounts of coffee were consumed constantly, to keep railroaders alert and awake. In the wintertime, it helped keep railroaders warm. When yard crews finished an assignment, they headed for the shanties and a good caffeine wiring.

# Chapter 8
## Tougher than Rail

One of the more sobering job assignments of the Central Pacific was the switchtender position on the other side of Lathrop Tower. Four tracks needed to have switches lined often, resulting from interchanges with many foreign railroads, local switching jobs, and all the run-through traffic. Many years later these switches would be electrically operated, but now they were strictly hand-thrown. This is where Central Pacific put their loyal but permanently injured employees for a relatively easy eight-hour shift. When Phil, Paul, and Barry caught the switchtender job, they were all amazed at the sheer guts of the individuals who held the job regularly.

There was a "Spooky" Landscome, whose mind had simply decided to vacate the premises. If it had been any other occupation, Spook would probably have had to resign. But it was proven he could handle the switches logically, so he was allowed to remain working after his mind sped away. He had been born Luke Landscome, and when he was a new hire, his nickname was Handsome Landscome. But over the years, his nickname from the railroaders had evolved to Lukey. He was very well-liked. His wife had run off with his best friend and taken his children, whom Luke never saw, ever again. No one was sure how that had all worked out. But Luke decided not to cope anymore. He wasn't violent. He wasn't even absentminded. He was just ... well, almost stoic, catatonic-like. The railroaders all thought he was much more lucid than anyone realized, but he rarely if ever talked. When he did talk, he quoted Bible verses that may or may not make any sense. When Spooky lost his family, he attributed it to his lack of biblical understanding, his logic being, "If I had been a good Christian, God wouldn't have allowed this to happen." Christians knew this wasn't the case. "It rains on the just and the unjust." And Jesus said further, "No matter if the world hateth you, it hated me before you." Leo Durocher simply put it this way: "Nice guys finish last." After the separation trauma had occurred, Luke developed a penchant for distrusting nearly everything that he presumed had the potential to harm him. He thought his food was poisoned. He thought his water was poisoned. He thought the air was poisoned. He would bring a large fifty-foot homemade wrap that he wrapped around his entire body when he worked the switchtender's position, leaving room only for his glasses and his nostrils. To him, it afforded him protection. Train and yard crews on the rails, passing by the switchtender's shanty, would see Luke through the window and remark how he looked like a mummy sitting in the chair. So "Lukey" changed to Spooky, or Spooky Lukey. It labeled both demeanor and appearance.

Most switchtenders endured the *physical* form of separation anxiety. Jeff Taylor had a leg cut off while switching in one of the grain elevator yards. He used crutches rather than a prosthetic limb, just happy to have survived. He never complained. There was Jim Cavanaugh, who had lost his right arm from the elbow down because of an engineer's incorrect perception of a hand sign. Jim had his arm torn off in a coupling move, the knuckles pinching and literally pulling his forearm away from his upper arm. He almost died from the accident and the resulting loss of blood. It had occurred many years before the advent of surgeons' miraculous reattachments. It was rumored that Jim's forearm was merely thrown into the Dumpster at the time of the accident, after his pinky ring was taken off. Yet he was happy to learn to write with his left hand and to be employed at a job he could handle, throwing switches and completing the necessary log of all the trains or jobs that passed, and which tracks they traveled.

Uncle Phil motioned for Phillip to come over to him once when young Phil was about six years old. They had just seen a man walking down the sidewalk with a crutch under his left arm for assistance, because the man had no left leg from the knee down. "Phillip Anthony, ... c'mere,

I gonna tella you somp-a-ting. I cried-a 'cause-a I hadda no shoes-a, until I saw a man-a that-a hadda no feet." Uncle Phil nodded down and sideways at young Phil, and squinted his eyes to ensure Phil knew he meant business with that remark. Phil didn't totally understand at the time, but later, understood the great wisdom of his godfather. Someone always had it worse. Don't whine about trivialities. When Phil first saw Jim Cavanaugh, his thoughts immediately went to his uncle Phil's comment, and the sage advice that was good for life.

Jeff Taylor worked mornings at the switchtender position, and Jim Cavanaugh worked nights. Spooky Landscome worked the afternoon shift. One time Barry caught the midnight switchtender job, to break in with Jim Cavanaugh. Cavanaugh was late arriving, so before leaving for the night, Spooky gave Barry the job briefing. He pointed to the ledger with his pencil, which showed that Barry and Jim had to be aware that three eastbounds were coming. Spooky smiled and shook his head up and down as he did so, to make sure Barry got the message. Barry smiled back, also nodding, to show he understood. Spooky then began unraveling his mummy roll for the trip home. Evidently he thought the air in his car with the windows up was safe. Then, uncharacteristically, Spooky spoke out loud with conviction, "Y'know, the other day I had a hard-on, but I prayed it away." Then he smiled and walked out the door.

Barry would think about that comment all his life, too. All the men working the switch tender position were in their mid- to late sixties, just biding time until they decided to retire. Barry just supposed a sixty-five-year-old would be happy anytime he had some wood in this pre-Viagra era. But sometimes over the years, Barry thought Spooky may have been "right on" about his hard-on, and everyone else was wrong. Everyone with a quarter of a cerebrum knows that since the beginning of recorded history, an erect penis has guided billions down the wrong paths, literally and figuratively. As Jim Morrison wrote and sang in "The End," "Ride the snake to the lake, the ancient lake, baby."

The hot days of summer in mid-July brought with them the familiar *zur-ee, zur-ee* of cicadas in the evenings, which signaled that fall was not far away. Barry liked the sound, but hated what it signified. He remembered when he was a child that this sound meant school was around the corner, and that the wonderful, carefree summer days of drive-ins, nature exploration at Grandpa McAlister's farm, and Little League baseball were about to end. Now there was no impending school … just railroading. Grandpa McAlister incorrectly called the cicadas "locusts," as did many farm people. Barry thought it might have been because farmers dreaded the real locusts so much. They could smoke your crop in no notes. A true locust was in actuality a grasshopper. As a little boy, Barry would see the cicadas in brainless crisis, fluttering on the ground under the lights at gas stations. Fran would allow Barry to take them home for observation. But their warning from the trees that summer was about to end would be an annual unwelcome sign for Barry. He always experienced a kind of sadness when he heard them, like something wonderful was soon to exist no longer.

After their ninety-day break-in period had been completed, Peter Steinman called in Phil, Paul, and Barry with the rest of the student switchmen who had made it. He gave each of them another orange sign passer, leather gloves, and a chromed caboose key. After another safety discussion, Peter told the class with the same hallowed tone in his voice, "Congratulations. You are now rails." Phil thought the term "rails" might mean that railroaders had the same toughness, strength, and durability of the seemingly indestructible steel ribbons that supported the never-ending parade of rolling stock, and the subsequent unimaginable cumulative tons of weight. Meanwhile, Phil, Paul, and Barry all enjoyed their new occupations, whether temporary or permanent, and they all had great summers.

At the end of the summer of '74, a notice went up on the personnel bulletin board that Tom Moffat was looking for management trainees, to which the Central Pacific referred as "officer trainees," the military background again being significant. But Phil, whom the air force had wanted to promote as an officer, offering him the Air Force Academy initially, and later, the Airman Education and Commissioning Program, declined the additional interview. A disappointed Tom Moffat had specifically called Phil, Paul, and Barry because of their degreed status as well as their now-relatively good idea of what railroading entailed. Phil didn't know why, but he never wanted to be considered "better" than anyone else. In the service, it bothered him that the military referred to "officers and their ladies," and "enlisted men and their wives." Why were the enlisted men married to just "wives?" Couldn't their wives be ladies, too? Phil remembered a cartoon he'd seen in the service of a two-tier outhouse, one on top of the other, rather than side by side. The one on top read "Officers," and the one on the bottom read "Enlisted." It was like in the movie *MASH*, when the doctor asked about the surgery patient, "Is this man commissioned or enlisted?" The answer was "Enlisted," to which the doctor replied, "Make the stitches bigger."

These observations didn't arise from nothing. It was this inequity that sort of naturally evoked a desire in Phil to stay away from any pecking orders, especially where he would be the "top pecker." It was uncomfortable for him. He was a natural- born leader, and he liked to lead. But he didn't like the authoritative, self-serving attitude accompanying many in leadership positions. He didn't like the appearance of one-way respect. Phil had been asked by his air force TI, his tech instructor, on the first day of air force basic training, if he thought he could handle the troops in the flight. Phil had thought it was because he had some college, and was required to take ROTC at Missouri University as a freshman, since MU was a land grant school. Phil had told the tech sergeant, "Yes, sir," and became the dorm chief for his fifty-man flight, all through basic. He did very well, and the new airmen respected him and Phil respected them. But when his flight was finished with basic, his TI asked Phil if he'd made his bed every day. Phil's answer had been a snappy, "Yes, sir, I did, sir." The TI replied, "Then you're a dumb sonofabitch!" Phil then questioned, "Sir?" The TI explained to Phil that he should have ordered a subordinate troop to make his bed. The thought had never occurred to Phil. First of all, Phil didn't think anyone could make it as decently as he could, since the beds had to be tight enough to bounce a quarter off of them. And further, wasn't it *his* job? Phil was uncomfortable with the idea of subservience, especially to him.

Paul, like his brother, shunned anything to do with honcho-ism. He had been the defensive co-captain in high school football, and like his brother, was a natural leader. But Paul basically didn't care that much about anything, especially the advent of leadership. His combat time in Vietnam had taken a lot of desire to achieve out of him. All he really cared about were his parents, Rosalinda, Phil, and Barry, and their families, an occasional female, and a more-than-occasional cold beer. In fact, child support had probably made Paul much more responsible than he'd have been otherwise. So when the bulletin was posted at the end of the summer of 1974 about the upcoming management interviews, Paul was asked by those who knew he had a degree if he was going to interview for management. Paul would smile, shake his handsome head, and say, "Yeah, right." When Tom Moffat called, Paul said, "No thanks, Tom, but I appreciate it anyway." Paul really didn't, but was being polite because he liked Tom. "Looks like you'll be the only psych major in management around here, Tom," Paul said with a grin.

"Okay, Paul, but it's our loss," Tom responded. "Maybe you'll change your mind later. It's there for you if you do."

"Maybe," Paul replied, but knew he wouldn't.

Barry, on the other hand, *did* interview, and was accepted to enter the Central Pacific Officer Training Program in Omaha, Nebraska. His officer background in the army had prompted him to accept promotion as a way of life. When you were offered it, you took it. During one of the few times Barry was actually able to spend time with his father, Bill, when he was a youngster, Bill told him, "Son, when someone hands you a ball, you run with it!" That had always been in Barry's subconscious. It was why he became an officer. And even though Barry was predisposed to view management with negativity, like Phil and Paul, he discussed the possibility with Susan, and they decided to give it a shot.

Barry had an additional interview in Kansas City, with Tom, and one more locally, when a midlevel management-type, Carl Banner, came down from Omaha to interview potential officer candidates. Since Tom and Carl were good friends, Tom had already conferred with Carl positively about Barry. Carl had a degree in business, like Barry, so there was already some common ground. And Carl, like Barry, was an ex-jock. Barry's interview with Carl couldn't have gone better. Carl scheduled Barry for a final interview in Omaha with the head of the Central Pacific personnel department, Vance Carlson.

Both Carl and Tom counseled Barry about Vance. "He deals in a stress interview, Barry," Tom told him. "Just be yourself. You'll do fine. Vance will ask you some off-the-wall questions and then study your answers. He's really different, but he's a genius in his own right. He's got a master's in business and an undergraduate in psychology."

"He's very cerebral, Barry," Carl added, with a serious "I don't envy you" look. Both Tom and Carl had had to interview with Vance when they became managers.

The CP flew Barry to Omaha on a Sunday evening in December 1974 to interview with Vance Carlson at 10:00 a.m. the next day. Barry spent a restless night that Sunday, even though both Tom and Carl called him, wishing him luck and encouraging him not to be nervous. The CP had arranged for Barry to bunk in at the Red Lion, a class-A Omaha hotel that was one block from CP headquarters on Dodge Street. Barry called Susan, who also wished him luck. He already missed her. On Monday, Barry had a ham-and-cheese omelet at the Red Lion restaurant. Even though the omelet was delicious, it didn't sit well in Barry's nervous stomach. Was his suit too old? Would his nervousness show? After additional cups of black coffee, Barry thought, Well, here goes, and got up from his table, leaving a generous tip for average service. He walked downhill toward CP headquarters. At 9:40 a.m., the sun was in Barry's eyes from the right as he walked eastward. The cool December morning was subconsciously serene as Barry buttoned another trench coat button and began to feel an unexpected confidence welling up inside. He walked through the CP front entrance and turned left to the personnel office, where he met Carl Banner for the second time. Carl had the corner office.

"Hi Barry! Good to see you again," Carl said, smiling, with an obvious attempt to put Barry at ease. He was well aware of the impending interview with the stoic Vance. "Did you get a good rest?" Carl didn't wait for an answer. "C'mon, Barry. I'll take you up to meet Vance. Let's get this party started."

Vance's office was on the third floor with additional personnel offices. Barry didn't feel the elevator ride. The third floor was also the home of the personnel department's sociological sister, labor relations. Through Vance Carlson's office door window, Barry could see a plain-looking interior. Vance was not one for art deco, or gung-ho encouragement statements printed on scenic posters. No, Vance was all he needed to be *inside*, without pretentious goo surrounding him on the walls of his office. There *were* some pictures of CP locomotives. Barry did like a large, framed poster on Carl Banner's office wall of a huge orangutan looking toward the camera with an expression of quiet indignation. The caption read, "When I want your opinion, I'll beat it out of you."

Barry began to be aware of his heart thumping. Through the window, he could see Vance staring at paperwork. He looked incredibly fit in an immaculate black pin-stripe suit, and appeared to be in his mid- to late thirties. Vance's hair was perfectly parted on the left side. He was tan and handsome. Barry thought Vance looked like he was at the top of his game. After Carl knocked, Vance, who already knew they were there, looked up at the two heads through his office door window, and with a bored semi-smile said expressionlessly, "Come in."

Vance shook Barry's hand, but didn't stand up all the way. Still, Barry could tell that Vance was at least as tall as he was. Somehow Barry knew Vance was attempting to not be overpowering. It was as close as Vance ever came to putting someone at ease. After the initial introduction, Carl left Vance's office, looking over his shoulder as he closed the door behind him, saying, "I'll see you later." Vance didn't reply, but stared at Barry for an incredibly long and psychologically painful thirty seconds, still sporting his half smile. He leaned back in his comfortable red leather chair. His fingers and thumbs were touching each other in a rhythmic silent tap as his wrists rested on his trim lower abdomen. Vance did not tell Barry to relax, but placing both hands behind his head, he leaned farther back in his executive chair, which squeaked softly, and asked, "Barry, how do you feel about life?"

The question really caught Barry off guard, but he answered quickly, "Pretty, good, Mr. Carlson, pretty good." (That was feeble, Barry thought.) This was to be the tone of the interview, and not atypical for Vance. Vance would ask nebulous questions, mixed in with very pertinent questions, and Barry would answer to the best of his ability. After a while, Barry began to exhibit some aptitude and wit, like a batter who steps in the practice box, whiffs a couple, but eventually starts stroking liners. During the interview, Barry had stroked a couple of "one-liners" that Vance liked a lot, but of course never reacted to, positively or negatively. When Vance finally ceased with the stress pitches, the interview ended. Barry felt like he'd just faced Nolan Ryan. "Thank you, Mr. Carlson. It's been a pleasure," Barry necessarily lied, wishing he were comfortably back home with Susan and Erin. Vance shook Barry's large hand comfortably and sincerely with his equally large hand, and characteristically unemotionally said, "We'll be getting in touch with you," which was Vance's cryptic way of saying, "You just hit one out."

After meeting with other midlevel managers, Barry called Susan, Phil, and Paul with the good news and flew back to Kansas City. The entire return flight was a jumble of missing Susan and Erin, recent recollections of everyone he had just met, a giant exhale, and a genuine concern about the future. What would this mean for the young McAlisters?

Phil, Paul, and Barry were temporarily laid off as switchmen on December 31. Typically, the railroads are busy with Christmas shipping from mid-November to mid-December, but after that, there is a lull in business. Shipping docks are empty, and no production occurs to fill them. Auto assembly plants shut down for annual maintenance. Demand, in general, is lessened. But the CP scheduled all three for two weeks' vacation, beginning January 1. They all thought that was pretty nice of the CP. Tom Moffat saw to it that Paul got a job at the caboose track while cut off as a switchman, where he cleaned cabooses and supplied them with distillate to burn in the stoves, and required paperwork for the conductors to fill out.

Tom also had arranged for Phil and Barry to work as District 3 clerks, which meant they would pick up crews in crew wagons and clean various buildings in janitorial service. At the beginning of March 1975, all three were called back to switching service, and in April, Barry was notified that he and Susan were due to move to Omaha in May for Barry to begin the officer training program. Barry and Susan were very excited at the prospect. Although neither knew what to expect, they both viewed the opportunity subconsciously as the *right* thing to do. "When someone hands you a ball, you run with it."

# CHAPTER 9
## HOW TO BE A HONCHO

Barry drove to Omaha on May 15, 1975, one year and one month after he, Phil, and Paul became railroaders at Kansas City. He was to meet with Harold Bader, supervisor of the officer trainees, the next day at 0800 in what was affectionately known as the "Big Brick," Central Pacific headquarters. Barry would find out that Harold was affectionately known as "the SOT," resulting from the initials of his title and his penchant for heading to happy hour as soon as his day at work ended. Barry would later learn that there was a reason for Harold to want to be delirious at day's end, ASAP. He would also learn that Harold had other, less harmless nicknames as well. Barry was to stay at the Red Lion Inn again. After checking in at 3:00 p.m., he took a walk around Omaha in the ideal spring weather. Omaha was a beautiful town. There was enough greenery growing near CP headquarters to allow the sweet smell of cherry blossoms and apple blossoms to overwhelm the vehicle exhaust odors, and the sun was a warm, comfortable 70 degrees. Birds were actually singing in the trees downtown. It all felt quite wonderful. It felt like success.

Barry reflected on the dizzying last few years of his life, and where he was at this point. Susan and her father were ecstatic about Barry's selection, as was Fran. But Barry's childhood supposition (it wasn't really a "dream") of becoming a dentist still weighed heavily on his somewhat cluttered mind. He knew he was in a position to be envied. He was a young man with a degree, had served as an officer in the military, and now had a shot at management in a very large, very successful organization. Many on the CP work rosters would have sold their souls to be accepted on the CP Officer Training Program, like Peter Steinman. It was a place to aspire to be. It was varsity Valhalla for railroaders. Barry would do well. He did well at anything placed in front of him to accomplish.

But Barry would always feel somewhat less than fulfilled, always wondering if he could have made it through dental school. He had taken the DAT, the Dental Admissions Test, once, and bizarre as it may seem, a janitor accidentally incinerated the tests that day. Barry and the other eighty-three students who took the test were given the option of retaking the test the next week or waiting for several months. Barry chose to wait, since the chemistry section of the test was a major-league challenge and he wanted to bone up. But he never retook the test. It was a rung on his personal ladder that would never be a step up. So, with the beautiful spring day filling his spirit with joy, and with the anticipation of his first day at the Big Brick, Barry attempted to forget his prior aspirations and grab a handle of the situation. As Barry thought Boz Scaggs sang in the "Lido Shuffle," now it was his turn to "wear the handle of the top." Or perhaps Bob Dylan was more to the point: "Try to be a suck-cess" in "Subterranean Homesick Blues." Barry would attempt to realize his good fortune to be here, and tried not to devote too much mental energy to the "what-ifs." Like Ned Lingle used to say, "If ifs and buts were candy and nuts, it'd be Christmas every day."

Barry continued walking east on Dodge Street, still smelling the fragrant aromas of spring blossoms and feeling the late afternoon sun filtering down from the Omaha skyscrapers, comfortably warming his back. There again, in all its glory, was the Big Brick, the heartbeat of the Central Pacific and Barry's new home. People were scurrying in and out the CP entrances, to and from all directions, exhibiting determined looks and immaculate dress. The building itself was an early-twentieth-century structure that had experienced a massive add-on in the fifties. Outside, it was almost painfully mundane, a block long and a block wide, except for the turquoise inlays between the windows, which set it apart from all the rest of the Omaha buildings. Barry would always wonder why the turquoise color was used, since the Central Pacific's famous colors were a pleasing yellow, red, and gray.

Barry walked toward the Big Brick with anticipation, and wondered at the substantial history involved and the fact that he would soon be a part of that history for better or worse. As he walked into the west entrance, he noticed the tight security, and the sign-in desk. He also noticed the extremely beautiful women. Management privilege, Barry thought, unintentionally chauvinistically, as if pretty women couldn't be capable also. Barry would soon be schooled in this sophomoric prejudgment in the ensuing weeks at CP. Many of those extremely beautiful women were also exceptionally bright.

It was close to the end of the workday, and human traffic was picking up even more. Barry thought he could best serve by exiting the building. The warm, fresh spring air subconsciously reminded him of Grandpa McAlister's farm and the wonderful feelings he had when school was out for the summer, long before the *zur-ees* of the cicadas were heard. He would go back to the Red Lion, have a good dinner, compliments of the Central Pacific, call Susan, Phil, and Paul, and have a good night's sleep. He would wake early the next day with nervous expectation, have a large breakfast, and walk east to greet his new life. Meanwhile, the beautiful spring afternoon that signaled the change in seasons also signaled a change in Barry's life. Was it to be good, or was it like the storm brewing, bringing the hideous carnival to town in *Something Wicked This Way Comes*?

The beginning of the first day of management left Barry feeling almost nauseated with anticipation. He was looking forward to meeting with Harold Bader for indoctrination and assignments. Harold's office was on the third floor of twelve at the Big Brick, the same as Vance Carlson's. Later, Barry would discover that Harold's other nicknames, besides Sot, were Bizarro, or Bizarro Bader, because his behavior was so bizarre. He was always laughing inappropriately at everything that was said, like a bad disk jockey, whether an attempt at humor had been made or not. Another label for Harold that reared its humorous head from time to time was Master Bader.

Barry, at the secretary's direction, was waiting for Harold in Harold's office at 7:50 a.m. Harold showed up at 8:20 a.m., and with an overacted look of surprise, shook his head, frowned, shrugged, and pursed his lips as he picked up some papers on his desk. Bader was short and plainly dressed, with short brown hair combed to the right in an out-of-date

1963 Princeton. He wore black, plastic-rimmed, thick-lensed glasses that made his beady little eyes even beadier and littler. Barry thought he looked like a mole. His body movements were quick, jerky, and multidirectional, but with no obvious task to be performed. He was just jerking around, absurdly, almost twitching. It was behavior that country folks would call "squirrelly." Barry thought some good rock music in the background would have been perfect. Harold looked up into his scalp, shook his head further, and finally, looking at Barry, raised his eyebrows and started to smile a "So, what's this?" smile.

"And you are?" Harold said, laughing for no apparent reason.

"I'm Barry McAlister ... from Kansas City," Barry said, already standing in respect for Harold when he entered his office. "I was to meet with you this morning."

Barry held out his hand, expecting a good strong handshake. Instead, what was returned from Harold was a feeble grab of Barry's large fingers, a gesture Paul always thought was a subconscious attempt at control. Paul Barnes's psychology training had rendered him forever consciously aware of the subconscious in people. He had often discussed human traits with Barry and Phil while growing up, long before he majored in psychology. One of the many personal behaviors they discussed was how much you could tell about a person by their handshake. Paul felt a good strong handshake represented the desire for honesty, fairness, and integrity to persist between the shakers. Conversely, grabbing one's fingers represented to Paul the desire to subdue the other person, or to hold him at a deliberate disadvantage if given the chance. To Paul, it was "You're not shaking my fingers ... We're supposed to be shaking hands." Many had learned to give a good strong, genuine handshake as a ruse and would happily screw you in the future. But today, Barry's higher calling was for CP orientation rather than psychological scrutiny, and he accepted Harold's version of a handshake as consistent with his rodentlike appearance.

"Harold Bader," Harold said, still smiling and still displaying confusion. "Are you a new trainee?" Harold easily guessed with asinine merriment.

"Yes, I am," Barry answered with a slight smile, but not cracking up foolishly as Bader was doing. "I *think* I was supposed to meet with you."

"Oh, that's right," Harold remembered. "I guess I almost forgot about you, ha ha. Couldn't let that happen, huh, Barry, hee-hee."

"No, sir."

"I have a lot of paperwork for you, Barry, which I want you to fill out now. It will take you a couple of hours to complete. You can do it in the trainee lounge. I'll show you where it is. This week will be basically an indoctrination week for you here at headquarters. You will be meeting with other company officers, as well as your officer-trainee cohorts, whom I assume you will get to know. You will have some assignments with them in the future. You will be meeting again with the director of personnel, Vance Carlson." Barry noticed genuine fear in Harold's face as he said Vance's name. He looked like a raccoon, with small, scared, beady little eyes in the headlights. His overly jovial, flaky demeanor ceased for a second to display genuine dread. Harold reported directly to Vance. Barry could not understand this at the time, since he liked Vance so well and vice versa. Barry would later learn that Harold was not Vance's choice to supervise the officer trainees. Harold was picked by a company officer whose rank was higher than Vance's, and with whom Harold was "sucked in," as it was termed at the time. This officer was about to retire, thereby taking Harold's protection with him, and Harold was feeling the pressure of an insecure, nonprotected future.

The "old guys," as they were sometimes referred to, could make or break careers. They were usually vice presidents or members of their staffs who could, one, positively affect people's careers, seeing that they were afforded the appropriate assignments and accolades; and two, keep anyone else from destroying their careers and ultimately, their lives. This wasn't *Sesame Street*. The most common name for these older, savvy, powerful gentlemen was "godfather." As is common knowledge, Barry would find out that hard work and dedication are no match for the "godfatherism" that had occurred in business since business first *was* business. You couldn't beat the good-ol'-boy network. This was another reason Barry, although grateful for this opportunity, remained reserved about his new status.

Fran had constantly referred with disdain to the baloney she witnessed from the zone managers interacting with the auto dealerships. She had often told Barry as he grew up, "Son, don't *ever* get into management. It's a cutthroat, immoral, dog-eat-dog existence." Fran had not minced words about her dislike for some of the disgusting unwritten precepts of management. Barry had listened for years to her scathing recollections of one manager selling his "best friend" down the tubes to attain advancement, or a boss taking his buxom secretary on a road trip with him, openly courting her, with a wife and three kids at home. There was alcoholism, adultery, thievery, envy, covetousness, and you-name-it. It was a smorgasbord of Commandment-breaking, and Fran didn't want any part of it, nor did she want her young Barry trapped in it as an adult. Her negative words forever echoed in both Barry's conscious and subconscious mind. Obviously, all managers were not like that, but Barry's early perceptions equaled total negative reinforcement for management in general. It was another reason Barry wanted to be a dentist.

Barry would later find out that Vance had, on several occasions, toyed with Harold Bader, entangling him in Vance's famous mind games. Harold wasn't a bad type, but deep down, management scared him to death, hence the flaky, silly smiles and frequent giggles. Harold's way of coping was to display the very opposite of what he felt inside: terror, panic, and general insecurity. He was suspicious of everyone, especially Vance. And Vance, who was a serious, straightforward, brilliant individual, viewed as fair game what he accurately perceived as superficial behavior in Harold. The result was that every time Vance had occasion, it was "let the games begin." Poor Harold would never win. And of course, Vance always held the rank trump card, although he didn't need to play it to surmount Harold.

"When you finish filling out the paperwork, Barry, see Miss Durrant, whom you already met, I presume, this morning. She will check over your paperwork and apprise you of omissions or corrections that are needed. Don't worry. You'll have some. Everybody does. Then, after lunch, come see me when you're finished, however long it takes. We want comprehensiveness, not speed. But meet with me, and I'll have your assignments for the next two weeks. Then, I have other stuff to get to." Harold once again dropped the false happiness, and looking at the paperwork on his desk, went deadpan for an instant. Then he recovered, and giggling, said to Barry, "Any questions?"

"No, not at this time. Thank you very much, Mr. Bader."

"Please, Barry … It's Harold, and you're welcome. See you after lunch," Harold said, managing a genuine smile. Like everyone, Harold liked naive, polite, honest, humble Barry.

Barry worked through his lunch hour on his paperwork, since he had already consumed a large, appetizing breakfast at the Red Lion. He had checked and double-checked, taking it as a challenge for perfection when Harold had told him everybody makes errors. When Miss Durrant returned from lunch, Barry gave her his forms, which she corrected amazingly quickly. He didn't have many, but he did have some errors. He then went back to Harold's office and rapped on the right side of the doorjamb with his knuckles.

"Sir?"

Harold looked up from his paperwork. "Hey, Barry. Turning in your paperwork?"

"Yes, sir."

"Well, I about have your assignments completed. You will, as I said before, be spending the remainder of the week here at headquarters. Then Monday, you will be heading for a week's tour in Pocatello, Idaho. You'll like it there."

Barry felt a twinge of stomach acid hit as he realized that the separation from Susan and Erin was to continue. This excursion to Omaha was just the second time he and Susan had been apart since they were married, the first being last December when he initially interviewed with Vance in Omaha. He really missed Susan and Erin. The trip to Pocatello would be the third time apart from his family. The separation times were beginning to mount up. It was another management red flag, with Barry not realizing at the time that the term, like so many in American life, such as *asleep at the switch* and *one-track mind*, originated in railroading. Red flags stopped trains. Sometimes metaphoric red flags stopped lives.

"One other thing, Barry," Harold said, becoming serious. He placed his forearms on his desk, with his hands clasped, and lowered his head with his chin about an inch above his hands. Then he said in a semi-whisper, his eyes reflecting panic, "I want to tell you something, Barry … There's a grapevine around here." Harold's voice was not strong, almost stammering. "Things get back to people, so expect everything you do or say to be common knowledge. It would behoove you to remember that. The 'vine' has destroyed a lot of people here at the Big Brick. Don't let it get you. Understand? I want to hear nothing but good about you, Barry. If you have any questions, don't hesitate to ask." Harold handed Barry his assignments for the next two weeks and shook Barry's large hand, grabbing the ends of his fingers.

"Yes, I understand, and thanks, Mr. Bader."

"It's Harold, and you're welcome. Good luck, Barry."

The following week was both enjoyable and confusing for Barry. He met so many railroad managers, he couldn't keep them all straight, even though he wrote down plenty of notes. He also met several other officer trainees who were back in town for that week. As much as possible, Harold had endeavored to alternate the weeks that trainees were in and out of town. Aside from the many interesting engineering feats such as tunnels, mines, coal loops, and strategically important rail yards the trainees would eventually visit, there was an inexhaustible amount of information to learn at headquarters.

During the next weekend, Barry and Susan moved, with the help of Susan's older brothers, to a little third-floor apartment in southwest Omaha. Barry had made decent money as a switchman in Kansas City, but he had taken a pay cut to be an officer trainee. This was standard for all trainees who came from the ranks. Those straight from college didn't know any better. The cheap apartment would suffice nicely until Barry was assigned with a promotion, which usually occurred a year after officer training. Susan's brothers were quite delighted with carrying furniture up three flights of stairs. Barry and Susan rewarded them with beer and brats. Sunday evening after her brothers headed back to Kansas City, with little Erin sleeping peacefully in the bedroom, Susan made a drink for herself and Barry, one she had labeled a "Moose Surprise."

Barry and Susan had played many games of Scrabble when they first became friends, when Barry worked with her father in the army. Then, when they were first married, they used to play Scrabble for sex. If Barry won, he got some. If Susan won, she got some. It was a good plan. There were no losers. They would close all the drapes and play the game in the nude, happily forgetting that the outside world existed. It was just the two of them, and it was very intimate and very sweet. Sometimes the games were pleasantly interrupted, with a prize being "awarded" before the game's outcome. Susan, who was 5 feet 4 inches, was always overwhelmed by Barry's height, a full foot taller. Because of this, and his large frame, Susan had nicknamed Barry "Moose," even though she realized he had another large-animal nickname from his youth, Bear. Barry didn't mind, and sort of liked the name Moose, since Susan said it with love and teasing. Usually, these nude Scrabble sessions, which Susan usually won, began with a drink, which was normally Barry's department. One time, all that was available was Bacardi Dark and half a can of Coke, not enough for two large rum and Cokes. Resourceful Barry had looked in the cabinets and found a can of fruit cocktail, which he put in the blender and beat to liquid. "What are you doing, honey?" Susan had asked, hearing the blender's whirr.

"It's a surprise, honey," Barry had answered. He mixed the liquid fruit cocktail with the Coke and added a shot-and-a-half of rum to each glass. "Here." Barry shook his head as he handed the new concoction to Susan.

"What is it?" Susan again questioned.

"I told you ... it's a surprise," Barry said again, not wanting to divulge the ingredients for fear of Susan's teasing.

"A Moose Surprise," Susan had said, laughing as she took the first sip. "Not bad, honey," she said, and it really wasn't. From that point on, Susan and Barry had indulged in Moose Surprises as their drink of choice, especially during Scrabble matches. It was a great personal tradition for the young couple to have established, the kind that keeps marriages intact.

As Susan handed the drink to Barry, they both scooted back on their comfortable blue velour couch, exhausted from moving, and sighed almost at the same time. Both pondered the life-changing circumstances.

"Well, honey, whaddaya think?" Susan asked with genuine concern and interest, since there hadn't been much time during the weekend move to discuss anything.

"You know, Suz, truthfully, I really wish I knew. I know I learned an awful lot about management I wish I hadn't learned, in only one week."

"Such as ...?" Susan questioned.

"Well, there are factions. It seems there are a lot of people on one side or another. If you are friendly with one side, the other takes it as an affront. And, honey, it looks a lot like it's the old 'who you you-no,' not *what* you know. People seemed to be well-thought-of for the most inane reasons ... because they can drive a golf ball well, because they can hold their liquor, because they're good with the ladies."

"You better not be good with any ladies but this one, Slick," Susan said, half kidding and half serious.

"That's a big ten-four," Barry needlessly agreed. "You know I wouldn't know what to do with it if it chased me up a tree. Besides, like Paul Newman supposedly said about Joanne Woodward, 'When you've got steak at home, why go look for hamburger?'"

"Thank you and Paul for the piece-of-meat analogy, Barry. Joanne and I appreciate it. You know some people *would* get tired of a steady diet of steak, and hamburger just might look pretty good sometimes."

"Not a chance, Suz, and you know that. Besides, you're much more than steak. You're mashed potatoes and gravy, and beans also. You're the whole meal." Susan reached across the couch and backhanded Barry on his huge shoulder.

"Really, Barry, what about this management stuff, really?" Susan was serious now.

"Well, I guess it's a very good thing I still have my seniority as a switchman-brakeman. It's an ace in the hole I don't want to have to play, but I see a lot a 'Danger, Will Robinson' in the management ranks. I honestly don't know if I can identify. It seems like they want you to be domineering to succeed. In one week, I've already met several people who are nervous as cats near a laboratory, and one guy who is just plain scared to death. It's obviously affecting their health and family lives. I don't want that for me ... or you."

"But what if I want that for you?" Susan spoke from the heart.

"What's that—early death and my insurance money? Remember Ray Stevens's great song from around 1968, '69, 'You better take care of business, Mr. Businessman?' Remember all the lines to that song, Suz?"

"No, honey, you misunderstand. I'm talking about the status you can enjoy being a Central Pacific manager. They do all right, you know, in the long run: the stock options, the company car, the paid vacations, and other perks. It may be for us, honey." Susan was being as wonderful a wife as she could be, trying to be positive about all of it. Inwardly, she too had reservations, her father being a non-com in the army. She recollected from her childhood the privileges of rank, which usually meant her father's lack thereof, given the direction poo-poo rolls. But Susan moved over next to her exhausted husband, and, putting her arm around his large shoulders, kissed him on the temple. "Now let's get you ready for Pocatello in the morning. What time do you have to be at the airport?"

Barry and Susan, too tired for Scrabble, just packed as they talked a bit more about their future with the management side of the Central Pacific. Their ultimate joint decision was a wait-and-see approach. They went to bed, kissed, said their "night-nights" and "I love yous," and turned to opposite sides of the bed with their backs toward each other, butts touching. Barry knew Susan was too tired for the husband-wife thing, but he also knew she would have provided if he had asked. He figured she needed her sleep now, to prepare for the next day of chasing after little Erin, who was very kinetic and very bright. Susan also had the massive task of unpacking, straightening, and arranging from the move. And Barry realized he needed some decent z's for the next day's festivities. He needed to be fresh for the trip to Pocatello. Sometimes it didn't feel so great to be responsible. Susan immediately drifted off into a sweet sleep, her breaths becoming long and even and relaxed. Barry looked at her curvy form, silhouetted by the white silk sheets just thrown on the unmade bed. Her naturally curly, now auburn-dyed hair was partially up on her pillow above her lovely head. The rest of her sculptured, thick hair was divided by her neck and right shoulder and had fallen on her lovely breasts, now expanding and contracting in a rhythmic peace. Barry followed her curves with his eyes. Susan's strong, square shoulders and ample, round, perfect breasts narrowed to a beautiful, trim waist. Then the silk sheets revealed her perfect, strong rear quarters, which then further narrowed to her graceful, dancer thighs and knees, with a mini-curve evident from Susan's calf. "Man, McAlister ... you sure lucked out," Barry thought to himself. "God *did* save this one back for you."

But Barry's blessing-counting soon gave way to a negative, rebellious feeling. His precious bride and daughter were again to be in a different city than he was for one week. Hadn't they just experienced that? When Barry was working as a switchman, he was used to working an average of six hours, being paid for eight, and then returning home to Susan. Sometimes when Barry worked midnights, Susan would stay up late, cleaning house or making some gourmet meal she and Barry and Erin could enjoy the next day. He, Phil, and Paul worked a lot of midnights, as extra-board switchmen. Barry always worried about Susan's lack of sleep for dealing with Erin, but she always managed extremely well. They were very close. But now, Barry felt his wife, and as a result, his life, beginning to slip away from him. He had noticed in just a week of railroad management that many of the midlevel and high-level managers were on their second or third marriages, and some even their fourth. Barry instinctively knew it was the work affecting the marriages. He tossed and turned restlessly all night.

The next day Susan had coffee on and breakfast cooking when Barry groggily rolled out of the rack. "Mornin', honey," she said energetically as she saw Barry's feet hit the floor. She had heard the alarm go off after the second time she had reset it for "snooze," so he could get a little more sleep. Miraculously, Erin was quietly watching morning cartoons on the tube, except for an occasional baby girl giggle. Susan took Barry a cup of coffee as she kissed him on the side of his mouth and patted him on the rear. "C'mon, Mr. Manager. The Central Pacific is waiting for your arrival so everyone else can start."

Barry shook his head, appreciating the humor. He was not a morning person, but had learned to be civil since Susan was. This morning he was not in the best of moods because he had to leave her and little Erin once again. He knew that a bad mood would reflect on his sweet, beautiful wife and be taken incorrectly, so he bit the bullet.

"Hey, wifey, that sure smells a-l-l-l-l-l right!"

# CHAPTER 10
## DERAILS ON THE MAIN LINE

They had a very nice breakfast together that passed all too quickly for them both. Susan and Erin drove Barry to Eppley Field for his flight to Pocatello. As he kissed them good-bye, he felt like he was leaving some of his own body parts. In a way he was, since they were both such an important part of his brain and his heart. They were his life. He loved them so much, and knew he didn't express it often enough to Susan. What if the plane crashed? Would she be okay? Barry stopped and bought some crash insurance for the round-trip in Susan's name, and then wondered: Who would check to see if he'd done so? Would the insurance company contact Susan, or wait for her to contact them? He would call and tell her. The Central Pacific did have an insurance program in place to cover such calamities, but though substantial, it wasn't enough money for Susan and Erin to suit Barry. To him, they were priceless, and no amount of money was good enough for them if he had to check out early.

He was to spend the week in Pocatello with Walt Morehouse, which he knew he would enjoy. It was to be their division tour, one of the trainee requirements. Walt and Barry had switched together in Kansas City, with Walt being Barry's switch foreman on several occasions. They liked each other. Walt also knew Phil and Paul. He'd been selected to go on the program a month before Barry, arriving in Omaha in April. Walt was taking a later flight since he was to meet with a midlevel traffic manager in Omaha that morning. He and Barry planned to meet at 4:00 p.m. in Pocatello and then have dinner.

Barry's plane screamed down the runway. He saw Susan and Erin waving behind the double doors below where his departure gate was. Barry put a big hand up in the window, knowing they couldn't see him, as a quiet little tear leaked out of his right eye. They *did* see him, and Erin jumped up and down, waving frantically as Susan smiled and shook her head, also waving. Barry didn't like this at all. After the flight attendant brought him some black coffee not nearly as good as Susan's, he leaned his head against the plastic panel that housed the window of the TWA 737 and sighed. A few minutes later, he gazed down at the ground now 28,000 feet away. It seemed like they were barely moving, but when Barry compared a speck on the window with the ground, he saw that the speck was moving right along, passing cars and farmhouses at six hundred miles per hour in the opposite direction from his wife and daughter. From this point on, that would sum up Barry and Susan's life together with Central Pacific. It would be a series of departures and arrivals, with very few layovers.

Barry arrived in Pocatello at noon. He rented a car and drove to the Lamplighter Inn, where he and Walt had reservations. As soon as he got his key, he called Susan.

"Suz?"

"Hi, honey," she said in a sweet, excited voice, scratchy and higher than normal. It sounded very cute. She had been watching the clock ever since she'd been back from the airport, anticipating Barry's location in the sky. And she had been crying, although she didn't want Barry to know that. "Did you have a nice flight, Bear Honey?" Although Susan still called Barry "Moose," she would often call him either "Bear Honey" or "Honey Bear," referring to the first nickname he'd received in high school from the football opponent. "Moose" was reserved for teasing times, and the latter two names for sweet times. This was one of the bittersweet times. "What's Pocatello like?" Susan really didn't care about Pocatello, but she cared dearly about Barry.

"The flight was okay, I guess, and Pocatello is pretty, honey. It's a valley between mountain ranges. At least that's what it looks like from what I've seen. I'm going to grab some grub and then meet with the local managers at the depot. Walt Morehouse, this black guy on the training program, is coming in at four. He's got his division tour assignment also, this same week. Besides switching with him in KC, we used to play ball against each other. He's a decent guy."

"Well, that sounds nice, Bear. It will be a lot more fun with him there, huh?"

"I guess," Barry said again, sounding unintentionally disinterested, when it was purely and simply longing for his wife. Susan's comment about "fun" lingered in Barry's mind. He hadn't looked at any of this in that manner. Maybe he should begin to do so. Maybe it was the only way.

"Can I talk to Erin?" Barry said with a sigh.

"She's takin' a nap, Dad." Susan tried to sound happy. "I finally got her to sleep."

"Well, okay, honey. Dad will bring her something." After some trivial verbiage that was designed to prolong the conversation to keep each other as "nearby" as possible, they said their "I love yous" and "good-byes," an unsanctified spousal railroad tradition. Barry promised to call Susan later, before bedtime. One thing the Central Pacific was good about: they expected their managers to use the WATS line as much as they wanted for both business and personal reasons.

Barry met Walt at the airport at 4:00 p.m. as planned. Walt was smiling, not only glad to see Barry but thankful he was off the plane. He hated to fly, always thinking his next flight would be his last. Barry had learned in the military when he had to take military hops that anytime he was the slightest bit concerned about air travel, all he had to do was look at the crew. They fly this thing day in and day out, he would think, and they're all still breathin'. Barry knew air travel was extremely safe and mileage-wise, the safest, but poor Walt was wobbly-legged.

"Let me get this car, and let's *eat!*" Walt said with a long exhale, as if he'd just cheated the Grim Reaper. "And cocktails will *not* be out of the question." The Central Pacific wanted all their managers to have separate cars at the work sites. Money was not an object. In railroading at this point in history, it never was. But in the future, WATS lines and separate cars and many management privileges would disappear.

"We have to go to the depot first. By the way, rough flight, Walt?" Barry remarked, noting Walt's been-through-the-mill look.

"They're all rough, Barry," Walt said, shaking his head.

"Hey, if you can take working daylights at Quindaro with Deacon Burdeau, you can handle a little ol' jet." Barry teased.

"You got that right, Bear," Walt said, shaking his head with a grin. "But that jet moved just a bit faster than Streakin' Deacon."

They got Walt checked into the Lamplighter. After that, they went to the CP Pocatello depot, a beautiful old building reflecting the great craftsmanship of another era, as most old depots did. Barry would never be a "foamer," the term that defined rail buffs in reference to their foaming at the mouth over railroad equipment, especially trains and locomotives. Nor would he be an FRN, the *RN* standing for "railroad nut." But it would always bother Barry when any railroad chose to tear down one of these beautiful depot structures rather than refurbish it. The depots Central Pacific had chosen to restore were literally works of art, and wondrous representatives of a different time in history. It was an era when excellent craftsmanship and aesthetic looks were the norm, rather than cheap imports, plastic, and pressboard. The Pocatello depot didn't even need restoration as yet. It was original and impressive.

Barry and Walt met with Assistant Division Superintendent Randall Kimball, a 6-foot 7-inch Mormon who had seven children. Kimball was a dandy. He was always making deadpan jokes with a lot of wit, coupled with very few smiles, as if he didn't have the time to acknowledge his own jokes, unlike Peter Steinman's snorting. Mr. Kimball was very mobile, always moving. He had come through the management ranks, hiring first as a telegrapher, then dispatcher, then chief dispatcher, then trainmaster, assistant yard superintendent, and yard superintendent, and was now the assistant Pocatello Division superintendent. He'd "been there," and he was one of the best.

He had already made up itineraries for the coming week for both Barry and Walt, with some assignments together, although most were individual. He took them through a quick rundown of the division on the large map behind his desk, and pointed out the primary yards and switching areas. Then he said, "Let's go," moving at a quick pace out the front doors of the depot to his white company Chevrolet. He gave the young trainees a quick tour of the Pocatello yard, showing them where arrivals and departures occurred, and where and how the trains were made up. Each would spend a time period with the Pocatello yardmasters for a closer look at the car classifications.

After a whirlwind-brief yard orientation, Mr. Kimball said, "Well, that's enough railroading for today" as he wheeled his car back toward the depot. "You're probably both tired from the trip. You'll have plenty of time to see and learn plenty. You two will be pulling some twelve-hour shifts this week, and maybe longer … Might as well get used to it. It's the way it's done. See you tomorrow, fellas, at 0700," he said, finishing his spiel exactly as he pulled up to the front of the depot. It seemed he was a master at time conservation, always planning in advance.

"Thanks, Mr. Kimball." "Thank you, sir." Barry and Walt spoke at the same time.

Barry and Walt had come in Walt's rental car since they knew they'd be together for the afternoon orientation. "Let's go wash the jet and railroad residue off our bodies and grab a bite to eat, Barry," Walt said with a grin. "Thompson tells me the Yellowstone Hotel right next to the depot has a good band every night, and decent food. Sound good?"

"Sure, Walt. It sounds fine," Barry said, trying to convince himself, and guessing Susan and Erin were probably thirteen or fourteen hundred miles or so away. "Meet you in about thirty minutes?"

"Make it forty-five. I need some phone time with my woman." Walt was single and enjoyed every second of it. The women loved him. He was a well-built black man with the proverbial pencil-thin mustache and an almost constant smile, except for when he had just stepped off a plane. He was almost exactly Barry's size and build.

"Forty-five sounds good to me, too. I need to talk to my woman also," Barry said, already looking forward to the contact with Susan. This call was shorter with Susan, and she seemed almost aloof for some reason. "Or was it my imagination?" Barry thought afterward. Erin was available for some sub-juvenile conversation with Dad. And without coaxing or directing from Susan, Erin added before saying good-bye, "Don't forget to bring me something, Dadd-e-e." After talking to Susan and Erin, Barry was even less sure about management, having been on the program only seven days.

Walt knocked on the door almost exactly forty-five minutes later, meeting Barry with his constant smile as Barry opened the door with his coat hung over his arm. It was still nippy in Pocatello in the spring. They sped down to the Yellowstone with Walt again driving. As they entered the front door of the Yellowstone, Walt whispered to Barry, "Kelly and Scotty enter the den of iniquity, expecting to find many enemy agents," referring to the great *I Spy* TV series with Cosby and Culp.

Barry smiled, and noticed the place was quite crowded. He and Walt sat at a table in the middle of the dining room, which also functioned as the seating area for the entertainment. The band was to begin at 8:00 p.m. What they did find, rather than enemy agents, was that the female sex was very well represented.

"The band any good?" Walt leaned backward with his handsome head intentionally lodged between two of the six girls who were sitting behind them. Four of the girls were Caucasian, and two looked like they had Native American blood. They all giggled at Walt's self-assured gesture and question.

"Yeah, they're real good. They're called The Quakers. Don't ask why. We're in Mormon country. We've been trying to figure that one out."

"We appreciate it. Thanks," Walt said, bringing his head back to his own table, but leaving his Drakkar aftershave at theirs. Walt leaned over to Barry. "Did you check 'em out?"

"Yeah, they're nice-looking," Barry said, not really caring that much, but noticing that Walt definitely did.

"That one in the purple top is F-I-N-E," Walt remarked with his patented, constant smile, now broader than ever.

"Would you gentlemen care for something to drink?" the waitress asked the two. Barry hadn't even thought about it. His mind was a mix of indeterminate thoughts. But when asked the question, he thought, Might be just what I need ... a little tour with nonreality for a while.

"You got any local beer?" Walt asked.

"We have a Canadian beer on tap called Molson."

"I'll take one," Walt said quickly.

"Make it two," Barry said almost as quickly.

When the waitress brought the beer, the two toasted each other. "Here's to our being senior managers in ten years," Walt said with deliberate false pomp.

"As long as I outrank you, Walt," Barry answered him with a grin as they touched their mugs and took swigs.

"Not bad," Walt commented, relaxing and feeling much better on terra firma than he had thirty thousand feet in the air.

"Definitely what Doc Yellowstone ordered," Barry agreed.

The two each ordered the brisket special, which was excellent, and at 8:00 p.m. sharp, The Quakers hit their first chord. The girls were right. The Quakers were good. They played a lot of Allman Brothers and Lynyrd Skynyrd.

When the second song of the second set began four Molsons later, Walt felt a tap on the shoulder. The girl wearing the purple top looked at him, smiled, and gestured toward the small dance floor directly in front of the band, saying, "How about it?"

"Absolutely," Walt said, and they did. Barry couldn't help but smile. As he grew up with Phil and Paul, they used to make fun of each other's dance styles. It was a natural for young men. It was hysterical watching your buddies move around while trying to look cool. Watching Walt out there on the dance floor doing a decent job with his own style reminded Barry of Phil and Paul. He could feel himself calming somewhat. The Molson was doing its job, anesthetizing him and uncluttering his mind from thoughts of Susan and Erin, their temporary separation, management ethics, not attending dental school, and so on. Now all he felt was relaxed, relinquishing some of the separation anxiety. He really wanted to go back to the Lamplighter, but he didn't want to rain on Walt's parade. And he was enjoying both the numbness the Molson was providing and the music The Quakers were providing.

As the evening progressed with more Molsons, the lead singer for The Quakers approached the microphone. He had a good, bluesy, husky voice, strained from screaming numerous high notes both this evening and past evenings. Sounding like Sugar Bear, another of Barry's nicknames, he said, almost out of breath, "We've got a request for 'Free Bird' by Lynyrd Skynyrd, which we just happen to do very well." Barry and Susan both loved the song. He looked over at the table at one of the girls who had been dancing with Walt. She was one who appeared to have some Native American in her family tree. She smiled and nodded. Barry raised his eyebrows as if to say, "Whaddaya think?" and motioned toward the dance floor with his head. He had no idea why he did it. She nodded again, still smiling as she gave her pretty, long jet-black hair a quick flip and began making her way through the crowded room to meet Barry on the dance floor. The dance floor was jamming with people wanting to move to "Free Bird." Walt was already there from the past two dances, and gave Barry five when he saw him next to him. The "Free Bird" dance was long, but the entire time, Barry never even touched the girl with his hands. There were some accidental body brushes during the dance, because of the crowded dance floor. The dancers got wilder as The Quakers kept increasing the tempo and volume, gradually playing toward the musical frenzy at the end of the number. The lead singer was right: the southern boys would have been proud. When the dance ended, both Barry and the girl smiled a quick smile, nodded thank-yous, and walked away from each other. It was as if the girl had noticed and honored Barry's wedding ring. Or maybe she had a husband or special boyfriend, although there was no ring on her fourth finger. When Barry got back to his chair, the girl was smiling and nodding, and waving another thank-you. Barry smiled and nodded back, and then suddenly felt sick to his stomach.

He realized it was the first time since he and Susan had married that he had danced with another woman ... maybe even since he'd known her. He felt like he'd committed adultery. He had never wanted to dance with anyone other than Susan. He really didn't even want to this evening. He just liked the song. He and Susan had never even discussed whether they could or *should* dance with other people. It seemed they hadn't had to do so. The situation had never come up. It wouldn't, with them always so close. The relaxation the Molson had afforded Barry was now of no value. He realized that he had just done something he never would have done otherwise. All of a sudden his brain took it a step further, to the "what if" arena. He understood in an instant how men cheated on their wives, because of being separated from them so much. At the same time he realized how haughty he had been about those who had done the deed, such as Chance Armstrong. He'd viewed them with disgust, when in actuality, circumstances played a great part. Not that there was *ever* any excuse. That's why it is a Commandment. But Barry was seeing adultery for the first time as being about 20 percent people and 80 percent situational. People were very fallible, true, but most, under normal conditions of daily contact with their spouses, could remain faithful. The days of the pioneer family, when husbands and wives worked together daily to provide for their families, were over. Now there were jets to take family members hundreds, even thousands, of miles away from their loved ones for weeks or months at a time. Barry not only hated the fact that he'd just danced with another woman, but the potential of what might happen after months, and no doubt years, of constant spousal separation. He wanted Susan, and he wanted her now, forever, and he never wanted to leave her again. Then he realized he'd told her he'd call her. What time was it, anyway?

He walked next door to the Central Pacific depot to call Susan on the WATS line. He noticed the big station clock was showing midnight. Good grief, Barry thought, … and she's been waiting for me to call. In his distraught state, he forgot about the time difference between Omaha and Pocatello. It was actually 1:00 a.m. in Omaha.

"Hi, honey," a sleepy, sweet voice said on the other end. "You okay?"

"Hi, babe. Yes, I'm okay. Walt and I are at this hotel next to the depot. Sorry it's late, honey."

"No, honey, I'm glad you called. I was worried."

She was worried about me, and I'm dancing. Good grief, Barry thought. I really didn't even want to dance that badly. It was a monotony breaker, he thought further, defensive but still feeling bad about it. Then he remembered the time difference and blurted, "What time is it there, Suz?"

"It's a little after 1:00 a.m."

"Oh no! I'm sorry, hon," Barry said, shaking his head as if Susan could see him.

"No, Bear Honey, I'm glad. I miss you. Friday when you get home, I'm cooking your favorite dinner, spaghetti and meatballs." Susan's spaghetti and meatballs was almost as good as Rose's. The reason was easy: Rose had taught her how to make it, and like with Carla, had even given her the sugo recipe from the old country and the females of the DeSimone family. Susan was very special to Rose. To Rose, Susan had married her third son, and that qualified her for the ingredients and preparation knowledge few would ever know. Barry was another of the many who enjoyed the exquisite taste, but was clueless about its content. Susan sleepily continued, "Then afterward we can have a couple of Moose Surprises, and you know," Susan yawned with a sleepy laugh, "… play some Scrabble." The sweet innuendo was there.

"That just sounds wonderful, honey. I can't wait. I miss you too, babe. I love you so much."

"Me, too, honey. Get some rest."

"Don't let the bedbugs bite, Suz."

"I wish I had one about six foot four next to me right now."

"Me, too, honey, and you know I *will* bite. Night-night, honey. Love you."

"Night-night, sweetie. Love you, too, Bear."

Barry walked back toward the Yellowstone to catch up with Walt. He felt better, and he felt worse. As Barry approached the Yellowstone entrance, Walt came out the front door, smiling. "Where'd you go, man?"

"I went to call my wife. How'd you do, Walt?"

"I got a phone number from Purple Top. We got a date tomorrow night, if we get in in time."

"Nice goin', Walt. Was there ever any doubt?"

Walt laughed. "C'mon, Barry. We better get our rest." That was rail-speak for "We have a long day ahead of us."

# CHAPTER 11
# LEARNING TO EARN YOUR BEANS

Barry and Walt were at the CP Pocatello depot at 6:45 a.m. Barry was to go with Assistant Supe Kimball and do some efficiency testing on the CP main line. Walt was to sit with the Pocatello yardmasters on both daylights and afternoons.

"Looks like a long one, Walter. We probably won't be able to get together this evening. Good luck with Purple Top," Barry said as Walt began walking over to one of the yardmaster towers.

"Later, Barry. Don't suck in too much today," Walt said, making a sucking sound and laughing, knowing Barry was probably the last trainee to ever do that. Walt himself considered apple-buffing beneath him.

Barry waited for Mr. Kimball to finish a few pertinent morning phone calls, and then they were off in what was now becoming the usual flash with Mr. Kimball. It was about a two-hour drive to the point of testing, and Mr. Kimball, like Barry and most railroaders, had an excessive fondness for coffee. They stopped once for breakfast, and several times afterward, to reload and unload coffee. Urine relief was one thing all railroaders had in common. Rarely was there a reason to look for a bathroom. There was no place like the great outdoors of the railroad to get it done right. Barry's Grandpa McAlister used to call it "watering the flowers" on the McAlisters' farm. Many a flower was watered on or near railroad property.

Barry noticed Mr. Kimball had an awesome control of the division. He was constantly handling phone calls from his car phone, and always carried his radio, which was also experiencing a lot of traffic. He could monitor train progress on his walkie-talkie, and call dispatchers for exact train location times, on both the walkie-tallkie and car phone. At 10:45 a.m., they reached the area for testing.

"Okay, Barry, now I don't know if you've seen the lineups yet, but the first train we're going to test is the PONA. It's due here in about twenty or thirty minutes. It's a good meet." A "good meet" was when a dispatcher could put a train in a siding just long enough for another train, usually opposing, to pass it. Sometimes, the train in the siding would still be moving when the red absolute signal they were approaching turned green, after the opposing train zoomed past them on the main line. Then the train in the siding could take right off, having never had to stop. It was called a good meet. No one was "laid out," and the freight kept moving. Everyone liked good meets. Plus, as usual, the name of the game was moving freight.

But sometimes, for a variety of reasons, such as there being no room in the yards for the train, a derailment, or just plain poor dispatching, a train might be in a siding for hours. As Barry, Phil, and Paul found out, sometimes this would happen when you were right outside your home terminal and really wanted to "get in," as it was called, and go home to see your family. This caused no minor frustrations. Railroaders might be only a half hour from their home terminal, thinking they would make it home to watch their son's or daughter's sports event, only to be put in a siding for four additional hours. But normally, the dispatchers attempted to dispatch good meets. In typical rail-speak, the term would be applied to describe any situation when everyone was where they were supposed to be at the right time. If everyone was able to get to a diner for coffee at a certain time (which was rare, for railroaders), it was a "good meet." Or, like Barry and Mr. Kimball in position for a test on the PONA, just a few minutes before the train's arrival, it was a "good meet."

"We're going to test the PONA to see if the crew members know what to do with a red intermediate signal. You probably remember, Barry, don't you?"

"Yes, sir. They're supposed to stop, whistle off, and proceed at restricted speed."

"That is correct, Barry ... Red signals with number plates. What are you slated for, anyway?"

"Personnel, sir," Barry said, somehow feeling like Mr. Kimball knew that already, the way he knew Barry was an officer trainee who came from the ranks and not a new hire from college.

"Ah-h-h," Mr. Kimball said, sounding slightly disgusted. "You need to be out here, son. I can smell good operating people. They're born, not made, y'know, and you, Barry, could help this company more out here on the ground than you could hiding behind a desk." It was the first time Barry would feel the presumed eminence of the operating department, and it would be far from the last. He was honored that someone he was beginning to admire, like Mr. Kimball, saw him as an operating officer. There was a loftiness about them that Barry would find out later was much deserved. They put in the time. They sacrificed everything for Central Pacific. Operating was like a giant chess match, where train and switching coordination were everything. It was not something everyone could do. It required panoramic thinking. Mono-faceted brain waves would not do. Barry would also soon find that although the CP employees felt a great camaraderie with one another, all other departments were satellite to the operating department. The operating department definitely was "where it was at." *All* railroad departments were ultimately created to support the operation of expeditiously moving freight from Point A to Point B. The operating department *moved it.*

Mr. Kimball pulled the company car behind a massive outcropping of rock. He had been there hundreds of times before. "They can't see us here, Barry. They know we *could* be here, because we test here all the time, but they don't know if we *are* here." One of the phone calls Mr. Kimball had made was to the Pocatello dispatcher, telling him to set the red intermediate signal at Milepost 291 to a stop indication, a red signal, before the PONA's arrival. The PONA squealed to a stop as the brake shoes pressed up against the huge steel wheels in ever-increasing pressures, proportionate to the amount of air the engineer set. On the CP, the brake pipe or train line between cars carried ninety pounds of air. The engineer set the brakes by exhausting air from the brake pipe.

In normal operations in the seventies with 26L brake equipment, there was a two-and-a-half times increase of pressure from the amount of air set by the engineer, and the amount of pressure on the brake shoes. If the engineer set ten pounds by removing ten pounds from the brake pipe with the automatic brake valve, there would be twenty-five pounds of pressure applied on the wheels from each brake shoe, and so on. How the engineer had decided to stop the PONA train was basically his business. In the train handling manual, there were several ways to accomplish braking, depending on train makeup or how it was blocked. Wind made a difference. Lading or shipper products made a difference. Power—the number of working locomotives—made a difference. Train weight made a difference. Train length made a difference. Ascending grades made a difference. Descending grades made a difference. Car types in the train made a difference. Ambient air temperature made a difference. Track curvature made a difference. One of the challenges of railroading was that there were rarely, if ever, the same circumstances with which to deal. Things literally were never the same. That's why it took years, and thousands of occurrences, to become adept in almost every railroad craft. It wasn't learned comprehensively in weeks or months.

The PONA whistled off with two long sounds of the locomotive horn, meaning the brakes were released. They began pulling, and reached a speed of 19 mph, which pleased Mr. Kimball as he checked them with his speed gun. "Just fine," he said as he entered the speed in his testing booklet, showing Barry what he was doing. "The boys are doing as good as they can for us, moving the freight and still staying within the boundaries of restricted speed. Do you remember the definition for *restricted speed*, Barry?"

"Yes, sir. I believe it is 'Proceed, prepared to stop short of train, engine, obstruction, or switch not properly lined, and be on lookout for broken rail or anything that may affect the movement of the train or engine, but a speed of twenty miles per hour must not be exceeded.'"

"That's perfect, Barry," Mr. Kimball said, smiling. "In other words, if you're going one mile an hour and hit something, you're fired, huh, Barry?"

"That's the way it looks, Mr. Kimball."

"That's the way it *is*, Barry. He wasn't proceeding prepared to stop if he hit something, now, was he?" Mr. Kimball said, referring to his example and enhancing Barry's solid answer, enjoying the operating discussion. "They're supposed to change that definition pretty soon, to 'Proceed, prepared to stop in one half the range of vision.' I don't know that I like that as well." That was another operating officer characteristic. They were ecstatic when discussing or arguing about operating rules. Barry would hear later that it was said of them, "Arguing operating rules with a railroad operating officer is like wrestling with a pig in the mud. Sooner or later, you realize the pig enjoys it."

"So Engineer Kohler on the PONA passes the test," Mr. Kimball said as he put away his testing booklet. "We've got an hour before the next train. We'll get some coffee and then test this LAAX. I think I'll get him with a 'light out' test. You know what the proper procedure is then, Barry?"

"Yes, sir. The engineer takes that signal as the most restrictive indication that signal can give, and he reports it to the dispatcher."

"*Bar*-ry," Mr. Kimball said, accenting the first syllable in Barry's name. "You better give some *serious* consideration to becoming an operating officer. You're halfway there already, young man. I got trainmasters out here who don't know the rules as good as you do." After both did some thinking, Mr. Kimball smiled at Barry and said, "This afternoon, we'll have five trains to test, counting the LAAX."

They tested a total of six trains, and arrived back at the CP Pocatello depot at 9:45 p.m., a fifteen-hour day. They had stopped three of the trains and boarded them, checking to see if the crew members had the proper paperwork required, such as train orders, general orders, superintendent's bulletins, rule books, and safety books. They also checked to see if the crews were properly attired. Wearing proper clothing was extremely important in keeping injuries in check. Walking on ballast at a 45-degree angle in tennis shoes was an invitation for a bad sprain. And they checked to see if the employees were wearing proper railroad-approved watches, and that these watches reflected the exact same time as the standard station clocks. Times were changing, and the old "onionskin" orders that began, "To C & E [conductors and engineers]" would soon be replaced by track warrants, issued by the dispatchers. Crews notified dispatchers when they were through the limits of a warrant. But until the change was permanent, lives literally depended on all employees ensuring their watches were compared with the standard clocks. With meet orders, wait orders, and work orders, the rails became joint property at certain times, and if you didn't protect, you'd simply be dead.

Mr. Kimball's white Chevrolet finally pulled up in front of the depot. "Well, that's enough railroadin' for today," he said, his standard end-of-day line. He was a machine. Barry could tell he could go forever. And he needed to, because the odds were very good that Mr. Kimball's railroadin' was *not* completed for the day. For higher-level operating officers, it never was. There was always the potential for derailments, injuries, dangerous trespassers, shipper inquiries, haz-mat spills or leaks, and so on. "See you at 0700 tomorrow, Barry. You've got the yardmasters tomorrow. *Very* nice job, son! Think about it now, will you? Come see me if you need to, while you're here in Pocatello, and you can always call me, Barry." Mr. Kimball was referring to Barry's becoming an operating officer. They had engaged in another conversation about it on the way home from the last train tested as they discussed operating rules.

Mr. Kimball had asked Barry if he thought he was going to like personnel. Barry had replied, "I think so, Mr. Kimball. It seems like it will be interesting, and challenging. I know I'd like operating, but ..."

"But you feel like you should dance with the one who brung ya, huh, Barry?" Barry couldn't have put it better.

"Yes, sir, I guess that's it." Barry had been slated for personnel, and Vance Carlson liked him. Mr. Kimball appreciated Barry's loyalty, but assured him that in CP management, it was like the Falstaff beer commercial at the time said: "We're all in this together." Mr. Kimball explained to Barry that production was the goal. In what department that occurred was only secondarily consequential.

Barry could easily tell Mr. Kimball was a good man and a good Mormon. He never swore ... something inherent in railroading. And he didn't drink. The CP used to be owned primarily by Mormons, and the Mormons had a great deal to do with the ultimate success of the railroad. Barry had learned about the Mormons' incredibly high standards and values and the importance they placed on family. But during this division tour, he also learned another term: Jack Mormons. They were evidently Mormons who *did* drink alcohol, smoked, and womanized. Mr. Kimball appeared to be a "perfect" Mormon, with the exception of his overkill on coffee. It wasn't enough to put him in the "Jack" category, at least in Barry's mind.

Barry couldn't wait to call Susan. He had thought about her and Erin all day, but he had to admit, he had really enjoyed efficiency testing with Mr. Kimball. He had already put the potential of his becoming an operating officer out of his mind, though. All that would mean was making Susan a "railroad widow" for sure, another wife constantly left alone, ever waiting for her husband to return from railroad work. Oftentimes these widows would wind up the wives of other men who had jobs that allowed them to be home every night. Barry knew in his heart and soul that it wasn't God's plan for husbands and wives to exist in this manner. It was antagonistic to the whole idea of marriage to be constantly separated. No, this was going to be a "bear" for the big Bear.

The week passed quickly, even though Barry's thoughts lingered on his family back in Omaha. He and Walt worked together a couple of additional times. They tested in the Pocatello yard with a local trainmaster, and Mr. Kimball had given them an encapsulated operating rules course that lasted four hours. He didn't test either Barry or Walt, but emphasized the value of learning the rules, saying for the record, "You guys can never have too much rules training. They are your entire world in operating. And keep in mind, general orders and superintendent's bulletins are always changing or modifying the rules. You *must* stay current."

Walt teased Barry on Thursday. "I heard you sucked in pretty good with Mr. Kimball."

Barry replied with a smirk and a smile, "Oh yeah? How's that?"

Walt, who was already slated for operating when he completed the training program, answered, "Seriously, Bear, he told me when we went testing that you are a natural operating officer. Maybe you should consider it, man."

"No, I think I'll leave that to the hotshots like you," Barry said.

Walt shook his head, laughed, and said, "You're a bitch, Barry. Remember, you got a lot of time to make up your mind. We could go testin' together sometime, maybe."

Friday morning, Walt and Barry had the same flight home to Omaha, but sat far apart on the plane. Barry would look at Walt and watch him squirm in mental and some obvious physical anguish. He noticed that Walt ordered several cocktails on the direct flight and had to use the bathroom often. Barry's thoughts were primarily on Susan and Erin, and having to tell Susan about the dance. He didn't feel good about it.

# CHAPTER 12
# HOME AT LAST

At Eppley Field, Susan and Erin mobbed Barry. "Hey, sweetie," Susan yelled as she grabbed Barry around the head, kissing him several times on his face.

"Hey, sweetie," little Erin yelled as she grabbed her daddy around the leg and Barry lifted her up with one big arm. "Whad'ya bring me, Daddy?"

"I brought you *me*," Barry said, teasing. "Isn't that enough, honey?"

"Oh, Daddy. C'mon. Whad'ya get me?"

Barry reached into his jacket pocket and pulled out a little bronze horse. "Hey, that's pretty cool, Dad," Erin responded happily, grabbing the horse for closer inspection. Barry had thought maybe Erin could keep it her entire life, since it was basically destruction-proof and might last a while. Then again, Erin was no amateur at destroying nearly anything, even a toy bronze horse.

"So what did you bring me?" Susan said, smiling as she deftly patted Barry's crotch so that no one else in the terminal could notice.

"I brought you *me*!" Barry kept it going. Actually, Barry had purchased a beautiful Indian necklace of turquoise and onyx at Pocatello to give to Susan later.

"It's about time, Bear." Susan had cried often during Barry's absence.

"Boy, I missed you, honey," Barry said with a sigh of relief to be with his loved ones. "Let's get out of here."

That night, with Erin sleeping soundly, Susan kissed Barry passionately after putting on a beautiful new black nightgown with lots of red lace. She had bought it especially for Barry's homecoming. And she *was* truly a beauty.

"How 'bout a couple of Moose Surprises, Bear?" she said as she opened the closet, pulling the Scrabble game down from the shelf. "This game may not even get started. I just may forfeit." She grinned, admiring her handsome husband in his boxers. After Erin had grown enough to observe some things, game-time nudity had been modified to present a more modest appearance. The little one could come in to check on Mommy and Daddy at any time.

"You were never that easy before we were married, Suz," Barry replied, trying to keep the mood cheerful but dreading telling Susan about the dance. He knew Susan would want to play Scrabble afterward, but he needed to get this out in the open first. He didn't want to have any secrets, ever, from his wonderful wife.

Barry put the Scrabble board out on the floor and began laying out the wooden tiles, upside down. Susan helped him, deliberately aligning her beautiful body next to his, touching him. Susan had stimulated Barry from the first time he'd ever laid eyes on her at St. Robert, Missouri, but he'd buried those desires because of her young age at the time. Although Susan was young then, she was womanly beyond her years. When Barry found out her actual age, he was determined to look at her with love and caring ... not lust. Still, her awesome looks were undeniable, and to not lust for Susan was one of Barry's toughest assignments in the military. The long-term payoff was fantastic, though. It felt so good to have her near him now, but first things first. Even preoccupied, Barry subconsciously tried to remember what letters were under what natural wood patterns on the backsides of certain tiles. Susan could tell something was on Barry's mind as all wives can. "What's wrong, Honey Bear?"

"You can always tell, huh, Suz? Well, I don't know if it's anything or not. It's nothin' bad." On the very rare occasions when Barry said, "It's nothin' bad," it always seemed to be worse for Susan than he expected. "You know when I called you late the first night from Pocatello?"

Susan tensed up but tried to be logical, knowing ... hoping, that with Barry, it couldn't be *too* bad. "You mean, when I was half groggy?"

"Yeah, honey. Well, Walt and I were at the Yellowstone eating, and this band, The Quakers, was playing. These girls were sitting beside us at another table." As soon as Barry said the words *these girls*, Susan's demeanor became serious, and she felt a sense of instability overwhelm her. She felt her body tense up further. She almost felt dizzy. "Well, The Quakers started playing 'Free Bird,' and one of the girls ... Well, we never talked about if it would be okay or not ... and ..."

"Barry, you *didn't*," Susan said as tears welled up in her large, beautiful eyes.

"Honey, it was just a dance. I know. I felt horrible about it, like I'd gone out on you or something. I never even touched her."

"Good night, honey," Susan said crying softly, heading for the bedroom. Barry watched his wife's exquisite form, in the red-laced, wonderfully slinky, black see-through nightgown, walk through the bedroom door and close it behind her. Her round, ample, womanly body moved quickly, but still rhythmically, perfectly. "Because the world is round, it turns me on," The Beatles once sang. But Barry's mental state was overwhelmed with feelings of regret and humility rather than luscious lust-love for his lovely bride.

Barry just sat on the floor looking at the two half-empty Moose Surprises next to the unplayed Scrabble game. Great. Just great, he thought to himself, feeling totally horrible. The love of his life was hurting because of something he did, and would *never* have done had they been together as marriage partners should be. Now *he* was hurting as well. It was like his stomach was being wrung like a wet washcloth. He turned out the living room lights, opened the bedroom door quietly, and slid into bed next to Susan, who was still sobbing quietly. He loved her so, so much.

"Honey?" Barry tried, placing his hand gently on Susan's shoulder. "Suz ...?" She was turned away from him in a fetal position.

"No!" she said in a firm but not unkind voice. She didn't want to fight. She loved Barry so much, but right now she wasn't feeling good. She went to sleep in a short time, calmed by the subconscious peace of Barry's nearness. It gave her a feeling of security she hadn't known the previous week in a strange town, with her young daughter. She wasn't happy with his dance with another woman, but she was very glad he was home. It was right. She had decorated the apartment beautifully, and it reflected her style. As a result, it had felt like home to Barry as soon as he'd entered it after a week away. It was Suz. It was now home. Barry didn't go to sleep for some time, and when he did, it was another restless sleep.

He awoke the next morning to Erin's loud giggling at Saturday morning cartoons on the tube and the great smell of a mouthwatering breakfast. Even the sound of the good stuff frying felt comfortable to Barry, like he was finally at home with his loved ones. Susan looked over her shoulder as Barry came into the kitchen.

"Hi, honey," she said, smiling, kissing him partially on his mouth and cheek. "I'm sorry."

Barry couldn't believe what a wonderful woman he was married to. He screws up and *she's* sorry. Barry grabbed her so quickly that the coffee she'd poured for him spilled on the kitchen floor. He just held her and rocked side to side, never wanting to let her go again. Susan felt Barry's sincerity, emotionally and physically. It felt wonderful to her, and she knew everything was all right. Little Erin giggled at the TV. A large, brown rock had just smashed the coyote into a flat disk with eyes, and he was walking around with two flat feet sticking out from the bottom of the disk.

"Never again, Susan," Barry whispered in her beautiful ear. Now it was Barry's tears that dripped on Susan's hair, ear, and bathrobe.

It was an absolutely gorgeous spring day in Omaha. Barry wolfed his great breakfast and slipped into the bedroom with his beautiful wife for some *real* R&R, while little Erin stayed occupied with the cartoons. After the fully satisfying, long-awaited reunion, Barry walked over to the closet door, where he pulled the necklace out of his jacket pocket and handed it to Susan. "Oh, Bear Honey," she said softly, her eyes tearing. "It's beautiful."

After Barry and Susan had experienced their proper "hellos," which they missed from the night before, Barry shouted, "Hey, let's go to the zoo!"

Little Erin screamed, "Yay!" They spent a wonderful afternoon at the Henry Doorley Zoo, a terrific Omaha attraction. All was well with the McAlisters, at least for now. The next few months would be periods of adjustment and growth with their new lifestyle.

But in general, management for Barry was a medium in which total adjustment seemed unlikely. To some managers, wives and families were obviously very much secondary. It wasn't necessarily the way they wanted it. Some wives were reduced to ornaments that looked good at luncheons and cocktail parties. Good-looking wives were very desirable assets in the management ranks. It was all part of the image, and image was everything … just more evidence of appearance seemingly being more important than substance. Children were easily sidelined at day care centers and showered with mundane items daddies would bring back from trips. In actuality, many young managers had begun their careers with mind-sets similar to Barry's. But time in grade necessitated that they eventually make the choice if they were going to stay managers. And more often than not, families were relegated to second place.

However, this selling out of family didn't exemplify all managers. Barry met some dedicated, decent people who were able to satisfy both management requirements and family duties. These folks usually Peter-Principled out in midlevel management positions, like Carl Banner. They developed respectable portfolios, but never experienced exceptionally big titles and the resultant big bucks. In contrast, there were also many haughty, selfish, superiority-minded individuals who exhibited egomaniacal personalities. They seemed to accept their positions as though they were a tail to be kissed, a shoe to be buffed, an ego to be stroked, an occupier of a throne at which to kneel. Mr. Kimball was the exception rather than the rule, and thankfully, there were a few more exceptions around like him. They had everyone's respect. But many were sewer rats.

Barry, who never had a very high regard for himself, found these self-serving rats easy to interact with for two reasons: his penchant for self-degradation, and their penchant for enjoying the superiority they felt as a result of being close to Barry. He always joked about his perceived problems. For instance in 1975, coifs were very much the thing for executives, undoubtedly a residual result of Beatlemania. Very long hair was still considered undesirable, but longer was definitely in vogue. Even the gray- and white-headed execs grew their hair longer, and the younger folks had to admit it looked good for the time. Bader's Princeton was definitely viewed as anachronistic stupidity. Baldness was definitely out, and Bear, who was male-hormonally enhanced in many ways, had a receding hairline resulting from male pattern baldness. One time during a break at one of the meetings, Barry and his fellow officer trainees and some midlevel managers were discussing fashion trends, and hairstyles in general. The majority of those present sported longer, styled hair. Barry, not feeling at ease with the conversation, commented that in high school, his hairline was voted "most likely to *recede*." Everyone cracked up and shook their well-covered heads. Barry made people feel better about themselves with his Rodney Dangerfield approach to life. It was this kind of self-deprecating humor that endeared him to many. Phil and Paul had grown up with it and loved it.

Barry was also liked because he was very sharp, mentally, and very dedicated. His input was welcome in any managerial endeavor. He was always expected to do the hard work while others took the credit. And Barry was not the type to whine when this occurred. The fact that he came from the ranks, one of the promoted-from-within crowd, was also a feather in his cap with the "old guys." They had all climbed the ladder in the same manner and tended to hold in disregard those who came directly from college to the officer training program, without having the benefit of working "the ground," as it was called. The old guys thought, not incorrectly, that a railroad manager needed to know how the railroad functioned from the ground up. And it was true. Barry noticed that the officer trainees who came directly from college without the benefit of learning the work on the many varied railroad jobs were never able to easily identify with the work or the workers who accomplished it. In the distant future, the importance of this ground-up learning approach to management would disappear completely. Instead, the approach would be to discredit the value of paradigm learning from experience, and embrace new ideas from nonrailroaders. The idea was that these new folks' thinking wouldn't be "polluted" by railroad experiences. The old head railroaders would consider this dipshit thinking by human resources: "Let's bring a bunch of fishermen into NASA for guidance." What, couldn't old head railroaders be capable of out-of-the-box thinking, with their railroad experiences as a basis?

Barry was well equipped for railroad management, in terms of background. He was the proverbial "good horse." In fact, when Barry had his second meeting with Vance Carlson, he had told Vance with a rare positive statement about himself that he thought he was a good horse. Vance had replied without expression, but honestly, "Good. We ride horses." Barry thought he noticed a wry, almost hidden smile as Vance said that. Barry had nervously smiled, appreciating both the deadpan humor and Vance's obvious honesty. He knew he and Vance understood each other. This definitely added to Barry's comfort level in the lower-echelon CP management ranks. Still, there was this burgeoning feeling of false superiority everywhere Barry turned. He was now with the "haves," and this wasn't altogether comfortable for unassuming Barry, who had grown up in the lower middle class.

He would never feel "better" than anyone else, and he thought very strongly that to do so was almost a mandate to be a good manager. It was the same principle as a great athlete knowing he or she would be successful in his or her attempts. There was a thin line between self-assuredness and cockiness. Barry also felt this approach to life was diametrically opposed to how God wanted us to feel about each other. "Love thy neighbor as thyself," and "Do unto others …" Barry knew management was a foreign approach to life for him, but still he would try his best.

Susan, who was a no-BS female, had a hard time identifying with the management lifestyle also, even though she was always supportive of Barry's management endeavor. Her father, being a regular army sergeant, the army's equivalent of blue-collar, was a straightforward, no-BS type himself, who harbored a constant disdain for army officers, especially the younger ones. He perceived them as taking the bows for his and other noncoms' accomplishments. It was Barry's easygoing, self-bashing nature, as well as his respectful approach to Susan, that endeared him to Susan's father, even though Barry *was* an officer. Susan was also attracted to these traits in Barry. It was what made him different. He cared about everyone. But Susan retained the basic dislike for overt honcho-ism she had learned from her father. Susan, too, was aware that in service terms, her mother, whom she had lost to cancer when she was only sixteen, was just a "wife" rather than a "lady." And, as officers' "ladies" were expected to do in the military, the "ladies" of CP officers were expected to entertain. Susan was very good at this unwritten SOP, but there was only one problem for the McAlisters: she hated it.

# CHAPTER 13
## TRAINEES AND HONCHOS

The CP officer trainee group looked as much like Jesse Jackson's Rainbow Coalition as possible. There was John Guttierez, and Sally Recturn, aka Silly Sally, who later would be referred to as "Lay Down Sally" after Clapton's great song and Sally's approach to seeking promotion in the management ranks. "Rectum" would also be one of her labels … a natural. Then there was, of course, Walt Morehouse, Barry's former switch foreman in Kansas City, and already Barry's good friend on the training program. There was a six-foot-five-inch Indian guy named Jim Thompson, who was sometimes referred to as Jim Thorpe or Runnin' Bear from the late-fifties song. Barry didn't bother to tell Jim that his own nickname had been Bear in high school, because Jim never heard these nicknames. They were not spoken in his huge presence. There was Nathan Alcord, who was the son of a friend of Bill Rogers, who was on the vice president's staff. Rogers had taken it upon himself to oversee the trainees over the last several years, and no one with any corporate power discouraged him. That's the way it worked sometimes. Management in general was never against anyone stepping up and taking on more responsibility. It was seen as very desirable, as long as you weren't overstepping into someone else's territory. Rogers liked the trainee association because he had the self-appointed authority to effect changes in the program, including who was allowed in. It gave him even more of a feeling of authority to feed his already massive ego-driven personality. That's also the way it worked. Power was what it was all about at the end of the day, when it ever ended. In operations, the "top guns" of the rail industry, power increased meteorically with rank.

Power, initially in operating, meant control over portions of yards, by yardmasters, in towers and shanties. Then, power increased to entire yard areas, with the rank of trainmaster, then assistant yard superintendents, and yard superintendents. This power increased again with assistant division superintendents and division superintendents, where power was distributed in hundreds of square miles. Then, general superintendents had control over three divisions. General managers had overview, where power and authority increased to thousands of square miles, each having ultimate control over several divisions. Finally, the power grid reached the last two rungs on the ladder, vice president and president, where ultimate authority was bestowed. These were the plateaus of unlimited expense accounts and million dollar–plus salaries, even in 1975. The railroad industry made so much money, no one could even imagine it. Barry remembered reading in the company magazine, *Railnews*, that the Central Pacific made two billion dollars in 1975. Of course that was not net, but it was substantial enough for off-the-scale salaries, and yellow, red, and gray Lear Jet taxis for the elite top brass.

There were many other nonoperating ladders to climb, each with their own hierarchy, and each with their own vice president at the top. There was a vice president of security and special services, the railroad cops, known on the CP as pussyfoots. There was a vice president of marketing and a vice president of sales. There was a vice president of labor relations. There was a vice president of traffic. There was a vice president of transportation. There were enough varied ladders of railroad management that almost everyone could find an area in which to excel.

There was Scotty Germain, who was as decent a man as a general manager as he was as a brakeman. It was rumored that his great-grandfather was present at the driving of the Golden Spike at Promontory Summit, Utah. Scotty was a Mormon and would not answer to "Mr. Germain," but expected everyone to call him Scotty, something his subordinates found painfully hard to do. When someone addressed him as Scotty, his whole face, which normally expressed a relaxed, pleasant demeanor anyway, would break into a wide-open smile as his right hand stretched forth in a happy greeting. If you called him Scotty, you were his friend. He was quite a guy. He never forgot where he came from. Everyone loved Scotty.

Conversely, there was "Neutron" Don Hudson, the vice president of transportation. Neutron received his nickname from his penchant for wandering through yard offices across the entire Central Pacific system at any given hour of the day or night. If he caught a clerk with his feet up on the desk, or anyone acting as if they had time on their hands, the job was gone, or "abolished," the next day. Another current position would assume the duties of the former job. As with a neutron bomb, the buildings were left standing, but all the people were gone. Everyone on the entire system feared Neutron. He had even been successful at removing high-level managers, a feat rarely performed. But secretly, Neutron had the green signal from the CP president, John Baker, to continue his missions. It was a numbers-proven fact that Neutron Don had saved the Central Pacific literally millions in the last few years with his hard-line approach. The only time Neutron ever smiled was when someone was feeling the sharpness and weight of his cost-cutting, life-destroying ax. And, although President Baker had the final say in command CP decisions affecting the railroad, the CP was ultimately run by the vice presidents, especially Neutron Don.

But Bill Rogers was beginning to slip. His decisions, which in the past had added considerably to the Central Pacific black ink, were now coming under some scrutiny by his superiors, Neutron Don specifically. Without Rogers being aware, Neutron had directed that his authority be slowly absorbed by other high-level managers. Neutron used Rogers's former self-appointment, as ultimate head of the officer training program, as the compartment for his waning managerial abilities, thinking he could do little damage in the ground-floor arena. Neutron and Rogers had chased girls and drunk beer together thirty-some years before, when they were young trainmasters whose territories butted up against each other. They had efficiency-tested together on hundreds of occasions. It was this past common history, coupled with the fact that Rogers had only six months before he retired, that rendered Neutron's decision much less severe than usual. In fact, it was Rogers who had handpicked Harold Bader to head up, on a lesser level, the CP Officer Training Program. Rogers was Harold's godfather. When Rogers retired, it would leave an open wound in Harold where Vance

Carlson could gorge himself. Poor Harold, knowing and feeling the inevitable, could be seen walking the halls of the Big Brick, laughing, jerking, and snickering to himself in uncontrollable panic.

Another of Bill Rogers's questionable decisions, like hiring and promoting Bader, was hiring Nathan Alcord. He had been on the training program for two years, longer than any other trainee. No one knew what to do with him, or where he could be assigned. Nathan had managed to isolate himself from every department he had visited as a trainee. His abrasive personality had not gone unnoticed. Since Bader was too much of a rabbit to suggest that a decision be made about Alcord, especially since Bill Rogers picked him, Nathan just lingered as the "oldest" trainee. He was also the self-appointed gossip columnist for the trainees. He seemed to think his longevity on the program elevated him to be Swami-Knower-of-All for Central Pacific Grapevine News, and relished the sharing of questionable information. The other trainees, including Barry, viewed Nathan with minor contempt, tolerating him only to a point. When they were finally maxed out on mindless, pointless, personal information, they would excuse themselves from Alcord's presence. And sometimes, they would just walk away when they saw him coming. But sometimes, Nathan would actually be right.

Officer Trainee Jim Thompson was a mountain of a young man. It was said that he could drive a golf ball a mile. In the "appearance is more important than substance" arena, Thompson was the ultimate example. He was literally tall, dark, and handsome, given his Native American heritage, and had been drafted by the Oakland Raiders at one time, although he was later released. This alone would have been enough to keep him in management forever. There was an association with prominence with which all managers identified. Success in one field of endeavor was always associated with success in another, especially if that field was sports. Of course, logic would tell even the most illogical that this was faulty reasoning. But it was nonetheless practiced, whether intended or not. In actuality, Jim was a mediocre individual mentally and in many other ways. But given his jock status, height, looks, natural air of superiority, and great drives down the fairway, Thompson's managerial road was paved in gold. Everyone loved associating with him. Psychologists who studied managerial behavior had concluded that individuals with greater-than-average height were promoted more often than those more vertically challenged. It was true, and it would also be a plus for Barry, as well as Jim Thompson.

Sally Recturn was a married railroad clerk who had gradually, over an eight-year period, worked her way to a bachelor's degree in sociology. The Central Pacific liked her because she possessed railroad savvy, having learned the ropes gradually and precisely. She had no children at this point, so the traveling required would not have a negative impact on her being a mom. Sally was smart and logical, and very much cutting-edge women's lib, a powerful force with which to deal in the seventies. It was whispered by the primarily white-male-dominated management ranks at the time that the new Batman and Robin team was a minority or female, and a lawyer. Previously untested arenas were indeed tested, with ramifications for the white males no one ever dreamed would occur. No one ever even bothered to check courtroom outcome statistics because of the slam-dunk results of the contests. It *was* the era of women and minorities. It was *their* turn, and the white-male-dominated management population was a-runnin' scared.

Sally was well aware of her power. She enjoyed cursing with the males and just generally being "one of the guys." She was famous for a comment that Barry had to admit he liked. She had said, "Womankind will know they have finally made it when they promote a mediocre woman into management." The point was well taken by Barry. Barry had watched his mother, Fran, practically run the car dealership by herself, as lead secretary, while the "boys" played golf and took the bows. He, Phil, and Paul had all three been very much attuned to the unfair predominance of white males in the honcho population. They were aware of the injustices that spawned the bra burning and the Black Power advocates in the influential, turbulent sixties. They had "understood," but never having experienced the prejudice personally, they could understand only to a point. All three of the young men had supported every effort for their brothers and sisters to be privy to the same opportunities that they, as white males, took for granted. If only their brothers and sisters of the same and other racial heritages realized that it was The Man who was the ultimate culprit. Granted, the majority of the "controllers" were of Caucasian extract. But the minority population never realized that the majority of white males were as socially debilitated by this head-man dominance as they were: reduced literally, in some cases, such as Ralph Dunne's, to "working stiffs."

But the pendulum, as always, didn't stop in the middle, and would swing far to the other side before any semblance of balance would ever prevail. Yes, Sally knew her power, and so did everyone else. But the odd thing was that, given her abilities, which were substantial, and the fact that she was female, which was a gold star, Sally still tended to attempt her ladder-climb from a horizontal position rather than vertical. And supposedly, this was the very type of behavior that spawned the women's lib movement in the first place, and to which the supporters of the movement were adamantly opposed. When people spoke of an entry-level position referring to Sally, it had a double meaning.

Sally, although married to some "simp-in-denial," thought it was her birthright to stalk and conquer males the way many males traditionally played the females—and she did, with a vengeance. Sally never wore any panties, and made no pretense about flashing her monkey long before Sharon Stone made the move famous on the big screen. Sally, because of her behavior, had earned and gained the obvious nickname of simply Rectum. Another nickname was The Wrecker, given her penchant for bedding down any male, married or not, and the potential outcome of that person's home. But the nickname that would last throughout her entire railroad career was by far the most descriptive, even more than Lay Down Sally. Railroaders are accustomed to calling out block signal aspects in the cab of the locomotive. They are made up of colors very similar to highway traffic lights, and provide information to the crews about required train speeds and routes. There were many different types of railroad block signals on the various railroads, a fact that drove the Federal Railroad Administration safety inspectors nuts. They wished, for the purpose of safety, that the signals were all standardized. But on the CP the signals were green, yellow, red, and white. "Red over Yellow" was a common signal called out (later called "Diverging Approach"). One time when Sally bent over sans panties, Bill Rogers, in the line of vision, called out the signal "Brown over Red." That became Sally's dominant nickname for her entire railroad career. And she never knew.

Walter Morehouse had become Barry's best friend in management. Because they'd previously worked together as switchmen, and had played some ball against each other, they had much common ground.

They even recalled certain plays, with each adding his particular twists to the recollections. Now, with railroad management in common, their common ground continued. Because they were the very same size, they exchanged clothes every once in a while, just because they could. Walt could get away with orange suits and violet suits, which looked great on him, and Barry could not. But Barry *did* look surprisingly good in a pair of Walt's fur-look, dark brown pants, which elicited wolf calls from the rest of the trainees when Barry wore them.

Walt and Barry also shared a "no-bull" approach to management, whereby they were unwaveringly going to succeed with hard work and dedication, rather than with godfathers. It may have been naive, but it was the only way either of them could approach the system. Barry had felt the Lord literally talking to him in inaudible ways, ever since his childhood, like Psalm 23 and the McAlisters' farm. And although Walt hadn't, as yet, felt the same as Barry with surety, he still had a lingering love for "Something Greater" as a result of his mama forcing him to church in his childhood years. Walt had been a wild man in high school and college, but in his early twenties, the foundation his mom had uncompromisingly laid years before was paying off. And Walt remembered one of René Descartes's quotes from philosophy in college: "Because I exist, there must be *something* greater." Walt began listening to the Holy Spirit when there were forks in the road, and now, he made good, positive, life-changing decisions for the most part. But like all of us, there was still some corrosion on the copper, like Purple Top in Pocatello. Both he and Barry would feel like strangers in a strange land on many occasions in management. But when they worked together, it was always a blast.

Barry, Susan, and Erin settled into a routine that lacked routine, as well as could be expected. Then one day, Barry, while assigned to the Big Brick for the week, was met with excited rumors of his assignment as division personnel officer (DPO) of the Nebraska Division. He was to meet with Vance Carlson about it. Vance was characteristically matter-of-fact with Barry, explaining to him what was expected and that he had scheduled the current Nebraska Division personnel officer to break in Barry for a month. Vance had been following Barry's officer training very closely, and was extremely pleased with his progress. He seemed to Vance to have excellent abilities, completing every assignment to near-perfection, although Barry hadn't felt like he had. All the input about Barry had been very positive, however.

But it was actually Neutron Don Hudson who had made the call for Barry to be assigned. Barry had been in the training program only three and a half months. But the employee who was next in line for the promotion to division personnel officer had zero operating experience. Barry did, having been a switchman for a year. So Neutron wanted Barry to get the call. Also, it just so happened that Neutron was godfather to Randall Kimball, the current assistant division superintendent of the Pocatello Division. Barry had so impressed Mr. Kimball from his division tour that Mr. Kimball had called Neutron Don to relay the information. Further, Mr. Kimball had apprised Neutron of Barry's potential in the operating department in the future. So Barry unknowingly had it made. That's also the way it worked. Sometimes godfathers sort of "happened."

He called Susan, excited at the prospect of first, being with her and little Erin much more often now, and second, with a salary increase to tell her about. It would now be about what he had made as a switchman. That was one discrepancy of railroad management. Initially, there was a salary cut. One had to work up to the level of assistant yard superintendent before the officers' salaries eclipsed the blue-collar transportation salaries, given the overtime rate and mileage. The real money was in the general superintendent and general manager ranks, and higher.

Al Roper, the current Nebraska Division personnel officer, really liked Barry. Al had learned his craft from the ground up, earning Barry's deep respect. As far as Barry was concerned, Al had a PhD in railroading. Al was not in the least bit jealous of Barry, as were many, because he was secure in his abilities. Odd how that works. Barry learned a great deal from breaking in with Al, and he would continue learning from him his entire life. Al was being promoted, and would eventually reach the rank of superintendent. He would graciously be Barry's mentor and friend throughout their railroad careers. At the time, Barry was unaware of the travel involved in hiring employees for the Nebraska Division, but he found out quickly from Al. Al was exceptionally thorough in showing Barry everything he needed to know to be a successful DPO, in explaining both the written and unwritten SOPs of the job.

Barry was relatively happy. It was his first promotion, and it happened quickly, considering his short time as a trainee. Now he and his young family could relax and perhaps enjoy life a little more. Or so they thought.

# CHAPTER 14
## MEANWHILE, BACK AT
## THE BONE YARD

Phil and Paul had tried to call Barry many times, attempting to stay in touch with their adopted brother. But in a pre–cell phone era, they actually had talked much more with Susan, since Barry had usually been gone. Back then, person-to-person was rarely a sure thing. But finally Barry and Susan had gotten in touch with Phil and Carla to tell them the promotion news and talk about life in general. Phil could tell they were somewhat disenchanted, but weren't ready to come back to KC yet.

In the summer of 1976, Tom Moffat again called Phil and Paul. This time it was about hiring them as engineers. Phil had unintentionally allowed the railroad world to become *his* world, and therefore he had developed RTV, "railroad tunnel vision," seeing life only from a railroad standpoint. It was easy to do. One, he worked at the railroad and spent a lot of time there. Surroundings were familiar. It was comfortable. It had become his turf. Two, his brother worked there. Three, his best friend worked there. Four, he'd made other good friends there. Five, it was making a good living for his family. It was as though the rest of the world had disappeared, like the *Twilight Zone* episode when the little kid wished everyone into the cornfield. Phil totally forgot about the outside world, about friends who went on to grad schools and professional schools. He was also somewhat happy. The later-felt burdening feelings of being unfulfilled as a college graduate hadn't yet surfaced from his subconscious. And as weird as some of the people he worked with were, there were also many sharp, decent people at the railroad. Phil took the humble attitude of "If it's good enough for them, it's good enough for me." Many years later, he would say, characteristically humble like Barry, "I strove for mediocrity, and I attained it."

But now, railroad tunnel vision was in serious operation, and when Tom Moffat called him to be an engineer, Phil jumped at the chance, especially when Tom told him about the money involved. Now Phil would have the "warmest seat on the property," as it was termed by railroaders. A railroad engineer was viewed as a very sought-after and respected position, both from within and without the railroad. Railroad engineers had the notoriety of pilots in the airline industry, and made as much money.

Paul declined the upgrade offer, once again not really caring that much. For now, Paul was content to work an average of six hours, be paid for eight, and drink beer and chase girls with New Man Pat Anderson. He happily saw Rosalinda every other weekend. It was a pretty good life.

"You'll hostle for a year or two, Phil, during which time you will mark up with an engineer-trainer for six months," Tom told him. "Then, you'll go to Engineman Training School at Cheyenne, Wyoming. It's three weeks long. Then you'll return and mark up with the same engineer-trainer for a while longer. Then, when they think you're ready, the road foreman of engines will observe you operating the controls and do the actual qualifying. At that time, you will mark up on what you can hold."

"Sounds great, Tom. Thanks a million! When do I start?"

"Be down here at 0800 on Monday. Peter Steinman will take you and the others through a quick course, after which other hostlers will show you how to move a locomotive. As a hostler, you can never move cars with a locomotive, but you can, and will, move consists of locomotives ... lots of 'em. You'll make up sets for trains that the diesel shop foreman assigns you. You'll put them on the head end of trains. You'll spot them for fuel in the diesel shop. You'll take them to the yards from the diesel shop and bring them back. You'll take them to foreign yards and bring them back. You'll trade them out for ninety-two-day maintenance inspection. It's usually a twelve-hour job. Some of the hostlers make as much money as anyone around here. Any questions?"

"No. As usual, Tom, I think you've been pretty comprehensive. Thanks again. See you at 0800 Monday."

Phil made the highest grade in the class of student hostlers. It was only a two-day course, with the rest of the week devoted to learning how to operate the locomotives. A railroad engineer was a time-honored profession. Basic instruction was simple for locomotive operation. There was an independent brake that operated the locomotive brakes. There was an automatic brake that operated the train brakes. Hostlers would use this brake valve only to do air tests on trains. There was a reverse lever, sometimes called a reverser, that selected a forward or backward direction for movement. There was a throttle. Place the reverse lever in the direction you wanted to go, forward or backward, release the brakes, pull out on the throttle, and you were moving. Shut the throttle down to idle, apply the independent brakes, and you were stopping. It was relatively easy, and it was fun.

Phil would find out later that "running a train," as it was termed, was nowhere near as easy. It was a whole different ball game. Phil learned you didn't "drive" a train. How could you drive something that already had the direction chosen for you? You couldn't "turn" a train, although one engineer who derailed some cars because of poor train handling was asked by a trainmaster what happened and replied, "I swerved to miss a dog." The English, Australians, and Canadians called their railroad engineers "train drivers." In America, the terms were "engineers, or operators," or the more degrading but accepted "hogheads." Sometimes this was modified to "hoggers."

Phil found hostling to be a strange livelihood. It was fun, with everybody joking around all the time and playing tricks on each other. But there was a reason for this. When you hostled, you worked only when it was needed. Otherwise, you were essentially on call at the railroad. Jobs would materialize, and the diesel shop foreman would call up to where the hostlers stayed and give out the job assignments, like making up sets. Sets were locomotive consists to go on the head ends of trains to power them. This was done at the diesel shop. Sometimes the hostlers left the power there, and the engineers took it out to the yards and attached the power to their trains. At other times, the hostlers would take the power out in the yards, and be picked up by the jitneys.

One of the most sought-after hostling jobs was the 0600 job. It made up sets at the diesel shop, and then after lunch, it would take the add-on power for the SKB train over to the Missouri Pacific yards, or the MOP, as it was called. It was an easy overtime move. The SKB was a daily train, so the hostlers made four hours overtime, at least, every day. The hostlers, glad to get the assignment, would sing, "Let's go to the MOP. Let's go to the MOP" to the tune of Danny & The Juniors' "At the Hop."

Phil enjoyed his new job and the crazy hostlers, but he didn't enjoy the time away from Carla and Angela. He had been accustomed to getting a "quit" as a switchman, and spending no more than six or seven hours away from them on any given day. But because of increased business, Phil was able to hold the 0600 job almost immediately, as the hostlers with greater seniority were forced out on the road as firemen. It was daylights, and it was good money with four overtime hours daily at time and a half. But with an hour's drive to work, and twelve-hours-plus daily, an hour's drive home, and Saturday work at time and a half, Phil was gone from Carla and Angela more than twice as much as before. The CP had now begun to take him away from his loved ones, just as it did Barry from Susan and Erin, and it wouldn't stop. He liked the work, but not at the expense of his family. He and Carla had bought a modest starter home, which, if baby boomers had had more of the Depression-era mentality, would have sufficed for a lifetime. The extra income really helped pay for the new house. But a precedent and trap had been set forever.

As a hostler, Phil would develop a high regard for the work done by the diesel shop employees. There were electricians, mechanics, pipe fitters, welders, sheet metal workers, machinists, and laborers. They did some phenomenal work to keep the locomotives moving. It was a constant schedule chase to ensure that locomotives were fixed in time to be used in yard or train service. Deadlines were a daily source of stress for the diesel shop superintendent on down to the laborers. Some of these individuals were artisans, not just journeymen. In the mid-seventies, there were still shop employees who had worked the steamers. Some of the machinists of the genre could actually *build* model steam locomotives that were replica miniatures of the big boys. These folks were real craftsmen. But modern design had dispensed with the need for such artisans. Rather than having to "build" and "form," shop craft employees now just "replaced." Everything was designed for speed, which meant prefabrication: unbolt the old, bolt on the new. Even the locomotive electronics were becoming modular in design at this time.

Phil would hostle for a while, and then he would be assigned to go out on the road as a student engineer. One of his hostling duties was to catch trains as they came through the yards and ride with the engineers to the foreign yards. When the jitneys picked up the crews, Phil and whomever he was working with would bring the locomotive units back to the "barn," again, the ultimate resting place for the "horses." "How many horses are we gettin'?" was a standard question referring to the number of locomotives for a train.

One day while hostling, Phil caught a ride on a train being delivered to the N&W yards. He was to bring some CP units back to the roundhouse. "Roundhouse", like "barn", was yet another name for the diesel shop, since the diesel shop design during the steam days was indeed a round house. Tracks occupied by the locomotives divided the house like a giant pie, cut in equal pieces. There were many comments referring to the old roundhouses. One such was that when a person is confused, "He's like a dog in a roundhouse looking for a corner to piss in." Another was Homer & Jethro's "So she'll meet him in the roundhouse, 'cause he'll never corner her there." There were very few actual roundhouses left, diesel shop design giving way to four tracks that went through the diesel shop and out the back to other tracks. But the roundhouse name still stuck in many railroad yards.

The N&W train Phil caught was a TC train or "Tom Cat," and the CP engineer delivering the train to the N&W was a big ol' hoghead, Beauregard Banks. He and Phil had a nice talk on the way over to the N&W. It began with a "Hawa yoo-oo-u, young may-an." Beauregard spoke in a slow, smooth monotone. He had been born three miles from Walton Mountain in Virginia, and his drawl was very evident. He had lost the musculature in his eyelids, so they were always at half-mast. It gave him an unintentional "I'm-too-bored-to-give-a-shit" look. The CP would put their own locomotives on the head end of westbound trains received from foreign railroads for cab signaling out West. Conversely, eastbound run-through trains naturally having CP units in the lead normally had the CP units cut off by hostlers at the CP yard. The hostlers would then take the CP units to the barn. Or, the hostlers would hop the run-through trains, ride the trains to the delivery point at the foreign yards, and then bring the CP power back to the barn. That's what Phil was doing with Beauregard Banks and crew today.

Beauregard's crew had set out their eastbound lead CP unit for a westbound CP train back west that needed power. So now, the lead locomotive was an N&W unit, with two CP units trailing, the ones Phil would bring back. The N&W locomotive had a whisker switch as a safety control device, a four-inch horizontal tight spring about the diameter of a ten-penny nail, sticking out of the control stand. A red light (a normal-sized lightbulb on the control stand) would come on, signaling for the engineer to hit this whisker switch with his hand. It was an automatic test of the engineer's coherence. If he didn't hit the whisker switch in time, the train would experience a full-service application of the brakes, unless the engineer recovered from a suppression position of the brake valve, which sometimes did not work. There were many types of these safety control devices throughout the industry. The CP had floor pedals. If the engineer took his foot off the pedal, the train would come to a normal stop from a full-service application of the brakes. It was known as the "dead man's pedal," referring to a not-all-that-uncommon reason for an engineer's foot to release the pedal: a heart attack. Other safety control devices required the engineer to move around in his seat. No movement by the engineer after a time, and neglect of answering the safety control warning feature, would elicit a full-service application of the brakes.

Beauregard had a string tied to his finger, with the other end tied to the whisker switch. When the red light would come on, he would flick his finger and the light would go off. That, coupled with his droopy eyelids, made Phil think Beau was pretty cool, when actually he was just pretty lazy. Beauregard was a huge man, bigger than Phil. He had fired on the local after World War II, when firemen were really firemen, shoveling coal during the steam era. Beau had shoveled coal all day long in a time when railroaders worked sixteen-hour days. His arms were huge. You didn't want to tangle with, or even arm-wrestle, these guys who used to "fire," as it was called, during the coal days. In the seventies, firemen were merely the equivalent of right seat pilots, who switched train operation duties with the engineers at the halfway point of a trip. A fireman would ride halfway while the engineer ran the train. Then they would switch off, and the fireman would run the train while the engineer observed the rest of the trip. This was a great opportunity for the fireman to gradually gain experience with an experienced engineer to oversee his abilities. Phil thought Beau's monotone drawl matched his give-a-shit appearance. The two hit it off and became friends.

Because of hostling duties, Phil and Carla's life with each other became modified to a life *without* each other. He had a separate life at work, and she had a separate life at home with Angela. Phil, who hated the separation from his family, did not know what else to do but keep working. After all, it was a *good job.*

Because Phil liked Beauregard Banks, he thought he'd mark up with him for training, since Beau was one of the engineers on the list as an engineer-trainer. But initially, Phil marked up instead with Bill Linden. Beau was marked off when it was time for the student engineers to mark up for road training, and Phil heard from everyone how good an engineer Bill was. He heard right. Phil wanted to learn from the best, and he did. Bill could stop "stretched," as it was called, on a dime. Stopping stretched was also known as power braking, where the engineer left the throttle in a "run" position, like Run 4, and gradually applied enough opposing force from the train brakes to override the throttle. The throttle would be reduced to idle as the train came to a stop. All the cars would be stretched, giving the caboose occupants a nice, smooth stop. Bill had been assigned to run trains in Europe for the Allies in World War II, when he was seventeen years old. He literally had grown up behind the throttle, and he was the best there was. Phil learned a lot about train handling from Bill. But after Phil went to the CP Engineman Training School in Cheyenne, Wyoming, again acing his tests, he came back to find that Bill was no longer taking students. At first, he thought it was because of something he had done, but later, Phil found out that Bill, who was close to retirement, did not want to train women, and there were some women in the class behind Phil. In the World War II generation, men worked, and women raised kids. So after engineer school, Phil marked up with Beauregard as originally planned.

Phil found out quickly that Beauregard was the antithesis of Bill Linden as an engineer. One time a head brakeman, Jack Ryan, was not happy as he boarded the locomotive in preparation for the trip. Jack never was happy when he had Beau as an engineer. Jack had carried many a knuckle as a result of Beau's poor train handling. As Jack checked to see if the lead locomotive was equipped with the proper flagging materials, torpedoes, fusees, red flag, and so on, he remarked, "Beau, you're the worst *&%^$^*&in' engineer on the CP system." Beau calmly looked at Jack and said, with his eyelids at half-mast in pseudo-cool, "That may be, but dey pay me da same as dey do da good ones." Of course, this just made Jack wilder, and the cursing continued, which bothered Beau ... not a bit.

Phil had already learned proper train handling from Bill Linden. He had watched Bill very closely, and tried to copy everything Bill did when he, Phil, was behind the throttle. But there was still a great deal to learn about being a good engineer. For one thing, there were "two railroads out there," as it was described. There was the road from Kansas City, Kansas, to Ellisville, and there was the road from Ellisville to Kansas City, Kansas. Downhill was uphill from a different direction, and learning the road was everything. In one direction you "pulled" into a pass, or siding, because it was uphill. Coming into that same siding from the other direction, you better be ready to brake, or you'd be out on the main line, at the other end past a red signal. So thankfully, Phil learned proper train handling from Bill Linden. He would learn the road with Beauregard.

In the old days, becoming an engineer took years, because of the years a person worked as a fireman. The road portion of the learning process was inherently learned, so when a fireman finally learned the mechanics of train handling, he already knew where he was on the road. One of the many concerns of the Federal Railroad Administration was the severe change in that practice by the modern-day railroads. After the fireman position was abolished in the eighties, there was no longer a gradual learning process. Once a person passed the tests, was okayed on the simulators, and okayed on the road, he or she became an engineer. Modern-day testing and simulations were excellent, but as all found out, nothing could replace actual experience for the best training. What used to take twenty years' seniority to hold the "chain gang" or the "road board" now sometimes took less than a year on some railroads. It was a scary thought for most informed, experienced railroaders, given the incredibly different characteristics of each train. People who knew railroading knew it took years to become a good engineer. It couldn't be accomplished in months. Experience was everything, and was directly proportional to safe operations.

The road board was referred to as the "chain gang." In the engine dispatcher's office, there was actually a huge Plexiglas wall that separated the office from the area where the engineers signed in and out on the Federal Register. It was composed of hundreds of slots made of wood and copper banding that was severely corroded and greenish from years of use and lack of cleaning. These slots all represented either job titles, such as "Quindaro" or "18th Street" or "Road," or employee statuses, such as "Vacation" or "Lay Off" or "Bumped." The job titles and employee statuses were painted on both sides of small wooden blocks and slid into the slots. They were painted black, with white letters. Each slot under the job title or employee status blocks contained blocks with employee names on both sides, who either held the job, or were currently in that status. They were painted white, with black letters to differentiate. As soon as a person became a hostler, they were given a block with their name painted on both sides. It was an honorable occurrence, because the person would then have that same block for their entire railroad career, through fireman and engineer statuses. The two-way wall was so the engineers could see the job assignments on one side of the Plexiglas wall, and the engine dispatchers, who took care of job assignments, seniority moves (called a "bump"), job bids, laying off, vacations, and so on could see the exact same setup on their side. An engineer, fireman, hostler, engine dispatcher, or railroad official could look at the board and immediately tell where everybody was at any given hour of the day. The "chain gang" referred to the engineer names that made up a long column of employee blocks—a chain—under the job title "Road," hence the name. There could be anywhere from fifteen to thirty-five engineers marked up on the road board at any given time, depending on business demands. An hour and a half before a train arrived, or was "made up" in the yards, the engine dispatcher would call the engineer "first out" on the road board, to take the train to Ellisville.

If an engineer "laid off," the only way to get time off on the road board, other than the normal layover, the engine dispatcher would put his block under the title "Lay Off." This would leave a "hole," which would be covered by the engineer's extra board, "Extra Board" being a job title. An extra board engineer would call in to the engine dispatcher to see how "far out" he was. Sometimes a wiseacre engine dispatcher would say, "Man, you're really far out," the old late-sixties jargon. A more common reply would normally be something like, "You're four times out, and there's two holes showin'." So this engineer might not get out, but then again, he might. One never knew for sure. Two guys on the extra board could lay off sick, and the third and fourth extra board engineers would "get out," meaning cover the two job vacancies. There were never any guarantees. Situations could change immediately. The engine dispatcher would give the engineer calling in a rundown on what to expect in the future. If an extra board engineer was ten times out, and there were no holes showing, he or she could pretty much figure he had some time to do whatever. But the railroads were all very unforgiving for missing calls. That was your assignment. That was your job. Dependability was the name of the game. Trains don't move if no one's present to move 'em. You might go to investigation if you missed too many calls, and at the least, be issued "brownies." So, most engineers had no lives. They were either working, sleeping (not much), or home waiting for a call to go to work in the pre–cell phone, pre-beeper days of the seventies. That was definitely another reason for the road board being referred to as the "chain gang."

The extra board engineers made extremely good money, since, quite often, they were called every other eight hours to cover a job. This was always at time and a half. During their eight hours off, they had to drive home, eat, and sleep (what little they could get), and then they were called an hour and a half before each job assignment. In other words, an extra board engineer was called in six and a half hours after he tied up at the railroad from his last job assignment. When he worked as a switchman Phil always wondered why the extra board engineers oftentimes went to sleep on the job. He sometimes had to pick up a brake shoe and bang it loudly on the side of a boxcar to rouse the drowsy engineer in the locomotive. When eventually he worked the extra board as an engineer, he found out why. Extra board engineers were rarely properly rested, covering jobs around the clock. He would pray to catch a road turn off the extra board, just so he could get his rest. He would rarely see Carla or Angela while he was marked up on the extra board. But he would make a lot of money. One time in 1984, he made five thousand dollars in one "half," what engineers referred to as two weeks' pay. Becoming an engineer would result in lucrative paychecks, but it would disallow anything but railroading.

But for now, Phil was just training. Before his marking up as a student engineer with Beauregard, he had to again take student trips, this time for engine service. When he took his first student trip to Ellisville, the engineer marked up on the turn was a classy engineer, Sam Watson. Sam looked over at Phil, sized him up, and then asked, "You know how to set air, kid?" Phil told him he did. Sam said, "Get over there," motioning to the engineer's seat. Phil was astonished, but not nervous, because Sam seemed very assured about it all. "Just do what I tell you to do," Sam said. So Phil had actually run the train all the way to Ellisville, totally under the control of Sam Watson, without a hitch. It was mind-boggling. Sam just sat over in the fireman's seat and ate his lunch, and talked to the head brakeman the entire trip. Other than to nonchalantly tell Phil, "Notch out a couple," referring to the throttle, or "Set minimum," referring to the air brakes, Sam seemed to pay little attention to Phil. In reality, Sam *was* watching closely. He just didn't want to make Phil nervous. It worked. It gave Phil some confidence for the future, even though he had no idea what he was doing other than following Sam's directions.

Phil also learned that he would have to choose between the United Transportation Union (UTU) of which he was already a member, and the Brotherhood of Locomotive Engineers (BLE), the traditional union of the railroad engineers. Phil chose the BLE, although the UTU-E was also a great union. The railroads had always enjoyed the fact that these two unions were rivals for the monthly dues of the railroaders. Control was always more easily accomplished when there was dissention among the troops. "Divided, they fell."

The local chairman for the BLE was a useless individual named Alex Suacausa. Suacausa would act like he was doing the BLE members a great service, when in reality, he would sell them down the river. He would tell them there was no negotiating on certain matters, when in fact he could have negotiated. He would do this for baseball tickets, hot dogs, and beer, and for the potential of becoming a CP officer, like Peter Steinman aspired to achieve. Suacausa was so good at what he did that few BLE members realized what a snake he really was. Some did, however, and referred to Suacausa as "Suckassa." When he was running for office, he, like all politicians, promised sweeping changes in the representation for the membership. However, as soon as he was elected, he thought he was the engineers' *boss*, rather than their *servant*. Phil would look at Suacausa and shake his head. Does it ever end? he would think. From a local chairman to the senators and representatives, to the president, we're supposed to be electing them to represent us. They're supposed to be *our* public servants. But once elected, they *all* think they're our bosses. Phil would vote for Ross Perot in the 1990s for that very reason. Mr. Perot would say, "I'll be your servant." Very few understood the concept presented by our Founding Fathers. How sad in a democracy.

# Chapter 15
# The Train in Training

After his initial student trips, Phil began immediately operating trains, with Beauregard sitting over on the fireman's seat occasionally mumbling directions. But most of the time, Beau was silent. One of Phil's first trains was a coal train, called out of Ellisville for Kansas City. It was more than fourteen thousand tons, about twice as heavy as a normal train. Modern-day coal trains would be about twenty thousand tons with distributed power, two locomotives on the head end, two locomotives in the middle of the train, and one locomotive on the rear end to push, rather than a caboose. But for now, a fourteen-thousand-ton train was considered a very heavy train. Going down the first hill after pulling out of Ellisville, it didn't take long for the speed to increase with fourteen thousand tons–plus shoving you in the rear. Phil had set the air at minimum reduction appropriately, at about 45 mph to stretch the train, or "charge" it, as was the terminology. Then, any additional braking should be smooth. Setting air at 45 mph also allowed for the natural and expected increase in speed caused by gravity on the descending gradient, and throttle-pull while the brakes were applying. An engineer always allowed for the increase in miles per hour going downhill. With a coal train you had to start the braking process a little earlier because of the extreme weight.

At the bottom of the hill, Phil saw the block signal exhibiting what was called a "flasher," or flashing yellow light. The appearance of a signal is called the "aspect." This flashing yellow signal meant that Phil and

Beauregard had to be down to 40 mph ASAP, because the next signal was probably a Yellow, with a red stop after that. With all this incredibly heavy weight pushing you, you'd better get busy controlling your train. Phil had put some more air in the train, which wasn't slowing down a bit, and in fact, was now up to 52 mph, two miles over the national speed limit for coal trains. The next signal after the flasher *was* a Yellow, which would be called an "Approach" in the future. But for now it was just termed a "Yellow," meaning trains should approach the next signal after the Yellow prepared to stop for a Red Absolute signal. Freight trains exceeding 30 mph were supposed to immediately reduce to that speed. Phil could feel panic setting in. At this point he had fifteen pounds of air set of a total of twenty-six, the maximum air available for a full-service application of the brakes with 26L equipment, other than an emergency application. When he saw the Yellow two miles away, Phil had set five more pounds.

If Beau was nervous, he sure didn't show it. He would just look over at Phil with his droopy lids and then look back out the front window. The head brakeman, Chip Downing, was an excellent brakeman, and he too seemed calm. Phil couldn't understand why, since he had no idea what he was doing. There was an old expression on the railroad, "It'll put shit in your neck," referring to the final resting place of the excrement once it's released in a panic mode, with your pants on, in a sitting position. There were plenty of instances on the railroad for this to occur. This was one of them. Phil was pushing with all his might, with his legs on this large, horizontal capped pipe, which some of the GE locomotives had as a design for a footrest. It was a subconscious and blatantly futile attempt to slow the train down. The additional five pounds of "whiz," another name for train-line air that Phil had set, had finally resulted in some braking being felt. They were now down to about 40 mph. As the retarding force continued, they passed the Yellow signal at 30 mph, as they were supposed to do. As they rounded the curve and continued downhill, Phil saw a Red Absolute block signal at the bottom of the hill, now only a mile away, and an opposing train entering the siding, the reason for the signal system stopping them. If Phil didn't get the train stopped, they were going to hit the opposing train. In a desperate but somehow instinctual move, Phil pulled the automatic brake valve handle to full service, all twenty-six pounds, and "let it blow," which referred to the air exhausting through the valve. Later design would have it exhaust through the floor, saving ear tissue. Phil didn't want to use "Emergency," which would give him maximum braking but could also cause a derailment and possibly kill somebody. The large, hundred-car, heavy coal train was now slowing down, and finally came to a perfect stop right near the block signal as the opposing train cleared up in the siding. Phil was glad he was sitting because he could tell his legs were shaking.

Big ol' Beauregard stood up and said, "Boy, you makin' me a nuvous wreck. Lez have some coffee, Pheel." He grabbed his thermos to pour Phil a cup. "Let me tell you sump'em 'bout dees coe trains, boy. You set ten pounds wit a coe train, you might as well hold yawr hand out ta winda."

Chip began to laugh so hard he couldn't stop. Beau had a way with words. Right then, Phil knew the extent of Beau's training regimen. He knew he'd better be on his toes. It was a minor miracle that everything had worked out. Phil knew that a one-second difference, or a little less air brake, and they could have blown by the red signal and hit the caboose of the opposing train before it cleared, possibly killing the conductor, the rear brakeman, and themselves. Phil learned a valuable lesson from the experience. It was "start early." Whatever an engineer wanted his train to do, too early was better than too late. Phil learned that, and he also learned that in attempting to slow down a coal train with ten pounds of air, he might as well be holding his hand out the window.

One time Phil and Beauregard were directed by the yardmaster to get off at the Mattoon Creek Shanty, as they pulled a train into the Kansas City, Kansas, yards. A yard crew was going to deliver Phil's and Beau's train to the MOP, and they were both happy about it. It meant going home four hours earlier than if they had delivered the train. A jitney was to pick them up. When they entered the shanty, Phil saw a friend of his he'd hired out switching with, Allen Henderson. Allen was an extremely unique and anti-norm, classy type. He was basically a biker, very bright and very capable, belying his hairy counterculture appearance. He had an enormous dark brown beard and long hair, and wore bib overalls and dark glasses. Allen was now hostling, and was sitting on the bench with his feet propped up on a stool, his arms folded across his lap. Allen had very wisely bought two 1964 Corvette Stingrays years before, one of which had matching numbers. Al bought them for practically nothing in Corvette dollars, about three grand a piece. They were both worth a mint now. He also had four motorcycles: three beautiful Harleys—a Softail, an Electra Glide, and a Sportster— and an old Indian. They were all in mint condition. Railroadin' didn't bother Al's family a bit, because he didn't have one. He would never get married. Al would just have a series of "old ladies." If they hung around, that was okay with Al, and if they didn't, that was okay, too. Just about anything was okay with Al. He looked up, and seeing Phil, started to smile a half smile, the most smiling Al ever did.

"Hey, Phil," Al said slowly. "How ya doin'?"

"Older and uglier and fatter and dumber," Phil said, and smiled, knowing Al would enjoy it.

Expressionless Al was slowly nodding in agreement with Phil as Phil listed the railroad-affiliated characteristics that accompany the passage of time. "You left out *poorer*," Al pointed out to him. They had a nice conversation till the jitney showed up.

Learning to be an engineer entailed a lot. Phil learned on the road, and he learned at the Cheyenne school. He learned things about in-train forces that the World War II jocks knew only by feel. Those guys had showed up for work one day, and there were diesel-electrics instead of steamers for them to run. The company said, "Run 'em," and they did. It was no wonder some engineers of that era, like Beau, never quite developed the expertise that Bill Linden had. The CP would, in the future, provide for their older engineers to go to school to retrain and learn what Phil and his fellow students would learn by virtue of the new training requirements.

In a moving train, potential always existed for extremely severe buff and draft forces with which the crews had to contend. "Buff forces" referred to the cars shoving against each other, or bunching. "Draft forces" referred to the pulling forces in a train, or stretching. Again, the Budweiser draft horses were called that because they pulled, not because it was draft beer. Sometimes, the severity of these forces were a result of train blocking, something yardmasters accomplished while making up the trains in the yards. Where the yardmasters put certain blocks in the train was determined by the order along the route where the train was to set out the cars in the block. For instance, if the first stop was a cement plant, the logical place for the cement hoppers was directly behind the locomotives. But it wasn't always easy for the yardmasters to make up a properly blocked train. There were schedules to adhere to, "the faster, the better" to keep shippers happy, so railroads wouldn't lose the contracts to one of their railroad competitors or the trucking industry. There was a constant desire for yardmasters to hurry, hurry, hurry, to move the freight. It all impacted money, and lots of it. There was per diem, and demurrage that cost the CP per car, or foreign locomotive, if the operating folks didn't get them moving and off the property. Other cars were "hot," which described high-priority freight. And still others were literally hot, such as amorphous sulfur in tank cars, kept hot by heaters.

Some freight, like autos or auto parts, were always hot. As a result, yardmasters were often more interested in making sure certain cars were *in* the train, rather than caring *where* they were in the train. Sometimes, for example, a train might have auto racks for hauling cars and trucks blocked in the middle of a train. These cars had cushioned drawbars for added protection from the in-train buff and draft forces. Then, the yardmaster might get a call from a trainmaster, explaining that certain loaded tank cars were hot priority. The tanks would then be added to the rear of the train just to get them "outta town," and the yardmaster would wave bye-bye. The engineer or fireman would be left the normally unsung and unappreciated challenge of getting the train, now a mile-and-a-half-long giant accordion, over the road in one piece. In general, railroaders weren't appreciated. They were paid. There was no provision for an entitlement mentality. Some of the old operating officers had the approach of "Hey, when I pay you, it's over." There was some peer support from the ranks, where railroaders would acknowledge and even occasionally praise each other's skills and accomplishments, like the way everyone thought very highly of Bill Linden's train handling ability. But for the most part, a great job was simply viewed as *a* job. The bottom line was that there was just no time for accolade. New Man Pat Anderson had told Paul at Quindaro when they first met, "Remember, nobody cares about you down here, Paul. You work, you're paid, that's it. On the railroad, your reward is the absence of criticism." Pat had further told him, "If no one knows who you are, you're doing a good job," referring to the unwelcome notoriety that came with tearing up equipment with poor railroad practices.

One day Phil and Beauregard were rolling down the rails at track speed toward Topeka, "Malfunction Junction." Beau, born in Virginia, had the nickname Ridgerunner, or just Ridge, referring to the Blue Ridge Mountains. He looked over at Phil, who was running the train, and said enthusiastically, "Phil, ma boy! Today, I'm gonna teach ya how to stop bunched!" Phil had learned stretch braking from Bill Linden, and that's the only way Bill ever stopped a train. Bill *never* got a knuckle, the term used to describe a break-in-two, usually a result of bad train handling. If you had too great a brake reduction and were still pullin' on 'em, throttle out, *pop!* you'd be in two. Rail terminology designated that a train broke in "two." On the rare occasion that a hundred-car train parted in two equal sections, between the fiftieth and fifty-first car, then conceivably, the reference could be broken in "half," given the amount of train on each side of the broken knuckle. But because that rarely, if ever, occurred, a train was always said to be broken in two. To a railroader, the easiest way to find out if someone was or wasn't a railroader was to hear them describe a train that had gotten a knuckle as "broken in *half.*" It would be cause for some eye rolling and head shaking.

Sometimes a break-in-two was the result of a bad valve on a car. If an engineer popped a knuckle, the brakemen would have to replace them. Modern knuckles weighed between seventy-five and eighty-five pounds. Carrying a knuckle forty or fifty car lengths was not "first out" on a brakeman's priority list. That's why Jack Ryan was not happy with Beau. He'd had to carry a lot of iron because of Beau's lack of ability. Beau's "they pay me the same as they do the good ones" attitude pissed off many of the CP trainmen, including the head brakeman this trip, Smittie. Today, Beau would give the rear brakeman and conductor a lesson in buff forces.

There were times when it behooved an engineer to stop bunched, like on locals. If you stopped stretched, the brakeman would have to bring you back on the cars to pull the pin, separating the cars. Otherwise, the pin wouldn't pull because of the lack of slack. If an engineer stopped bunched, the slack was already "in," and the brakeman could easily pull the pin and give the engineer a "take 'em ahead" sign, or command. It saved a move, something railroaders always tried to accomplish. Over an entire trip, stopping a local bunched saved many moves. And locals usually never had too many cars to bunch.

Today, coming into Topeka, Beau was going to teach Phil how to stop bunched. Beauregard had begun the process by telling Phil to "feather" (Beau said "featha") the independent or locomotive brake. This meant to apply slight brake cylinder pressure to the head end, then release. This caused the cars to begin to stack up against the locomotives. This process was to be repeated until all the cars in the entire train gradually nestled in against the locomotives, now totally "bunched." This had to be done carefully, and with great skill; otherwise you'd hammer the rear brakeman and conductor on the caboose with severe slack action. Today, Phil and Beauregard had a 150-car AKO train, not a good train to attempt to bunch, because of its excessive length. It was almost two miles long with many extended-length cars. But at the time, Phil didn't know the process was flawed from the git-go, and was just following Beauregard's direction, which Phil was learning, wasn't always the right direction.

Coming into Topeka from Kansas City, westbound track speed, which could be 60–70 mph, reduces to 20 mph over the Topeka public crossings. Jake Jacobson, the local trainmaster, would get on the radio, and praise the run-through engineers for being right on the 20 mph mark, which Jake checked with a radar gun. Being right on 20 was important. Faster than that was a violation, and Jake would have to explain to the mayor and the superintendent why it was allowed. Less than 20 mph "laid" trains out, and cost precious time. So Jake would go against unwritten company policy, get on the radio, and actually praise engineers for doing a good job when they were right on 20 mph. The Central Pacific higher-ups hated it, but the engineers loved it, and as a result, really tried to be on the money at 20, for Jake. It's odd how people respond positively to positive reinforcement. Jake was a class act, his own man, and extremely decent in dealing with subordinates. In later years, he would be president of the Copper Basin Railway, and receive Railroader of the Year honors bestowed by *Railway Age* magazine. Jake would make the cover of the magazine. Someone would even refer to him as Railroader of the Century. Those who were fortunate enough to know Jake knew it was not only well deserved ... but true.

Phil had actually managed under the misdirection of Beauregard to slow the train to the required 20 mph before reaching the yard limits, as the timetable, and Jake, prescribed. But not without some extreme displeasure voiced from the rear end. The conductor, Ben Hudson, had been teasing Beauregard from the trip's beginning by keying the radio several times after leaving KC and in an intentionally comically gruff voice saying, "I dunno what you're doin' Beau, but you're turnin' this caboose upside down back here." Every few miles, Ben would key the mike and tease Beau with the same statement. But now, Ben's voice displayed genuine worry: "That's about enough of that, Ridgerunner!" When Phil had begun to bunch the cars, he had started the process gently and felt the cars respond equally gently, nestling in against the locomotives. Again, the secret to good train handling was to allow enough time for the entire train to respond to your controls before attempting a further form of control. So, start early. But Beauregard had directed him to "not be afraid," and had walked over to the control stand and jammed the independent brake to a fully applied position before releasing. This resulted in some serious *boom-boom-boom* run-in on the head end as the cars in the train slammed toward the locomotives with too much independent braking power applied. The *boom-boom* of the buff forces made it hard for Beau to keep his balance standing up next to Phil by the control stand. Phil's coffee spilled, and he could not imagine what it felt like to Ben and the rear brakeman on the caboose. Smittie, rocking back and forth in the head brakeman's seat, just shook his head and wondered how long it would be before he'd have to carry and replace a knuckle. "Ridge, knock it off," Hudson yelled into the radio from the rough-ridin' caboose. Ben was worried they were going to derail, and maybe die.

As the head end neared the point where Smittie was to get off to pull the pin and shove down in the Topeka yards with the cars to be set out, it became evident they were going to overshoot where they needed to stop, without additional braking. Beauregard yelled at Phil, "Set aya! Set aya!" which was Virginia hillbilly for "Set air! Set air!" Phil reached for the automatic brake and pulled off a full-service application, all the train brakes possible except for emergency. They came to a perfect stop, allowing Smittie to cut off in the clear of the yard lead. This allowed

Phil to be able to shove the set-outs by their train for yard storage, before they picked up their cars for Ellisville.

Simultaneous with the stop, Glen Forbes, a local Topeka engineer working a yard switcher, keyed the radio and said, "Anyone got a giant spatula to get the conductor and rear brakeman off the front of the caboose on this AKO train?" Phil's heart sank. He knew then that the stop on the rear hadn't been as smooth. The train was only partially bunched, maybe the first three-quarters. When Phil set air, the air reduction at 540 feet per second, the rate for a normal service reduction, got back to the rear of the bunched portion at the same time the head end was "setting down," and the caboose had run into a brick wall.

Phil finished shoving the set-out cars into Track 10 in the Topeka yard. Smittie tied a hand brake to hold the cars, and closed the angle cock on the locomotives. Then he pulled the pin and gave Phil an "A-head" sign. There was a loud *p-s-s-s-s* as the air vented to atmosphere from the brake pipe of the set-out. The cars were now secured with an emergency application, as well as a hand brake. Brakeman Smith had done a fine, safe job. It was another railroad no-no to "bottle the air." If you left the set-out with no hand brakes, an air reduction to hold the cars, and closed angle cocks at both ends (called bottling the air), it could lead to disaster. Many times this was cause for death, injury, or destruction, because the air would "bleed off," gradually releasing the brakes, and the cars would go bye-bye.

Brakeman Smith was now taking Phil and Beauregard into Track 13 for their Ellisville pickup. The rear brakeman for the AKO was Bob Bromley, Big Mike Bromley's older brother, who was about six feet five inches and 260 pounds. He always stayed marked up on Conductor Ben Hudson's turn, and was walking alongside the pickup toward Phil, checking the cars for Ellisville. He was normally a nice guy, but today his face was red, and he was not happy.

Uh-oh, Phil thought. Bromley walked up from the caboose on strong, unstable legs to help with the pickup and give the train a roll-by when they left town on single track for Ellisville. As Bromley slowly walked under the engineer's window, he looked up at Phil and said, "Young man, I'm gonna stick that short handle right up your ass." "Short handle" referred to the independent brake valve handle for the locomotive brakes, as opposed to the longer handle on the automatic brake valve for train brakes, the preferred choice for the caboose occupants, for obvious reasons. Indeed, some engineers referred to the automatic and independent brakes as the automatic and the "acrobatic," meaning the conductor and rear brakeman "flew through the air" because of an engineer's misuse of the independent brake. And it usually wasn't done "with the greatest of ease." Nothing else was said to Phil, either in Topeka or Ellisville. Both Hudson and Bromley knew it was Beau's faulty guidance that caused their bruises. Unfortunately it was normal with Beau.

When they were preparing for the return trip the next day in the Ellisville yard office, Beauregard, with eyelids at half-mast, asked Hudson, "Hey, Hudson ... you stamp up ye-et?" referring to the rubber ink stamps Central Pacific employees were given to stamp their official time slips. The stamps had the employee's last name, first, and middle initial, and their respective employee numbers.

Hudson replied, "Why, no, Beau. Why?"

Beau mumbled with droopy lids, "Iss a litta hawd to do up-sy-dowon."

A story that had been around for years on the CP, although no one was exactly sure of the origin, told of a train coming into Topeka and stopping with a rough stop. Allegedly, the conductor had gotten on the radio and excitedly screamed at the engineer, "You just turned this stove over on its side back here."

The engineer purportedly calmly replied, "Don't worry. I'll set it back up when we take off."

It occurred to Phil that the jitney drivers were the unsung heroes of the railroad, yet they were treated like second-class citizens. In actuality, they were District 3 clerks, some who could have bid on many different jobs, other than driving a jitney. But as time progressed, the computer slaughtered the clerical jobs. Those holding the remaining clerical positions, and assuming the extra work, had tons on their respective plates. To them, the CP's prevailing attitude was "Oh, that job has a computer now. Much more work can now be accomplished." Of course it was severe job overload. So some of the clerks, even chief clerks, would mark up on the District 3 jobs, calm down and drive the troops around, and make the same money without the hassle. Undoubtedly, they'd live longer and, for sure, happier, less-stressed lives.

One jitney driver Phil really liked was a very quiet African-American man named Clarence Jackson. Clarence was a huge man, but had a very gentle spirit, the kind a person could just feel when they were around it. Clarence was an former heavyweight boxer. It was rumored that at one time he was one of Floyd Patterson's sparring partners. He, like Phil and Paul's father, had boxed in the service, but Clarence was "in" during Korea. Clarence was also a preacher, which was probably the reason people felt the "good" coming from him, although Phil realized all preachers didn't necessarily have this aura of goodness. But thank God, literally, that many did. When Phil or Paul would catch Clarence as a driver, they would talk boxing, since Clarence was definitely an aficionado. One time, Phil remarked to Clarence that he and the family were going to try to take a quick vacation down I-44 to I-40, to see the Petrified Forest, Carlsbad Caverns, and so on. The season was late fall when the desert wouldn't be as hot. The forecast in Kansas City was for freezing rain. When Clarence let Beau, Phil, and the rest of the crew off at the yard office to turn in, Clarence said to Phil, "Wait a minute, son." It was the *son* that got Phil. It was a black man sincerely calling a young white man *son*, and it really sounded wonderful, because it *was* sincere. Clarence was "fathering" him. Clarence had gotten out of the jitney, and as the rest of the crew went in to tie up, he grabbed Phil by Phil's hands. Phil had very large hands, but Clarence's hands dwarfed Phil's. "Let's pray together, son," Clarence said as he bowed his head. Phil did likewise. Clarence began, "Dear heavenly Father, watch over this young gentleman and his family during their trip to the Southwest, and keep them safe from harm. We ask this in Jesus' precious name. Amen." Phil would think about wonderful, caring Clarence the rest of his life. And the young Barneses had no trouble at all on their vacation.

While training with Beau, Phil met an interesting character who was his head brakeman on several occasions,. The accent was on *head* brakeman, because this guy, Groove Whitfield, was definitely in a holding pattern from 1968. Groove was a great guy and quite talented, playing a very clean guitar. He still sported late-sixties/early-seventies sideburns, and had an earring long before it became trendy. He asked Phil to get high with him one time, but Phil declined, explaining to Groove that he had long since turned in his roach clip. Groove laughed at the answer. Phil and Groove sang the great late-sixties songs plus a few songs Groove himself had written. One time, Groove asked Beau if he would mind if he played guitar while they ran to Ellisville. Beau looked over at him, displaying his normal unintentional nonchalance caused by his droopy eyelids, and said, "S'long as you don't play while I'm on da radio."

Groove answered him, "No problem, Beau. I don't know that song anyway, man." It zoomed over Beau's head. Groove looked at Phil and made a backward motion over his head with a flat hand. Beau missed it, but Phil enjoyed it. Groove then said loudly, in a deep Johnny Cash voice, "What this country needs is another good railroad song." Then he began happily and vigorously playing a song he called "Railroad, Railroad."

Rollin' down the rail doin' sixty,
Listenin' to the track going clickety-clack.
All I wanna do is get a trip in or two,
And keep the officials off my back.
Left KC at four o'clock this mornin'.
Shot past Lawrence about four twenty-five.
My whistle and my bell got their own story to tell.
They say, stay off the track, and stay alive.

Chorus:

Railroad, Railroad, never stop a-rollin'
From the time you were first built with muscle and sweat.
Railroad, Railroad, I guess I'll never leave you,
'Cause you just ain't got the best of me yet.

Won't be long before another trip has ended.
Won't be long before my feet are on the ground.
And if everything goes right,
I'll be in Ellisville one night.
Tomorrow, I'll be Kansas City bound.
Don't know if I'll get a short, fast hot shot,
Or a train with fourteen thousand tons of coal,
But I know this for a fact,

I'm gonna keep 'em on the track.
I ain't ready for the Lord to take my soul.

Chorus:

Sometimes, it seems that all I do is railroad,
And leave the wife and kids somewhere behind.
But the money, it ain't bad,
And though I'm a long-distance dad,
It seems the best old job that I could find.

Groove then began singing lower and slower. It was hard to hear over the whine of the locomotive diesel engine turbocharger. There was a sadness in his voice.

Twenty years and lookin' to go thirty.
Days and weeks and months all seem the same.
And although time goes by fast,
I know this job won't always last …
And I'll never get to ride another train. (Groove was speeding back up)

Then Groove speeded up all the way and sang loudly for the last chorus, "Railroad, Railroad …"

"Ya oughta try to publish dat, Groove," Beau said. "Sa-ounds pretty goo-ood." Phil really liked it, too. He could sure identify with the "long-distance dad" line. He rarely was able to read or tell a story to little Angela when he was home. Phil, or Carla, or his beautiful little daughter would be sleeping. Groove had written the song while he was still married to his second wife. The railroad had gotten both of Groove's marriages. It wouldn't be getting a third. He wouldn't even think about marrying again, at least while he was still railroadin'.

Just as Groove's song accurately portrayed railroaders as never being home, Carla *was* feeling like a railroad widow. Phil had already told her that if he were to be killed at work, she should avoid the CP claim agent and get a lawyer. Now the CP was just killing their marriage. And now that Phil had learned his craft, even though he would not have considered himself a good engineer at this point, he knew what he had to do to be one. Time would make him a good engineer ... time away from Carla and Angela.

# CHAPTER 16
## THE BEAT GOES ON AND ON AND ON ...

If Barry had an Achilles heel, it was the feminine sex. Actually, it wasn't his heel that affected his thought patterns so much. It has been said that God gave man a brain and a penis, but only enough blood to operate one at a time. Fran had told him that when he was a little two-year-old, he would grab the legs of his female cousins, aunts, even Grandma McAlister. "Pee-ey 'egs! Pee-ey 'egs!" (for "pretty legs") little Barry would yell in delight. It was a reaction to the beautiful stimulus that would never leave Barry. It was both a blessing and a curse. It embarrassed him to hear from Fran years later that he had reacted like that, since Barry always tried to be the epitome of a gentleman as an adult.

Barry could understand totally Charles Grodin's character viewing a young Cybill Shepherd in Neil Simon's play-into-movie, *The Heartbreak Kid*. In one excellent scene, Cybill explains to Charles that they should play a game while in her father's cabin in the mountains. The game is that they both take their clothes off while standing at opposite ends of the cabin and slowly move toward each other without actually touching. With no light other than the fireplace flickering, a beautiful, young Cybill Shepherd disrobes. "Thank you, God" is the comment from Grodin's character. Barry definitely understood. After watching that scene, anytime Barry would see a beautiful woman, that was his reaction: "Thank you, God." Barry would always be "affected" when there was an attractive woman nearby. He didn't know if other guys felt this or not. And he still never even dreamed of messing up on Susan. Yet he always felt the tug.

It had been both a very vivid and confusing time when Barry learned about sex. He had known insects mated to have babies from the McAlisters' farm. Dragonflies, Barry's secret to his baseball hitting ability, would be flying around in tandem, in mating posture. Although Fran would rarely walk around the pond with little Barry, once in a while, she did. One of these times Barry had asked her why the dragonflies were flying "together." Fran had explained to Barry that it was necessary in order for there to be little dragonflies, and that it was called "mating." Barry noticed butterflies also flew "together," and from Fran's dragonfly answer surmised that this also led to the butterflies laying eggs to create more butterflies.

But it wasn't until a Cub Scout den meeting in the fifties that Barry would learn about human sexuality. Rose was Barry's den mother, which Barry totally enjoyed. He was her "star pupil." The local Cub Scouts had a rule that a den mother's own children had to attend the den of another Scout mother rather than their own. It assured fairness, and worked well. On this particular day, Rose had chosen taffy pulling as the Scout activity for her den, and it was a beautiful spring day to accomplish this project. She began by showing the Scouts the ingredients, which she cooked on the stove. Then she poured the taffy into little aluminum foil bowls for cooling off. When the taffy cooled enough to handle, she and the boys, who totaled six including Barry, went outside to pull the taffy.

There was much laughter as the boys began to knead the taffy and pull on it as Rose directed. The taffy was initially clear in the aluminum containers, but as the boys pulled, it turned opaque. The laughter never stopped as some of the young Cub Scouts pulled and rolled way too long, creating ropes. One young Cub dropped his taffy on the ground, and it became taffy, leaves, and dead grass. Another had rolled his taffy into a ball and was playing catch with another Scout, who had draped his own taffy over his shoulders like a towel. One of the ones who created the ropes began to jump rope with his until it pulled apart. Every time it came in contact with the ground, the sticky taffy picked up dirt and leaf pieces. Of course Rose corrected them immediately. "Hey, you guys gonna take-a this-a taffy home-a to your-a families! Do a good-a job!" Barry had simply done as he was told, and was pulling his taffy so that it had become a silvery, opaque mass as it was supposed to do. "Look at-a Barry. That's-a what it's-a supposed to look-a like."

At this time Harold pulled up into the Barnes's driveway in their new 1954 Ford Fairlane. "I'm-a gonna go in-a for a minute-a, boys, and fix-a Hal a cup-a coffee. You keep-a pullin'-a that-a taffy. And don't letta it hitta the ground." Now, the Barneses had a beautiful little black-and-tan female miniature dachshund named Victoria. She was an "indoor dog," and when Rose went in the house, Victoria came out. She knew to stay in her own yard, even though it was not fenced. As the taffy pullers neared the completion of their task, Barry noticed Victoria "stuck" to another dog, a cocker who lived up the street. The dogs were facing the opposite direction and seemed both confused and immobile with their predicament. The young Scouts had all gathered around the two dogs, wondering what could be keeping them together in such an absurd position. It reminded them of the doggie magnets sold in the stores at the time. Finally, Barry could stand the curiosity no longer. He ran into the Barnes's house to ask Rose what was going on. She was in the process of handing Harold his nightly after-work coffee. Harold was comfortably relaxed in what in the fifties was called an "easy chair" and had the evening paper opened across his lap in quiet, fact-absorbing comfort. As he took the coffee from Rose, he noticed Barry flying into the room excitedly, his taffy balled up in his hand. "Thanks, honey. Hey, Barry, how's the taffy pullin' comin', young man?" Harold asked, sounding excited for Barry's sake.

"It's comin' just fine, Mr. Barnes, but there's a dog out here stuck to Victoria," Barry said with anticipation of a great answer. Barry didn't realize he'd just summoned Batman. Responding to Barry's description, Harold calmly put down the paper and headed for the garage, with Barry and Rose following.

"Now-a Harold," Rose injected unnecessarily to calm him. Harold was never *any* other way but calm. Harold picked up the kerosene can in the corner of the garage and headed for the backyard. When he reached the two dogs, he placed the kerosene spout between them and upended the two-gallon can.

The cocker yelped and whined, and pulled apart from Victoria, who watched in further confusion. The cocker then, still whining, pawed out of the yard with his front legs, dragging his rear end on the ground, rear legs up. It was like the dog was moon-walking forward while sitting. When he got to the road, he began to run, still whining.

The puzzled Cub Scouts stood by in amazement while Rose took Victoria back inside. Batman took the kerosene back to the garage. After washing her hands, Rose returned to the backyard, with wax paper for her den denizens to wrap their taffy in for the trip home. Phil and Paul were returning from their Cub Scout meeting, and Barry ran up to them to see if they knew what had happened with the dogs. "You guys missed it!" an animated Barry shouted. "Victoria was stuck to another dog, and your dad poured kerosene on them! What happened!? Do you guys know!?"

Phil, always the one who seemed to "know" about such matters, put his arms around Barry's and Paul's shoulders and pulled them together so the other Scouts couldn't see. All three had their arms around the others, with their heads together, looking at the ground. "I'm not for sure …"—Phil pulled his lips inward and pushed them out again—"but I think it has somethin' to do with *this*." As Phil said *this,* he cupped his left hand and placed the middle finger of his right hand in his left, as if showing Barry and Paul a special secret. Barry and Paul were no more enlightened than before, although Phil was quite satisfied he had given them the extent of his knowledge on the subject. Fran would get some questions tonight. Barry had noticed his mother pulling her 1950 Olds into their driveway two doors down. He went home to see if Fran could be a little more explicit than "It has something to do with this."

Barry explained the whole scene to Fran as soon as he entered their house. Fran said, "Barry, you know how the dragonflies mate at your grandparents' farm pond?"

"Yeah, I do, Mom." Barry felt like he was going to receive information that probably wasn't going to make him feel better about things.

"Well, other animals higher up the evolutionary scale must also mate to create babies." Before young Barry could absorb the enormity of that statement, Fran dropped the Hiroshima tidbit: "And humans, too, must mate to have babies."

Eight-year-old Barry's first reaction was to think, No-o-o, couldn't be, followed by thoughts of how, when, where, and so on. Then Fran explained about why moms and dads sleep together, and how she and Barry's father, Bill, had lost a child when she had a miscarriage, explaining that, too. She said she had tried to have children with her second husband, Dennis Slater, with another miscarriage as the outcome. Barry's young mind was swirling at this point, thinking all at once about the prospect of almost having little brothers or sisters living with him. He also thought about his real brothers and sisters from Bill McAlister's second family, whom Barry loved dearly, and the distinctly uncomfortable knowledge about people having to mate in general. Barry would probably have rather had his father, Bill, expound on this subject, but Bill wasn't there.

Then Fran dropped the Nagasaki tidbit when Barry asked her, "What does *it* feel like?"

She told him, "Well, the first time it hurts the woman a lot." This would cause Barry some performance anxiety in his later years as he, Phil, and Paul launched into the sex-prone mid-to-late sixties. In his first attempts, Barry was afraid he'd hurt the girl, and if it didn't hurt her, did it mean she was a "dirty leg" if she let him try? Plus, Barry felt in his heart and soul that it was wrong until marriage. Doesn't God say that? Why was everyone going crazy? The approach should have been "Stick by your guns about your guns." Of course the boys were also taught to respect women who didn't want to be respected at the time, reflected by Mama Cass with "Words of love, so soft and tender, won't win a girl's heart anymore." But the anxiety didn't last long, because Barry found during this time that he really, really, really *loved* the opposite sex. One time in the service when Barry and his buddies were having a beer and discussing how they had learned about sex, one of the men remarked, after hearing Fran's comment, "Why didn't she just tell you your dick would fall off the first time you had sex?"

In seventh grade there was a gorgeous young girl who just seemed to like to show Barry her legs. Her name was Belinda Edwards. Her nickname was Lindy. It was during Common Learnings (how appropriate) that Lindy, who sat to Barry's right, would turn her lovely young body with its very beautiful legs toward him, cross them, and read her book in her lap. She hadn't yet gotten out the razor, and her beautiful legs were covered with fine blond hair. Sometimes she'd be wearing poodle skirts with petticoats, and sometimes dyed-to-matches, which were tight sweater tops with tight knee-length dresses of the same solid color. Either fashion just made Lindy's legs look that much finer. When Lindy crossed her excellent legs, Barry couldn't believe how great it looked, and the incredible feeling it gave him. Barry would leave Common Learnings with steam shooting out of his ears, like an old-time powerful steam locomotive, and with a banana in his pants. It was embarrassing. Every time he slow-danced with Lindy at teen town, he was wired to the max with the blood rushing toward the middle of his body, manifesting into the proud McAlister extension. Like one of his service buddies used to say, "Looks like a little boy with an apple in his hand." One time during one of these slow dances, like the instrumental "Sleep Walk," Lindy asked, "Barry, do you like me?" obviously stimulated from Barry's protrusion.

Barry's response was "Yeah-ya, huh, I do," totally clueless at the time about what had spawned the young lady's question. He felt like Jethro Bodine.

When Barry, Phil, and Paul were sophomores in high school, they used to tease one another about sexual situations they encountered. Barry, on one occasion in his second home with the McAlisters, had fallen asleep on their couch. It was after a sandlot tackle football game on Sunday, standard practice for the neighborhood boys, tackling each other before they tackled homework. Barry would walk down to Fran's afterward and hit the books. Phil and Paul, too, crashed for a short time after these enjoyable but physically demanding football games.

As Barry slept he had a wet dream, sometimes called, absurdly, a "nocturnal emission." It not only sounded like something an astronaut would be involved in clandestinely at night, but simply wasn't accurate. These emissions weren't necessarily nocturnal, to which any male who has been fifteen can attest. Barry slowly, groggily woke up, but as he felt the warm, wet semen in his dirt- and grass-stained jeans, minor panic overtook him. His immediate thought was, Where are Harold and Rose? Then, looking down on the floor at Phil and Paul still asleep, he thought he'd quietly slip out and head for Fran's. Bailing out seemed like the best approach at this time. It wasn't a time for explanation.

As Barry got up from the couch, he noticed a stain on the dark red velour. It wasn't small. Great, Barry thought, just great. Kinda like, Think I'll just leave my calling card here before I go. As he tried to quietly maneuver around Paul and Phil, Paul woke up stretching.

"Where you goin', Barry?" Barry, not wanting to be discovered, kept walking toward the door, but Paul wasn't up for that.

"Barry! Wait a minute. What's your hurry?" For some reason, Barry decided to turn around, showing the obvious darker area covering the crotch of his old, overly washed jeans. Paul studied him for a moment and then realized what had happened, and why Barry was leaving. A broad smile formed on Paul's young, handsome face.

"Dumped 'em, huh, big guy?" he said, teasing and laughing.

"Yeah, and look at the stain on your parents' nice couch. Isn't that cool?"

Phil was reviving also at the time, and Paul, after calming the laughter somewhat, said, still smiling, "Check Pop's chair, Barry. See that discolored area on the cushion? I had one there … Same deal … Took a little nappy-poo and voila, damp dream. I tried to get the stain out with Clorox. You see how wonderfully that turned out. And, the reason it isn't turned over is that Phil got the other side of the cushion about two months ago."

"Let's face it: we're all sperm machines," Phil philosophically and sleepily muttered. "I load up my bed all the time. Mom never says anything. It's natural. I'll just tell Mom I did it, Barry." This made Barry feel a little better.

"Thanks, Phil. Somehow it doesn't seem as bad in your own home. I'm going to throw these jeans in the washer."

Around this same time, Barry was over at the Barnes's home when Uncle Phil was there. The boys were watching the June Taylor Dancers of the *Jackie Gleason Show*, and their great legs, on TV. Uncle Phil walked in the room and turned the TV off. "C'mere, boys-a. I gonna tella you somp-a-ting. I know you been-a lookin' at-a da women. You will be-a doin' it-a all-a you-a lives-a. But I wanna tella you somp-a-ting. You don't-a getta somp-a-ting for-a nuttin'. Remember-a dat." The boys would find out their entire lives that as usual, Uncle Phil had said a big 10-4 with that one, referring to females. There were always "things" that happened. It wasn't that easy.

Although Paul was the youngest of the three, he was the first to really make out with a girl, and he never looked back. By the time Phil and Barry turned sixteen, fifteen-year-old Paul was already developing the self-assured charm that would make him irresistible to the opposite sex for the rest of his life. Phil and Barry always viewed the opposite sex from their vantage points, like it was all initiated by what they thought and felt. Paul viewed them with a more dynamic approach, like women too had sexual feelings, something Phil and Barry, and society in general, rarely considered at the time. When Phil or Barry, both new drivers, would say, "Let's go out and look at the girls," Paul would say, "Let's go out and let the girls look at us." Later in life, Paul would amplify this approach to making a quiet *p-s-s-sh-sh* sound when he, Phil, and Barry entered a club full of females. Paul explained that this was the sound of a "panty splash," which Paul surmised the girls were experiencing in physiological delight upon seeing the boys enter the place. Phil and Barry would just roll their eyes, smile, and shake their heads.

A couple of years later when the boys were seniors, Barry was fixed up on a blind date with Rachel Montgomery, one of the most beautiful and sought-after girls in the Northland area. Phil had fixed him up, and they were going to a party. Paul would also be there with his date. Rachel did not go to school with the boys, or with *any* boys. Instead, she attended a private girls' school. Her wealthy father wanted an excellent education for Rachel and did *not* want her educated in sexual experiences at an early age. Although this logical and moral approach has greatly diminished in America since the late sixties, both reasons were working for Rachel's father. Rachel had a reputation for being "the ice woman." You got nothing, nada, no way.

At the time, in 1964, boys would try, and the majority of girls would stop it. It gave the young men a sense of security knowing that in a pre-Pill era, they wouldn't be fathers at too early an age. Plus, it gave them a sense of decency, knowing that the girls they dated weren't "whores," the word usually used for girls who put out, even though it wasn't for money. But unbeknownst to Barry, Rachel's hormones were in overdrive that night. She had known about handsome Barry for some time, and had even fantasized about his body being on top of hers. That was Rachel's first sexual thought, one that would have sent her father running for a nun's habit. But it felt good for her to fantasize like that. Youthful hormones were always a challenge for either sex. Few of the young men of this generation ever thought their female counterparts thought like that.

The party was very enjoyable with the lack of chaperones, another logical, sensible tradition of the early sixties for the junior high crowd who, without oversight, were basically guns without safeties. Morality was taught and monitored in the early years, so as seniors, everyone knew their sociological sexual limitations. Everything was gradual, like learning how to properly operate a train. The safeties were on that night. As the evening progressed, the music changed from fast to slow. Barry's favorite song had been played, "Surfin' Bird" by the Trashmen, and he and Rachel had "rocked out" before the term became popular. Barry was always mad that The Beatles, whom he loved later on, knocked the Trashmen out of their number one slot with "I Wanna Hold Your Hand." So the slow stuff was now in everyone's ears, and kissing was certainly looked upon as a desirable goal. It's how you knew your date liked you, and it wouldn't create unwanted babies with someone you weren't in love with.

"I Can't Help Falling in Love with You" by Elvis began, and Rachel grabbed Barry's big hand and pulled him onto the makeshift dance floor, a living room with the chairs and tables pushed against the walls. While they were in each other's arms, Rachel looked up in Barry's eyes, something she'd dreamed about many times. Barry had no idea Rachel ever even knew who he was. When Rachel, who was known for not even kissing (yes, there were even girls like that in the Jurassic Era), looked up at Barry with a kiss in her eyes, Barry thought to himself, Well, here goes, McAlister.

When Barry slowly kissed the sweet lipstick-y lips of the beautiful Rachel, a wild thing happened. Chastity-governed Rachel went nuts. She animalized Barry, kissing him all over his face and French kissing his mouth. This caused a lightning-quick atten-hut! from the McAlister manhood. It was off-the-scale sensual for Barry and yet, at the same time, embarrassing. Rachel continued this onslaught for the entire Elvi-song. Barry felt like an Erector Set made of real full-sized steel. As Barry opened his eyes to see if anyone was staring during the festivities, he caught a glimpse of Paul sitting with his date on the couch. Paul had a smirk on his face. His right hand was over his eyes with the fingers opened, and he was shaking his head. After Elvis stopped singing by slowing down the title words at the end of the excellent song, Rachel, who was now a mess, as was Barry, regained some composure. Barry felt like he'd been systematically mauled by a female roller derby team. He absolutely loved it. Rachel's white shirt was pulled out from her immaculate jeans, and the second button of her blouse was unbuttoned, even though Barry hadn't touched it. Her pretty dark brown hair, though well sprayed, was sticking out everywhere.

"Oh," she said, as if finally realizing she'd "lost it" temporarily. Regaining composure, Rachel leaned toward Barry and said quietly, "Barry, will you excuse me for a minute? I'm going to freshen up."

"Sure, Rachel." Then Barry pole-vaulted over to sit down on the other side of Paul on the couch.

"We-e-e-l-l-l. Bear … What's up, big fella? Looks like the big fella *is* up! Man, does she like you!"

Barry leaned over and whispered to Paul. "Pauly, my testicles hurt like crazy. I mean there is some p-a-i-n down there."

"You got blue balls, Bear. You're gonna have to jack after you take Rachel home. That's what's causing the pain. It's a monumental sperm buildup. The only way to get rid of the pain is to relieve the pressure from those critters." Barry pondered it as Rachel returned from the bathroom. She looked incredibly perfect.

The party ended about 12:30 a.m., but Barry and Rachel were long gone because Rachel had a midnight curfew, another aspect of dating in the early sixties when dinosaurs used to roam. On Rachel's parents' front steps, Barry and Rachel made small talk, then said good night, and kissed very gently and sweetly. Rachel's father was still up to make sure the time constraint was obeyed.

Barry, who was still in testicular pain, thought he'd take Paul up on his suggestion when he got ready for bed at his own home. Fran was not there, being on a date, so Barry had the run of the house. He brandished the tissues for action and got his release. It felt *so g-o-o-o-d*! No more pain, and the release wasn't bad either. Later, when Barry heard that some writer had described life simplistically, yet perhaps accurately, as merely "tension and release," he understood. If you weren't busy building up tension, you were busy releasing it. Though simplistic, it made good sense.

Barry would think about Rachel's beautiful figure for years, how perfectly she felt in his arms, and how she had excited him to the point of ecstasy and pain. It had been a wonderfully powerful combination of how she looked, felt, smelled, sounded, and tasted. It was sensory synergy. He and Rachel would become friends, always glad to see each other, but Barry would never ask her out again. It wasn't that he didn't want to, but with the Vietnam War heating up, most of the young men were soon to be either college or military bound, and high school relationships were rarely continued. Phil, Paul, and Barry would be involved with both college and the military for years.

But he would think of Rachel from time to time all his life, as he would other incredibly attractive females who bombed his brain with their attractiveness over the years. Certain moments with them, how they looked, what they were wearing, and so on were always near his thoughts. He didn't even have to know them. Certain females at a ball game he never even met, and how they looked in their shorts, halter tops, or whatever stayed in his mind in a permanent mental imprint. As early as Barry could remember, he was enamored of the female anatomy. A beautiful breast, a curvy calf, a dynamite thigh, a great rear, a slim waist, beautiful hair, pretty eyes, and sometimes, admittedly, an attraction on which logic had no bearing would always have their effect. Barry knew that in some cases, if Phil or Paul had been present for the bird dog "Hey, guys, look at that," they would have responded, "Barry, you need help." It was an individual deal ... always was "in the eyes of the beholder," sparking such low-grade, chauvinistic Chance Armstrong comments as "One man's meat is another man's poison." But Barry knew he would always be knocked off center by an unexpected view of the feminine gender's natural beauty. It was the way it seemed it *had* to be. There would always be that longing in the loins.

Susan could feel it. All wives can. It made Barry very uncomfortable as much as he loved Suz, but "those curves, that skin, that face, those eyes ..." When Barry saw these feminine "superchargers," his mind leapt back and forth in asinine scenarios that were totally devoid of logic. And if the beauty was exceptional, the vision would appear in his mind for months and sometimes years. The beautiful, reoccurring, stimulating visuals were like discovering a tantalizing snack in the cupboard that one had forgotten was there. Unfortunately, men were visual freaks, and most wives would never understand this, understandably.

Barry knew that probably only God was aware of the point where admiration became lust, but he did have an idea, and sometimes let the fantasies continue beyond that point. It felt in a way like he was going out on Susan worse than when he had danced with the pretty Native American girl in Pocatello. But he always told himself, No big deal. The psychologist Dr. James Dobson says that males are visual responders, that the view of an attractive female causes electrochemical responses in their bodies over which they have no control. Gabe Grundy, an old switchman who held the 16th Street shanty job for years, paraphrased Dr. Dobson. He said, "I tell my ol' lady when I quit lookin', she can bury me, 'cause I won't be any good for her either."

Barry viewed masturbation merely as a tension reliever. It was amazing to him how a semen buildup could "control" his mind. Supposedly, Mozart experienced an unwanted orgasm while composing the *Unfinished Symphony*. It was evidently why the symphony was unfinished. But Barry just wanted to think about his current task, rather than his "task at hand." When Paul was in school, he researched a paper for his Adolescent Psychology class that he titled "Masturbation: A First-Hand Account." Barry's buddies always teased him about the ritual, and he teased them back, but in actuality, he really hadn't partaken until the evening with Rachel. From that time on, he thought masturbation was a great way to get your mind off the pretty legs, the nice breasts, the awesome figures, and so on. Then he could think straight again. It was like, I'm thinkin' about her legs … Now I'm not thinkin' about 'em anymore. Semen buildup … Mind on babes. Semen gone … Mind now logical. Maybe there was an as-yet-undiscovered part of the brain other than "right" or "left." It seemed there should be a "middle" part of the brain for thinking sexually about the female of the species. One thing was for sure: nothing worthwhile could be accomplished mentally till those thoughts subsided.

Phil had told Barry of Elia Kazan's book *The Arrangement* when they were discussing the semen control of the male brain. When Phil was overseas, one of his service buddies had it, and had lent it to Phil to read. One of the characters in the book is an executive who wants his female "bunkmate" to disappear as soon as he experiences his massive neurovascular discharge. It is yet another example of the semen-affecting-mind thing. "I want you here … I'm off … I don't want you here."

In college, one of Barry's friends was reading the Kinsey Report out loud. "It says here," the college sophomore read loudly, "that 95 percent of all single males masturbate."

Another guy down the hall yelled, "And the other 5 percent don't have dicks." The Kinsey Report went on to say that 65 percent of all married males masturbate. It was considered normal, but later, both Barry and Phil would consider it what the Bible called a "work of the flesh," like substitute fornication. There was one way God wanted us to enjoy sex: with one wife, for life. Barry wondered how many individuals could claim to be half of a couple like that. They were the ones who had *really* done it right.

To Barry, another very degrading fact about masturbation was that it was a waste of great manhood. He, Phil, and Paul had discussed that about the phenomenon at length. So what was the choice? Wet dreams forever, if there were no female outlets? And once in discussion with Ned Lingle about the subject, Ned said he thought *any* sexual substitution excepting husband and wife was wrong. Ned had compared it to the "abomination of desolation" discussed in Daniel, where the Antichrist was sitting where Jesus was supposed to be. Ned thought *any substitute* for other than what God intended was abomination.

Barry thought there was a place in the Bible where it said, "God did not give us the spirit of lust." Barry did not understand this. What then allowed us to be attracted to our wives? But on the other hand, he could understand it from the standpoint of what he knew, disgustedly, he did. The apostle Paul in Romans says he sees another law in his members, warring against the law of his mind that brings him into captivity to the law of sin which is in his members. Good to know Paul, a chosen apostle, had the same problem that Barry and the majority of the males on earth deal with during most of their waking and sometimes sleeping hours.

As a division personnel officer, Barry had to notice that some of the women who wanted to be hired by the prestigious Central Pacific were slam-dunk gorgeous. Not to the point of ever thinking about skating on Susan, but various anatomical parts lingered in Barry's mind. Some of the women sat in front of Barry's desk and crossed their gorgeous legs and smiled, and it was pure heaven and hell for him. He tried successfully not to be led astray, although some of the females made no pretense at all about their desires with handsome Barry. He always surmounted the situation. But it was tough when it seemed to be everywhere. And although Barry never slipped off the curb, someone always knew something about someone who was having an affair at the Central Pacific ... the old grapevine Bader warned Barry about. And it *never* turned out well for any of the parties involved. As Uncle Phil said, "You don't-a getta somp-a-ting for-a nuttin'."

# CHAPTER 17
## TO BE OR NOT TO BE

Although being a young officer with Central Pacific carried a lot of prestige, and although Barry couldn't have been doing better, he and Susan planned to leave Omaha and CP management. They had come to the realization that if Barry was going to swim with the sharks, he had to grow teeth, and it just wasn't in his nature. Things had occurred, such as Susan's father having to undergo back surgery. She had left with Erin for two weeks to be with her dad, who had no one to daily look after him. Barry had gone out with the local CP officers to watch the Golden Gloves fights and have a few beers. After the fights they wound up at the house of a gal whom everyone referred to as "437." It was her phone extension at the Big Brick. "Extension" was the operative word, because 437, as far as Barry could tell, would accept any "extensions" pointed her way. She evidently would have sex with anyone at any time, and many of the company officers tapped her resources. Barry had not known where they were going when they went to her place. When they arrived, a couple of other company officers were already there. When Barry asked, "Where are we?" an officer he was with said, "This is 437's place." Barry thought, Uh-oh; the notoriety of the infamous extension being common knowledge.

Inside the house, 437 slithered up to Barry and put her snake-y arm around him. She was attractive. "How are you, big guy?" she gurgled.

Barry answered, "Fine" and sat down on the couch with a beer, deliberate body language that told 437 he wasn't "getting in line."

The woman's young son was walking among the gathering crowd, looking lost. He was wearing a black cowboy hat and had two toy six-guns strapped on him in their holsters. It made Barry very sad. "Occupy yourself with your toy guns, young man, while Mama gang bangs. Maybe when you grow up, you can use real guns on people and will feel good about it, thanks to chaste Mom." Barry couldn't believe people actually lived like this. It made him sick. And there was a haughtiness, an air of "this is what adults do," that Barry would never be able to identify with, just as he couldn't identify with "adult movies." It's "adult" to be immoral animals. Yeah, right. What a trick of the devil. Barry thought very strongly that whatever a man and wife did sexually was *their* business, and "Katy, bar the good ol' door." God gave them to each other, and that was one of his great purposes. But Barry also felt very strongly that sex outside marriage was outside God's Commandments also. Even though he knew the lust gremlin kicked his tail now and again, his wedding vows before God were sacred. He was totally out of his element here. He always told Susan everything, like the dance in Pocatello, but this was one he'd keep to himself. Where was Walt Morehouse when he needed him? Barry waited painfully while everybody did their after-hours business with 437.

Barry was still traveling a lot more than he expected, most often for a week at a time, hiring new employees on various parts of the division. And Susan was pregnant again. On those nights when she didn't feel so hot, and Erin was being a young wild child, there was no hubby to help her. Barry was gone as usual.

As Nebraska Division personnel officer, Barry had instant status. He had gone from a lowly trainee to a high-visibility position. Of course, being that close to headquarters, many senior officers from the Big Brick called to get their relatives jobs. One of the senior officers was a friend of a local college football coach. He had told the coach he would arrange for the college's football players to work on the track gangs for the summer. It would definitely keep them physically fit. The only problem was that when the forty-three football players showed up, Phil had to tell them he already had 125 section workers laid off, and that they had to be called back before he could hire any more. "Damned if you do, and damned if you don't" was a prevalent management sentiment.

Then there was the piss fight with the operating department about the hiring of women and minorities. Personable Barry had developed a great rapport with local minority agencies such as Chicano Awareness and the National Urban League. He had hired some really top-notch people from these agencies, but the old hard-line, redneck operating officers wanted only white males. Too bad. This was the way it was. The times, they still are a-changin'.

Barry enjoyed the challenge of the job, but as time went on and demand for employees grew, he, like most CP officers, was jammed with work. He took it home on weekends, when he was in town. Tom Moffat, who was an old hand at it, and now Barry's peer and mentor, always offered his help. The laid-off section workers were all called back to work, and Barry was able to hire the football players for the gangs. There were machinists, pipe fitters, welders, electricians, switchmen, engineers, section men, clerks, and others to be hired. Each newly hired employee had to fill out no fewer than twelve forms, which were sent to personnel. Each had to have a physical scheduled, with Barry checking the results as soon as possible. There were back X-rays at the time for those hired in transportation. Those with back problems would not fare well holding on to the sides of railroad cars for extended periods.

Then there were the calls, the endless calls. Barry had no secretary, so he was his own answering service, and *everyone* called the Central Pacific personnel office. This was before the era of the blessed answering machine. People wanted to know if they could get a job. People wanted to know if they had gotten the job. People wanted to know if they passed the physical. People wanted to know if they passed the back X-ray. People wanted to know if they were close to being called back to work. People wanted to know what jobs were available. Then there were the miles of "walk-ins," who wanted to know *everything* and fill out applications. It was endless.

Although Barry met many sincere, decent, caring company officers who outranked him, he met some extreme creeps also. One such mega-creep was Albert Vaccaro. Barry was leaning up against a hallway wall at the Big Brick talking with Carl Banner one day when this thin, short, middle-aged, nasty-looking individual goose-stepped up to them with his arms back and his little chest sticking out. He had on a white shirt, one size too large, a black tie and black pants, and pointed black shoes. He wore black plastic-rimmed glasses, which were the opposite prescription of Harold Bader, enlarging his black, joyless eyes. With his large, hooked Roman nose and the black plastic glasses, it looked like he had the fake nose and glasses on, minus the mustache. This person was obviously overwhelmed with his own perceived importance. He was smiling, but it wasn't a sincere smile, like from the eighties song "Smiling Faces." "Smiling faces show no traces of the evil that lurks within." Again, the great lines from Dylan's "Like a Rolling Stone" were pertinent. There were plenty of both jugglers and clowns in CP management. Vaccaro was a little of both. He actually made Barry a bit physically sick with his presence, like Stephen King's great central character in *The Green Mile*. He barked some orders at Carl, still fake smiling, intentionally ignoring the much larger Barry. Then, gripping his "illegal pad," he stepped off in a quick self-important huff. Carl just sighed and shook his head.

"Who was that guy?" Barry asked Carl, still a little nauseated from his presence.

"That, Barry, was the famous Al Vaccaro, one of the most disgusting individuals you will ever meet."

"I've heard of him, and I've seen him around. I actually felt a sickness when he walked up." Barry still felt somewhat uneasy.

"Well, your gut reaction was correct. He is the king of dirty tricks and low-rent deals. He and I were up for the same promotion a few years ago. He spread a rumor to our superiors that I was sleeping with a certain female personnel employee who shall remain nameless. Well, as you've guessed, Vaccaro got the promotion. It wasn't because the senior officers thought that what was alleged was wrong. It was that one of them actually *was* banging this gal, and the false rumor that was true for another got me punished. I assured some of the committee members who made the ultimate selection that the rumor about me was absolutely false. But from what I understand, the senior manager, who shall also remain nameless, never quite believed I wasn't doing something. Let's go to the cafeteria, Barry." There, Carl continued talking about Vaccaro's background.

At the cafeteria, Carl lowered his voice and moved his head closer to Barry over the table. "Vaccaro evidently supplies women from his 'contacts' for any company officer who desires them," he continued.

"Then he gets a 'bonus' at some point and 'rebates' some of the amount back to the 'ladies,' and I use the term as loosely as they lead their lives. It's how he gains promotion."

"Sounds like the 'oldest profession' to me," Barry said, offering rare editorial comment.

"That's exactly what it is, but welcome to the sterling sub-level of railroad management, Barry. And what do you think that makes Vaccaro? Walt Morehouse says all Vaccaro needs is a broad-brimmed purple hat with a matching purple suit, stack-heeled shoes, and lots of gaudy gold jewelry around his neck. Supposedly, Vaccaro's management philosophy can be summed up by his frequently stated, self-composed adage, 'Don't promote anyone who can surpass you.' He's only good to those who can do him some good. He treats everyone else with the same disdain you witnessed." Carl almost hated to enlighten decent Barry. Barry's effect on people was always the opposite of Vaccaro's.

"What a wonderful human being." Barry couldn't help the comment, which was common rail-speak for just the opposite. If a yardmaster gave railroaders a rotten move, they might say, "That was nice of him" and "I'll make it a point to send him a card at Christmastime." It seemed to lessen the blow. Probably every organization has at least one Vaccaro, a miserable, self-serving, measly slime of an individual who will do literally anything for a promotion. Paul always referred to these people as "sniveling." They were sub-human vermin who knew how to play the game, and play it viciously. It was their mission to get ahead at all costs, not only without regard for how many lives they destroyed in doing so, but also taking a sickening measure of pride in accomplishing their destructions. Barry surmised that Al Vaccaro, being short, of slight build, and rather wimpy in appearance, had, from childhood, *way* too much physical and metaphorical sand kicked in his face. Now he was in a position of power, and he was going to kick dump trucks full of sand *back* at someone as long as he could kick.

"Vaccaro is living, breathing proof of the old adage 'Never give a little man a lot of power,'" Carl continued. "It's not the stature or lack thereof, Barry. It's the size of the heart. Look at Mr. Woods, the VP of security and special services. He's about as nice a person as there is on this planet, and he's five foot two. He has a huge heart. Have you heard what he does when he is not railroading? He helps with the homeless."

"I have met him, Carl," Barry said with a reverent smile. "He has a huge presence also ... such class. He's so quiet-spoken, yet when he speaks, you want to listen. His stature is immaterial. He's a giant of a man."

"Yeah, he's the antithesis of Vaccaro."

Carl further enlightened Barry that Vaccaro's nickname was The Vacuum, because he sucked in so consistently and effectively with the brass. There was also the obvious alliteration with his last name, Vacuum Vaccaro. One of the midlevel CP managers had commented, "The Vacuum is a great name for Al, since he's such a dirt bag." Al was one of the first people in America to receive a corrective operation for carpal tunnel syndrome. When his peers learned of the operation, two of the comments were "Probably from excessive masturbation" followed by "Yeah, of the vice president's staff." Al Vaccaro would eventually make it to the level of assistant vice president of sales—no doubt because CP had made no provision for vice president of pimps.

Carl Banner would never be promoted much higher because he possessed such characteristics as honesty, frankness, conscientiousness, conviction, humility, and discretion, as evidenced by his refraining from naming names to Barry. He would hang around for years, doing great work, eventually having a "Senior" attached to the beginning of his Manager of Personnel title. He was always his own man, and that was an excellent, dedicated man, but oftentimes those types aren't promoted. Human garbage like Vaccaro is what gets promoted most of the time. Barry knew he wanted away from people like Vaccaro, and away from a management system that promoted the likes of Vaccaro and held back people like Carl Banner. Then there were wonderful examples, such as Mr. Kimball and Mr. Woods. It was confusing.

After six weeks on the job, Barry got a call from Walt Morehouse. "Hey, Bear Man. Guess what? I just got assigned!"

"Really, Walt. Where, man?" Barry shared Walt's enthusiasm.

"With *you*, man! I got assigned to the trainmaster job in Council Bluffs!"

"Walt, that's just outstanding! Now I'll have someone to whine and dine with at lunch."

"Cheese and whine, Bear … Can't beat it! I'm due over there next Monday. Looks like we can go efficiency testing together after all, even though you pussed out with the king of Nebraska personnel officer job."

"Yeah, real impressive, huh, Walt? I don't even have my own secretary. I'm nothing more than a clerk with a tie. Some have referred to this fine assignment as the Nebraska pissing post position."

"Sure, Barry. You are useless. Right. All I ever hear is good about you, man. Anyway, now I can help you handle Payne."

Garrison Payne was the division superintendent and Barry's ultimate boss. Barry was still in the Vance Carlson hierarchy in personnel and labor relations, but now he reported to a division superintendent as well, and it was Garrison. There was a local yard superintendent and assistant in charge of the Council Bluffs yard. But Garrison was the commander-in-chief of the Nebraska Division, and everyone within earshot knew it. At least they better have known it. All the managers within the division thought Garrison should have spelled his name P-A-I-N because he inflicted enough of *it* on *them*. They referred to Garrison's daily rippings as "getting their vitamins." The funny thing was that if Garrison didn't like you, he wouldn't even bother to chew you out; he'd simply get rid of you. So being chewed out by Garrison was somehow *honorable*, and related to job security. Garrison carried on a time-honored CP tradition of verbally hammering subordinates. It was more than just a common Type A approach to management. It was SOP in railroading.

Garrison was a Mormon, and definitely of the "Jack" variety. He was Jack to the nth degree. He even drank "Jack": Jack Daniels Black Label … Black Jack. He smoked ready-rolls to the point that his fingers were yellowish. He drank constantly, and those younger operating officers who efficiency-tested with him knew they could expect several booze snorts from Garrison during the testing period. Black Jack was a perfect shot for a Jack Mormon. Garrison's father had been a CP officer, and his great-grandfather had been at the driving of the Golden Spike at Promontory Summit, Utah, like Scotty Germain's. So he was quite the blue blood … a blue blood on Black Jack. Garrison was known to say, "I work twenty-four hours a day, seven days a week. Happy hour is when *I* say it is." It was Garrison's version of Alan Jackson's "It's Five O'Clock Somewhere." The Jack came out when *he* wanted it. Garrison pretty much felt that way about anything ... It happened when *he* said it did. And it did. And Garrison never, ever acted drunk. He was always ready for the next challenge.

Barry thought Garrison was a closet genius because he had such a command of the division, just like Mr. Kimball. He knew literally everything. Nothing escaped Garrison's scrutiny. Barry was in charge of hiring for the entire state of Nebraska for the Central Pacific. Cecil Henry was the Nebraska Division roadmaster in charge of maintenance of way, the track structures and roadbed, and so on. Don Malley was the head of bridge and building for the division. Bruce Stallings was manager of the storehouse and saw to it that the proper amount of supplies was constantly delivered to the field and immediately replenished at the storehouse. Hugo Waller was the superintendent of shops, whose job it was to see that the CP locomotives, the total motive power for the railroad, were properly and expeditiously overhauled, inspected, and ready for service. Evelyn Chambers was the office manager and the head of all the clerical functions on the division.

Garrison Payne knew *all* the functions of *all* these departments better than the people who ran them did. At division meetings, the division managers sat semi-petrified, expecting Garrison to embarrass them by discussing pertinent division items of business that they should have known about but didn't. Garrison *always* did. If any one of these division manager support groups dropped the ball, it had a negative impact on the Nebraska Division, and Payne would drop the wrecking ball on them. He was a maniac. Barry would welcome Walt's company on the division, and he would welcome his company in these division meetings and dealing with Payne in general. Walt's presence lessened the stress. Garrison Payne affected Barry and the other division managers the way commercial jets affected Walt.

When Barry had first been assigned to the division personnel officer position, Vance Carlson had introduced him to Garrison. Garrison was uncharacteristically polite at the time. Then, just a week later, when Barry had hired his first switchmen's class and was feeling good about his choices, hoping to please both Vance and Garrison, he received a call at 0730:

"McAlister! Get the $&#* over here!"

"Yes, sir!" Barry had dropped everything and rushed to Garrison's office. He was totally caught off guard, and anxiously searched his mind for a reason why he was being called on the carpet. Garrison's division office was on the Omaha side of the Missouri River. Barry didn't even remember driving over there from his office in Council Bluffs. When he arrived at Garrison's office, Garrison's demeanor hadn't changed from the time of the phone call.

"Get in here, McAlister! Will you please enlighten me as to why we hired these new &%#@* clowns? Where did you find them, Barnum and Bailey?" Garrison had evidently overlooked the fact that Barry had submitted the resumes for the new-hire switchmen the week before and that Garrison himself had signed off on them. But Barry was wise enough to let Garrison vent and bellow, because his basic instinct told him that silence was in order at this moment. This was not the time for logic and principle and showing Nebraska Division Superintendent Garrison Payne the error of his ways.

Garrison's father had seen to it that Garrison learned railroading from the ground up, literally. Garrison's father was a superintendent at Pocatello, where Mr. Kimball was assigned. In fact, Kimball, Payne, and Germain all had common railroad histories. That was the way it worked for the real brass. Garrison began his railroad career working on the section gang, pounding spikes with a spike maul. His father knew it would toughen him up. In fact, that was where Garrison began his drinking, or "learned to drink," as Garrison put it. Most of the section men drank. It helped take the edge off their aches and pains, and gave them the courage to return the next morning. Sometimes they never left the railroad, sleeping near the tracks on blankets, in an open, stored boxcar, or in their cars.

But after Barry understood Garrison's rough edges, he learned to respect and admire him. Garrison Payne, like most everyone, admired Barry. Also, Garrison's "kick ass, take names" attitude viewed Barry's large frame as "there goes one of my boys," not to mention the fact that Barry was extremely conscientious and never embarrassed him. If you wanted to get on Payne's poo-poo list, embarrass him by poor performance or lack of knowledge about your craft. All the division superintendents were in constant competition. There were always differing nuances to every division, but the vice presidents had a way of scoring, known only to them, that put all the division superintendents on a level playing field. Garrison was one of the best, and he wanted to keep it that way. His division moved freight, and many multi-tons of it.

With Walt secured as local trainmaster, Barry's life as a personnel officer was better but still uncomfortable. Garrison liked Walt very much, too, and always asked for him personally to inspect his business train when Garrison left town on his business car to inspect his division from the rails. Barry and Walt used to call and ask each other on a daily basis if they'd gotten their vitamins yet, referring to Garrison's penchant for blowing out his subordinates. Usually, either young company officer's answer was yes. Garrison started early, like a good engineer controlling his train.

# CHAPTER 18
## SWITCHING OUT THE BAD
## ORDERS IN YOUR MIND

After Barry had been handling his new job for about a year, a middle manager, Herman Boyce, told him not to shave before he came to work on the next Saturday. He told Barry to wear a tie, as usual, but to leave his top button unbuttoned and to pull the tie's knot down a bit and pull his tie sideways. Barry said, "Okay," trusting Herman, but knowing that obviously Herman had something up his sleeve. He'd shared this with Susan, and she, too, was curious. Barry was to meet Herman at the International House of Pancakes on Dodge Street at 6:30 a.m. for coffee. Herman liked Barry and was concerned for his career. Technically, he outranked Barry. Most did at this point. Herman thought Barry was an exemplary young company officer, but needed to mingle with the troops a little more, just to ensure that his rising star would continue to rise. Herman was aware of Barry's notoriety with Neutron Don and Mr. Kimball, but thought he could use some continuing exposure. Herman was very bright, and positioned in the marketing hierarchy of the Central Pacific. Barry walked through the front door of the IHOP at 6:25 a.m. and saw Herman sitting in the second booth on the left.

"Hey, Hermy. What's goin' on?"

"Hey, Bear. Today we go on a premier trip."

"A premier trip?" Barry questioned.

"You know who Bob Huston is?"

"Sure, he's the vice president of marketing," Barry responded.

"That's right," Herman said, like he was about to explain an attack strategy to Barry. "He's my ultimate boss. He likes me, and I happened to have overheard him talking to Neutron Don on the conference phone. He had his door closed, but the volume was loud enough so that I could hear. They were talking about *you*, Barry. Neutron said good things, you know, but Mr. Huston said he didn't know you. Well, today, he's going to know you. We're gonna go pay him a Saturday morning visit. You look great, like you've been up all night. That was the idea."

"Oh, now Herman, I ..."

"No, don't 'Herman, I' me," Herman said with an authoritative, self-assured smile. "We're goin'. I already set it up."

Barry felt like a manipulator extraordinaire. This definitely wasn't his deal. Reluctantly, he went with Herman to the twelfth floor of the Big Brick to meet Mr. Robert B. Huston, vice president of marketing.

The twelfth floor was a whole other world. Stepping off the elevator, Barry and Herman stepped onto a mega-plush carpet with a magnificent olive-and-blue pattern. As they made their way to Mr. Huston's office, Barry looked into the offices with the doors open. They were huge, and looked like suites. One had a beautiful, brass steam locomotive whistle mounted on a massive block of polished marble with a brass inscription plate, too far away for Barry to read. The walls of the hallways and offices were covered with huge colorful paintings and pictures of locomotives, train wrecks, and trains. The ceilings were at least twenty feet high. There were archways into some areas. The place was palatial.

Barry looked at Herman, just shaking his head, overwhelmed at the opulence. But he did not speak. After they rounded a corner and walked down a long hallway, Herman grabbed Barry by the arm and pointed to a large office. Smiling a smile with canary feathers sticking out, he silently mouthed, "This is it." The door to Bob Huston's office was open. Through it, Barry and Herman could see a beautiful, massive high-backed, dark green leather chair, turned away from the door toward a wall-sized window. Blue-gray cigar smoke was rising from the chair. Herman knocked on the doorjamb. The massive dark green leather chair turned slowly around. Barry was about to jump out a window. He had never become totally acclimated to this stuff.

"Well, hello, Herman," Mr. Huston said jovially. "Who we got here?"

As he shook his boss's hand, Herman, sounding quite relaxed, said, "Hi, boss. This is a good friend of mine, Barry McAlister. Barry's the Nebraska Division personnel officer."

Barry had been moving closer to Mr. Huston's desk. "Well, hello, Barry. I've heard good things about you," Mr. Huston said, the standard greeting of acceptance. It was the white-collar version of the blue-collar "Come back anytime."

"Hello, Mr. Huston. I've heard *great* things about you," Barry said, surprising himself with his own candor and sincerity.

Mr. Huston smiled pleasantly. He loved it. He could easily tell Barry *was* sincere. Mr. Huston had a suck-butt meter that was as sensitive as any in the industry. Barry's comment didn't even require a measurement. "Well, that's nice to hear, Barry. I'm glad my reputation precedes me. What brings you two young pollywogs tryin' to swim upstream to my office?"

To Barry's delight, Herman took over. "Actually, it was my idea, Mr. Huston. Barry and I were meeting for coffee, and I suggested we come see you. Barry doesn't get out much." This was a politically preferable way of saying, "Barry doesn't meet many high-level officers" or "Barry doesn't have a specific godfather."

"Well, Barry, you'll have to come around here more often. Did you come to us from college, Barry?" Mr. Huston asked, for his own information.

"No, sir, I was a switchman in Kansas City," Barry said with pride, although he didn't know why. Barry humbly neglected to say that he *did* have a degree. Bob Huston knew that already anyway, just like he already knew Barry had been a Kansas City switchman.

"Really?" Mr. Huston said in his strong, assured, yet pleasant voice. "Thirty-three years ago, I hired out in Kansas City as a switchman. Been all over the system since then, and wound up here. I'm blessed if I know why." Barry then knew why Herman had set this up. Both he and Mr. Huston had begun their railroad careers in Kansas City. It was the kind of association that was always pertinent. "Well, I don't want to rush you guys off, but railroadin's waitin'." Mr. Huston referred to a meeting he was to have in fifteen minutes. "Herman, thanks for dropping by, and

Barry, awfully nice meeting you, young man. We'll see you later. Now you two go make some money for us."

As Mr. Huston said this, he shook both their hands, putting his Cuban cigar back in his mouth as he did. Barry felt like doing an about-face as he used to do leaving a colonel's office. He noticed that Mr. Huston was unshaven, and that his top button was unbuttoned, with the knot on his tie pulled down a little. Barry and Herman walked toward the elevator in silence. When they got in and the doors closed, Barry breathed a sigh of relief.

"That was *perfect*, Barry," Herman said, laughing. Barry was hearing that statement a lot.

Barry was laughing, too, but more at the relief of being able to leave. "I see what you mean about not shaving, and wearing your tie pulled down."

"That's the standard dress code on the twelfth floor on the weekends. Some of those guys literally don't go home on Friday. Most of them have showers and bathrooms in their offices. 'If we gonna keep ya, we gonna keep ya comfortable.' And that comment, 'I've heard great things about you,' that was *all right*, Bear."

"Well, it's true. I *have* heard awesome things about Mr. Huston," Barry semi-defended himself to himself.

"Yeah, Bob Huston is the classiest of class acts. He's like Scotty," Herman said, referring to Scotty Germain. "Y'know … you may just have you a godfather … Both big guys, both nice guys, both Kansas City switchmen. You just may, godson." As he let Barry off at the pancake house, Herman said, "See ya, Big Bear. Nice job."

"Thank you, Herman. Thanks for lookin' out for me. I owe you one, man. Blessings, now." A strange feeling of belonging began to permeate Barry's psyche, like he had felt watching Shock Theater on Friday nights with Phil and Paul at the Barneses' … like when Rose would bring them popcorn with lots of butter, before horror movie time with Frankenstein or the Wolf Man. Barry always enjoyed the few times he got to meet Phil and Paul's uncle Phil. He knew Uncle Phil was Phillip's godfather, and remembered thinking at the time when they were all young kids how Phil had a father *and* a godfather, whereas he was growing up with neither. He was never jealous of this, but just thought it was nice for Phil. Uncle Phil had imparted his wisdom to Barry a time or two, and he'd loved it. Now the term associated with Mr. Huston sounded like contentment to Barry. Maybe he did have a godfather after all.

Barry drove over to the Nebraska Division personnel office. Let the punishment begin, he thought as he imagined the numerous phone calls and endless paperwork, some of which he'd taken home and spread out on the apartment floor on Friday night. A Scrabble game with Susan would have been much, much more enjoyable. They weren't happening at all anymore.

Barry was still dizzy from meeting Mr. Huston. It was actually pleasant, but at the same time, it seemed somewhat lacking in integrity. And yet, it was just tradition, no more, no less. Herman was a good guy. He was wise in the ways of management and just wanted to help Barry. Barry wanted to deliberately remain unwise. The twelfth-floor meeting was just the way it was done. It dawned on Barry that years ago, Bob Huston and a young officer buddy had probably done the same thing at his age: deliberately didn't shave, and wore their ties crooked, with top buttons unbuttoned, to talk to the top brass. The tradition continued. Barry psyched himself up to deal with the considerable personnel challenges just minutes away. The work was insurmountable. You didn't do it well. You just did your best, and acted like you did it well. At least that's how others represented the position. Thomas Moffat had made it all look so easy.

Still, it wasn't the demanding work that bothered Barry. It was the seeming lack of morality everywhere, like Vaccaro, and his cronies, and 437. There was a story about an assistant division superintendent and a yard superintendent who used to get drunk together and then show up in the yard of this female clerk who put out. They would go to opposite ends of the yard, run at each other, and butt heads. They did this until only one of them was left standing. Then the "winner" got to go in and have sex with the lovely sleaze-bag clerk. There were stories like that everywhere. Barry even had one female job applicant tell him in the personnel office that she'd do "anything" for a job, and she was not kidding. There were lots of innuendos, but this had been blatant.

There *were* some princes in management. Scotty, Mr. Huston, Mr. Kimball, Vance Carlson, Herman, Tom Moffat, Walt were all wonderful, dedicated men. But the "crumbs" were more numerous, or so it seemed. Maybe it was just that they had the most notoriety from their evil approaches. For sure, they were affecting Barry. It wasn't so much that he had a "holier than thou" attitude. He had seen a lot of immorality in the service. It was that he was desperately afraid he'd change and be just like them, and hurt Susan and Erin. He did think the female of the species was quite wonderful. He didn't know if, after countless times in compromising situations, he'd be strong enough *every* time. Although proximity to 437 made Barry feel sickeningly similar to the nauseated way he'd felt when Vacuum Vaccaro walked up to him and Carl that day, he had to admit that he thought she was physically attractive. In fact he thought she was *very* attractive. It's always dangerous for a man to be around an attractive female he knows will "give it to him." He thought the best solution was to never allow himself to experience any more potentially dangerous situations, family-wise. And that meant bolting from management. Barry didn't realize that other managers wrestled with the same thoughts.

Barry had been in touch with Phil and Paul more than usual lately. Paul had stayed on the Quindaro jobs, happy to get a quit and earn enough for Rosalinda's child support, which was another way of saying "free money for Ramona," in Paul's estimation. He managed by sharing a crummy, low-rent house with a couple of other railroaders who were single, one of them Paul's friend New Man (Pat) Anderson. On those rare occasions when Paul got to have Rosalinda for the weekend, he would rent a motel room for himself and his daughter. That way, Rosalinda would have nice, clean surroundings, and her own clean, comfortable bed. Also, it didn't cramp the other house residents' style if they wanted to watch a ball game and drink beer, which they usually did. And females were usually around the place on the weekends, too, something Paul did not want Rosalinda to be around.

Besides the fact that Barry and Susan were both disenchanted with things in Omaha, they missed everyone back in Kansas City. One of life's sidebars in taking promotion was that oftentimes people were permanently displaced. Phil had found out from Tom Moffat that CP was to hire some more engineers in Kansas City. He had told Barry about it, telling him honestly that he liked the work but disliked the time away from Carla and Angela. And Carla, like Susan, was pregnant again. Phil also told Barry he would make more money as an engineer.

"Heck, Phil, I'm away from Susan and Erin now—way too much. It's got to be better," Barry said. "At least I'll be able to identify, stay away from compromising situations, and make more money. Heck, we might even be able to barbecue together once in a while with the families. Both the girls are pregnant, and Erin and Angela are about the same age. It all sounds pretty good, huh?"

"You bet, Bear, and you'll know for sure you have a home to go to, to live in for a while, at least a couple of times a week. With you in management, they could tell you they want you in Portland, Oregon, tomorrow."

"That's true, Phil. I've already seen that happen to guys. This guy Brad Hackett ... He and his wife had just built a beautiful home in this very nice part of western Omaha. It was their dream home. His wife had a good job here. He was notified on a Friday that effective Monday, he was to be in Evanston, Wyoming, as assistant division superintendent. It was a promotion, but they loved Omaha and figured they'd retire here. Thank God they didn't have any kids to uproot from school. You think Tom would want me as an engineer?"

"Are you kiddin', man? He thinks you're the greatest thing since nighttime baseball."

"Okay, I'll call him. Thanks a lot, man. Talk to you later, Philsy."

"See you, Bear. It'll be great having you and Susan around again. Our wives can go through pregnancy together. They sure can't do it with us being railroaders, huh?"

When Carl Banner heard of Barry exercising his seniority for a return to the blue-collar ranks, he called him to meet for coffee. "It's a trade-off," Carl wisely told him. "We definitely hate to lose you, Barry, but I'd be lying if I told you I didn't understand. If I had seniority behind me, I might have left several times myself." The coffee break ended with a hearty, sincere handshake, and with Carl asking Barry to please stay in touch. Barry thanked Carl for his faith in him, and apologized for his decision that in many ways said to the remaining company officers, "I don't like your lifestyle." Barry would never talk to Carl again.

So Barry and Susan moved back. Tom Moffat *did* want Barry as an engineer, and quipped when he set him up with a training schedule, "Barry, you'll have to sharpen your goosing techniques again, going back into the blue-collar ranks. You may even need some student trips. Also, there are some redeemable aspects … You'll be able to fart, spit, and piss about anytime again." Tom knew Barry would be a good employee wherever he was assigned. It didn't matter to Tom where Barry worked. Because of work demands, Barry was able to hold the road as a fireman *within* a year, and make good money. Firemen made about 85 percent of what engineers made. Susan and Carla did enjoy being pregnant together, and had their children a month apart. Susan had a beautiful little boy, Graham Michael, and Carla had another beautiful little girl, Margo Marie. Susan and Carla were great friends and comforts to each other while the railroad owned their husbands' souls.

# Chapter 19
## Up Jumps the Devil

Barry, like Phil before him, very much enjoyed the challenge of learning to be an engineer. The way the business forecast looked, there was to be a downturn in the early eighties, followed by an overwhelming period of growth. This meant that even though Barry was behind Phil seniority-wise, both would see engineer promotion very soon. Another reason for the relatively quick promotion was attrition. Most of the World War II-era engineers would be retiring in the late seventies, and all through the eighties. So the engineer's board would have an entirely different look by the end of the eighties. And both Phil and Barry would gain seniority very quickly, especially compared with the Korea-era engineers, some of whom hostled for twenty years before they even got to work as firemen.

Barry had marked up with Engineer Higgenbotham for training; he was supposed to be almost as good as Bill Linden. Higgenbotham was a good engineer, but tended to be gruff. He also did not like the fact that Barry had been in management. As a result, Barry did not have the good relationship with his engineer trainer that Phil had with both Bill Linden and Beauregard Banks. Higgenbotham was fair, though, and his training did eventually make Barry a very good engineer.

One time while Barry was running the train, the dispatcher called on the radio: "Ellisville dispatcher to the CP Extra 3458 West, over." Higgenbotham stood up out of his seat and came over to answer the radio, allowing Barry to concentrate on the train controls. "This is

Engineer Higgenbotham on the CP Extra 3458 West, dispatcher, over."

"Yes, Engineer Higgenbotham, do you have an engineer trainee on the train with you, a Barry McAlister?"

"Yes, I do, dispatcher, over."

"He has a family emergency. We're gonna let him deadhead back to Kansas City on the SLKC. I'm putting the SLKC in the hole at Sullivan." Railroaders referred to the sidings as "holes." "Stop there, if you will, and let him off."

"Okay, dispatcher, we got it."

"Okay, thanks. Ellisville dispatcher out."

"CP Extra 3458 West, out."

Engineer Higgenbotham uncharacteristically patted Barry on the shoulder. "C'mon, kid, I'll take 'em from here."

Barry got up from the engineer's seat in total confusion. This one had come from left field ... from the ground up. The CP dispatchers never discussed on the radio exactly what the emergency was. All the crews working who heard the transmission always hoped for the best. Still others prayed. It was a radio communication no one ever wanted to get. Barry went through the precious list: Was it Erin? Was it Graham? Was it Susan? Was it Fran? Was Dad okay, his family? In a pre–cell phone era, the railroaders had to wait for a phone, something that was not available on the locomotives.

When the SLKC arrived in the yards, Barry bailed off at the Mattoon Creek shanty where the first available telephone was located. It had been a little more than two hours since they'd received the dispatcher's call. He was a nervous wreck, mentally running the gamut of possibilities, none of which had a happy ending. He dialed Susan, barely able to control his fingers. When the receiver picked up at the other end, Barry didn't wait for a response.

"Suz?!"

"Barry, it's your father. There was a problem at Cameron."

"Is he all right? What happened?"

"No, Barry. He didn't make it. He was shot by a guy trying to break into the grocery store. The bullet went through his renal artery. You know he was out of shape. Nothing too bad ever happens in Cameron."

"Until now," Barry muttered. "I'll see you in a bit."

The funeral was horrible for Barry. Bill McAlister had died shortly after the ambulance arrived at the emergency room entrance at the hospital. He had not only lost a tremendous amount of blood but was overweight. The strain on his heart caused by the trauma was the reason for his death, as well as the blood loss. He'd suffered a fatal heart attack, and flatlined before the attending emergency room physician could even take action other than to attempt futile heart shocks. The flatline stayed flat. His partner had apprehended the man who shot him. After he'd shot Bill, he'd thrown down his weapon, not having intended to shoot anyone. Backup had arrived after the ambulance was called.

Phil, Carla, and Paul were at the funeral standing next to Barry and Susan. But Barry didn't feel their presence. He didn't feel anything. He had not been able to see his father as much as he'd wanted when he was a youngster. But there was this amazingly powerful bond between them when he did. And when he was not able to see Bill, Barry always *knew* how much his father loved him and how proud he was of him. It was enough. Combined with the Barnes family's love and caring for Barry, it was enough. Fran had always seemed to be biding time with Barry, like she was waiting for it to be over so she could get to something else. Barry felt she cared, but further felt it was only to a point. But with Bill, Barry always felt things were as they should be. Barry was never special to Fran the way he was to Bill. So Bill was always extra-special to Barry. And now, that extra-special person was gone from the face of the earth. Barry would miss him every day for the rest of his life.

Phil and Paul's uncle Phil was standing next to Harold and Rose Barnes. After the service, he slowly sauntered over to Barry, and was actually the first person Barry acknowledged at the funeral. Uncle Phil was quite a bit shorter than Barry. He reached up to Barry's suit-coat shoulder and grabbed it, gently pulling Barry down toward him. "Barry, c'mere, son. I gonna tella you somp-a-ting. Your papa, he's-a witta God now. You willa see him again-a, and-a it-a willa be better than-a this. You unnerstand?" Then Uncle Phil hugged Barry, and Barry completely broke down, crying out loud and hugging him back. Uncle Phil patted him on the back. "It's-a gonna be okay, son. It's-a gonna be okay." But it wasn't. Barry was never the same afterward.

As if this wasn't hard enough on Barry, another dismal life occurrence reared its ugly head some months later. Fran McAlister, who was still attractive, had allowed herself to be romanced by and eventually married to a devil of a man named Don White. White was a retired foreman from the local Ford assembly plant. He was married when Fran met him at the local bowling alley, but he lied to her, saying he and his wife were separated. Fran had followed him home one night to his wife, but it didn't seem to make a difference to her, even though she caught him in the first of what was to become an endless parade of lies. He was the antithesis of Fran. Fran was so overwhelming in her presentation of monumental happiness to the world that no one could ever say they'd seen her in a bad mood.

White *was* Fran's total opposite. He wore a constant scowl on his booze-red face. His hair hadn't grayed like most who age and refrain from the desire to dye it. That was because the hair covering many alcoholics doesn't turn gray. Something about being blitzed nightly with booze represses the body's mechanism that stimulates graying. Many alcoholics have younger-looking hair color perched directly above *The Portrait of Dorian Gray*. It's diametrically opposed to two quotations from Proverbs: "The hoary head is the crown of glory, if it be found in the way of righteousness," Proverbs 16:31; and "... and the beauty of old men is the grey head," Proverbs 20:29. So White had this blond-brown hair on top of a craggy, hideously ravine-laden, red, angry, swollen puss. His head was shaped like a peanut. His eyes were diluted, hazy light blue, inset, too close together, with a red background, where most healthy people had white. They were always watering. And they were totally joyless, devoid of anything but hatred and distrust. His nose was always dripping in hung-over sinus drainage. He went through several hankies a day. His arms, which were normally folded in defiance and obstinacy, still showed some muscle, with sagging skin. But his narrow shoulders looked almost misshapen. White's constant scowl set it all off.

Why Fran could be attracted to him surely was not physically evident. Maybe it was because he was married to someone else when they met, and it was the lure of forbidden fruit. He was a real keeper. He hated everyone. He even hated his own children. He definitely hated Barry, *and* his family. Why wouldn't he, if he hated his own kids? His own daughters had excelled both scholastically and athletically in college, and White hadn't spoken to them in years. One of his grandsons won the basketball version of football's punt, pass, and kick contest. White never even called him. He even hated Fran, but she never mentally addressed it. The weirdness of their relationship was right up Fran's alley, maybe literally. It allowed Fran that great pleasure of hers, of covering up a secret to be kept. Fran also enjoyed rebelling against logic. The more those who cared attempted to offer reason that would make her life better, the more she rebelled against it. White was a mean, demonic drunk who had whaled on Fran many times, even before they were married, unbeknownst to anyone. Fran's secret nature saw to that. And in a way, she must've liked it, because the behavior continued for years. If Barry had known about these incidents at the time, he'd have twisted White's head off like a mayonnaise jar lid. Yes, Fran and White were total opposites. It was as if Fran had no bad side, so she married it, and White had no good side, so he married it. But that was initially. As time passed, in Dr. Jekyll–like fashion, Fran began to become more and more like the evil White.

Everyone has seen the cardboard clock bar displays that say "No Drinking Until 5," and all the numbers on the clock are fives. Well, White actually didn't drink until 5:00 p.m., but exactly *at* 5:00 p.m., in true alcoholic compulsive-reactive fashion, he would set a quart of Jack Daniels Black Label down in front of him and ceremoniously begin to unwrap the top. From that point forward, he wouldn't get up except to drain his lizard, or harass Fran, until the Jack also was drained. Fran saw to it that his glass always had ice. And Fran drank with him, but not as much. After a certain point, White would begin to become verbally abusive, cutting either Fran down or her family. She would answer, continuing the sick conversation, like two little kids picking on each other. Then White would reach a point when his verbal abuse changed to physical abuse. He would get violent and begin swinging at Fran, sometimes connecting. During these nightly, drunken, ghastly soap operas, Fran sustained many bruises, as did White, from falls. White also destroyed many of the antiques Fran had collected over the years. White's horrible mouth cursed everyone Fran was related to, or knew, thousands of times, and he would continue to do so for years to come.

And there was beaucoup smoking. White would ritualistically put two Winston Gold cigarettes in his mouth, light them, and hand one to Fran. ("Here ... Let's kill ourselves together.") It was his version of class. This happened dozens of times in a twenty-four-hour period. The two smoked at least five packs of cigarettes daily, sometimes more ... rarely less. White would contribute further to his impaired version of class when, after Fran refreshed their drinks, he'd say, "Let's bump butts, honey." He and Fran would toast by touching booze glasses with a *tink*. They would then encircle their arms and attempt to drink, clumsily and noisily slurping and spilling Jack on the floor in amorous ignorance. The amount of Jack on the floor was directly proportional to the amount previously consumed. Because of the massive overindulgence in booze and smokes, White's voice was modified by a load of mucus that was always stacked against his vocal cords. As a result, his low, guttural, gravelly voice sounded even more disgusting than Chance Armstrong's. And it would crack because of the mucus modification. It was worse than an irritating foghorn. And the drunker he became, the louder the irritating voice became.

The evening festivities always ended the same way, with White, again ceremoniously, getting a can of Schlitz beer and slowly pouring it down. It was usually around 12:30 a.m. Then he would creep down the hall to his bedroom. The next day would be a groggy beginning with coffee and cigarettes, after which White and Fran gradually cleaned up, assessed the damage, and stuporously went to Shoney's for the salad bar. During these afternoons, White was civil, although not necessarily nice. He still didn't like anybody, but he just glared rather than voice it all the time. It may have been that secretly, Fran felt the same way about people. She may have thoroughly enjoyed the horrible things White said about her family. But given her penchant for exhibiting constant happiness to the world, and hiding her true, weird feelings, she was content to let White be the mean guy, like good cop, bad cop.

The two absurd actors, mindlessly embroiled in their own gruesome play, would eventually leave Shoney's after copious amounts of tobacco and coffee, and return to their little hell on earth. At exactly 5:00 p.m., the quart of Jack would hit the table and the whole performance would begin anew. Fran endured years of this behavior, with no attempt to see the total insanity of it all. In her sick mind, it wasn't insane. It was the life she'd chosen, and it was good.

While pickled, White had referred to Barry many times as "that filthy fxxkin' son of yours," and Fran had no reaction at all. When someone who supposedly cares about them says anything as degrading as that about their children, no matter what age, most people take extreme exception. Not Fran. White had been, as usual, drunk one night, and referred to Susan as that 'two-bit hair," which followed his first wonderful statement about Barry. He normally referred to Barry and Susan as "that filthy fxxkin' son of yours and that two-bit whore he's married to." This time the alcohol produced *hair* from White's ugly mouth rather than *whore*.

Fran's response would be to lessen the sordid behavior in her mind by thinking, Oh well, he's just drunk. But as time went on, she began to change. It was the first time Barry had witnessed what he thought was a demonic influence. Psychologists would have said that it was merely the influence of Fran's environment and that she was adapting the best she could. Perhaps they may have suggested mild dementia. And they might have said it was *folie à deux*, where two people share the same delusion. But Barry saw something else. He saw genuine evil. Fran not only began to hold Barry in low regard, aligning with the disgusting White's assessment of him, but began saying bad things about her brothers and sisters herself, something she'd never even considered before. This is, of course, what White did. He would constantly cuss Fran's brothers and sisters, as well as his own, and Barry and Susan, always with no reaction from Fran whatsoever. Was his control over her so overwhelming that she ignored his horrible, unwarranted hatred for her son, daughter-in-law, and brothers and sisters? Was she so masochistic that she thought she deserved it? Was she so sadistic that she thought her family members deserved White's immeasurable, nonstop contempt and cussing? Was she so afraid of being by herself? Who, indeed, *was* "herself" anymore?

On those rare occasions when Barry was able to stop by in the evenings, White was always drunk and Fran was always tipsy. White was always railing about someone or something. Even drunk, he knew not to push Barry too far, though. He did, however, push the boundaries of decency. He pushed them down, and down, and way down. Fran would go to the refrigerator to get ice for her and White's drinks. White's chair was next to it. He would grab Fran's posterior, and say in one seriously grotesque, loud, drunken, bullhorn-slurring voice, "What a cute little fart box your mom has! What a cute little fart box!" To Barry, this was the absolute lowest, most degrading, and vilest form of humanity he'd ever witnessed. He just couldn't witness his mother descending to these depths. Fran's reaction to the ass-grabbing and comment was to smile, as if flattered, as though White had just told her she had class.

When Fran went to go to the bathroom, White would tell Barry what he did with Fran sexually, and it always involved his hands. "You put your thumb here, and your fingers here ..." It was like an absurd bowling lesson. It was sickening for Barry. It was just a monumental disgrace. Should he just double up his fist and put it completely through White's hideous puss, like Billy Budd did to the captain in Melville's novel? Should he just put White out of his misery, and save everyone else more misery? Or should he just consider the source, which was now his mother's husband, and let it go? As much as White drank, his hand was probably the only part left of his anatomy that resembled hardness. White's hands were large, although nowhere near as big as Barry's, but he and Fran were both quite proud of the fact. When White prepared to shake anyone's hand, he would raise both hands in the air and open them so wide, with his fingers absurdly spread, that he looked like a big, stupid, drunken tree frog. Too bad the Violent Femmes didn't come out with "Big Hands I Know You're the One" till years later. It would have been a great theme song for White. Then, as White shook the other person's hand, he would grip too firmly and say, "You'll never find a better one." To Barry, this was clown stuff, but Fran was always impressed. The Fran whom Barry grew up knowing would have thought White's handshake ritual absurd. But now she admired and wanted it. Sadly he also knew what she didn't want. She really didn't want him around anymore. He really didn't want to be around. He didn't recognize his mother anymore. Many, many times in Barry's life, he would wish he had never returned to anywhere near Fran after the memorial service for Bill. Then he could have remembered her for the fun mom she *used* to be, and would not have been subjected to this other thing.

Barry was the only one who witnessed Fran and White's bizarre behavior. When anyone else was around, the two hid their nastiness. Fran had since moved from the neighborhood where Barry grew up next to the Barneses. She had sold her home, taking advantage of good real estate value at the time, and bought a smaller home several miles from the Barneses, banking the difference. So Rose, who never would have dreamed that Fran could stoop to these depths with White, never knew. But she did know Fran was becoming different.

# CHAPTER 20
## DEALING WITH THE DARK SIDE

Barry not only tried not to judge his mother, but also tried to speak with her about God. On these occasions, Fran was so combative it was reminiscent to Barry of the Dracula films made by Hammer in the early sixties. When Peter Cushing as Van Helsing brandished the cross, Christopher Lee as Dracula, and all the pretty young female vampires, would back up and hiss. Fran's reaction to Barry's wanting to discuss Christ with her was so oddly and vehemently negative that it seemed almost like the vampires hissing at Peter Cushing. Her abhorrence to anything dealing with the Lord actually compelled Barry to entertain the conclusion that there just might be some evil spiritual influence controlling her. Again, it made no sense to him, because Fran was the one who had taken Barry to church and instilled Christian values in him when he was a child. She even taught him to say his prayers before bedtime, a wonderful habit he still practiced.

But the main reason Barry thought of demonic influence as the basis of Fran's behavioral peculiarity was that he actually saw, at times, the same snarl and vicious expression on his beautiful mom's face that White wore permanently on his own. Any time Barry tried to talk with Fran about it, she portrayed it as if he, Barry, were at fault. It broke his heart. He wasn't the one hating and cussing everybody. He wasn't the one beating on Fran. He wasn't the one trying to make her choose, like White was, between her family and him. Yet it was almost as if in her becoming-schizoid mind, Fran did indeed hold Barry responsible. *He* bore the responsibility for the physical and mental bruises that the evil White inflicted. The devil is the great accuser of mankind.

Any attempt at logic with Fran was worse than futility. It was a vicious, horrible game whereby Barry attempted to defend himself by saying, "Mom, I helped put myself through college with sports and the GI Bill, I made dean's list grades, I am honorably discharged, I've worked hard all my life," and so on. Barry's sorrowful, defensive, bottom-line logic was "I'm not such a bad kid." Fran would viciously interpret these sad, desperate attempts to rekindle her caring and logic as *opposing* her. So when he laid his loyal, loving head on the block, she gladly and purposefully cut it off, like a medieval executioner. Motherly cruelty like that is a crime against nature. It was as if she waited until after Bill McAlister's death to really turn on Barry. It was as if she knew that with Barry's father gone, he had nowhere to turn. From this point forward, Barry began experiencing an inexplicably evil, systematic destruction process spearheaded by his own mother. When someone's severe cruelty has evolved to the point of cognitive dissonance, the game is already over. Prayer is always the best approach. The attempt to impose logic on the vicious ones just provides them with a forum for even greater cruelty. Fran would dispense with the flaky smiles during these Barry-hating sessions. Her countenance would reflect that of a pissed-off pit bull ... like White's. But she never let anyone else, like Rose, see it. Fran was always crafty in hiding her true emotions around the Barnes family members.

Barry responded to the hate by working, and working, and working, eventually becoming an excellent engineer, as did Phil. One good thing about the railroad: you could get away from horrible family situations, and make good money doing it. But sometimes the absence was the cause of the situations, like with the bum job jocks. It killed Barry to have Fran be so unloving to him. He had felt her being distant many times in his childhood, but never just plain hateful. But what was the secret here? White demanded only a few simple stipulations: hate your only child and his wife and kids, allow yourself to be a human punching bag, and drink and smoke with him. What was so hard about that? It was ideal to White. And Fran, strangely, didn't find it hard to comply. The boozing and constant smoking was beginning to modify her natural good looks, depleting oxygen and water from her cells. Her facial features began to have a mild, mummylike appearance, an effect that worsened over the years.

As if the physical loss of his father and the emotional loss of his mother weren't traumatic enough, Barry had yet another bad hand dealt to him. Susan had, for some reason, ceased to refer to God at all. She also ceased to regard Barry with high esteem, rarely calling him Bear and rarely even saying his name. It was "*You* think this" and "I guess, if that's what *you* want." Susan had developed a counter-life with Fran, Erin, and Graham, apart from Barry. Further, Susan not only failed to see the change in Fran, but also aligned *with* her *against* Barry, just as Fran had done with White. When they looked at Barry, they saw a much different person than Barry actually was. It was like a mean-spirited devil filter disallowing Fran and Susan to see their son and husband in a good light. They thought it was a correct assessment. Barry, monumentally hurt and confused by it all, just kept on workin' like a huge ox strapped to a yoke on a descending circular path to hell.

Now Phil, Paul, and Barry were all "together" again, but they only occasionally saw one another at work and rarely had the time off to get together with one another or their families. The barbecues didn't occur. They were normally all working at different times, although they did occasionally see one another at work. The challenge of railroading had vanished for Phil a long time before. It was replaced with tedium, boredom, and the resentment he felt because the job took him away from Carla, Angela, and little Margo. He became agonizingly aware of all the wasted time at the railroad. A crew would do nothing if they had to wait for another job to use the same track, and they would have to stay in the clear. A crew might be pulled up to a red block and the dispatcher or control operator was not able to "take" them, as it was termed, for some time. These stops or blocks could last hours. Both Phil and Barry would replay their thoughts at these times: My former classmates have gone to grad schools, some even getting PhDs. Some even went to professional schools, like law school or dental school, and I'm stuck behind this friggin' red block from 2:00 a.m. to 6:00 a.m. What is wrong with this picture? They had unconsciously, as young men, accepted the railroad as their world … as *the* world. Paul, as always, didn't really care that much. He made much less money than

Phil or Barry, but he worked fewer than half the hours they did, and never left town. The railroad was tolerable for him. He had no family at home to miss.

Not only were these red block stops monotonous and life-killing, but there was the waiting to "get out," both at the home terminal and away terminal. If you were close to being called at home, you had to be available for a call. This drove Carla and Susan nuts. They either had to go places without their husbands, or go with them, with Barry and Phil constantly having to call in to see how close they were to being called to work. If they were called, it meant the wives had to return, too, unless they'd taken separate cars. Then there would be a "What's the point?" atmosphere about the outing. So Susan, Erin, and Graham just started going out with Carla, Angela, and Margo, leaving Barry and Phil home to wait for calls. In future years, most railroaders on call would buy beepers, or cell phones, to keep from having the railroad dictate their personal lives, at least as much. But the technology wasn't there yet for the average citizen in the early eighties.

At the "B" end, or away terminal, most were in a hurry to get back to their families, although once they returned home, they would have to eat, sleep, and get ready to "get back out" again. Time flew by, and husbands, wives, and children frequently lost each other. As Groove wrote, "Days and weeks and months all seem the same." Phil had imagined Marlon Brando saying, "The boredom, the boredom" in the great character-portrayal voice he used playing the renegade colonel in *Apocalypse Now,* when he said, "The horror, the horror." To Phil, the waiting to get back to Carla and the kids *was* a horror. And he had no control over it.

Phil had watched many good guys go bad, simply because of the boredom. They might go to have a few innocent beers, and wind up with an Ellisville "Queen for a Day," just because they were bored. From *The Music Man,* Phil remembered the lines, "The idle brain is the devil's playground" and "We've got trouble right here in River City."

Railroaders were no different from other workforces in that they were made up of extremely moral individuals on one end of the spectrum, and some extremely immoral on the other. But all had the same trouble with boredom. Some took up golf, which seemed to make them somewhat happy. On one end they were with their families. On the other, they were playing golf or sleeping while waiting for a call. Of course wintertime had its effect on these folks. Some decided to hunt or fish, always allowing for a crew member to retrieve them when they were called to work. Some read books and periodicals, even the Bible. Still others would drink and screw around on their wives. It didn't take long, observing human behavior, to realize that if a man screwed around on his wife, he was screwing around on his kids also. God wasn't messing around with the family as a sacred unit, or the marriage vows before Him. All were intertwined and indivisible. United, we stand. Divided, we fall. The dividing came from a prevailing thought among many to be a "good-time boy." The railroad was a place to make good money and have fun ... a halfway house for loveable rogues. Most males got silly when there were female body parts around. Phil, Paul, and Barry all spoke often of the "Never-Never Land" quality of railroading. Some guys never grew up but had the Peter Pan syndrome: lots of grab-ass, laughter, goosing, and most definitely a total lack of understanding that the same behavior yields the same results, three or four divorces, and bankruptcies down the road.

One could expect literally anything. One time at the dormitory in Ellisville, the fellas had arranged for one of the cleaning girls, whom they had named Mammoo, to go in and suck the toes of this old, very nice engineer, Melvin Hobbs. Hobbs had even planned to preach when he retired. He and his wife, Edna, had been married forty-nine years, and Hobbs had worked for the railroad for fifty. He could retire literally at any time. Mammoo actually had an incredibly beautiful face, with jet-black hair and huge bright blue eyes, luscious lips, perfect teeth, and flawless skin. But from the neck down, she was a Holstein, hence the nickname. She was about 5 feet tall and 225 pounds.

They waited until poor Hobbs was asleep and then Mammoo, who of course had a key, opened the door and knelt down by the foot of the bed. Hobbs was snoring away. She very deftly pulled the covers out from the bottom of the bed, folding them back over Hobbs's shins. Hobbs stirred a bit. Then, with half the railroaders in the dormitory looking on, she bent over his toes and started sucking on them. Hobbs jumped up, wide-eyed, yet in a half stupor, amid peals of laughter. "You bitch!" he screamed. "Getoutahere! Now!" It was the first time Hobbs had raised his voice since he could remember. He hadn't even used the word "bitch" except to describe the female beagles he and Edna enjoyed raising. The laughter didn't subside for some time. Melvin Hobbs retired after getting back to Kansas City. He didn't tell Edna why. Phil didn't like humor like this. He remembered his uncle Phil's words, "Phillip. C'mere I gonna tella you somp-a-ting. You know-a, it's-a notta funny, unless-a everyone-a is-a laughin'."

Over the years, Phil had observed many of his railroad counterparts ending up divorced from their screwing around. They would then remarry, oftentimes marrying those they'd screwed around with, and keep screwing around, resulting in another divorce. Phil heard one conductor say, "Next time I want to get married, I'm gonna find some gal who hates me and give her ten thousand dollars and my house and car. Why waste time?" They never realized that the same behavior yields the same results.

Carla had been the best. She was always there when Phil called, and like other railroad wives, was horribly neglected, as were the kids. Phil realized that days, weeks, months, and years were slipping by, with the kids growing up and he and Carla growing older. It seemed there was never enough time for the family. He and Carla were both exceptional accomplishers. They began as the best of husband-and-wife teams, but they were losing each other.

As the railroad and time rolled on, Phil was aware of always hearing Carla say to Angela and Margo, "Shh, your dad's trying to sleep." He also realized that although he was *there*, he was not really there *with* his beloved family. He would hear Carla and the kids playing Super Mario Brothers, hear the infectious, catchy tune of the popular program, and hear them laughing. He would sigh in the bed, realizing he needed to get his rest to be called to work in a few short hours, but wishing, fervently, that he could be in the living room with his dear ones instead. How he loved them. More than one railroader had his marital pink slip served to him without having a clue it was coming. Another odd thing Phil, Paul, and Barry had witnessed over the years was that often, the *best* guys were the ones served with these divorce papers. Some guys would screw around their entire lives, some actually hoping their wives would divorce them, and the wives never would. But others would be thoughtful, exemplary husbands and fathers, and they'd be the ones to receive the divorce papers. It might be more evidence of Chance Armstrong's "Treat a whore like a queen and a queen like a whore."

One time Phil was at beans with a trainman, R. K. Hammon. Hammon said, "Well, it won't be long before I'll be able to go home to my castle I work my ass off for and get screamed at by the queen."

"You're not married to one of those, are you, R. K.?," Phil responded, and smiled with nonenvy.

"Oh yeah, Phil. And I can guaran-damn-tee you, I'd never have married her if I'd known what she'd be like. She talks to the dog better than she does to me. She always has that disgusted tone with me, and then it's a sweet, happy, 'Are you ready to go outside and poo-poo?' to our dog. I make her mad all the time, no matter what I'm doing. And when she knows I'm enjoying myself, which is rare, she *really* gets mad. I think women in general don't want you to enjoy yourself."

"I hope it works out for you, R. K."

It was rumored that some worthless railroaders would actually call some wives and tell them their husbands were fooling around when they never were. It was just to get back at them for something. How rotten was that? Allegedly, some had even gotten divorced over this. Once again, Phil could hear Uncle Phil's words: "Phillip. C'mere. I gonna tella you somp-a-ting. People, dey try-a to get away witta whatever. Dey don't-a care who dey hurt-a in-a dis-a world. But God-a, Phillip … He's-a takin-a notes. He knows-a everyt'ing. He's-a takin-a notes."

Phil, Paul, and Barry were very much underemployed at the railroad. They had stopped climbing at a very low rung for their capabilities. They had "Peter-Principled" out. Barry had at least seen the management end of railroading, and had really enjoyed parts of it. But the "not who you know, but who you you-know," the inherent supposed superiority, and the immorality sickened him, hence his return to the blue-collar ranks. Barry didn't realize that the only way he was truly going to escape immorality was to eventually reside in heaven. He certainly hadn't escaped it by returning to the blue-collar ranks. Phil and Barry now felt like drones. Paul, as usual, really didn't care that much.

# CHAPTER 21
## NICE DAY FOR A RIDE
## IN THE COUNTRY

In Centralized Traffic Control territory, if there is a shunt on the tracks—a shunt being anything that breaks the electrical code on the track—there is a fail-safe mechanism that displays a red block signal aspect to the entrance to that track. Further, it displays an approach signal two miles before, and an advance approach two miles before that, or wherever the preceding block signal might be placed. If a rail were to break, for instance, there would be an interruption in the circuit. The code in the rail would then be zero, which always produces a red aspect at the entrance to that block. This fail-safe signal system works very well, except when conditions that initialize this provision occur *after* the train enters the block.

On October 5, 1981, Engineer Roger Warren, Conductor Joe Hiles, Rear Brakeman Jack Gilford, and Head Brakeman Cliff Halover were called in Ellisville for the GNOB train, or The Knob or G-Knob train, as the railroaders called it. The GNOB was a "good train," because it ran straight through to Kansas City and rarely stopped. The Central Pacific did not have many hot eastbounds, but this was one of them. It carried auto parts. The GNOB had a 60 mph runnin' order.

It was a beautiful sunny fall day. The birds and insects weren't sure if summer was actually over or not, and the heat of the day was causing activity among the nature denizens to peak. Railroaders were always treated to a "wide-screen" view of nature. At dusk, deer were everywhere, and raptors owned the skies all day long. At night, owls were prevalent. Many engineers felt a twinge in their stomachs as they ended the lives of possums, raccoons, deer, and others. Most would blow their horns and flash their headlights, which, if left on solid bright at night, tended to blind the animals. And although many animals made it, there was still a lot of carnage. Just like on the roads and highways, there were always dead animals between the rails and on either side. Animals, like some uninformed, unsafe, and unfortunate people, did not expect trains.

On this day like many others, the entire crew was looking forward to getting back to Kansas City. They were called for 8:00 a.m., which should put them home around 2:00 p.m., 4:00 p.m. at the latest. Engineer Warren was happy with the prospect of being off and catching up on his sleep. It looked like a good layover, about thirty-six hours. And, since it was Friday, Warren would be spending it with his wife, watching their son quarterback his high school team. Life was good.

The crew wagon delivered Hiles and Gilford to the rear end. Warren and Halover walked across from the yard office and boarded the lead locomotive. Since the GNOB was a run-through train, it didn't need inspecting at Ellisville.

"We're all ready back here when you are, Roger," Conductor Hiles happily shouted after keying the radio.

"Here we go," Engineer Roger Warren hollered back as he pulled out on the throttle one notch. His spirits were high, elevated by the beautiful day and the prospect of being in Kansas City by late afternoon.

"Movin'," Conductor Hiles politely informed the head end.

"Movin'," Engineer Warren repeated, as was the procedure. He then began to throttle out. "Beautiful day, huh, Cliff?" Warren looked happily over at his head brakeman, Cliff Halover.

"Nice day for a ride in the country," Halover answered him with a smile. That statement was made all the time on the Central Pacific, when conditions were as nice as they were today. The inference was that all the crew would do was ride and enjoy the beautiful day, since there was no physical work to do on this train, the GNOB.

The GNOB began slowly pulling the seven-mile hill eastbound out of Ellisville. This was the point where the crews found out if they had a "screamer" or a "dog." If the train pulled the first hill easily, the crews knew they had a fine, quick trip ahead of them. If it was a hard pull, just barely making it over the hill, they knew the trip might take a while. They might even "lay down" on some of the more challenging ascending grades, such as Aikens Hill, and need to be "pushed over" by the locomotives of a following train. The GNOB pulled the first hill easily, adding to the crew's anticipation of spending the rest of the wonderful afternoon with their loved ones.

At the crest of the hill, the GNOB Train speed began increasing as soon as the locomotives were over. They would be at maximum authorized speed quickly. It would be up to Engineer Warren to "hold 'er back." This was going to be a sweet trip.

The GNOB was runnin' on "Clears" or "Greens," which meant the block signals were all max speed, another excellent indication of a quick trip home. You could be authorized for 70 mph, but if the dispatchers had other problems to deal with, you might be stopped by red signals. But there was nothin' but "Proceeds" today.

As the train rounded the curve at St. Mary's, Engineer Warren noticed a half-double-wide trailer was high-centered on the rails. Years of practiced reflex action caused him to "plug" the train, or put it into emergency, although it was futile at this point. They were going to hit. On impact, a two-by-four from the double-wide's roof structure penetrated the cab window of the door in front of Brakeman Halover. Continuing its split-second javelin path, it penetrated his body. He died instantly, the two-by-four taking out his entire chest.

Because they were on a curve when Warren put the train in emergency, they derailed after impacting the trailer. The three locomotives and the first four cars rolled over on their sides and down a slight hill, crushing three trailers in the Happy Acres Trailer Park, killing one occupant. The right fuel tank ruptured on the lead locomotive and was spilling diesel fuel everywhere. On the rear end on the caboose, Conductor Hiles and Rear Brakeman Gilford didn't feel a thing. All they heard was the *p-s-s-s-s-s-s* exhaust of air as the train went into emergency and came to a stop. The stop was more abrupt than normal, with a run-in, but not enough for Hiles or Gilford to suspect anything out of the ordinary.

"What happened, Roger?" Conductor Hiles called up to the head end. "Roger?"

Miraculously, Engineer Warren received only minor scratches and a bruise over his left eye, which was mousing up pretty good. He was in shock, however, and not functioning well, mentally or physically, as he climbed vertically out the locomotive window, since the locomotive was now on its side. But he would see his son's next football game, missing the one on this day because of the battery of medical tests he would undergo at the hospital. Halover wouldn't see anything ever again. What was left of him was an open, shattered chest cavity spraying blood, with a broken two-by-four still sticking out. The sirens were immediately audible as Hiles and Gilford started walking up to the head end.

The police were the first to arrive, followed by ambulances and emergency response teams. Emergency response teams are composed of firemen, policemen, hazardous materials specialists, and others. A huge crowd was gathering, being cleared back by the police. They were evacuating the trailer park, and attempting to contain the diesel fuel spill. There was temporary chaos in Happy Acres. As the unpleasant smell of diesel fuel permeated the air, there was panicked shouting, screaming, and crying, dogs barking, with more background sirens growing louder and louder. Happy Acres wasn't very happy today.

Halover's wife would get the news from Jake Jacobson, the Topeka trainmaster, a job Jake did not relish and had had to do only one time before, when he worked for a superintendent in Nebraska. That was when a switchman had been coupled up, every railroader's worst fear. Allegedly, the crushed nerves were not sending any pain signals to this switchman's brain. He was still alive, and actually felt quite well. His family was called to say good-bye to him, because as soon as the cars were pulled apart, he would be like the animals in the road or between the rails, or like Ralph Dunne. Jake had made that call also. He hated it.

That's the way it was on the railroad. Most days were ordinary, without incident. But it took only one extraordinary day to change your life, or end it, like in Halover's or Ralph Dunne's case. And after a few years on the property, most railroaders would be subjected to the news of a death at work. But it was so much better now. At the turn of the twentieth century, the late 1890s to the 1900s, a couple of thousand a year died on the railroad. Now it was single figures, or only a few more, nationwide in the span of a year, but one death was always *one too many*.

Semis carrying propane tanks usually meant instant death by explosion when impacted by the locomotives. Then there were school buses. Both instances made the engineer and head brakeman nightmare list.

Hulcher, a derailment cleanup service, would arrive at Happy Acres and do the seemingly impossible. Railroads used to clean up their own derailments, but Hulcher had become so expert and cost-effective, they always got the call nowadays. Train derailments do not look logical. The sheer mass of the equipment stacked up in a twisted mountain of wreckage defies conception. Even lifelong railroaders who witnessed many derailments over the span of their careers were always awed when witnessing the latest one.

Every so often someone would find a bizarre picture showing the aftermath of a derailment and put it up on a wall. There was the caboose that looked like an accordion in the pushed-together phase of operation. It got that way from being rear-ended by a train whose engineer ran a Red Absolute signal. Both the rear brakeman and conductor were killed. They had to be separated from the caboose piece by piece. It was as if they had become part of the caboose like Brundlefly in Jeff Goldblum's excellent portrayal in the modern version of *The Fly*.

There was the weird incident where a crew unintentionally shoved a flatcar through the electric dual control switch onto the main line as a train was passing by. The flatcar jumped the track at the switch, somehow became airborne, skewered the engineer through the cab of the locomotive, and kept going. The result was a macabre scene with the dead engineer dangling from the end of the flatcar sixty feet in the air. A railroader would remark, "It was definitely his time." Literally anything could happen in a train wreck.

Warren was lucky, plain and simple. Did he or any crew members do anything incorrectly? No, just like with Mel Landers when Ralph Dunne experienced his last night at the railroad. In railroading, one never knew what was "around the curve," on the rails or in life.

News travels extremely quickly on the railroad. When Phil, Paul, and Barry first hired out, there was a tired joke around, about the three quickest means of communication: telegraph, telephone, and tell-a-woman. But railroaders made all these means look slow. By the next day, almost all the local Central Pacific employees knew about the crash. Almost all of them either knew, or knew of, Halover. Some were very close to him. When a railroader died on duty, it was like losing a member of the immediate family. It was that gut-wrenching grief and loss, plus the realization that "it could have been me." For Phil, Paul, and Barry, dealing with Brakeman Halover's death was disheartening and unreal. It wasn't supposed to happen.

Phil had often thought how cruel big business in general was. After reading *The Jungle* by Upton Sinclair in college, he was always aware of the potential evil side of Big Business. Aside from Brakeman Halover and Ralph Dunne, Phil had known of other deaths on the railroad. They weren't close friends of his, the kind he'd watch football with, but friends whose funerals he'd attend, because he had worked with them or knew of them. Ed Slovic, Phil had known when he was a hostler. Ed was an electrician who oftentimes rode the nose of the locomotives in the shop area for the purpose of positioning them for work. He did not run the locomotives, but threw switches and removed derails and so on for the hostlers to move the locomotives. While performing these duties, he was working as a "hostler helper." As his last move of the day, Ed was to spot four locomotives for fuel inside the diesel shop. The hostler, Dan Grimes, was shoving six locomotives, and could not see Ed on the head end as they rounded the curve outside the diesel shop. There was not enough clearance to ride the steps of the locomotive into the diesel shop with one's body extended. There was only about eight inches of clearance on each side. On one side was the elevated iron diesel shop floor, which was constructed to be at the same height as the locomotive front platforms, allowing easy access to the locomotive cab for the shop workers. On Ed's side was the steel-reinforced outer wall of the diesel shop. Over the many years, railroad equipment had gotten bigger. Diesel shops built in the steam era were constructed with clearances in mind for that era. As the locomotives became wider, the clearances became smaller. This day, Ed had made the fatal mistake of leaning outward, facing away from the locomotive, his feet on the lower step and his hands grasping the grab irons behind him. He had spotted locomotive units for fuel literally thousands of times, instinctually knowing where he needed to be clear of the walls of the pit. But that day, he misjudged. He was looking backward, trying to keep visual contact with Grimes, since diesel shop personnel rarely carried radios. Ed did that just at the wrong time as the locomotives entered diesel shop Track

1. The initial contact with the steel-fortified concrete wall had spun Ed in a vertical, clockwise spinning motion, trapping him between the steel-reinforced concrete wall and the locomotive. Grimes continued to shove the locomotive consist into the diesel shop. Hostler Grimes had lost sight of Ed while shoving around the corner, but he knew, as he knew Ed knew, they were spotting four of the six locomotives for fuel, and he knew exactly where to stop. He knew Ed would be all right. He did not know that in a moment of mental lapse, Ed would lean away from the locomotive and spend the last moments of his life being rolled into an eight-inch cylinder like some bleeding, grotesque Hungarian sausage. The steel-fortified wall wasn't going to give, nor was the four-hundred-thousand-pound locomotive. That's what a small error in judgment would net you on the railroad.

Phil had known of others who had not lost their lives, but had had them forever changed as a result of accidents. Mark Parker was an eternal jock. Phil, Paul, and Barry had all enjoyed working with Mark, because he, like they, had very much enjoyed playing sports. As a result, they enjoyed talking sports also. But unlike Phil, Paul, or Barry, Mark, who worked a regular job with regular hours, was still very much involved with softball, basketball, and bowling. He was between the rails one time while working a local, coupling air hoses, when a car was mistakenly kicked in on him. Railroaders are supposed to always be aware of this possibility, and Mark was always conscientious, much more so than most. In fact he enjoyed the inherent athleticism involved with switching, like climbing the ladders to the high hand brakes, tying the hand brakes, pulling pins for uncoupling, and the constant walking. He performed his job energetically and happily. It kept him in shape.

But on this one day, he stepped in between the rails with only one foot, as taught in switchman's class, and bent down, grabbing both hoses to couple them. With one foot still out of the Red Zone, a railroader can quickly move backward to safety if there is enough time. When there are a number of cars, a trainman can hear slack running toward him from car to car, if a car is kicked into the track he is lacing up. Because of conservation of momentum, he can hear the *bang-bang-bang-bang* as each car moves the same direction as the car that was kicked into the cut. This banging grows increasingly loud, the closer it gets. The trainman has time to step out before the cars move where he is. That's why the other foot is left out from between the rails. The irony is that car men, by railroad rule and government law, are to be protected by a blue flag while connecting air hoses. This means that no cars can be kicked into the cars they are lacing up. The switches to that track on both ends are lined away from movement into the track, and locked. However, trainmen like Mark Parker are on their own, with no protection when coupling hoses.

Since there were only two cars between Mark and the car that was kicked in on him, he had no time to react. The foot that was between the rails was cut off before any reaction was possible from Mark. It happened just that fast. Greg Alston, who found Mark after hearing him yell, found him smiling and saying, "Well, guess there goes my basketball for a while." The wheel that pinched off Mark's foot also pinched nerve endings, like when the switchman whose family Jake called was coupled up. It wasn't uncommon. Mark felt zero pain, at least for the moment. He later accepted a dispatching position with the Central Pacific, something that was usually offered to employees who were injured on the job. This was done for two reasons: one, to show loyalty to the employees and ensure they had a chance at self-esteem and productivity; and two, to deter potential lawsuits. Not uncharacteristically, a job offer could be a function of a lawsuit settlement. Railroading could be brutal. The Central Pacific paid for Mark's prosthetic foot and subsequent rehabilitation. Mark became a very good train dispatcher and an expert bow hunter. Mark was the type who never quit, *ever*.

But like in Sinclair's novel, it wasn't just the transportation industry that was brutal. Carla's father had retired from the steel mills, and had told Phil stories of men falling into the furnaces and becoming instant fireballs. It was just for an instant. Big business in general for years had pinched, cut, crushed, beaten, scorched, mauled, choked, poisoned, contaminated, and generally killed and maimed their employees.

Then there was the destruction of the family. How often Big Business requires family separation. Phil remembered being taught the Judeo-Christian ethic in college sociology, whereby the initial settling of any country in the past had been done by homesteading and farming. The family worked together as a unit on a daily basis, raising their own crops and livestock, relying on each other. Money was unnecessary. Barter was the way to acquire the family needs. The dad was the undisputed head of the household, and if he was a good dad, he backed up his word with God's Word. Children were economic assets. The more children a family had, the more work would be done, and the more everyone would eat.

But as soon as industrialization hit, the man went away from the home to work for the first time. And essentially, because of Big Business again, wars were fought on foreign soils and the dads now had to leave the country, some not ever returning. Rosie the Riveter was born, and women no longer needed a man for support. The result was the breaking down of the family. Divorces and abortions increased dramatically, and the country gradually became more and more unstable as a result. The only stable organization was the military, which the government finally turned on its own people after they rebelled in eventual anarchy. There are correlations in Babylon, Greece, Rome, and look out, USA. It was ever thus, and all because of family separation and, most important, the lack of God in people's lives. Railroaders rarely got to church because of working weekends.

# CHAPTER 22
## THE ROAD TO NOWHERE

Little Margo was just one more loved one for Phil to miss while at work. Phil had bid into the yard on a bum job, and Barry had stayed out on the road. Overtime was a dreary, drawn-out way to make money, compared with quick trips over the road. And still, Phil had no time for Carla and the kids. It seemed like he caught only glimpses of them in the short time he was home. The money was very good, but he was home to eat and sleep only, and then back to work. As the months and years continued to roll past, Phil didn't know if the road would be better or not, but he figured with a twenty-four to thirty-six-hour layover, it would allow him *some* of the proverbial "quality" time with his family that all the Phillip Barneses had consciously missed for years. On the bum job, Phil was gone before the kids woke up to get ready for school, and home about the time they were calming down and ready for bed. He really enjoyed telling them stories before they went to sleep in their beds when they were younger, all tucked in for the night. He told them Cabbage Patch Kids stories. The little pudgy dolls would come to life in the local toy store after the lights were out and all the employees went home. The Cabbage Patch Kids would then go on great adventures, and be back in the store before the next day would begin. Angela's eyes would get big as if lost in the story, and little Margo, also wide-eyed, would suck her thumb and giggle, listening intently to her father. The girls loved the stories. The stories would end for good when Phil went on the road the first time, and the girls were now growing up minus a home dad.

Granted, trips over the road weren't all quick, but many were, and the ones that weren't were quite lucrative. Barry had told Phil some road engineers were making $55,000 a year at the time in the early eighties. So Phil marked up, and after taking three student trips, he was on his own and enjoyed it immensely, work-wise.

But as it turned out, family-wise it was SOS: same old separation. It proved no better than when Phil was marked up on the bum job. For Carla and the kids, it again became the unwelcome "Shh, your father's asleep" ritual, since Phil never knew what time of day he would get back. Or Phil would get in, and Carla and the kids would be asleep. When Phil first worked the road, he would get in sometimes at 4:00 a.m. or so, fairly exhausted. But he would wake Carla, having missed her, and they would do the husband-wife thing. But then as time went on, Phil knew that Carla needed her rest to deal with the kids and life in general, as he needed his. So after a few months on the road, this sweet, tired coupling ceased. Phil would just nestle in beside Carla and put his arm around her, or put his foot over hers. Sometimes he would get home dead tired, just as the family was getting up. It was an adjustment, but it allowed Carla and Phil to live in a nicer home, and have nicer things for themselves and the kids. So Phil stayed on the road. He felt like a robot. He wished dearly that he would have had more insight into life than the "fishbowl mentality" he'd developed about the railroad in such a short time, when Tom Moffat asked him if he wanted to be an engineer years before. He began to not like himself and what he perceived to be classic underachieving. It wasn't a status thing ... far from it. If Phil had been like that, he'd have accepted Tom Moffat's offer of officer training. It was Carla, and Angela, and Margo. If only he could make the same or even better money and be with them much more. Why couldn't it happen? The railroad was a good job ... one of the best. But why couldn't there be more time for family?

The road *was* very good money. There was initial delay where trains in the yard longer than thirty minutes were paid for that time segment that began after the thirty minutes, and ended when they finally departed. It was not uncommon to be stuck in the yards for two to three hours because of brake problems, traffic volume, waiting on add-ons, and so forth. If the train did not get out of town, it was not the fault of the crews. Then, final delay began immediately when the trains entered yard limits at terminals on the other end of the run. Again, it was no fault of the crews if they were not picked up after they yarded their trains. So they were paid for the time segment that began when they entered the yard limits until they were picked up by the van and taken to finally tie up. These agreements kept everyone honest.

There was overtime after eight hours, which when accrued had to be figured to determine if it was more or less than initial and final delay, because train crews couldn't claim both. Air pay and other "arbitraries" allowed the crews more pay under certain circumstances. Sharp conductors and engineers could make hundreds of dollars extra per year when their heads were in the ball game, by knowing what they were entitled to. And then there was the wonderful mileage, equivalent to almost a dollar a mile in 1980, and the main reason guys marked up on the road. It was 147 miles from Kansas City, Kansas, to Ellisville, Kansas, 145 on the return trip. This was because the Ellisville yard was two miles long and the return trip to Kansas City began on the east end of the yard. The crews were already two miles closer. So the trip guaranteed crew members at least $292 before arbitraries. Crew members were guaranteed more than $300 in a twenty-four-hour period, not bad cash for 1980, and the crews were paid mileage, whether the trips took four hours or twelve, plus tow-in time.

Another compensation was in the form of "penalty time." Penalty time began to accrue when the crews were stuck at the "B" terminal for longer than sixteen hours. After this time, they would again go "on the clock." If these bylaws were not in effect, nothing would preclude the railroads from holding the crews at the away point until a train arrived, heading in the direction of the home terminal. This would be at no extra expense to the company, but at exceptional expense to the crews, time-wise, money-wise, and family-wise. So penalty time was a blessing. If you had to be kept away from home, you might as well be paid. But another by-product of being held away for a long time was being first out or close to it, when you returned to your home terminal. It was "Hi, honey. Bye, honey."

Ellisville, Kansas, the "B" end of the run on which Phil marked up, was not an atypical railroad town. It had developed along the tracks of the basically east–west Central Pacific, like hundreds of other railroad towns. Businesses appeared, such as cafés, a barbershop, and a hotel, catering to the needs of the incoming and outgoing railroaders. Railroad towns gradually expanded northward and southward from the tracks of an east–west railroad, as the Central Pacific was for years. Towns that had north–south-oriented railroads running through them expanded eastward and westward from the tracks. As time progressed, the railroad area often became the grotesque part of town, and the outskirts were the clean, decent areas. Railroaders were relegated to hanging around the former areas for proximity's sake to be available for a call.

Since railroading began, no one had any problems with a beer before, after, or even *during* work. It was before the time of mandatory drug and alcohol testing. Some of the crew members still got stoned also. But many railroaders had the occasional beer with a meal and thought nothing of it. Even the railroaders considered to be good family men would go to the local joints, if they got in on a Friday or Saturday night, and have a "cold one" before turning in for the night. There, they would "view the zoo," not unlike the yard railroaders going to Champlain Truck Stop for beans. Some of the zoo inhabitants were Ellisville locals, and some were railroaders. Byron Schilling, known for his ability to drink constantly, attempted potential romance with some of the local Ellisville talent. Byron was single, divorced three times. He would develop gas as a result of excessive beer drinking, and then attempt to pass it, unnoticed. But oftentimes, the intended gas would be produced as a liquid or solid in his shorts. Byron always smelled like do-do. But the beer had anesthetized his sense of smell so that he smelled nothing. His sweet talking would continue, and occasionally he would actually pick up an Ellisville queen in his sulfur-bomb condition. Sometimes it's hard to disguise class, no matter how hard one tries.

While on the road, Phil had some extremely interesting conversations. On the railroad, continual learning took place. Someone always knew how to do something well. Whether the subject was the ingredients in a recipe for barbecue sauce, roofing a house, or changing a water or fuel pump out, there was someone who knew the process. And many times the conversations would be individual philosophies, and uh-oh, politics and religion. Opinions were not hard to come by on the railroad.

One time Phil was called to deadhead from Ellisville to Kansas City. When a deadhead was called, the crew first out would ride, and the second crew out would operate the train. A deadhead crew was paid only mileage on the road. The operating crew was paid mileage, plus initial and final delay, overtime if accrued, and other arbitraries. Some crews liked to deadhead, being paid well for no work and just riding. Other crews would rather have the extra money for operating the train. Also, it was often necessary to deliver a train to a foreign yard after arriving at the home terminal. The operating crew delivered the train. The deadhead crew never delivered, but were let off at the home terminal. It wasn't because the CP cared if they saw their families or not. It was because they wanted the crews rested as soon as possible, to man the trains.

The train they caught was a TC-4 or "Tom Cat," as the railroaders called it. It might deliver, and it might not, depending if the Norfolk and Western (N&W) had room for it or not in their yards. The conductor on the operating crew was McGee Brown, Phil's good friend from working in the Kansas City yards. McGee had gotten his conductor's rights and come out on the road a few months ago. When they marked up, it was reunion time.

"Hey Phil, my man, how've you been kickin' it?" Brownie smiled with delight at seeing his old friend.

"This railroad's been kickin' me, Brownie," Phil said, also smiling.

"I know the feeling ... Me, too ... along with life. Phil, why don't you deadhead on the caboose this trip? It's quieter, and we can talk."

When deadheading, crews could ride in the trailing locomotives on the head end of the train, or the caboose. The CP didn't care. On the head end, you might get to eat diesel fumes all they way back, and it was noisier.

"I'll do that, Big Mac."

When they were taken to the caboose by jitney, Brownie filled out his necessary paperwork and climbed up in the cupola. The cupola was the raised housing on top of the caboose, where the rear brakeman and conductor had "almost" lounge seats to sit in and view the train on inside curves. They would be looking for hotboxes, or any other detriments to safe train operation. Brownie hollered down at Phil:

"Hey, Phil ... George [Brownie's rear brakeman] usually takes a coffee crap for a half hour, a few minutes after we leave town. Come on up here when he does."

"You got it, Big Mac. See you in a few."

A few minutes later, George West came down the ladder from the cupola with his thermos and a newspaper, heading for the caboose toilet. The caboose toilet flushed into the middle of the tracks, where Mother Nature would take care of the mess. Phil climbed up into the cupola, occupying the comfortable seat across from Brownie. Phil felt it nice that he was able to view the beautiful countryside without having to control a train at the same time. He would watch the train on inside curves on his side, for Brownie and George.

"So what's been happenin' with you, Brownie?" Phil asked, genuinely interested.

"Well, we've been doin' okay family-wise, but the other day, my daughter Lisa came home from school crying because some kid called her a nigger. It broke her heart, and it broke mine and Donna's. She cried all night."

"That makes me literally sick, McGee. Lisa is such a beautiful, bright, and sweet little lady. Makes you want to throttle the little bastard, like Billy Jack."

"Yeah, that was my first reaction, Phil. But I thought better of it. You know me. I don't think I have any prejudice in me at all. I mean, that would be pretty stupid to be prejudiced against the race of my wife, now, wouldn't it? I guess the kid was white, but it just as easily could have been a black kid calling her an Oreo or something, because of her mixed-race heritage. A fact of life is that kids are cruel."

"Unfortunately, that is right," Phil agreed.

"I called his parents, who were genuinely shocked and said they never use the word and have taught their kids never to use it. I believed them, whether they were telling me the truth or not. They were going to question him about it and punish him, talk to the school and all that."

"Well, that was good of you to believe 'em. I believe it was Edgar Cayce who said, 'It's better to trust a heart that's untrue, than to distrust a heart that *is* true.' It's a hell of a world we're passing on to the kids."

"You got that right, Phil. Y'know, I was going to write my congressmen about this black-white crap, and the labels we have inherited without questioning why they came about, and why we have to claim them. I mean, people *learn* they're black or white. It's nonsense."

"Whaddaya mean, Brownie?"

"I mean you are not white, and I am not black, literally. You are beige and, I notice, tan darkly in the summertime. Heck, *I* tan in the summer. The guys call me high yellow. *Beige* and *brown* would be better defining terms, if we must label ourselves as to our appearances. They're not as far apart. I mean, what are black and white? They're opposites, man, like good and evil. Because of those inaccurate labels, I think there is a subconscious lingering in the minds of all of us that says, 'If I'm black and I'm good, then if you're white, you must be evil, because we're opposites.' I think it's the same the other way with folks of Caucasian heritage. I saw a *Star Trek* episode one time where there were two checkerboard dudes who were just the opposite, representing matter and antimatter. They were each other's nemeses, and when they got together, there was to be this big explosion. It's not like that with us ... not *at all*! I think the devil wants us to believe that. We all want ... well, I won't say *all* ... but guys like you and me, Phil, we want the same things: a good job to provide for our families, security for the future, a good education for our children, good health insurance, and so on. Not only are we not opposites ... but we're the *same*."

"I totally agree, McGee. Makes a lot of great sense, what you're sayin'. But what would we call ourselves then?"

"How about *men* and *women*? It would sure save a lot of BS. God is no respecter of persons. Why should we be? The Good Book says genealogies just lead to strife. No doubt. Like I said, I was going to write this idea to my congressmen, to, you know, suggest we just drop the opposing labels and be men and women."

"Why didn't you write your congressmen, McGee?"

"Basically, I just figured none of them would deal with it, realizing the false labels were too deeply imbedded in either heritage. And you know, Phil, most people of either heritage would be outraged. They think it's their *right* to have prejudicial beliefs. It's racial pride or some such bull."

"Pride goeth before a fall," Phil quickly added.

"Amen, Brother Phil. Amen!"

"I don't want to do any labeling myself, Mac-10, but there seems to be a correlation between intelligence and prejudice. The dumber you are, the more prejudiced you are. Anyone who prejudges anyone until they get to know them, which is where the Latin root for *prejudice* comes from, is not swift."

"I wouldn't disagree, Phil."

Phil continued, "I've always found women of African heritage to be extremely attractive. Hell, women of *all* races are attractive. That's one of the most wonderful things about being a male. I always felt somewhat cheated in my younger, single years, because all I ever dated were Caucasian women. I think God gave us the power between our legs, not necessarily just between our ears, to alleviate the problem. If we all had been interbreeding all these years, look what a beautiful race we'd all be. I mean your daughter, Lisa, is a real beauty, with that dark golden skin and those big blue eyes. And speaking of *Star Trek*, I saw some blue-green women on there who were gorgeous. And how about that Lieutenant Uhura?"

"Yeah, Nichelle Nichols is a real beauty. How lucky was the man who got to have that?" Brownie added with a smile. "And thanks for saying that about Lisa. She is beautiful, and she can marry whomever she wants. Flip Wilson used to do a joke about that: This white father hollered up the stairs to his wife, 'Hey, honey, our daughter wants to marry a black man.' Flip then in his Geraldine voice hollered back, 'Honey, she can marry whoever she want.'"

"Hey, you two finished with the bullshit up there?" George yelled from down below. "This railroad's payin' me to do a job."

"They just paid you while you were doin' that last job in the toilet, George," Brownie teased.

"Hey, that was some of my best work," George joked as he waited for Phil to descend the ladder from the cupola.

"I wouldn't argue with that, George ... not for a minute," Brownie continued the teasing. "It's probably the only bad order you do a good job of setting out."

When they arrived in Kansas City, Brownie's engineer slowed the train down to a speed that would allow the head end and rear end deadhead crews to jump off. They were going to deliver the train to the

N&W. In the future, railroads would dictate that the trains come to a complete stop before crews board or step off the trains. Before Phil dropped off, he reached up to McGee and shook his hand.

"Blessings, man," Phil said with great sincerity and great respect for Brownie. "If you ever need an ear, you got one." As he said this, Phil made the railroad sign for the radio, a circular motion with his finger beside his ear.

"You too, Phil. Always a pleasure, man. God bless you and yours. I might take you up on that."

One day Phil caught a turn with Groove Whitfield, now assigned to the road as a conductor. Phil knew he would enjoy working and conversing with witty Groove. They caught a work train, and were headed in the sidings by the dispatchers all the way to Ellisville. As Phil pulled to the west end of a siding, bringing his train to a stop, Groove grabbed his nose bag out of the refrigerator. "Nose bag" was rail-speak for "lunch sack" sometimes, again with the horse association. Groove took the rear seat on the fireman's side and, turning the seat in front of him sideways, propped his feet up on it. He unfolded the wax paper from around one of his homemade sandwiches and took a bite. "So Phil, my good man, how's married life?" Groove didn't ask the question to be haughty about his single status. He genuinely wanted to know.

"Okay, I guess, Groove. Carla and I never see each other, and just seem to be going through the motions. The kids are growing up and I have a good job, so I guess all is well. But I have to admit, sometimes I do wonder about our existence. I really don't know if Carla is happy or not. I guess I assume she is, because bills are paid and kids are healthy. But it does feel like we have lost what we had. How're you supposed to keep it out here? I know you said you'll never do it again, Groove."

"No, once was enough, and I had to do it *twice*. What a moron."

"What was the deal, Groove?" Phil asked, genuinely concerned not only for Groove but for his own potential.

"Well, my first marriage was great. And let me say, I got two great sons and a daughter from the first marriage, and there could be no greater gifts."

"I know what you mean, Groove," Phil quickly responded. "So, go on."

"Well, my wife, Sharon, was a terrific wife. She was a great cook, and a wonderful mother, and a fine companion. We were both counterculture kids when we met. I guess I still am a bit, at heart. But we mutually decided to leave a lot of that behind when we found out she was pregnant with our first child. We still enjoyed the occasional joint now and then, but quit the wild partying. We sucked up and became 'dependable.' I guess you could even say 'responsible.' She was great with the kids, and I never missed work. But after about fifteen years of me doin' this, I could tell she was unfulfilled, but I didn't know what to do about it. Once all the kids were in school, she tried cooking classes, sewing classes, college classes, and nothing did much to change this indecisive mood she seemed to be in all the time. So one day I suggested she take an aerobics class, since she had gained a few extra pounds over the years. I thought she still looked great, but she thought she was heavy. Well, she started to look extremely great, and eventually ran off with the aerobics instructor."

"Sounds like a modern-day fairy tale," Phil added.

"Yeah, I thought it was quite nice. I mean, do the wives think we're out here because we're all foamers? Anyway, I was bitter for quite a while. It screwed the kids up, too, as well as me. I became one of those guys who are just down on women."

"And?"

"And then I met Alice. Alice was quiet, lovely, loving, and only had eyes for me. She loved my guitar playing. She sang along with my guitar ... had a great voice. She appeared to be on my side. She said I brought her peace, which was a great compliment. And she brought me peace. It was great. She had been married once, years before, and her husband was killed in a military accident, a helicopter crash. She'd been a widow for some time, and her kids were grown. We went together for almost a year and decided to get married. We never had an argument. Almost as soon as the 'I do's' were spoken, she began to change, and I mean that *very* day. Something agitated her, and the corners of her mouth turned down. I'd never seen that before. Then, over the next few months, the beautiful woman inside and out became violent, horribly bitchy, controlling, and rebellious. I felt so betrayed, I couldn't stand it. She would jump on me and pound on me and interrupt me when we tried to talk about anything. She was always screaming and hollering.

She would scream and holler about stuff that she misunderstood, but wouldn't shut up long enough to let me explain. She hated me buying anything. She got violently mad because I ordered an eleven-dollar knife, yet I never *once* said a thing about stuff she bought. In fact, I encouraged it. If she wanted it, I said, 'Get it.' She went nuts when I had to buy a railroad watch for this job, after my old one shot craps. And I was the one making the money! She complained about everything I did."

"She sounds charming," Phil added with rail-speak sarcasm, still listening intently.

"You know, I used to ask her when we were dating, 'When are you going to unzip the wonderful woman suit and let the demon jump out?' because she *was* so incomprehensibly wonderful. The demon's been out ever since the 'I do's.' She was always the perfect lady when we ate out. But after we were married, she started eating like a pig, like some of these guys out here. Now, I know it may sound weird, and people would probably think I'd be the last one out here that this would bother, but I cannot stand to see people eating with their mouths open. I grew up on a dairy farm, and had to feed and shackle the cows before I was old enough to milk them. So I stared many a Holstein in the face for years. Phil, nothing looks stupider, and I mean *nothing* looks stupider, than a big ol' dumb Holstein chewing her cud with her mouth open. Alice—again, only after we were married—began to chew with her mouth open, slurp her soup and coffee, and chew her gum like the Holsteins. I mean it was like living with Larry, Moe, and Curly. Then she began to pop her gum incessantly, of course while chewing with her mouth open."

"I could never stand that either, Groove. My mom and pop always taught us to eat with our mouths closed. Thank God, Carla never did any of that. She's always been a quiet eater, with great manners in general."

"I bought Alice this dog, y'know, to keep her company while I was out here," Groove went on. "Well, the dog occupied her lap twenty-four seven. I mean the damn thing would literally dig into her business. I've never seen anything quite like it."

"Maybe he was trying to bury his bone." Phil couldn't help inserting the obvious.

"No doubt. The dog literally took my place. I used to lay my head in her lap at night. Nope, there's the dog. When I told her about it, she said I was jealous of the dog. And if everything else wasn't enough to make a guy run like Bob Hayes, she began to dispense with her feminine cleanliness."

"Perfect ... A female trifecta."

"Yeah, I thought so. I didn't quite know how to approach the uncleanliness. I knew it was going to be touchy, but I said, 'Honey, the smell is pretty rough. I don't know if I can perform at all with it being as bad as it is.' Well, as you can imagine, she started crying uncontrollably, and I comforted her as best as I could. I said, 'We can do something, honey. Don't worry.' All she did was keep crying. She tried one douche, and somehow she actually smelled worse. So more tears. After that, she refused to attempt sex anymore. It was my fault."

"Of course. You were there. God forbid she see a gynecologist and attempt to correct the problem," Phil said, again suggesting the obvious.

"Yeah, it wasn't like I said, 'You smell like a buffalo fart' or anything like that. I just wanted to clear it up, for both our sakes. You'd think she'd try something. I couldn't see a doctor *for* her. But if the situation were reversed, I *would* see a doctor for her. Hell, I'd see a doctor for me. Why wouldn't you want to quit smelling?"

"I think I've heard that when there is a strong, stenchlike aroma, all is not well in that department. I think the smell may be from bacteria," Phil added.

"Yeah, I thought it was cooties of some kind. So, anyway, our sex life went down the tubes quickly, along with her not being nice, ever. And as if all that isn't enough, Alice didn't like my kids either."

"Why would she? ... She didn't like you. That's probably a natural also ... Too close to the first Mrs. Whitfield. Whatever the reason, in probably 90 percent of the cases, the second spouse will not like the children of the first spouse, no matter how decent they are. Granted, sometimes they are a mess. But I've noticed that with some of the guys out here. When they get remarried, a whole lot of 'em hate the kids of their new spouses. I think some are actually jealous, which is the ultimate in stupidity. It's not the same kind of love ... Hello! Personally, I would not like a woman who didn't hold their children in the highest regard. My brother, Paul, has stopped dating some real beauties because they treated their kids like do-do. So you finally got divorced?"

"Yeah, the entire marriage went from really bad to horrendous, and we eventually got divorced. And I will *never* trust another woman again. I will never look for that special one, because I thought Alice was it. She turned out to be the *absolute opposite* of what she was when we dated. I felt really cheated … All these characteristics that I cannot live with, and she absolutely had them all, and hid them all, while we were dating. I'm not sayin' I'm right. There's someone out there for her. It just wasn't me."

"Who, Jack the Ripper? Leatherface? Did you ever talk about the fact that she *was* so different after you two were married?" Phil asked, although he thought he probably knew the answer.

"Yes, we did. It was always a joke. Nothing positive, ever, occurred. She said she knew she had problems, but that I was different, too, after we were married. Yeah, I was different because I hollered back and was moronic enough to try to reason with her when she was insane. Y'know, we're probably all different after marriage, whether we want to admit to that or not, but I *know* that Alice got *no* surprises from me. With me, what you see is what you get."

"Yep, everyone out here can attest to that, Groove. No cultural relativism for you. You are real, man."

"Thanks, Phil. I really do try to walk it like I talk it. When I was a kid in college, in this English course I took, we studied H. L. Mencken, an early-twentieth-century journalist. He said something to the effect of, 'Every man thinks he loves the one woman that's different.' What a statement. No, I do not dislike women. In fact, I still love them, and definitely appreciate how God made them look. But I will *never* trust another one again. I can't be jaded enough to think they're all alike. Chance Armstrong says, 'Stand 'em on their heads, and they're all sisters.' I can't be like that. I'm sure there are some who are married, who are like Alice was *before* our marriage. But I'm *never* looking again. I know everyone tends to be on their best behavior when dating, but Alice was Ms. Hyde. I don't know what I'm supposed to do for an outlet, but I think I know what I will do. I also think I know how God would feel about prostitution as an outlet. So there you go. My mom was sure good to my dad."

"Mine too," Phil responded quickly. "But that World War Two generation was something special. I think there was only about a 7 percent divorce rate among them. They worked things out, evidently, and maybe they were calmer, too. The world is harder to cope with by the day. My uncle Phil said to me when I was about twelve or so, 'C'mere, Phillip. I gonna tella you somp-a-ting. When-a you-a fine-a a girl-a to-a marry, look-a atta her-a mama. If-a her-a mama is-a good, she will-a be-a good. If-a her-a mama is-a bad, she will-a be-a bad.' And I gotta admit, my uncle Phil was right on, as he was with everything he said. What was Alice's mother like to her father?"

"She was mean to him. She hollered and screamed at him. She disrespected him constantly, and she verbally abused him all the time, like, 'You can't do anything right.'"

"So Alice learned from her mom, huh? What did her dad do when her mom was going off on him?"

"He just sat there and took it. He'd just shake his head and smile. I never saw anything like it. I guess when you're used to the same woman, and have kids and grandkids with her, you can take it."

"But why would you want to?"

"I didn't, and I couldn't. One thing good about the railroad: the women I see around the railroad haunts, and I do mean haunts, are not very appealing. So the temptation is just not there, except for Amy Johnson. She may be the most remarkably beautiful girl I've ever seen." A broad smile formed on Groove's face.

"Amy Johnson *is* the most beautiful girl I've ever seen, Groove ... If it just weren't for that track record. Most of the women who share her lifestyle have that road-hard look. Amy seems to be immune."

"I wrote a song about that once, Phil. Well, at any rate, I'm a happy guy now, and I plan to remain that way. No more crap shoots or turkey shoots where *I'm* the turkey."

"Gotcha, Groove. I just hope I have Carla for life. I can't imagine another one."

Both Barry and Phil had been on the road four years when Phil finally talked his brother into "coming out," as it was termed. He knew Paul needed a change, and besides, he missed his brother. Unless you were marked up "regular" on a job with the same people, it might be months before you would see certain people. At least with Paul on the road, Phil would catch him as conductor sometimes and see him in Ellisville a lot, marked up on a different turn. And it would mean much more money for Paul.

So Paul, after much prodding from Phil, had marked up on the road board as a conductor on July 4, 1984. What really changed Paul's mind was the money differential. He'd have more money to spend on Rosalinda. Paul marked up on the conductor's extra board, which meant he would be called to work sporadically, and quickly, which would mean mucho extra dinero for Paul.

Phil was always the proverbial "good horse" when it came to supporting Carla, Angela, and Margo, and never laid off. Again, laying off was the only way anyone on the railroad who held a job without scheduled days off was afforded time off. Some of those who marked up on yard jobs had regular days off, the highest seniority jobs having Saturday and Sunday off to correspond with spouses who worked and children who attended school. Other jobs were seven-day jobs. Those who worked days in the yards had more normal lives, but the money wasn't significant unless the jobs were bum jobs. Phil remembered when he was first training as a switchman in 1974, Sid Schwann, a switchman who had held bum jobs all his life, said at Kaw Tower, "Well, my daughter is graduating from high school tomorrow, and I don't even know who she is." Phil then knew he never wanted to do that to members of his family ... but he was doing it.

Paul had been working the afternoon job at Quindaro yard in Kansas City, Kansas, for years. He went in at 3:59 p.m., worked till about 9:30 p.m., and either grabbed a beer at some local joint with New Man Anderson or went home and grabbed a beer. It was a great job if you wanted the least CP attachment possible, and Paul basically did. Unlike his brother or Barry, all Paul wanted was to be left alone. He wanted Ramona to quit being vindictive and let him see his daughter. He wanted the Division of Family Services (DFS), what Paul perceived as a nasty, mean-spirited group of feminazis, to get off his ass. From the time of his ill-fated marriage to the present, it had been one continuous piss fight, and it looked to Paul like no matter how hard he tried, prayed, and was patient and conciliatory, the lousy DFS believed everything Ramona told them. Paul thought DFS stood for the "devil's finest stooges." Pat "New Man" Anderson, Paul's buddy who was also paying

DFS-monitored child support, said DFS stood for "dames for Satan." Whatever DFS wanted, they got. To Paul and Pat, it was all one-way. Paul played defense constantly, and of course with a substantial amount of his salary going to child support, he didn't have the money to take Ramona to court to rectify visitation with Rosalinda. That was the socialistically hideous Catch-22 that was heaped upon all good divorced fathers like a giant feminine-woven shad net. He didn't even have enough money left over to buy Rosalinda *anything* on those rare and wonderful occasions when he got to have her with him. He barely could afford to take her to eat. One thing judges never consider is that fathers who pay high-dollar child support still need money to travel to see their children, feed them, and buy things for them, over and above the basic child support they pay. At one time, Paul considered giving up beer to allow him extra money for Rosalinda, but the thought lasted only a second. Besides, was he supposed to drink water when he and Pat went out? Paul also really believed the beer helped him cope with what he perceived to be the absurd hand life had dealt him: a disloyal wife, and a much-loved beautiful daughter he paid dearly for but wasn't allowed to see.

So he had to "lie there and take it," a totally foreign circumstance to Paul, who was used to flicking off offensive blockers like gnats while concentrating on a would-be hole for the opposing tailback. As the tailback advanced toward the hole, Paul would thrust his titanium-hard helmet, powered by a nonfat 225-pound muscle mass and twenty-inch neck, as far through the tailback's sternum as he could. That was how Paul normally dealt with life. It was like on *Laugh-In* in the late sixties when they said, "The Vietnam War ended today when John Wayne flew over and punched it in the mouth." That's how Paul imagined dealing with everything. He wasn't necessarily a brute when off the field, but if he was physically challenged past a certain point, it was "curtains" for whomever. However, this current situation was one only time would heal. Meanwhile, it was Feminazis 14, Paul 0.

Paul had a severe problem with modern social agencies because it was an era when the guy was bad and the woman was wonderful, which even the lowest of low-grade morons knew couldn't be the case *every* time. And yet every talk show at the time had as a subject "Deadbeat Dads." No talk show *ever* had vindictive ex-wives who wouldn't let the fathers see the kids. No, the dads were vilified, and vilified well. Phil had always told him, "Remember what Uncle Phil told us, Paul: 'God is-a takin-a notes-a. Heaven is-a forever. This-a is-a just-a temporary.'" And as much as Paul wanted to believe that way, he was still stuck with the present physical world and hated the bureaucracy that spawned the crap in which he had to exist. He couldn't go up and punch DFS in the mouth, John Wayne–like, or stick his head through their sternum. But he sure wished there was some way he could.

To make matters worse, Paul had become more disenchanted with life in general than usual. Ramona had made it all but impossible for him to see Rosalinda, who missed her daddy tremendously but knew better than to bug her mother too much about it. She gradually learned to live without her father, having a stepfather spoon-fed to her by degrees on a daily basis. Over the years, Rosalinda accepted the situation. Paul certainly didn't blame her. He just loved her. Multiply by millions, and you had America. Seven out of ten prisoners come from homes without dads. Two-thirds of teen suicides occur in homes without dads. And the devil succeeds as brain dead, ostrich-syndrome America buries her feminine freakin' head. Some dads *were* bad, but most, like Paul, were not. Why would the United States of America, self-appointed judge and jury of fair play and equality, condone a system that beats on dads and then allows their former spouses to disallow visitation with their children? Jesus is coming, folks. Get your licks in while you can.

And although Paul never thought Rosalinda's stepfather was the type to be "Lester the Molester," he didn't totally trust him about it. Paul always wondered how stepfathers could look at a developing young woman who wasn't theirs by birth and not be naturally attracted. He felt very strongly that molesting stepfathers should have their scrotums nailed to a stump. Step two would be to have their balls smashed with a ball-peen hammer, one ball at a time. Step three would be to have their penises cut off with bolt cutters, so they could bleed to death in a public place. His psychology studies had been enough proof to Paul that these molesting incidents affected individuals detrimentally for their entire lives. He also thought the wives who knew and yet still allowed their children to be molested should have their own organs obliterated. Jesus says something like it would be better for those who harmed these little ones if a millstone were tied to their necks and they were thrown into the lake. (Where did that thought come from?) Paul would like to do the tying, with a ball-peen hammer nearby.

Paul did enjoy working with Pat "New Man" Anderson and the rest of the guys, like Jethro. It was a rather comical comfort zone at times. One day, Jethro was peeling an apple as Paul and Pat entered the shanty at Quindaro. Jethro stopped peeling, looked straight ahead, slowly grinned a brainless, toothless grin, and summoned up a visual. "Ol' Bwue got in 'na chicken yawd de udder day. He keel twee chickens befoe I cud stop 'eem. I had ta waf. I tawt, Ol' Bwue is smawt! He *is* a burd dawg. He jus' don' know what kinda burd." Then the silly grin vanished, and Jethro concentrated on the apple peeling. Paul had to smile. But the humor and the daily comfort couldn't replace the much-needed bucks.

So Paul *did* need a change. One of the advantages of railroading is that with a few seniority whiskers, individuals usually have a choice of several jobs they may hold at any given time. So with Phil's input, Paul thought the road might just make a difference. Little did he know ...

Phil had been cut back from engineer to fireman in June 1984. Some engineers loved firemen because again, the position was equivalent to the right seat pilot. The engineers would run half the way, the firemen the other half. It made for a nice trip. The fireman position was originally necessary when the fireman had to shovel just the right amount of coal for the task the locomotive was to perform. Engineers and firemen had to be a great team. Shoveling the coal was intense labor. Rex Aiken, a yard engineer for years who had been a coal-shoveling fireman years before, referred to the work as "a good kinda tired." Phil knew what he meant. Many engineers who were nearing retirement when Phil, Paul, and Barry initially hired had huge, strong arms like Beauregard Banks, from shoveling coal all day in years past. In the steam days, the relationship between the engineer and the fireman was one of a serious nature. Trust was definitely involved, and the unity of a good fireman and good engineer was paramount if the trains were to proceed safely and efficiently.

But some engineers hated firemen. After the steamers were replaced by diesel-electrics, firemen were merely extra baggage to some engineers, yet the position still existed. Although some engineers liked the sharing of duties—"Charlie, you run to Topeka, and I'll run to Ellisville"—

others did not like the pay cut they automatically got by virtue of labor agreements when a fireman marked up with them. So some engineers looked upon firemen as parasites sucking up some of their pay. Some also didn't like sharing the duties of train operation, and therefore, didn't. They were brought up in a railroad era whereby they earned the warmest seat on the property, and relinquishing the seat was not in the cards, even if it was only for the seat across the cab. Again, in the minds of some, the engineer's seat was one of honor, one for which they worked very hard. In the old days, becoming an engineer meant *memorizing* the entire operating rule book, no small accomplishment. Engineers were required to write the contents word for word. Very few railroaders in other crafts were required to do this. Would they have been capable, if required? And the responsibility was enormous, ensuring a safe trip, especially in the steam days.

Paul *was* ready for a change. Life had been SSDD, "same stuff, different day" for years. His "basically, didn't care that much" attitude was changing. He felt the same pangs of life-waste that Phil and Barry were feeling, and very much felt that he was on the 'Road to Nowhere,' like the Talking Heads song

# CHAPTER 23
## THE ROAD TO SOMEWHERE

Paul had finally marked up on the road board, and with a little sharpshooting help from Phil, had caught the first turn with his brother, since Phil's conductor laid off this trip. Paul had not been on the road since his student trips ten years before. They were called for the KCNP-3 train, which stood for Kansas City, Missouri, to North Platte, Nebraska. It was a van train, or "piggyback" train, which referred to the trailer containers used in the trucking industry loaded on flatcars. At some point the containers would be unloaded by "piggy packers," giant machines with giant arms designed to grab the trailers and lift them off the flatcars. For years this feat had been accomplished by truckers, Teamster members, to be exact. Portable ramps were placed between the flatcars, and truckers literally drove the trailers on and off the cars. The proper name for these trains was TOFC, for "trailers on flat cars." Similarly, COFC stood for "containers on flat cars" used in barge traffic, both for river and overseas shipping, as well as for railroad shipping.

Local rails referred to the train as the North Platte Van, or NPV. It was a desirable train to catch, because it was called between 6:00 p.m. and 7:00 p.m. every day but Sunday. It had a 70 mph running order and was a priority train. Other trains, both in opposing and the same direction, "went in the hole," or took the siding for the van trains, and especially the NPV. Being a priority train and called at the time of day it was gave the crews a chance to have a meal and a beer before going to sleep at a decent hour in Ellisville.

Phil and Paul, though having grown up in the same house, still enjoyed the advent of being together after all these years. The NPV was called for 6:15 p.m. on this July 4, 1984. They had still been able to enjoy some of the (for them) brief holiday with Harold and Rose and Phil's family, and managed to down a few burgers and a gallon of iced tea. They had time to shoot off some fireworks with Rosalinda, Angela, Margo, Erin, and Graham, but the effect was somewhat lost with the sunlit sky. Paul was able to see Rosalinda because Ramona was "busy," and it worked to have Rosalinda's time occupied. Barry had already been called to work at 1:00 a.m. that morning, so he missed all the festivities. Later, Harold and Rose were taking all the kids to the drive-in for a three-movie night and a giant fireworks display. Susan and Carla were going to a baseball game where they too were to be treated to a huge fireworks display during the seventh-inning stretch, and again after the game. Then they were going to hit a few nightclubs.

Phil and Paul had previously, as usual, checked with the engine dispatcher (for Phil), and the crew dispatcher (for Paul) and found out they "stood" for the NPV. If they had to work on the Fourth, that was the train to catch. They had given Harold and Rose's telephone number to the engine dispatchers. So when they were called for the NPV train, they drove to the depot together in separate cars. As they marked up on the Federal Register, Allen "Paunch" Phillips, Phil's engineer, came through the door.

"Howdy, fellas! I got you two tonight?" Paunch had received his nickname during the years of the TV series *CHIPS*. It was Erik Estrada's character, Paunch, that put the name commonly before the public, but it was Allen's penchant for drinking beer and overeating that put his considerable belly "before" him, earning him the name. Years after the series had run its course, Paunch's paunch continued its growth spurt almost as if his stomach was subconsciously fulfilling the description implied by the label. Of all the engineers at the Central Pacific, Paunch was one of the best. If there would be any "iron carrying" (again, referring to replacing knuckles from train separation) this night, it wouldn't be because of improper train handling.

"How are ya, Paunch?" Phil said. "This is my brother, Paul. He's been out at Quindaro for ten years. He just marked up on the conductor's extra board, and caught us first trip." Phil had deliberately marked up as a fireman on Paunch's turn. Paunch was one of the engineers who liked firemen and enjoyed teaching those who would listen all he knew from his years of experience behind the throttle. Phil would listen and learn.

"Oh no, *two* Barneses to deal with?! One is plenty. Paul, are you as dense as your brother? It looks like you may be as ugly." That was Paunch's version of rail-speak, whereby a person said just the opposite of what they really thought. Both Phil and Paul enjoyed the reverse compliment.

"He's okay, Paul. He's just a typical engineer. You just have to explain things ree-ee-al slow to him," Phil returned the compliment. "He doesn't leave *too* much iron for you to carry, though."

The depot door opened and Bob Simpson and Hal Evans entered. "Hey, guys," said Simpson, the rear brakeman who would occupy the caboose with Paul. "Who we got here, Paunch?" he asked, gesturing toward Paul, since he knew Phil.

"You aren't going to believe this, Bob, but would you believe there are *two* of these animals?" Paunch said, shaking his head and pointing a thumb at Phil and Paul. "This is Phil's younger brother, Paul. He's been hidin' in the yards all this time. Up until now, he's been too afraid to come out here with the *real* men."

"Oh no, you don't mean ..." Simpson grimaced, keeping up the teasing. "Another Barnes?"

As he shook Paul's hand, Simpson asked, "First trip, Paul?"

"Yeah, Bob, and I can use all the help I can get," Paul said sincerely for the record.

"Well, this is a perfect learnin' train. We'll have it made, kid. All we'll do is some minor paperwork, maybe take a leak or two, and ride and make money, that is, if this ol' hogger can keep 'em on the rails."

"You just worry about that caboose seat cushion, and I'll get us there," Paunch said, feigning some disgust. "And take care of that new Barnes."

Hal Evans, the head brakeman, had been on the road about sixteen years and was a very private, quiet person. Paul had introduced himself to Hal, who wouldn't have taken the time, not because he was uncaring, just shy and withdrawn. Hal was nice.

Bob Simpson had been on the road for thirty years and had deliberately not taken promotion to conductor because he could hold better turns as a brakeman. He had been holding the Salina side as rear brakeman, which was more money, but he wanted to be home more often since his son was soon to begin summer football practice. Bob went to his son's practices as well as his games when he could. He went to the Ellisville side, where the board turned faster, allowing more time at home and more potential to catch a practice and later, a game, without having to lay off. And if he had to lay off a trip, he could.

"Here's the jitney. Let's get this show on the road," Paunch said with enthusiasm, happy to catch such a good train. He was looking forward to his usual fried chicken dinner with lots of gravy and five beers at May's Place, which equaled a good night's sleep, minus a urine break or two. The jitney dropped all five crew members off at the head end by the locomotives. Paunch, Phil, and Hal boarded the locomotives, and Bob and Paul stayed on the ground. Paunch would begin this trip running the train, and Phil and Hal would jockey for position for one of the two seats situated one behind the other on the left side of the locomotive cab. Some brakemen liked to sit in the front seat, giving them a better view of the road, and some liked to occupy the rear seat, making it easier to look at their train out the back window of the locomotive for hotboxes on an inside curve. This time Hal sat in the front seat. Bob and Paul would stand beside the tracks on opposite sides of the locomotives and give the train a roll-by inspection as they departed slowly. When the caboose got to them, they would climb aboard. They would be checking for sticking train brakes, a hand brake that would need to be released, shifted lading, or anything else that might affect the safety of the train. It was a required inspection.

The roll-by was completed at 6:45 p.m. and Bob and Paul boarded the caboose easily, since Paunch was moving at only three or four miles per hour. Again, in the future, movements would have to be stopped before trainmen could board or get off the equipment. Bob picked up the microphone of the caboose radio and said, "All aboard, Paunchie. Warp speed, Mr. Sulu."

"Rocket J. Squirrel," Paunch replied. Federal law prohibited extraneous comments from crew members using the radio, but these rules were not policed very much. It was a way of self-expression. "Did you buy that truck, John?" and "Anyone hear the score of the game?" were commonplace in radio chatter. Use of profanity on the radio was about the only thing that could get you busted, and some even got away with that. Occasionally, someone's mike would get stuck open, and those on that frequency would get an earful of collective cussing.

It was long noted among railroaders that Ellisville was the home of black squirrels, fat girls, and hundred-dollar cars. The black squirrels were a compliment of God and were really beautiful animals, with a jet-black sheen to their coats in the sunshine. They were the counterparts of the famous white squirrels of Olney, Illinois. Phil once had a conversation with his buddy McGee Brown about the squirrels. McGee had been on the road for quite a while now.

"Hey, Brownie," Phil began to ask, "do you suppose if the black squirrels of Ellisville were introduced to the white squirrels of Olney, Illinois, their populations would mix?"

Brownie thought quietly for a few seconds, and a grin began to form on his handsome face. "You mean, would there be a squirrel version of Mariah Carey and Halle Berry? I don't know, Phil, but I bet the male squirrels of either group would hope so."

The fat girls were also an integral part of the landscape, and could frequently be seen grazing at the local Ellisville lounges. It *did* seem that there was an overabundance of women with an overabundance of body blubber. Perhaps it was diet, Phil had thought at one time, but later he changed the thought to, It *is* diet. The locals, men and women both, ate large amounts of biscuits and gravy, butter, chicken-fried steaks, and other fried fatty foods. In essence, they ate themselves into land beasts.

The hundred-dollar cars came into existence because of a government law enacted in the late seventies that made it unlawful for railroads to build housing for their crews less than one and a half miles from a railroad depot where switching operations occurred. So now there was a new dormitory built almost exactly one and a half miles from the depot. Railroaders permanently assigned to the road were understandably not content to wait for one of the two jitneys used for crew movement. They were never available anyway. So they bought cheap cars in Ellisville, for the sole purpose of going to and from the dorm. It also allowed them to eat when they wanted to, the majority of the eating establishments being closer to the railroad in downtown Ellisville. Some of these cars were so visually painful, they were hysterical. They were either wrecked, or rust buckets, or both, and a few of them were rusted out so badly that one could see the street through the floorboards. This earned them the name Fred Flintstone cars, like you could stick your feet through the floorboards and run. But some of the railroaders bought some pretty nice older cars from the Ellisville locals.

When Phil was first training as an engineer on the road in 1977, crews were still staying at a hideous fleabag called the Pacific, undoubtedly named after the Central Pacific. It was right next to the tracks in beautiful downtown Ellisville, and was probably not a bad place in its time. However, its time had long passed.

Trains had for years, just as now, arrived and departed Ellisville twenty-four hours a day, seven days a week, each one blowing their horns with two longs, a short and a long, for every crossing in Ellisville, as prescribed by law. With six crossings in Ellisville, that was a lot of horn. This was extremely detrimental for the crews housed next to the main line tracks, in terms of decent sleep, and was just one of the many reasons railroaders drank. With a load on, it was easier to bear the incredibly loud horns with decibel ranges that easily penetrated the thin walls of the Pacific Hotel. With a load on, it was easier to bear everything. Booze was the forerunner of Tylenol in transportation and industry.

Phil had to initially stay at the plush Pacific when first being indoctrinated to road life years before. He remembered feeling like the whole thing could go up in smoke at any time. There were nine floors, and railroaders were constantly falling asleep from fatigue or liquor-induced stupors with their cigarettes still burning. There were dozens of burn marks on all the old furniture in every room. If the place caught fire, the Pacific Hotel would have instantly become a giant roman candle. The only good thing about a fire was it would have fried an abundance of rats, mice, and cockroaches that shared the fine quarters with the crews. It was unnerving to hear the rodents scurrying through the walls at night. Railroaders never knew if they had uninvited "company" in their rooms while they were asleep.

The rooms smelled like a combination of smoke, mildew, and puke from those times railroaders alcoholically overindulged past the point of a good sleep coma. When the Pacific was first constructed in the late 1930s, the support timbers, which were strong and made of oak, as were the floors and stairs, were more than adequate. But gravity and entropy had, as usual, won out over the years. The big timbers now sagged with age, and both the floors and stairs were warped, and worn, and creaked severely. There was no interior insulation. It seemed there was almost a constant *tramp, tramp, tramp* up or down the stairs by heavy railroad boots. One could hear the person above, below, and on either side, pacing the floor. Phil had heard poor old Adam Walters one night, obviously drinking, moaning to himself and coughing and hacking, literally for hours. "Terrible thing, terrible thing," Adam would mutter, and then he would cough to the point of not being able to catch his breath, which he needed desperately for the next coughing spasm. It sounded to Phil with every spasm that a succeeding inhalation was not possible, but at the last moment before what Phil assumed would be unconsciousness or death, Adam managed another wheezy breath. Phil then knew why Adam always looked extremely tired and worn, with huge, red eyes and eye bags every time he saw him. Adam also could be seen at various times sitting on the rails, a real no-no in railroad safety. This earned him the name of Rail Tail, not to be confused with Rail Head Reed, a war-decorated engineer who was awarded his nickname from a piece of nonremoved shrapnel buried in his right temple from World War II. When one of the younger railroaders would see him, they'd intentionally say, "Hi, Rail Head," to which Reed would smile broadly and reply in good fun, "Boy, you ain't been here long enough!" referring to the unwritten railroad law that if you tease him about his nickname, you better have some time in on the railroad. In other words you had to *earn* the right.

The basement of the Pacific was a haven for twenty-four-hour card games. The basement was a lovely suite, complete with not only all the wondrous odors of the rooms, but also with the added aesthetic visual of protruding limestone walls from the Pacific's ancient foundation. It had a dirt and concrete floor, which was usually speckled white and tan from cigarette butts. The air was blue, both from cigarette smoke and Olympic-caliber cussing. The proprietor, an old man everyone called Easy Money, would come down and sweep up a huge pile of butts and dirt once or twice a day. This caused the air, what there was of it, to be filled with dust particles, which you could actually taste if you were "fortunate" enough to be there when Easy Money swept. The air would then turn blue brown in color, reflected in the lights. Most would cuss and run up the stairs when they saw him coming; that is, if they weren't holding a good hand. The place was a real palace. In fact that's what the crews had named it: the Pacific Palace. Many crew members who were on the road permanently used their good salaries to rent their own places in Ellisville, leaving the horrible conditions at the Palace for others to endure. This provided them some semblance of better living conditions and a shot at feeling semihuman.

The Pacific Palace days were long gone. It was now a parking lot. The dorm was completed in 1978, and was hellishly mundane. But now the crews at least had clean living conditions, free from smells, vermin, the horrendous noise of constant train horns, and Easy Money's broom. The rooms were very small, not for the claustrophobic. There was a small day room with a TV, but there were always arguments about what shows should be watched, unless it was a ball game. The dorm did, however, still house Big Mammoo, who worked out on the toes of Engineer Hobbs, literally sucking him into retirement. Talk about "that giant sucking sound." Ross Perot was so right ... Mammoo ... and jobs being sucked out of the country.

Phil had not yet bought a car because the probability of him being "bumped" off the road was high if business slowed any more. He was unable to hold the road even as a fireman until 1980, and was forced back in the yards as soon as his training was over. Usually at least one person on the crew had a hundred-dollar car, so transportation was not a problem.

# CHAPTER 24
# THE ROAD LOOKS GOOD

The KCNP-3 arrived in Ellisville at 10:15 p.m., in plenty of time for Paunch to satisfy his appetite, which *was* rather insatiable, and again, directly proportional to the great, distended belly that earned him his nickname. For years the phenomenon was referred to on the railroad as Dunlop's Disease: his stomach done lopped over his belt.

After Paunch, Phil, and Paul registered their times, they picked up their grips and headed for Paunch's hundred-dollar car. It was a 1969 Ford Fairlane that had been wrecked and never fixed, but the engine was still breathing. The driver's side door did not shut all the way. Paunch had a makeshift latch invented from an old belt. The tires were marginal, but sufficient for one three-mile round-trip each time Paunch went to Ellisville. The thing would run forever under those conditions. Bob and Hal were taking their respective cars to the dorm.

"You guys want me to take you to the prison, or do you want to stop by May's with me for a bite first?" asked Paunch.

"Oh, we'll come with you for some hair and swill." Phil smiled as he patted his belly, as if expecting delicious cuisine. Phil had eaten at May's many times. The food *was* good, but there was an occasional hair. Mike Bromley said May's was too close for comfort to the barbershop next door. At one time Mike suggested that May's waitresses ran the orders by the barbershop for additional hair before delivering them to the railroaders.

The three climbed out of Paunch's Fred Flintstone car, walked into May's, and took a knotty pine booth directly across from the door. May's was the only place open at this time of night that served real food. May's contract with the local unions and the Central Pacific required her to stay open twenty-four hours and cater to the crews. A small, local truck stop was also open at this hour, but served only microwave food and cold sandwiches. May put out a good cheeseburger, thanks to May's fine and fresh meat supplier, Rolf's. It was the local meat market, and had excellent Angus beef. The artery-clogging fried chicken, Paunch's favorite, was delicious, but had plenty of deep-fat-fried white flour and chicken skin … Good taste, bad health. May served both beer and coffee around the clock, which was the basis for Groove Whitfield's song "Up on Coffee, Down on Beer." Someone was always looking for assistance in one direction or the other.

May herself was a former local bar lizard, which is a genre unto itself in small railroad towns. She had eventually married one of the older railroaders who was twenty years her senior. She'd physically abused him for years, as she had many others. He'd died years before and left May a goodly sum with which she'd opened May's Place. This allowed her to continue her railroad-associated lifestyle, all she knew, therefore providing her a certain continued comfort level. May, who at one time *was* pretty, still flirted with the railroaders, or the "boys," as she affectionately referred to them, although there were no takers these days. She was now fifty-eight, and looked ninety as a result of *way* too many cigarettes, which she still cherished and chained. The 500,000 gallons of booze she had consumed hadn't helped her appearance either. She was now gray, wrinkled, bearded, fat, and toothless, but she was nice.

Marge, one of May's waitresses, was walking toward Phil, Paul, and Paunch to take their orders. Marge was both loud and dumb, a great combination and an all-too-common waitress trait that was tough on forced listeners. "How're you-all today? You just git in? You guys look like you could eat anythin' … ha ha, tee-hee." Then Marge turned in a circle in a sort of a clownish dance, as if to show them what she was referring to. After the mindless flirting and loud babbling, she finally began to take the orders. Paul, right in the middle of ordering a cheeseburger basket, stopped with his mouth open, staring at the door. He was staring at *absolutely* the *most beautiful* female he had *ever* seen.

She was wearing a pink T-shirt that had a white Nike insignia on the front. The Nike insignia was complimented by a beautifully sculptured bustline pushing the symbol outward and upward. The T-shirt was tucked neatly into a pair of mid-thigh, pleated, size nine white tennis shorts, from which protruded the most gorgeous, golden-tanned, curvy legs Paul could ever remember seeing. The thighs were strong and beautifully protruding, and the knees were small and chiseled. The calves were artwork, and the ankles, slim. These masterpieces entered into thick white socks, turned down once, which occupied a pair of white Lugz with thick soles. Her dark auburn hair was short, and Paul could see from across the room that her eyes were a bright bluish purple. They were like bluish-purple visible-spectrum lasers. She was amazingly stunning, and here in Ellisville with the fat girls.

"She runs," Phil said, leaning over to Paul, referring to the obvious excellent physical appearance of the extremely pretty female holding Paul's gaze.

"From guys?" Paul asked.

"No, *after* guys," Phil said with emphasis. "Pauly, that's Amy Johnson. She's caused more divorces around here with what's under her beautiful belt than the entire rest of the railroad babes combined. She's a machine."

"She's exquisite," Paul managed, still initially stunned and only half hearing his brother.

Amy turned around to speak with her two larger feminine companions. As she did, Paul noticed her rear quarters were exquisitely formed, strong and hard, but not overly muscular. Amy was 150 pounds and extremely curvy. At 5 feet 10 inches this 150 pounds was perfectly proportioned. Her measurements were 37-21-38. She reminded Paul as being built the way Al Capp used to draw the women in his comic strip *Li'l Abner*. When Phil initially went on the road and had first seen Amy, he too thought she was quite exceptional, beauty-wise, and thought of Jay Leno's great line about how he liked a woman who looked like she could throw a toaster about two hundred yards. Phil knew what he meant. He and Paul had identified with Jay anyway, being half Italian, and they both always liked luscious, strong women. That skinny crap was appealing only to the anorexic jocks. Nipsy Russell once said, "Don't nobody like a bone but a dog." Phil and Paul were not the types to be dictated to by the media about what their likes should be. Carla was a statuesque beauty herself, as was the senseless Open Kimono Ramona, the mother of Paul's daughter, Rosalinda. Amy was awesome. Many railroaders seeing her for the first time said she looked like a movie star, and she did.

"She's bad news, Pauly," Phil continued, attempting to derail his brother's obvious powerful attraction and curiosity. "Uh-oh." Phil had finally seen it on his brother's face. He had long thought Paul was immune to the "thunderbolt." Mario Puzo discussed it in *The Godfather*. All Italian males had heard about it. He himself had certainly experienced it with Carla, but Paul never seemed to be affected in that manner by any of the substantial number of females with whom he had been involved over the years. Phil was worried. His handsome brother could just about pick and choose, and this was one woman he would not have chosen for him. There were rumors of abortions, many of which were the result of Amy's sleeping with several of the married railroaders as well as some townsfolk. Indeed, when she became pregnant, there was always a dartboard lottery of individuals with whom to contend, to determine who the parenthood prize would go to. But Amy never gave birth, at least locally. She had always "taken care of it." It had been rumored that Amy did have a son and a daughter resulting from sex with two different drug dealers in the San Antonio area of Texas. The children were supposedly being raised in foster care. In the cases of the alleged Ellisville pregnancies, Amy never knew with certainty who the fathers actually were. This was because of her basic inability to be with one person at a time, and no one was volunteering for blood tests.

The railroad provided a perfect medium for Amy's behavior, with different guys in town every trip. Absolutely no one, not even the best-trained, most experienced psychologist, could have looked at this incredible beauty and managed an intelligent guess at exactly what her past or present was. Paul was well aware of the dangers of "judging a book by the cover," but that didn't stop him. He, like Chance Armstrong and most all others, allowed the physical to overwhelm the mental and, most important, the spiritual. Paul was not making that leap of wisdom past initial attraction that Alex Hollander had expressed to Phil and Chance years before at the Champlain Truck Stop. Men have the questionable ability to disregard everything but looks. Nothing else matters. Most of the railroad rags exhibited physical appearances that perfectly displayed their lifestyles, like May herself. They just looked nasty, and like they deserved the terms "lizard", "snake", and the more modern "skank." They had that "rode hard and put to bed wet" look, which had been their MO for years. They were just "holes," nothing more, nothing less. Groove had written a country song:

> Well, she's been rode hard, and put to bed wet.
> You know that woman never, ever had a chance to dry off
>     her sweat.
> Now them good times, she ain't seen yet.
> She's been rode hard and put to bed wet.

Groove had also composed his own version of Tommy James's song "Hanky Panky," where he substituted "Skanky Panky," cracking up a few railroaders with his always-changing lines.

But Amy Johnson didn't look like the rest. She *did* look like a movie star.

She had moved to Ellisville by herself at age twenty-six, from where, no one knew for sure. She had made friends extremely easily, and had called Ellisville her home for three years. Some said Amy had talked of Texas as being her birthplace, but she rarely talked about her younger years. She was concerned with the here and now. "The here and now is all that counts, ah-ooo, ah-ooo. The here and now in large amounts, ah-ooo, ah-ooo," as Adam Ant sang in "Room at the Top." Barry had told Paul that "Adam Ant" came from the word "adamant."

One time Amy had gotten drunk and stoned, two of her addictive passions as well as sex, and had told a local she was molested by a stepfather from age ten to fourteen. She had no memory of her life before that. Her marvelous mother had evidently known this was occurring, but had chosen to ignore the fact, since this guy had done a good job exercising her own "business." Ah, motherhood … Ain't it great nowadays? Sell out your kid for a good diddle. One of Ned Lingle's observations was "Love is when someone else's needs are more important than your own." Phil, Paul, and Barry thought that made great sense, but didn't see it in operation in too many sectors of life anymore. "Look out for number one," like Amy's mother, was a much more common approach. Mother Teresas were rare, unfortunately.

"She's an ex-coke addict, Paul ... Crack cocaine, I think," Paunch mumbled as he chewed chicken, leaning toward Paul as if to whisper but saying it louder than he had planned. A glob of chicken gravy was stuck on the left side of Paunch's mouth. "Carson is a good friend of mine. He attends AA meetings up here, and he says Amy is always at the meetings, so at least she's tryin'. Carson says there are as many at AA meetings for drug dependency nowadays as there are for alcohol dependency ... maybe more."

"Poor kid," Phil said as he too stared at the statuesque beauty. Phil and Amy were friends, as she was with anyone who would notice her, which was everyone. He had, after meeting her, sung the first line of the chorus of Vince Gill's terrific song when he was with Pure Prairie League, "Amie, what you want to do?" Phil was exceptionally faithful to Carla, and was never the type to hold as *desirable* any woman who just about anybody could have. But Phil was never "holier than thou" either, realizing we all fall short of the glory of God, that our righteousness is as filthy rags. Phil desperately did *not* want to be a Scribe or a Pharisee. Jesus had problems with them. Jesus loved sinners. Phil treated Amy like he did everyone else: with respect, and she liked and respected him for doing so. And perhaps it was yet another example of Chance Armstrong's "Treat a whore like a queen and a queen like a whore."

Amy's reputation always preceded her, but she chose to ignore it. She chose to ignore reality in general, constantly seeking "a good time," some sort of buzz, to attempt to satisfy her insatiable appetite for new experiences and people. But at this point, Paul was not scrutinizing her behaviors or personalities, however many of either there may have been. Paul was still mesmerized when Amy began walking sensuously over to their booth. Every inch of Amy was moving in physical perfection and desire. The lust gremlin was overwhelming Paul much more than usual.

"Who's the stud muffin?" Amy asked as she smiled a gorgeous, gentle smile at Paul, making her look even lovelier.

"Amy, what you want to do?" Phil sang to her in his baritone, opposing Vince Gill's higher singing voice. "That stud muffin is my brother, Paul, and you can't have him, Amy. He's not easy, like the rest of these goons."

"Calm down, Phil. Let's not be hasty," Paul quickly responded with a smile.

"Excuse me, Amy, I may be wrong, and he *is* a goon," Phil said equally as quickly.

Amy's beautiful, deep auburn-colored hair and the short style with the intentionally uneven part on the left side pointed to her athletic leanings. The style suited her perfectly. Amy had been a softball star in high school. She had told one of the locals she had even qualified for the Olympics, but was pregnant at event time, the normal outcome of a young, fertile woman who had lots of unprotected sex. Amy was incredibly beautiful, incredibly sweet, always laughing and teasing, and incredibly tragic, in both her lifestyle and, as a result, her life. She had been raised literally on the streets of San Antonio, and had no idea what good parenting was all about, or what a good life in general might be. Her mother had divorced her father and gone through the proverbial string of men until marrying the molesting stepfather. Amy was left to fend for herself, learning very early in life about sex, drugs, and alcohol, the norm for abandoned children with or without homes. Her winsome mother was totally self-indulged in her own pleasures. Amy's mom, Linda, would at least leave food in the fridge that Amy could microwave, but Linda never cared about Amy's whereabouts or her welfare in general. Linda was totally self-indulgent, a trait Amy subconsciously inherited, either from environment or DNA or both.

In her childhood, Amy's only decent outlet was softball. She spent a good percentage of her teenage years at the local community center practicing her pitching and having sex with whomever. Ellisville residents and railroaders who had played catch with Amy could easily see how she may have indeed qualified for the Olympic team. She could really bring it. And those coaches who admired Amy's early development as well as her softball abilities were able to enjoy either for the asking. Most of the time, they didn't even have to ask ... Amy offered. It was Amy's way of showing friendship and gratitude. No one ever told her it was wrong, and she certainly couldn't have derived that conclusion from watching TV, the movies, or her mom, Linda. In fact, the media merely reinforced in her subconscious that her behavior was correct. "This is what people do." It was "adult" behavior.

Amy superficially seemed always in a good mood, but sometimes, when she would indulge in the addictive behaviors that warranted her attendance at AA meetings, she would cry relentlessly as the drugs and alcohol forced her to review her life. Most people who abused controlled substances found it numbed their abilities to ponder their lives. With Amy, the opposite effect sometimes occurred. Sometimes when she was high, Amy, who in everyday life naturally suppressed those thoughts, had all the horrors of her past mentally appear in living color. She would stressfully recall abortions, rapes, sexual perversions, being molested, and the emptiness left in her from a father she'd never known and children she'd rarely seen. It would all be projected in front of her like a massive IMAX presentation. These horribly emotionally devastating visions sometimes left her bordering on suicide.

But most of the time those thought processes didn't occur, whether she was high or not. And she was able to easily engage in behaviors that many in society still considered disgusting, even though social liberalism had won out in many sectors over the years.

After becoming Christian, Phil always thought that God allowed the United States to experience calamity *after* participation in sinful pursuits. He thought the stock market crash of 1929 and resulting Great Depression was a direct result of the immorality of the Roaring Twenties. Some people's great-grandparents weren't all that chaste, a thought most would find appalling. Biblically, it sure worked out that way for Israel. When Israel repented, God allowed prosperity. When they sinned, God allowed capture and slavery. Phil thought this was so obvious, he wondered why it was not accepted as the most common of common knowledge. He had discussed this with Paul and Barry on many occasions, but Paul had not yet completely aligned with Phil's total dedication to God. Paul knew God loved him, and he knew he loved God. But he didn't feel like he was going through life with Him, as did Phil and Barry. So Paul bought into part of Phil's Christian reasoning, but not all.

Phil knew this retribution for sin worked with individuals, because he had certainly felt the wrath of God a few times more than he wished in his own life. When he repented of his sins, he was again blessed. "Just what about that is so tough, conceptually?" Phil would ask himself. Pastor Adrian Rogers of Memphis said, "God is a loving God, but He will take you to the woodshed once in a while." Yes, He will.

Amy had been to the woodshed many times in her life. Her constant, existential pursuit of the physical, "If it feels good, rub it" had netted her some real horror over the years. But she was trapped and spinning in a brainless, continuous, pleasure maelstrom. She could never slow down long enough to try to understand. Paul would add to that maelstrom, rather than rescue her, which was pretty much the way it was with Amy. Many had used her, which she liked. She used them. This brought her loss of children, divorce, isolation from her family, physical abuse, which she learned to accept and sometimes *like*, and even some jail time. For all anyone knew, Amy might even have been presently ducking authorities, her reason for choosing Ellisville as her home. But her behavior never changed. It was literally all she knew.

Very occasionally, someone came along who genuinely tried to help Amy. Once, while in jail in San Antonio for drug charges, she had met an older Christian woman, Sally Benson, who regularly visited the prisoners. Sally had helped Amy to realize that there was a spiritual side to life, and that this side, though unseen, was the most important one, even though it was a faith trip. Amy, while incarcerated, had read certain scriptures Sally had recommended, and they had actually helped Amy cope with life much better. But as soon as Amy was released, she forgot all about them. Amy had also been diagnosed with attention deficit hyperactive disorder (ADHD), a perfect foundation for an addictive personality. She couldn't hold still, and she couldn't keep focused on thoughts or individuals. She just kept spinning. She was very beautiful externally, but internally, she was a psychological tornado.

Paul was still admiring the beautiful external while Phil mulled over the tragic, psychologically shattered internal. "What are you doing later, Amy?" Paul smiled and reached out for Amy's hand at the same time she reached out for his. Their touch was an electrical storm.

"Going with you somewhere, I hope," Amy replied playfully. Her voice sounded like music to Paul. It had a scratchy, sexy, Kim Carnes–like quality, and was extremely high-energy and exciting. When she spoke, she was always almost laughing, and usually teasing. Amy reeked with desire. Everything she did was seductive, and it came naturally.

But she'd deliberately learned additional attractive behaviors that gave her physical pleasure, both sexually and materially, like men buying her cars and jewelry. And Amy didn't associate the sins with the tragedies. Short-term pleasure was always her primary goal. The majority of her seductiveness was a street-learned ability. It was no more or less effective than an orchid mantis, which looks like a beautiful flower until an unsuspecting insect attempts to pollinate it and instantly becomes mantis pizza.

Phil inwardly moaned, and Paunch inwardly snickered. Both knew what the outcome of Paul and Amy's "date" would be.

"Let me get showered and cleaned up, and I'll meet you somewhere," Paul said excitedly.

"How 'bout if I pick you up at the dorm at midnight?" Amy said, giggling.

"That will work for me," Paul said, still smiling like a possum about to indulge in incredibly tasty garbage as Amy walked back to her friends.

"Paul," Phil again tried, although he knew he would be unsuccessful. "She's caused more trouble out here than any hundred women. Guys have gotten divorced, almost killed. A North Platte engineer is serving time for attempted manslaughter. George Bingham, a conductor whose wife had already left him because of Amy, came back to find Amy in bed with this North Platte guy. George swore he would get this guy, when this guy was only doing what everyone else does with Amy. When the North Platte guy went to work, George was waiting in the parking lot of the yard office. George swung at this guy, and they wound up fighting by the tracks. George was on top of him, choking him, and the North Platte guy picks up a brake shoe and hammers George on the side of the head. Guys who saw it said it was a sickening *crunch*. George went to the hospital, and he's still off. They say he'll never be right. It's been a year now. The other guy went to jail, got out on bond, and went to jail again. This wasn't an isolated incident. Guys fight over her all the time. She's going to get somebody killed. But it's like two Komodo dragons fighting over a piece of rotting wild pig. Whoever wins ain't got much. She's bad news, Pauly."

Paul wasn't listening. He was still concentrating on the most beautiful woman he'd ever seen. He knew he would be with her very soon. He hadn't had a woman in a long time, and he felt about them like Pacino's great Oscar-winning portrayal of Colonel Slade in *Scent of a Woman*. He loved everything about them, and waking up with them all warm and funky. At one point, he *had* semi-listened to his older brother, and realized he couldn't find a way it would please God to have sex outside of marriage. "Yeah, Phil, it's easy for you. You're married," Paul would say. "You can have it anytime you want."

"Yeah, right," Phil would just say, and he'd smile, shaking his head. "Please tell that to Carla." It was tough on marrieds, but both agreed that it was extra-tough on singles, men and women both.

Paul had long thought that although fornication was a sin to God, it wasn't heinous enough in God's eyes to be a Commandment. He knew it *was* considered sinful to God, since in the Bible it said, "He who committeth fornication sinneth against his own body." But Paul thought the real sin, bad enough to be a Commandment, was the sin of adultery. Still, he had tried to stay free from either of late, opposing both his and Phil's approach to life when they were younger. He was beginning to reason that God was a wonderful, forgiving God who constantly referred to the "sins of your youth," as if we all had some leeway when younger. He also petitioned, referring to Amy, "C'mon, Lord, I have attempted to be so good. Please make this turn out. You can do anything. And please don't kick my ass for this."

Something else had happened to set this stage. About three months before, Paul, who almost always thought he could handle anything, was sitting alone in his apartment one evening. He had moved out of the apartment shared with Pat "New Man" Anderson and John Summers and a couple of different railroaders at different times. It was just easier if he had his own place on those rare occasions when he got Rosalinda. On this particular evening, he hadn't felt like walking to the local bar for a beer. But he looked up on the mantel at the Sacred Heart of Jesus picture his uncle Phil had given him years before. He said out loud, "Father, is this what you want for me? Do you want me to go through the rest of my life alone? If you do, I can, but I'd like to know." Paul was not melancholy or crying in his beer, but matter-of-factly talking to his maker. He hadn't received an answer. But now, just three months later, this tantalizing meeting had occurred. Was Amy the answer? Paul did not know if God had sent Amy or not, but he figured he might be due. Paul never categorized these thoughts as irrational thinking. But given that he and Amy hadn't even had their date yet, the thoughts were not all that logical. Did Paul know something, deep down in his inner being?

Phil and Paul ate their excellent cheeseburgers and fries, and Paunch wolfed the last of his fried chicken dinner, complete with a couple of quarts of beer for further belly enhancement and a good night's sleep. No hair was present at this meal. Amy had left after speaking with Paul, just getting a Coke to go with her larger, less-proportionately attractive friends. She would shower, and put on Tommy perfume at strategic points on her perfect body. She would change to a completely new outfit, this time a white short-sleeved summer sweater top, with white pearl beads around the collar and arms, a red miniskirt, no doubt to show Paul and others even more of her exquisite legs, and black patent leather shoes. No, she didn't need panty hose. Her legs were a perfection of color and form. She was physically magnificent.

# CHAPTER 25
# THE ROAD LOOKS GREAT

The evening was a warm, comfortable July 4. Fireflies were strobing everywhere, and fireworks were still occasionally heard and seen as Amy pulled up to the sidewalk leading to the front door of the dorm a little before midnight. The air was sweet, and scented with a hint of detonated explosive powder. Phil watched from his room as his big handsome brother walked out to Amy's car, a 1963 red Plymouth Fury that a former "acquaintance" had purchased for her. He watched as Paul, carrying his grip, opened the passenger side door and leaned across to kiss the beautiful and tragic Amy. The kiss lasted a long time. Phil wondered exactly what that meant for his brother, feeling like no ultimate good could come of it. Phil also wondered how many dozens, or was it now hundreds, of times the red '63 Fury had pulled up to the dorm. The thought of the female black widow spider devouring the male black widow after coitus crossed Phil's mind.

Amy had taken the initiative to pick up a fifth of rum, not knowing that rum and Coke happened to be Paul's favorite drink. He had been weaned on it by a Delta Upsilon active member at a fraternity rush at the University of Missouri in Columbia in the spring of 1965. He had gotten sick on it, but loved it anyway ever since. Amy already had Cuervo Gold at her apartment for her margaritas, her drink of choice.

"Wanna stop by Fred's for a little dancin' beforehand?" Amy teased, the word "beforehand" referring to the obvious outcome of the evening's festivities.

"Sure," Paul replied happily, thinking to himself how wonderful the road looked at this point. He had checked the lineup at the dorm and his turn was fourteen times out, and there were only seven trains coming. If they didn't deadhead, his turn would not get out until the next afternoon. They might even make penalty time. "What's Fred's?" he asked as he cupped his left hand behind Amy's lovely auburn hair, which ended at the back of her neck.

"Just a local place. They have good bands, and the Hounds are playing there tonight. They're not bad." Ellisville could have about any type of music playing in the local pubs. Country was a sure thing, or "thang," but rock and roll was also quite popular. Tonight, to both Paul's and Amy's satisfaction, the Hounds played rock and roll.

Amy and Paul walked into Fred's and immediately went to the dance floor. The Hounds were playing "You Can't Always Get What You Want" by the Rolling Stones. Paul and Amy reached out to each other at the same time, and slowly and naturally, sensuously, barely touched each other, gradually increasing the tension of the touch at the same time. They were staring directly into each other's eyes, and the rest of the world was quickly vanishing. Paul had slipped his large hands around Amy's waist, and gradually pulled her closer to him, his hands passing behind her twenty-one inch waist, one above the other until his big arms were totally around her.

Although Amy was tall, she reached up for Paul's shoulders, first placing her hands on both sides of his huge upper torso and then moving herself toward him, her forearms crossing behind his large football player neck. They looked into each other's eyes, both feeling something neither had ever felt before. Considering the experiences of the two, they both knew they were experiencing something extremely special.

Phil and Paul had discussed electromagnetics many times. They both thought it was the basis for many human feelings and reactions, as well as scientific reactions. It may explain why people born at certain times of the year have certain characteristics, a platform occupied by astrology jocks. It may explain why we are so complicated as individuals in many respects, and why psychology, although important and certainly part of the mix, may still take a back seat to physiology and physics. DNA and electromagnetics may ultimately be much more influential on human behavior than environment. Everyone is aware that children of the same parents brought up in the same manner in the same home are quite often very different. And there is a physics formula for the gravitational attraction of bodies.

The semipermeable membranes in the body function because random charges govern the area when a liquid flow is *not* desired. When a flow *is* desired, the charges line up, positives on one side of the membrane, negatives on the other, and a flow is allowed to occur. We are, in our most basic form, matter and energy. We know where the matter goes eventually, at death: ashes to ashes, dust to dust. But where does the energy go? Since the first law of thermodynamics says that matter and energy can neither be created nor destroyed, our "energy" has to go somewhere.

To Phil and Paul, it was great *physical* proof of Christianity. Supposedly, immediately after dying, corpses were all twenty-three grams lighter. Some theologians felt like this energy, peripherally, was what formed the basis of our spiritual bodies. Phil and Paul had seen shows on Kirlian photography whereby a portion of a leaf was cut off, but a Kirlian photography picture taken of the cut leaf showed the outline of the original, with the life force still there. Paul also knew his buddies in Vietnam who had unfortunately lost arms or legs reported feeling like the missing limbs were still there at times. Maybe they *were* there … in another dimension. Could the electrical impulses involved in thought processes be present in another dimension?

Phil and Paul both knew for sure and had discussed many times that although most women felt nice to touch, once in a while, touching a certain woman was like the physical version of Zarathustra. It may be the physical version of the visual phenomenon Uncle Phil called "da thunderbolt-a" that he blamed on Aunt-a Josephine. It may be the reason the majority of us are here. Thank you, God and electromagnetics!

For Amy and Paul, it was Zarathustra to the twenty-third power. People have referred to the feelings as "fireworks," apropos for the Fourth of July. Wherever Amy and Paul's skin touched, an extremely powerful, indescribable, massive-surge feeling occurred. Besides each of them subconsciously liking the textures (and perhaps electricity) of the other's skin, there was much, much more. It was like it became *one* skin. Amy and Paul never wanted to let go from that first moment of holding each other. The Hounds were into the long ending ... "You can't always get what you want, but if you try sometime, you just might find, you just might f-i-i-i-i-i-nd, you get what you need." All the dancers were enjoying the old song, including Amy and Paul, but Amy and Paul both desperately wanted more. They frantically exited Fred's to get what they needed.

On the way to Amy's apartment they didn't even realize they hadn't even had a drink at Fred's. Now, at Amy's apartment, they were too involved in each other to think about anything else. Technically, Amy wasn't supposed to be drinking, ever, with her addictive personality. But she reasoned she went to AA for drugs, not alcohol. It was faulty reasoning.

From the minute they had touched at May's, Paul and Amy felt they had to be touching in some manner. It was a feeling both knew was extraordinary. Both of them had had many sexual partners, but neither had ever felt what they were feeling now. Amy had ahold of Paul's right hand behind her with her left hand, leading him to her apartment, unlocking and opening the door. She subconsciously didn't want to stop being in contact with him. Paul, also subconsciously, wanted to feel her touch at all times. Although he had just met her, he felt he had known her forever. Amy felt the same way.

Amy pulled Paul toward the bed, barely even giving time or thought to closing and locking the door. She did not bother to turn on the lights. Her window shade was up, and the streetlights let enough light in to reflect a black-and-white image of everything in the apartment, including Paul and Amy. Outside in the moist summer evening, a skyrocket exploded into a green-and-gold umbrella. The now less often and faintly heard fireworks, coupled with the crickets chirping, added a relaxed, comfortable, auditory background to the sweet air of the pleasant July night. Fireflies lit in unison with each distant mini-explosion of the lingering fireworks. Amy's apartment smelled like expensive perfume and incense, with a hint of gunpowder blowing in through the screen in the open window.

They did not tear into each other, but quietly, purposefully, and tenderly unbuttoned buttons and shed clothing, all the while kissing and caressing gently, each feeling that they had found their "place" in the other. The touching and kissing was an unprepared orchestration.

The building excitement was the physical version of "Bolero." Each sound of rustling covers, each sound of a kiss, and every little noise of passion and yes, *love*, was a symphony to Paul and Amy. It was all *so* perfect.

They explored every inch of each other, which both thought was the most perfect example of the opposite sex either had ever seen. Amy was even more perfect than Paul could ever have guessed. And for Amy, Paul's rock-hard body heightened the already seemingly insatiable passion she felt for him. At the same time, his physical virtues gave her a deep sense of security. All these feelings, the intensity of which could not be measured in one union, was a physical perfection neither Paul nor Amy had ever known. When, after an immeasurable time period, Paul finally entered her, the crescendo was a ten on the Richter scale … total annihilation. Two bodies were decidedly one, and *only* one. Their union was an unforgettable massive power surge.

The two of them just lay next to each other saying nothing, enjoying each other's breathing and the unusually extreme closeness. Amy was trembling. There were tears in her bluish-purple eyes. They were overwhelmingly happy lying side by side, as if joined together at the hip and the head. Reality didn't exist, except for each other. Although Amy smoked, she wasn't even thinking about a cigarette now. Her abnormal need for nonstop stimulation of any kind was temporarily put on hold. She was totally satisfied. Both knew something exceptional had just happened, far and above being simultaneously orgasmic. They rested side by side in peaceful, gentle bliss, a moment never to be forgotten by either. They were both too spent, and too satisfied, to even consider a "where do we go from here?" thought. They just enjoyed the unexpected and unforgettable moment.

Finally, after an imperceptible time segment passed, Paul said, "Well, I've had better."

"Yeah, right," Amy countered, laughing, secure in the fact that she knew he hadn't. "What do we do now?" she asked, half teasing and half serious, knowing the potentially life-changing ramifications of what had just occurred.

"I don't know, Amy." There was more silence. Three or four minutes later, Paul again spoke softly. "I know I wasn't counting on this happening, *ever*, let alone on my first trip to Ellisville. I heard all that was up here were black squirrels, fat girls, and hundred-dollar cars. Brother never told me about you."

"He probably didn't want you knowing about me, Paul. I do have a reputation, you know."

"You know, Amy, I'm a firm believer in 'Let he who among you is without sin cast the first stone.' No one will be throwing stones at you, ever." Paul could feel a protective nature surfacing, another feeling he had never felt before, except in reference to his own family members. "To me, what either one of us did before this is of no consequence. But from here on, it *is* important, if you felt what I did." Paul knew she had.

"I did. You know I did, Paul."

"Then what happens from this point forward is all that's important. The rest is just history, and history's gone."

It was 5:43 a.m. Neither Amy nor Paul were remotely concerned with time, but it had passed ridiculously quickly. Paul called the depot to find out the latest lineup and found out their turn was second out, and there were two trains coming. Things could change quickly on the railroad. They had deadheaded several crews to get them back to Kansas City and rested for trains originating there in the next twenty-four to thirty-six hours. They had run a ballast train out of Ellisville to work extending the siding at Piedmont, and had to use a turn in the Ellisville pool for that purpose. So what had been a pretty safe bet of not getting out till the afternoon had changed, not surprisingly, which is why railroaders were always short-rested.

"I'm going to be called, Amy," Paul said, sighing, and thinking crazily for a split second that there might be a way he could stay there with her, although he knew it couldn't be done. He felt a sickness he couldn't explain.

"Don't go, Paul, *no!*" Amy grabbed him and they held each other tightly, each trying to cover as much of the other's body as they could with their own. Paul felt he could never, *should* never, let Amy go at this moment. This desire was too wonderful, but this was also nuts.

The phone rang. Amy answered, and Paul imagined it being one of her "pasts" or "presents" calling, something Paul knew he would be dealing with, and not very happily, but necessarily.

"It's your brother," Amy said, handing the phone to Paul.

"Hey, Pauly, we're called. Did you get any sleep?"

"None, brother. How'd you get this number?"

"It's known, brother. Hey, we're called for 7:30. Paunch and I will pick you up at 6:45 for breakfast, okay? Amy can come, too."

"Why don't we just meet you, brother?"

"Sounds good, Paul. There's a little café two blocks down the street from May's. Amy knows where it is. See you then."

"Well, Amy, a brief but brilliant beginning is coming to an end. Phil wants us to have breakfast with him and Paunch. We're called."

"I don't ever want to be away from you, Paul. It's crazy, but I know that in my heart." Amy *was* speaking from the heart, something she was not accustomed to doing. But she was also thinking of her penchant for fulfilling Stephen Stills's 1970 advice, "If you can't be with the one you love, honey, love the one you're with." The thought of anyone else *ever* was so distasteful-sounding at this point that Amy thought it absurd even to consider it. However, she knew how she'd been, how she'd *always* been. She tended to love whoever happened to be in front of her at the time. So here was the dilemma: She *knew* Paul summed up all she ever wanted in a male, by light-years. But she also knew she could not focus. Actually, she could not focus on this thought very long.

"Let's take a shower, Paul," Amy said, laughing as she snapped him with a towel. He grabbed her and hoisted her up onto his broad shoulders as she screamed with laughter, throwing her lovely head back. Neither had put their clothes back on at this point. The shower was nothing less than more physical perfection between a man and a woman. Paul felt like every cell in Amy's beautiful body was attached to his cells with an electrical charge. They had very simply, and very quickly, fallen deeply in love. Logic did not exist.

Paul got out of the shower first, drying off, and noticed Amy's apartment for the first time in the morning light. There were candles and Beanie Babies all over, and a couple of incense-burning miniature adobe huts. There were balloons losing their helium both on the floor and halfway up the wall. There were magazine pictures of various CK models, both male and female, cut out and Scotch-taped to the walls. There were stuffed animals, including a dog, a penguin, and a large Tasmanian devil, Paul's namesake when he was younger and crazier.

Amy's apartment was decorated like a typical teenager's room, though Paul did not consider this at the time.

"Whaddaya think?" Amy said, smiling as she stepped out of the shower holding the towel in her hand, which rested on her beautiful hip as she shifted the weight to that side of her body.

Paul couldn't think. He just stared. Would he ever stop seeing more and more beauty in this awesome young female? Amy's hair was puffed out all over her pretty head in the most beautiful look Paul had ever seen … *again*! It was as if Amy, while showering, had somehow managed to have the most expensive dreadlocks hairdo done. Her auburn hair looked like Raggedy Ann hair, a look that some women paid hundreds to achieve, but like so many of Amy's attributes, she achieved naturally, with her awesome DNA. Paul just looked at his moppet-haired beauty. Yes, *his* moppet-haired beauty. He inwardly thanked God, but was he right to do so?

They had breakfast with Paunch and Phil at Bob's, a little café that had been there as long as anyone remembered, but with different owners. The early-1950s black-and-white paint-peeled neon sign above the entrance no longer worked. It was mounted to the building by rusty steel brackets and simply said, vertically, "Café." No one talked specifics at the quick breakfast. After breakfast, Amy drove her Fury to the depot with Paul, a scene that had occurred hundreds of times before, only without Paul on the passenger's side. "Just My Imagination," the great Temptations song of spring 1972, was playing on Amy's car stereo, and the two sang along. The words almost seemed prophetic. Crews coming in noticed Paul getting out of Amy's car.

"Amy's latest, huh?"

"I guess. She's a busy one."

Paul and Amy embraced, and neither wanted to let go. Although this scene too was a common one at the Central Pacific Depot in Ellisville, the difference this time was that Amy Johnson was truly in love for the first time in her life.

# CHAPTER 26
# B & B

After their train arrived in Kansas City at 3:30 p.m., Paul and Phil finally had a chance to talk. In Ellisville before departure, Paul hadn't been able to speak with his brother in private. After signing in, Paul and Bob Simpson were taken to the rear end of the train by jitney, whereas Phil, Paunch, and Hal merely boarded the train at the yard office depot, where the North Platte railroaders pulled up the eastbound trains in the Ellisville yard.

At the Kansas City terminal, the opposite was true. The jitney picked up the head end, Paunch, Phil, and Hal, and Paul and Bob got off the caboose and walked to the depot. They all arrived about the same time.

"Well, brother, are you in love, heat, or what?" Phil said, with both kidding and some concern.

"Probably, 'or what,' brother," Paul said smiling, with a hint of confusion in his eyes, "but definitely in heat, *and* in love. I'm still not sure what went on. It's like I'm in a different dimension."

"The Twilight Zone?" Phil further attempted to add humor to the situation.

"The Amy Zone," Paunch broke in while tying up on the Federal Register, enjoying the brothers' banter and teasing. "It's quite a membership. There have been many *members* involved."

Paul just shook his head, managing a semi-smile, still mentally and emotionally blitzed from the time with Amy.

Quiet Hal also shook his head. Being the quiet type, he had observed years of railroad insanity. He had seen guys who people never in a million years would have thought capable of stepping out on their wives ... step out. He had seen absurd fights, arguments, physical ailments, and tragedies, and he had seen Amy Johnson seduce literally dozens of railroaders. With few exceptions, most of them fell in love with Amy, given man's basic inability to differentiate between love and sex. Hal was a quiet Christian who respected all and had a great propensity for empathy with his fellow railroaders. No one knew, because Hal was quiet. He did not like to see behaviors that ended in sorrow, and usually, anyone "connected," in any meaning of the word, with Amy somehow ended up in sorrow. To Hal, there seemed to be a malevolent spirit associated with her. Hal said a quiet prayer for the new guy, Paul.

"You got some time, brother?" Paul asked Phil.

"Always," Phil replied. "Let me call Carla and tell her I'm in, and that you and I are going to have a little B & B." "B & B," or "beer and brother," was what Phil and Paul called their times together when something needed to be discussed. Carla knew the code, and she trusted Phil and knew he would never get too much of a snoot full, especially with the advent of seeing the children, who were Phil's "gifts from God." Carla also knew that Paul was extremely important to Phil, as he was to her as well, and understood the necessity of their closeness. She had seen the excitement on Phil's face when he found out Paul was going with him this trip. And Carla was, at times, like Susan was with Barry, beginning "not to care" about Phil's whereabouts as much. She was getting used to a life without him. Phil's "missing in action" a little longer was no big deal to her.

Paul and Phil said their "so-longs" to the rest of their crew and stopped in at a little pub in Kansas City called The Village. There were only a few people in the bar at this time of day: some locals and two manure-faced alcoholics who were there all the time when they weren't picking up their welfare checks.

"Well, Pauly, are you gonna marry her?"

"C'mon, Phil, I'm nuts now. I have never, ever felt like this about anyone. She's so different."

"Different, how? Got an extra leg ... P. T. Barnum stuff?"

"No, *I* do. That's the problem. Really, I don't know how she's different. I can't put my finger on it."

"Sounds like you put *more* than your finger on it."

Paul shook his head and smiled. "I can't exactly tell you what the deal is, Phil. I know I really feel like I *need* her."

"Would it do any good if I told you I've seen more than a few railroaders feel the same way toward Amy Johnson? No, probably not," Phil mumbled, answering his own question with a sigh of futility. "Paul, speaking of P. T. Barnum, have you ever heard, 'Never overestimate the intelligence of the public'?" To Phil, that quote coupled with Gore Vidal's extremely pertinent observation, "Living in a free society, we have the freedom to screw ourselves up," summed up a lot of American life ... probably life throughout many parts of the world.

Paul ignored the Barnum quote, being dominated totally by the physical. He was thinking of Amy's perfect legs, and their incomparable texture. "Phil, you know how we've always talked about electromagnetics?"

"Sure."

"Well, if I multiplied all the tactile sensations I have ever felt by one hundred thousand, that might be close to what I felt when I felt Amy's skin against mine. Even when we first touched hands at May's, it was electrically overwhelming ... I mean, it's crazy."

"Yeah, that *is* crazy. Is it love Paul, or lust?" Phil said now, with seriousness in his tone, still worrying about potentials for his brother. "She's been around, Paul ... I mean *really* around. She *is* a beauty. She's one of the most beautiful females I have ever seen ... maybe *the* most beautiful. But she is a substance abuser, supposedly cocaine, and crack cocaine, and who knows what else. She's addicted to everything. She cannot have enough men. I'm sure that's some form of addiction, too, and I'm sure you used protection, right, Pauly? Did you, Pauly? Paul!?"

"No, actually, Phil, I honestly didn't even think about it."

"You bed down the one woman in Ellisville who is Olympic status in sexual activity, and you don't use a raincoat? Paul, you better have an AIDS test. I've heard stories of Amy burning certain guys with clap, but I always figured with her track record, there would be a more serious STD to consider." Phil did not approve of any form of sex beyond a basic, godly, heterosexual marriage, but he did not pontificate with Paul. One, he had faith that his brother would eventually do the right thing. Two, he'd "been there" in his younger years, and three, he was Paul's brother, not his God.

Paul sipped his beer, just staring off into nowhere. He had all sorts of things on his mind at once. For one, he was wondering, Just what *was* Amy doing now? and he definitely did not like thoughts like that. Paul had never been the jealous type. Phil was, but Paul normally, basically did not care that much ... *until now.* These were not normal, familiar feelings for Paul. Now he could feel himself being drawn into a situation whereby trust was not even to be considered a factor. How do you trust someone like Amy? Or are you ever supposed to? Are you just supposed to "enjoy" her as she is? It wasn't a question of "if" she would ever be with anyone else. It was a question of "when."

"Well, I'm there for you, brother," Phil said unnecessarily, but Paul always appreciated it anyway.

"Thanks, brother. Give Carla and the kids a big sloppy kiss from Brother and Uncle. Throw in the tongue for Carla."

"You bet, Paul." Phil had a sudden feeling of dread for his brother. He had never seen Paul this hung up on a female, and of all females, it had to be Amy Johnson.

Paul and Amy called each other fifteen times before he was called to work again. Sometimes they talked three or four hours. It was shaping up like John and Yoko.

The next trip, Paul caught the KCBL-5, or the Kansas City Big Loser, as the crews called it, since it was a work train. It had been called for 10:00 p.m., and was an agonizingly slow train for Paul. He didn't mind the work involved. He had done much more switching in the yard per shift, by far. But he almost couldn't stand being on the way to see Amy but not yet there. The disgusting but potentially correct thought of her being with someone else would also enter Paul's brain.

Amy had been almost a different person while waiting for Paul to return to Ellisville. The usually flirtatious Amy had stayed totally away from railroad hangouts, something she'd never done before, no matter whom she happened to be going with at the time. Once she had made herself a fixture at the railroad hangouts, she always occupied those haunts, except when having sex, which she accomplished somewhere nearby. Actually, nobody ever had really "gone" with Amy. They just thought they had. As soon as they left town, Amy was with whomever, whenever. That was just Amy. She was the perfect companion for Paul, the way he *used* to be. In fact, Amy was Paul's female counterpart. Amy hunted men the way Paul used to hunt women: sow and reap. But her behavior now was very different.

The KCBL-5 arrived in Ellisville at 10:00 a.m., working twelve hours, the maximum allowable, as prescribed by the Hours of Service Act. Though tedium was evident with twelve-hour shifts, the last four hours were time and a half, which was okay, because it was sweet money. If you couldn't get in for a quit, then overtime, or "OT," was just fine. What railroaders hated was "splitting the whistle," which meant completing their work after exactly eight hours and not receiving either a quit or overtime. In 1968, the act had been amended to allow only fourteen consecutive hours of work, down from sixteen. It was again amended down to twelve hours in 1970, where it remains today. When railroaders worked sixteen straight hours, some never even bothered to go home after a shift, given the substantially short time they would have before having to prepare for work in the morning. Again, it was no wonder they drank.

As the caboose rolled across Main Street, Paul could see the depot, and the red '63 Fury that was parked in the parking lot. Some railroaders Paul did not recognize were leaning toward the window on the driver's side. Paul just sighed.

Paul stepped off the caboose on one side as his rear brakeman, Don Arthur, stepped off the other. "Hi, Paul," a high-energy, scratchy and excited, musical voice yelled from the parking lot. Amy was waving wildly.

"Amy, what you want to do?" Paul sang like his brother to Amy, and couldn't help but smile. He actually felt like his feminine side, his "completion," was in the parking lot waiting for him. Ned Lingle—Paul, Phil, and Barry's friend who played high school football with them—was now a Baptist preacher. Ned said he thought that in God's eyes, the "perfect person" was a man and a woman together. Ned definitely had a spiritual gift.

Paul made several mistakes tying up, which Don corrected. On the trip up, he had mentioned to Don he was going with Amy, and watched

Don stare down at the floor, trying to hide a grin. Don knew Paul would be as dizzy as most who had been involved with Amy.

Amy was waiting outside the yard office when Paul opened the door. She ran and jumped on him, throwing her arms around his neck and her gorgeous legs around his waist. Paul was in heaven on earth. Nothing else mattered right now. He was where he was supposed to be: with Amy.

Amy was giggling, she was so happy to see Paul. They drove immediately to her apartment, and again launched into the precious Amy and Paul Electromagnetic Review. The song "Feels Like the First Time" by Foreigner went through Paul's stupor-engulfed head.

This time, rather than lie next to each other, Amy and Paul just held each other … and held, and held, and held. Paul, who was extremely "short-rested," as railroaders called it, from working all night, substituting work for sleep as railroaders often did, eventually closed his eyes. Amy, who also hadn't slept, with the excitement and expectation of Paul's arrival, closed hers about the same time. They were soul mates, at least for now, if not forever.

They awoke about the same time. Amy had awakened just before Paul, and was staring at his incredibly handsome face, watching him breathe. She had kissed his cheek tenderly, which woke him. They just continued holding each other, staring into each other's eyes and saying nothing. They both felt an overwhelming, massive concern for the other—again, something previously very foreign to them both. Eventually, the cherished staring gave way to more tactile stimulations, and they were again two bodies as one, each never feeling as complete as they now felt. They showered with constant teasing and laughing, with Paul once again marveling at Amy's incredibly beautiful thick, wet hair. Boy, did God bless this one physically, he thought.

Then the phone rang, an unwelcome reminder that there was an outside world. Paul had two thoughts simultaneously: I wonder which one of her former conquests this is, and I forgot to see how many times out we were. Amy reached for the phone.

"Hello," she answered musically.

"Hi, Amy."

"Hi, Judy! It's Judy, my sponsor," Amy happily semiwhispered to Paul. "You what? Well, maybe. Remember me telling you about the guy

I met? Well, he's here, now. No, that's okay. We just took a shower. Can I call you back? Okay, bye," she said sweetly.

"That was my sponsor, Judy Grant. Paul, I go to Alcoholics Anonymous meetings—y'know, AA? I was addicted to crack at one time and this local church lady said I should go to AA to make sure I have the support from others who have past addictions. I met Judy there. She's sort of a mother for me. She's older and has been clean for ten years. She's an alcoholic."

# Chapter 27
## Sometimes the Baggage Is Too Large to Carry On

"Are you clean, Amy?"

"Been clean a year."

"That's good stuff, Amy." Paul would later buy Amy a gold bracelet. He would have it inscribed, "Good Stuff, Amy Johnson" to represent her being drug-free for a year, although he was not entirely sure she was.

"I'm doin' real good, but I want to tell you, Paul, my life has been one long crazy situation. You have no idea. I know I'm not right. I've got problems, you know. And I feel like I'm really in love with you … *really* in love with you!" The words sprang out of her before she realized what she had said and repeated, but she continued. "I feel like you are a part of me, Paul, *already*. It's like you're supposed to be my man, the special one I've never had. Am I crazy?"

"Well, if you are, Amy, it's folie à deux."

"It's what?" Amy said, obviously totally confused.

"We learned it in psychology. It's when two people share the same delusion." Paul could tell Amy had not spent much time in the educational world. "In other words, I love you, too, Amy, and I love you ridiculously strongly. And no, it doesn't make sense."

Amy looked relieved. She wasn't sure at first if what Paul was trying to explain was good or bad. She felt inferior, just one of the many feelings that motivated her various behaviors. "Paul, this is all new to me. I almost don't want to have to feel this way. I can tell it was easier not to care."

"I know exactly what you mean, Amy. I was always happier when I didn't have to care. There's responsibility in caring. And then you have to care in the correct manner. It seems better not to care much, and I really haven't, until now."

"I don't think I ever have either, Paul. All I know is, I feel *so* different with you."

"Me, too," Paul agreed. There would be a lot of conversations like this one between Paul and Amy over the next few months. One would say something, and the other would feel exactly the same and say, "Me, too."

"Judy wants to come by to meet you. Can she, Paul? Or maybe we could all go out to eat together. Okay?"

"That would be fine, Amy."

"I'm starved. Let's go to May's. I'll call Judy and have her meet us there." Amy was excited about the prospect of Paul and Judy meeting. She loved them both so much. Judy had met Amy the first night she attended AA in Ellisville three years earlier, and had asked her if she needed a sponsor. The two had immediately bonded, probably because of the void they filled in each other's lives. Judy had one daughter who was grown, but didn't associate with her because of Judy's actions when she was involved in her alcohol addiction. Part of the role of AA is to have the members come to grips with their own behaviors, and make restitution with those whose lives they hurt while addicted. Judy had said and done some horrible things to her daughter, who thus far had not forgiven her. It had caused many a lonely, crying, suicide-thought-filled night for Judy. She had tried to make amends with her daughter, to no avail. Amy filled the daughter void for Judy.

And Amy needed a mother since her own mother had little to do with her, ever. Amy's mother had divorced her father before Amy was born. Amy never knew her father was always there hiding behind the bleachers as she struck out the side, or hit home runs many times in softball. Over the years, she hadn't seen him much at all. All Amy had was her son and daughter, whom she tried to put out of her head, because thinking of them and being unable to see them was too painful. Later, Paul would look back on their relationship and realize that much of Amy's outward joy was a cover for the tragic losses she suffered in her life. She had no dad or mom around, or siblings. Her children were with whomever—she didn't know. She just knew they were somewhere in San Antonio, and hoped beyond hope that she'd see them again someday. She fantasized about how joyous that day would be, not unlike Whoopi Goldberg's great character in Spielberg's fantastic *The Color Purple.* Meanwhile, many men had come, and many men had gone (some women, too). But in the three years Amy had been in Ellisville, Judy had remained as her friend, guidance counselor, and mother figure. The only problem with this arrangement was that Judy's elevator did not always access the top floors, because of the billions of brain cells she had destroyed with her years of drinking. In some ways, Amy having Judy as her sponsor and mentor was akin to "the blind leading the blind."

At May's, the Angus burgers were smelling very good. As Amy and Paul entered, they heard, "Over here, you guys." Railroaders from Kansas City and North Platte were diving into May's good-tasting food, and noticing Amy's latest conquest. Paul felt the stares, but basically did not care that much.

"Paul, this is Judy. Judy, this is Paul," Amy said with the standard merriment in her voice.

"Hi, Judy, how are ya?" Paul asked, only minimally caring to really know. He had unintentionally, but correctly, assessed Judy as possessive when it came to Amy. Paul wasn't so sure that the two of them hadn't sailed off to the Isle of Lesbos, as Cliff Clavin used to say on *Cheers.*

"Just fine, Paul. Nice to meet you." Judy smiled a polite but flaky smile at Paul. Amy didn't catch any of this. "We're going to the meeting tonight, Paul. Did Amy tell you?"

"No, this is the first I've heard."

"I have to go to the meeting tonight, Paul. They meet every night. The first year, I went every night. You have to. But then, when they think your addiction is under control after a year clean, you can cut down to three times a week. They don't like to see you going less than that."

Paul wondered if these meetings were a way for Judy to keep Amy close, over and above the obvious good AA did for people. He would also wonder later on if the meetings were just a social event. But he didn't give it much thought. With his psychology training in college, he knew that AA was a great organization, and that through it, many had experienced success where only heartache and failure had been before.

"It's from 7:00 to 9:00 p.m., Paul," Amy said. "I'll take you by the apartment after we eat, and I'll just come right back there when the meeting's over. Is that okay, honey?"

"Sure it's okay, baby," Paul said, the love talk already coming naturally for both. "I'll check to see how far out I am." Knowing how precious their time was together, both had second thoughts about the meeting, but they also both knew it was necessary. They finished their burgers, and Paul and Judy said their flaky good-byes to each other outside of May's. Then Amy and Paul drove back to her apartment.

Paul did a shoulder roll on the bed, a move he'd done since he was a child. Amy playfully jumped on him, and they began to laugh and pinch and wrestle. This gave way of course, to the powerful, sensation-intensive Amy and Paul Electromagnetic Review. When they were again through, if they ever really were, they once again looked into each other's eyes and saw what they both thought to be their absolute destinies. It was almost eerie.

"Paul, I may hurt you, honey," Amy said, surprising herself by speaking totally from the heart.

"Amy, this ol' heart is so full of gristle and scar tissue, I doubt if you can. Now don't take that as a challenge, but let's just say it's unlikely. I'm a big boy. If it happens, it happens, but I'm not going to let that possibility ruin the absolute joy I feel just being near you and touching you."

"Good, Paul. Good." Amy smiled a not-so-self-assuring smile. "I'm not right, you know. I've got a real bad past, and I really don't know if it *is* past. They say there's only a 15 percent chance I will stay off crack, Paul. I've slept with a lot of guys. I'm a mess. My mind changes sometimes. But you know, I've never had a one-night stand."

Paul thought Amy's comment might have been a cryptic way of saying either, "I've always stayed at least two nights" or "It didn't occur at night."

"Paul, I've been married, and I have two kids, Jason and Megan." Amy did not tell Paul they were not from her husband. "See?" She pulled pictures out from a dresser drawer. "Aren't they beautiful?"

"Yes they are," Paul smiled, admiring the children's heritage. "Look who their mother is."

"I can't keep their pictures out to see them all the time, Paul. It hurts too much, because I can't see 'em in person." Tears were forming in her beautiful bluish-purple lasers.

"Why not?" Paul asked, thinking he may be able to help.

"It's too complicated, Paul. When I was in my addiction, you know …"

"I understand." Paul tried to be supportive, knowing all the possibilities. "Maybe I can help, Amy."

"Maybe someday, Paul," Amy said with a look of half hope, half hopelessness, as she dried her tears with a Kleenex. "Right now I don't even know where they are. The state took them. My mom doesn't care. She's nuts. She's only concerned with herself. I can see why she wouldn't like me, 'cause I'm so screwed up. But I don't understand how she couldn't like her own grandkids. They didn't do anything. They deserve more." Amy's tears began again, knowing her own pitiful approach to motherhood was the basic reason for any suffering her kids might be undergoing. She knew it shouldn't be her mother's responsibility. Amy felt like getting high. That's why she was going to AA. And that's the way it was with addicts. Which came first, the chicken or the egg? Their behaviors in their addictions rendered their past, and sometimes present, lives so unbearable that they would slip back into their addictions to escape, exhibiting more disgusting behaviors, leading to more horrid history to escape from, with more drugs and alcohol. This extremely vicious circle made the devil very happy; the Bible says he has definite purposes: "to kill, to steal, and to destroy." So far, he'd stolen and destroyed Amy's family and, to a certain extent, her life. "I'm no good, Paul."

"You're all right as far as I'm concerned," Paul semi-lied. What that meant was, Amy was all right in his eyes because he loved her, but he was aware she had problems. "Amy, I haven't exactly been a monk … More like a mink, myself. I'm not proud of that, but it's truthful. I've got a kid, too, Amy. Rosalinda is living with her mother, who rarely lets me see her. It's really hard sometimes." Paul shook his head as he showed Amy a beautiful billfold picture of Rosalinda.

"She's gorgeous, Paul. She looks like you. Paul, would you think I was silly if I thought God put you in my life?"

Paul immediately felt a comforting warmth and peace literally flow over him. What a wonderful thing for Amy to have said. He thought about that evening in his house three months ago, and the conversation with God, through the Sacred Heart of Jesus picture Uncle Phil had given him.

"Not only would I think it was *not* silly, Amy, but I have wondered that myself, about you. I have never felt this way about another female in my life. Maybe God *did* put us together for some purpose."

"I mean, in AA, we're supposed to get in touch with our higher power. I haven't really known much about God, you know. One time, when I was in this place in San Antonio, you know, I met this older lady. She was real nice. She showed me some things to read in the Bible. It made me feel better, really."

"That's great, Amy. My brother and I talk about God a lot. You know Phil. He is real devout. He tries to be like Christ. Our parents are real good people, never missing church. Me ... I know I could do better. For instance, Amy, ever since we've met, as much in love with you as I am already, and love being intimate with you, I keep feeling like we've been *sinning*." Paul felt the word squeeze out of his mouth, and wondered why he had even said it. "That thought has never crossed my mind before."

"*Does* it feel like sin to you, Paul?"

"A little, honey, but mostly, it feels like *love*," Paul said as he reached for Amy's cheek and caressed it with his thumb while his fingers held her under her perfectly chiseled jaw and well-sculpted right ear. "Awesome love."

"Me, too, Paul," Amy said, tearing up a bit. "When I do it with the other guys, it's like going to the bathroom, you know. It's like my body thinks it needs it. I'm not even sure sometimes if I really do need it. But when I first saw you, my knees were knockin', Paul. Could you tell? That's never happened to me before. Guys are guys. I was so nervous when I walked over to you, I thought you'd see me shakin' for sure. But after we made love the first time, I asked God, 'Did you give him to me, Lord?'"

"I've asked Him, too, Amy. I want to do what's right in His eyes, but I know I don't. And I really want to do right by you."

"Thanks, Paul," Amy said, feeling the emotional wear and tear beginning. "You want to play some catch before I go to the meeting?"

"Sure."

# CHAPTER 28
# PERFECT FOR PAUL

Amy tossed the catcher's mitt to Paul as they walked outside behind the apartment building. "Stand up against the wall, Paul. I may be wild. I'll warm up first."

Amy fired an underhand fast pitch to Paul that totally impressed him. "Where did you learn to throw like that? That's a warm-up?"

"All I did when I was a kid was play softball, Paul." Amy's arm seemed like it could go forever. She got stronger and stronger, and the ball made a loud *POP!* when it hit the mitt. Paul pulled his left index finger out of the mitt and put it behind the index finger of the glove, giving him extra padding. "You're awesome, Amy." He looked at her comprehensively, thinking, What a total package of womanhood. He imagined he was playing catch with the woman he was always meant to have, his *real* wife. He looked at the smiling beauty and her fluid motion, and imagined what an awesome child they could have … Talk about "Welcome to Fantasy Island." He had met this girl only four days ago. What he didn't know was that Amy was thinking the exact same thing. She had been admiring the way Paul had scooped her low pitches out of the dirt, and watching his suntanned, muscular body move in fluid motion. The motherhood instinct was surfacing.

They finished playing catch, and Amy left to pick up Judy and head to the meeting. Paul called in and found out he was three times out with four trains coming. He would get out that evening. Amy had told Paul, although the meetings were only from 7:00 to 9:00, that they stayed afterward and talked about the meeting, something Amy, and especially Judy, felt was extremely beneficial. The time went by like days to Paul. Every second with Amy was valuable, and he was losing precious hours here. At 8:30 p.m., Paul was called for 10:00 p.m. on the eastbound NPKC-6, the sister van train of the westbound KCNP train that had initially brought him to Amy just four days before. At 9:45 p.m. Paul heard Amy's keys rattling outside the door as the lock disengaged.

"Honey, I'm home," Amy teased.

"Honey, I'm gone," Paul responded.

"What? What's the matter, honey? Oh, no!" Amy's demeanor changed immediately from playful to sorrowful.

"I got called. We're leaving in fifteen minutes."

"Darn it, honey." Amy grabbed Paul. "You just got here. I'm sorry, baby." Amy was referring to her absence for her AA attendance, knowing it took away from their precious time. "Here." Amy stretched her hand toward Paul with a card in it.

Paul took the unsealed envelope and lifted out the card. There was a little Precious Moments girl on the front with a beautiful, shy smile. When Paul opened the card, he saw the words, "You're in my heart. You're in my mind. You're in my prayers. I love you. Amy."

Paul grabbed her and pulled her on the bed, where they just held each other until five minutes till ten. Amy and Paul then sped to the depot, allowing for only a quick kiss and hug. After the kiss, Amy had a devilish look in her eyes that Paul found almost as a sign of multiple personality disorder. It was a change in demeanor from sorrow for Paul's leaving to almost impudence.

"You think you can handle me, Paul?" Amy teased.

Paul thought to himself, No man can handle you, Amy ... but God can. (Why didn't he tell her that?)

"Sure!" Paul yelled over his shoulder as he ran for the yard office. Paul managed a laugh, but was worried at the thought of Amy's comment almost being a challenge, like, "How much crap can you take, Paul, because I plan to issue you some."

As Paul zoomed into the yard office, Don said, "It's okay, Paul. I already got you in."

"Thanks, Don. You're outstanding."

They arrived in Kansas City at 9:45 a.m. Paul was pooped. He got in his Ford F-150 truck after tying up, and went home, his mind a mix of love, what-ifs, jealousies—yes, *jealousies*—and worry. Paul wasn't used to this. This love stuff was baloney. He thought about the J. Geils Band, when they put out "Love Stinks."

The next few months would find Amy and Paul in Ellisville like "The Incredible Two-headed Transplant," except for the evenings Amy attended AA with Judy. Paul tried his best to be understanding of Amy's AA meetings, knowing the ultimate good it offered her. But at the same time, he was feeling like he wasn't part of "the gang." He had gotten to know many of Amy's closer friends, men and women in the group. Amy had told him stories about the different affairs that were spawned within the group by the affiliation with one another. It had sort of worried Paul, especially one guy named Lance Alward. Lance had been going to the meetings for several years, and was one of the keynote speakers. He was a local success story, starting his own construction business after he had "cleaned up." He then had hired many of the group members to work for him.

As a result, Lance was a local hero, and Paul was not really comfortable with Amy's obvious admiration for and attraction to Lance. Evidently, some poor woman who had fallen into the addiction of alcoholism had come to one of the meetings a couple of years before. She was extremely attractive. Lance had made it his business to personally counsel this woman, who was married. An affair ensued between the two. The woman had come to AA seeking healing. But instead, at the hands and other body parts of Lance, she had severely damaged her first attempt to become "clean." The situation had provoked her to drink more, feeling hopelessly torn between her loyal husband and Lance. Eventually, she was able to re-rail herself and return to her understanding husband, saving her marriage. Lance, however, hadn't fared as well, and was still in love with this woman. Every time she came to a meeting after their breakup, Lance had to leave in emotional distress.

Of course, Paul naturally thought this a potential for Amy also. The word was taught to him by a service buddy years before: "propinquity." Propinquity described the attraction between people that occurred from working together, or experiencing the same things, that eventually turned into love. Examples were the boss-subordinate, doctor-nurse, or perhaps, local AA hero–Amy. Paul could see that as a potential, but at the same time, he didn't want to throw a wet blanket on what was only potential. He had to admit, he didn't like the way Amy revered Lance. She made a point of saying how beautiful the woman with whom Lance had the affair was. It seemed to matter to Amy that Lance could get someone beautiful. It evidently did not matter to her that she was a married woman who had come to AA for help. Paul had met Lance and wasn't impressed, but then, he wouldn't have been. Paul felt many times that although there were many very nice, sincere people in AA, many of them acted as if those who were not addicts were the ones with the problems. It was a defense mechanism that said, "We're the cool ones. You're the odd ones." Everything is perspective. It all depends on which side of the glass you're on. Paul learned a lot in the next three months, and at times felt he might be hurting Amy's recovery more than helping it.

He wasn't good with sharing her, and Amy loved to be shared. And for a complete recovery, she *needed* to be shared with AA. Amy had rented the film *When a Man Loves a Woman*, with Meg Ryan and Andy Garcia, to help Paul understand what it would be like to be in love with a substance abuser. He had to admit, it really helped him to understand. But in the movie, Andy at least had Meg and the kids for a while, before he had to share her with the AA entourage. Paul was just *beginning* his relationship with Amy by sharing her. It wasn't easy.

Sometimes Amy would leave her Fury for Paul to drive while she attended the meetings. She would ride with either Judy or Lance. When Lance would bring Amy home from the meetings, and they sat and talked in the apartment parking lot in Lance's truck, Paul would be livid. Maybe it was selfish, but Paul would reason, "I'm going to be called anytime, and she's talking with him. She could do it when I wasn't here." Amy would finally come in, and Paul would not be in the best of moods, and they would not feel good toward each other. This was a major relationship difference from the feelings of celebration that usually occurred between them. This further convinced Paul he might be detrimental to Amy's ultimate well-being, a thought totally distasteful to him. If Paul even glimpsed a potential for his presence being detrimental to anyone, he was *gone* in a Nike Swoosh.

At one point, a couple of months after their initial contact, Amy asked Paul if he wanted to have a baby with her. Paul thought it would be wonderful, much to the chagrin of his brother, Phil. "Paul, are you out of your box?" Phil would ask. "You haven't known her very long. The girl is not stable. What if she goes on a crack binge while she's pregnant? Then you can raise a little crack baby by yourself. Or what if she runs off? Have you had an AIDS test yet?" Paul knew there was a lot of nonexistent logic in this relationship, but it was those darned electromagnetic sensations. And all Paul could visualize was the offspring, boy or girl. What a little beauty he or she would be, and what awesome potential. Of course, neither Paul nor Amy ever gave any thought to a potential like the supposed verbal contact between Marilyn Monroe and Albert Einstein. Purportedly, Marilyn called Albert, suggesting that they have a baby together. "It would be terrific to have a child together," she supposedly said. "With your brains, and my beauty, the child would be perfect."

Einstein evidently replied, "Ah, Marilyn, but what if the child had your brains and my beauty?" But in the case of Paul and Amy's offspring, the looks would be there from either side, that is, unless Amy screamed and jumped back into crack while pregnant. Then the result would be a total crapshoot, with dice loaded for craps. Paul was never much of a gambler either.

But reality checks were few and far between. All Paul could see was Amy. The thought of having a baby with Amy had been so much fun, however absurd the prospect. It was a very good thing Rose and Harold didn't know about this. They only vaguely knew about Amy, and didn't know her background. Mercifully, both Phil and Paul referred to Amy as a pretty Ellisville girl. It would have cost Harold and Rose a few sleepless nights if they had known the whole story. But Amy would get her little calendar out, and count backward and forward from her periods, trying to calculate the days to make sure they "did it" at the right time of the month to create a child. And on those days, they would make love all day. Then they would worry that they were doing it so much that Paul's sperm count could be lowering. Amy also thought she might have been injured during one of her abortions to the point of never being able to conceive again … just a wee bit different from *The Donna Reed Show*.

Amy would giggle and get so excited about the prospect of being pregnant with Paul's child that she would buy and use test kits too early for the pregnancy hormone to show up. Then they would have to buy additional kits. It was great fun asking the local pharmacist questions about conception. One time the ring appeared like she was pregnant, and Amy missed her period that same time. The prospect of conceiving and parenting a child made both Amy and Paul feel even more deliriously happy and in love. Amy even had names picked out, which Paul liked: Roman Carlos if a boy, and Alison Rose, after Paul's mom, if a girl. They felt like their lives of coexistence were indeed predestined. But Amy did not get pregnant.

# CHAPTER 29
# GOOD RAIL TO BAD RAIL

Paul and Amy were browsing in J. C. Penney one time, and looked at rings. Amy really liked the thought of marriage with Paul. Having him home with her in their little house was a dream too wonderful for her to totally conceive. "In a cozy little home in the country with two children, maybe three," the Temptations would harmonize in her pretty head from "Just My Imagination," one of Amy's favorite songs. She remembered the first time she and Paul were together when they heard it on the oldies station Amy left on all the time in her Fury. They had heard it on the way to the depot after leaving breakfast with Phil and Paunch that first morning. Amy had begun to sing, and Paul had chimed in. Neither spoke to the other until after it was finished. "That was beautiful," Paul had said.

"You know it," Amy said in a soft, sweet voice. The song had remained on Paul's mind all the way back to Kansas City that first trip out. It had been Paul's favorite song in the spring of 1972. It fit in with the warm days of spring the way hot butter did on popcorn. The song became *their* song from that point forward. Amy bought the CD, and listened to it for hours when Paul was in Kansas City. The beautiful visual of "a cozy little home in the country, with two children, maybe three," coupled with the Temps' beautiful falsetto harmonies, was so relaxing and so pleasant to her, thinking about the future with Paul. The thought and the music were beautiful, and soothing to Amy's normally cluttered mind.

When Paul came to town and they went to her apartment, Amy would put in the CD first thing, and they would dance slowly and lovingly, holding each other in the perfection that was theirs only. The rest of the world would disappear. Amy and Paul would sing the song softly together, and when it came to the "cozy little home" part, they would look into each other's eyes and visualize that maybe there *would* be a reality for them someday to have that. When the "with two children, maybe three" part came, Paul and Amy would both sing, "with three children, maybe four," allowing for Rosalinda, Jason, Megan, and one of their own. Amy loved it. It was sweet ... sometimes very sweet. Amy, who always needed contact with others, *any* others, was amazed at how most of the time now, all she wanted was Paul and the children. All she needed was Paul and the children.

Paul really wanted Amy as his wife, but obviously, only with the assurance that she would remain clean and decent. Even assuming that, would her ADHD even allow her to *be* home once in a while? As much as he loved her, he wasn't sure he could love her enough to share her constantly with the world. He understood easily that individuality was also important. And he knew couples needed time for individual pursuits, as long as those pursuits weren't detrimental to either. But Amy seemed always to be going somewhere, or meeting someone, usually associated with AA, and Paul didn't know if he could handle that on a permanent basis. Maybe that was not proper love, or at least not enough understanding love for what Amy needed. Maybe she *would* be better with someone from AA. He wanted what was right for Amy, and maybe he *was* more of a detriment for her total recovery than a support. So he had reservations. One time when he, Amy, and Judy were having coffee together at May's, Amy went to the bathroom, leaving an uncomfortable silence to linger between Paul and Judy. Finally, after about a minute that seemed like fifteen, Judy said authoritatively, "Paul, you know if Amy doesn't complete her recovery, she won't be any good for you or anybody else."

Paul had suspected that Judy viewed him as a complication, rather than a help to Amy's recovery. And although he correctly assessed Judy's comment as based somewhat on jealousy, he also knew Judy genuinely cared for Amy. He nodded in agreement as he pondered her comment. But given his monumental love for Amy, surpassing anything he had ever felt for any other female, he figured in the long run he *would* be good for Amy. Whether or not he was with her, he was always aware of the desire he had for her, well over and above the physical. But Amy, it seemed, was always on the move. If Paul wanted, like Ashford and Simpson wrote, and Marvin and Tammy sang, to "stand by you like a tree," to stand by Amy, that tree would have to be planted in a big pot on wheels.

The ring Amy liked in J. C. Penney was constructed simply, but tastefully beautifully, with a row of five marquis-cut diamonds, her favorite shape in her favorite stones. It was absolutely beautiful, and Amy knew she would never have it. Paul bought it for her and surprised her with it one evening while they walked together at Ellisville Park. He got down on one knee and proposed. Both were laughing with joy as he held the ring up toward his beautiful fiancée. "Amy, will you marry me?" he asked, knowing the answer and looking into those awesome bluish-purple smiling eyes. Amy stopped laughing and didn't say anything kidding or in jest. Her loud, happy demeanor changed to one of quiet, joyful peace. Tears immediately formed in her bluish-purple laser eyes. Her hands began to tremble. A calm, pleasant smile formed on her exquisitely beautiful face. As she took the ring from Paul, she said simply, sweetly, and seriously, "Yes."

The next few weeks were to be so poignant for them that neither would ever forget the closeness that definitely defied logic. They constantly exchanged cards with each other, all with gentle, considerate thoughts written inside. Once Amy gave Paul a card she had made herself. It had a cartoon of a little cleaning lady on the front with a cute smile and a mop in her hands. Amy had cleaned houses and trailers for extra money at times. On the inside, Amy had put in her own honest words what she loved about Paul. He had never had another card like it in his life. He took it to Kinko's to have it laminated. He kept it with him in his grip while on the road at all times, taking it out when he returned to Kansas City and putting it on his dresser. He thought that even though Amy had a tough time remaining sincere, when she was, she *was*, and the card exemplified it. He would cherish it forever, no matter what.

They even had their own star. Without first conferring with each other, both tended to gaze at a certain beautiful star while walking through Ellisville Park in the evenings. Ellisville Park was built on a slight hill surrounded by huge oaks and sycamores, except on the west side, where the park was open into a huge field. This opened up a large portion of the western late summer sky. The magnetically bright star capturing both Paul's and Amy's attention was to the left of the Big Dipper. If the curvature of the arc of the Big Dipper handle is followed, it points to this beautiful star. One of Amy's young AA friends was taking an astronomy class at the local community college. Amy had asked her if she knew what star it was. She told Amy it was Arcturus. Amy had pointed out the star to Paul and told him the name, telling him the star reminded her of him. She said she had started noticing it when they first became a couple. Paul told her he had thought exactly the same thing, only he hadn't known the name of the star. It was another "Me, too." Why had he and Amy both fixated on Arcturus at the same time? Was God directing them? *Something* seemed to be. Arcturus then became *their* star.

They also shared a mutual love and appreciation for exotic animals. To Rose's ultimate dismay, Paul had always liked snakes and lizards as a kid. He still did. Rose could always handle (not literally) the lizards, but hated snakes. Amy had a pet ball python she had named Rex. She also loved guinea pigs. Rex would have loved them, too. Pets, as well as the children, became a part of Paul and Amy's vision of "a cozy little home in the country" together.

No, this was not an ordinary relationship. Too many coincidences occurred for it all to be chance, and yet Paul never once thought that the joy he and Amy had shared in these last few months would be anything more than fleeting. Unlike Paul, Amy rarely gave a sustained thought to the potential pitfalls of their union. Her life history on the streets did not allow her brain to think in those "what-if" terms. Amy was a reactor, not a thinker. It wasn't as though she sought out the "no good." Amy never had evil intent. She simply responded to stimuli in her environment. She was going to survive in any social situation, and was just as comfortable in an AA meeting as she was when she was into crack addiction, street life, or group sex, or when she was in prison. It was all the same to Amy, who had been left to fend for herself on the streets of San Antonio from childhood. All this extra baggage was not easy for Paul. He used to think, Everyone's got baggage, but Amy's could fill a C5-A. But more than compensating for this baggage was the corresponding almost delirious happiness Amy was able to give Paul. It was like the opening sentence in *A Tale of Two Cities*: "It was the best of times, it was the worst of times ..."

And that's how it went, an uncertain future, but with each holding the other in higher regard than each held themselves, a real change for them both. Again, Ned Lingle hit it on the head: "Love is when someone else's needs are more important than your own." Amen. That's the way it was with Paul and Amy, at least for a few months. Amy had told Paul this was her first normal relationship, and it felt wonderful to her. It *was* a wonderful time, but as Paul always knew, it was only a matter of time. As much in common as Amy and Paul had, there was that darned baggage from Amy's inescapable past, the foundation that was truly and literally "cracked," Paul thought. Paul was certainly willing to forgive and overlook, but the habits and traits Amy had developed over the last twenty-nine years were indelibly printed on her emotional and psychological makeup.

Phil and Paul talked often, but one time, about a month after Paul and Amy met, Phil called to see specifically if his brother was okay emotionally. "Hey, Pauly, everything copacetic?"

"So far, so good, brother," Paul answered, knowing exactly what Phil was asking about. "She's just wonderful."

"Paul, as your brother, I need to ask you this: Have you ever thought about what God wants out of this deal?"

"All the time, Philsy. Amy and I pray for each other and our relationship daily. We kneel side by side by the bed, and say the Lord's Prayer."

"Is this before, or after the fornication *in* the bed?" Phil asked, not trying to be judgmental, but just to put the idea before his brother.

"I guess sometimes, both."

"Well, the devil makes a whole lot of things look, feel, sound, smell, and taste good ... All of the above, with Amy. Look at the horror she's caused in people's lives she's touched. I know it's not totally her fault, but reality is reality. I think you would agree, Amy has done some of the devil's best work, and totally mindlessly at that. Remember how Mom used to tell us the devil is not going to appear to us as a fifteen-foot-tall red cat, with horns and a tail? She said if he tipped his hand like that, people would hammer him with God and the Bible. So he appears in a manner that is pleasing to our senses, a trick of the angel of light. I just don't want you to be a victim, Paul."

"I understand," Paul replied with a sigh and some reluctance, but knowing his brother was right. "I think maybe the Holy Spirit has been convicting me, because I've been thinking a lot about it lately, actually. We were in bed one time, and Amy was still asleep. I reached for the remote and clicked on the tube. Pastor John Hagee was on. He was right in the middle of a stern warning when the sound first began. He was saying, 'The Bible doesn't say to merely walk away from fornication, but it says, *"flee fornication!"'* Pastor Hagee shouted it." Phil and Paul both liked John Hagee because not only was it obvious that he was a devout man who spoke with the spirit's voice, but he was *tough*, like Phil and Paul were. They also thought they'd heard that Pastor Hagee had played football at the University of Missouri, Phil and Paul's semi–alma mater. "I thought he was talking directly to me, Phil."

"Maybe *he* wasn't, but maybe the Holy Spirit *was,* through him," Phil suggested.

"But you know, Phil, remember that part in Corinthians? I can't remember if it's first or second Corinthians. I have started to read the Bible, and it stuck in my mind one time. I think it says you can do it with them if you marry them."

"It's Corinthians 7:36, I think. What it says is, 'But if a man behaveth himself uncomely toward his virgin, if she passeth the flower of her age, and her need so require, let him do what he will, he sinneth not. *Let them marry.'"*

"That's *it,* Phil! It sounds like if you marry the woman, and I asked Amy to marry me"—Phil winced on the other end of the phone—"it's okay, if you make an honest relationship out of it, eventually joined together before God, you know?"

"First of all, Paul, I don't think Amy has passed the flower of her age at twenty-nine. There have been enough bees pollinating that flower to prove that, so that right there trumps the whole deal. But I'm not sure what is meant there. I've heard it refers to a woman's hymen, and I've heard it refers to the cessation of menstruation, quite a wide age range in the female physiology. I honestly don't know. Anyway, according to the scripture to which you're referring, if you don't marry the girl, it's like retroactive fornication. But what I do know, Paul, is that in James

4:3 it says, 'You ask and receive not because you ask amiss, that you may consume it upon your lusts.' In other words, God is not even going to answer prayer while you are lusting and fornicating. You and Amy might as well be playing bingo as expect prayers to be answered while you're sinning. If you marry her, that's a different story."

"It doesn't feel like lust, Phil. It feels like love," Paul said slowly, thinking about it, and about the joy he felt with Amy. "But," he added reluctantly with a sigh, "sometimes it *does* feel like sin."

"Pastor Adrian Rogers says, 'When God saves you, He doesn't fix it so you can't sin anymore. He fixes it so you can't enjoy it anymore.' Ask for God's guidance, brother. You'll get it," Phil assured his brother.

"This is just great, Phil … A little good news and a little bad news."

"I know, Pauly. God bless, brother."

"God bless you, too. Phil, will you do me a favor? Will you pray for Amy and me?"

"Sure I will, Pauly. I will pray for you both. I always pray for you anyway. See you."

"I love you, brother," Paul said in a quiet voice. "See you."

Phil prayed.

There was to be a Halloween party at Ellisville for the AA members. Amy had been all excited about it, and was going as either Elvira or a female werewolf. She didn't make up her mind until October 30, when she finally bought the Elvira costume. She felt good about the choice. She had tried it on for Judy and Lance. Naturally, she looked incredibly beautiful, her gorgeous, perfect leg protruding through the slit in the black dress. The black wig that came with the costume accented her bluish-purple eyes. Paul hadn't seen the costume yet. On Halloween, the night of the party, Paul arrived in Ellisville at 9:00 p.m. He had gotten a ride to Amy's apartment, for which he had a key. He knew ahead of time Amy would be at the party. In the parking lot he saw the red Fury, for which he also had a key. He figured she must've gone to the party with either Judy or Lance.

When he opened the door, there was a note on the table: "Hi, honey. I love you. I'll call you, okay? Love, Amy." Paul had previously, as usual, called Amy to tell her what time his train would be arriving, so she knew he was in town. Amy never called. Paul knew where the party was, but was afraid of what he might find when he got there, so he didn't go.

Also, Amy hadn't actually invited him to come. It could have just been oversight with Amy's cluttered brain, but Paul felt she was somehow ambivalent about his being there. Amy could be having a sexual relapse, or drug relapse, or too many margaritas, or all of the above. Paul was tired. He had two rum and Cokes and went to bed.

The next morning, Paul awoke to the jingling of Amy's keys banging on the door as she turned the latch. He had barely slept at all, expecting her at any time all through the night. When she pushed open the door, he sat up in bed and sleepily scooted back to the headboard for support. He clasped his big hands behind his head. Amy was still wearing the Elvira costume, but had her black wig in her hand. Her hair was a mess. She looked as if she'd just gotten out of some bed.

"I guess you're pretty mad at me, huh?" Amy looked guilty, like a dog that had gotten into the trash.

"*Mad* probably isn't the word, Amy. Maybe *disappointed* would fit better," Paul said, trying very hard not to be emotionally controlled by the situation. "But I guess I have nothing to be disappointed about. It was inevitable. You did tell me a time or two this might happen. And lately I've felt that your desire to be with me is not what it used to be."

"That's not true, Paul."

"It's okay, Amy. My mom taught us that actions speak louder than words. Too bad you never met her. I think you two would have gotten along. Your actions are showing me you're not as in love with me as you used to be." Paul was cool, even though he didn't feel like expressing "cool." He felt like having a Taz flashback.

Tears began to form in Amy's beautiful bluish-purple eyes. One dripped down the left side of her little turned-up nose. She loved Paul more than any other man she had ever known. She walked over to the bed and just sprawled across Paul like he was a beanbag, and began sobbing. For the first time ever, Paul did not put his arms around her. His hands remained clasped behind his head against the headboard. Amy could not stand Paul not holding her. It was making her physically ill.

"I don't know what's wrong with me, Paul. I told you I was screwed up. You know I love you," Amy said with a puzzled expression, shaking her head as if trying to understand her own behavior.

"Was there another guy there, Amy? I mean *another* guy, like *I* am to you?"

Amy didn't answer, but continued sobbing. That was answer enough for Paul. Amy could never lie to Paul, something she found extremely easy to do with everyone else. Paul had a mental glimpse of the "other guy" being Lance, to whom he had referred as "Lancelot" once before, which got him a swift rebuff from Amy. He had felt Lance's attraction for Amy, and vice versa, and considered the possibility that before his entering Amy's life, she and Lance had a tryst on the Round Table. In that same mental glimpse, Paul imagined throttling Lance, Taz-like. Almost immediately the biblical words "Take no thought," referring to evil toward one another, entered Paul's mind, and he terminated the thought immediately. The Holy Spirit had definitely been tapping at Paul these last few months.

Finally, he put his hand on Amy's beautifully formed rear and patted it. "Honey, I don't think people in love are supposed do this to each other." They both instantly knew they had run their course. "I can share you with AA, Amy, but I'm just not the kind of guy to share you with another man. Sorry. I'll always love you, Amy."

Amy kept crying as Paul dressed quickly and walked slowly out the door to go to the dorm. Amy began sobbing more loudly. When he was about half a block away, he heard the bottom door of the apartment entrance open. "I'll always love you, too, Paul," Amy yelled, crying, and then she screamed it again, louder, in frustration, seeing that the words had no effect on Paul. She coughed from the strain on her voice, not totally accepting the obvious at this point. It was the kind of reaction that exhibited pure truth, without regard for how it looked or sounded to others. And somehow, Paul believed that the two of them would remain "in love" in some parts of their beings forever. He knew there would be a sacred place in his heart for Amy, no matter who he may be with in the future, and he knew he would occupy a sacred place in Amy's heart forever, too. This did not feel good. "Don't think twice. It's all right." Dylan scored a monumental triumph with that one. "But good-bye is too good a word, gal, so I'll just say, fare thee well."

Paul thought about the time when he, Phil, and Barry were teenagers, and Uncle Phil told them, "You don't-a getta somp-a-ting for-a nuttin'." How true, like all of Uncle Phil's statements, that was. There was *always* some type of penance to be paid ... always a piper demanding payment. Might be an unwanted pregnancy, often leading, very unfortunately, to an unwanted child. Might be a horrendous sexual disease. Or, like Paul and Amy, might just be broken hearts. But one thing was certain: it was *never* something for nothing.

Paul couldn't wait to catch the next train home. He knew he was already the laughingstock of the railroad for even remotely trusting Amy, but he didn't care about that. It wasn't about trusting Amy. It was about knowing her like no one else had ever known her. It was a beautiful love, and in a way, Paul was relieved. He knew there were way too many red flags in the relationship to equal "forever and ever." What he didn't know, but had surmised a time or two, was that all he'd really known was the tip of the beautiful iceberg. Amy had been married when she was twenty, and had remained married for three years. Her mentally sick husband, Steve, had enjoyed sex by watching her with other men. Amy learned during these years that to be "loyal" to her husband, she had to be disloyal sexually. Her husband used to bring home "acquaintances" with whom Amy would perform all types of illicit sex while her goon husband watched. It was unfortunately not an abnormal path for a young woman who had been molested as a young person. Sometimes these people paid Steve and Amy. Much alcohol was consumed, and many drugs were bought, sold, and taken during this sad time period. Two of the more frequent visitors were well-known drug dealers and the sources for Amy and Steve's cocaine. Amy surmised, by counting backward, that they were also the sources for her two children, Jason and Megan. They certainly were not Steve's, because Steve never touched Amy ... he just touched himself. After Amy and Steve separated, she lived with several couples who enjoyed threesomes, until she finally ran off in a drug-induced flight to Ellisville. The children became wards of the state, and eventually were placed in the foster care system.

Although Paul knew Amy had been married, he had no idea that she still was. Amy and Steve had never bothered to get a divorce. So all those wonderful Paul and Amy Electromagnetic Reviews, too many to number, were actually adultery and not "just" the fornication that the Holy Spirit, John Hagee, and Phil had convicted Paul of as being wrong. Amy wasn't kidding when she told Paul he was her first normal relationship. Paul just hoped he didn't see her in Ellisville before he was called for an eastbound train, and he didn't.

# CHAPTER 30
# BROKEN RAIL

When Paul returned to Kansas City, he checked with the crew caller and found out he could mark up on a yard job again, which he did immediately. Paul was in pain. He called Phil. He hadn't talked to him lately. "Hey, brother, I just got in." It was November 1. He and Amy's relationship had lasted a mere four months. But both of them had felt enough wonderful feelings to last a lifetime.

"Hey, Pauly, What's up?"

"You got time for some B & B?"

"Always," Phil replied, extremely glad to hear from his brother. "Meet you at the Anchor Bar in thirty minutes, okay?"

"Okay," Paul replied, feeling a certain amount of relaxation and stability coming to bear just from the familiar sound of hearing his older brother's caring voice.

At the Anchor, Phil was already waiting and had a beer ordered for Paul when Paul walked in and sat across from him. "What's up, dude?" Paul said, and smiled at his older brother, whose mere presence greatly helped his emotionally shot state.

"What's up wichyou," Phil mimicked back, like they were stereotypical Italians from the American Northeast.

"Well, Philo, it's over," Paul said with sadness yet conviction. "I always knew it would be."

"I knew you knew, too," Phil commented quickly, "even as much in love with her as you were. I mean, I've never seen you like that, Pauly."

"I know."

"You knew it was a temporary situation. You know, Paul, all relationships are temporary. They're just time segments. Some are longer, and some are shorter." Phil felt the philosopher unintentionally slipping out of him. "What you two evidently had was more than some people ever experience who meet, get married, have kids, and grow old and die. That intensity you two shared *was* off the scale."

"Yeah, I've felt that for sure, Phil. You're right. Amy can't help the way she is. She's the product of an uncaring mother, an absentee father, and a molesting stepfather. She never had a chance. And as a result, I didn't, and *we* didn't. I knew it was a pipe dream. But I think I'm okay with it, brother." Paul spoke without much conviction.

"Well, for what it's worth to you, Paul, I heard from literally everyone on the road that they had never seen Amy like she was when she was with you. They said she never went to the bars and never went with any of the other railroaders, which was always her behavior when she was with anybody else."

"Well, she's finally been 'with' someone else. Past practice finally won out, old habits being hard to break and all that good stuff," Paul said wearily, with a sigh.

"Who was it, just for curiosity's sake?" Phil asked as nonchalantly as he could, attempting to view it as a matter-of-fact situation and wondering if it was a railroader he knew.

"I think it was this Lance squirrel she goes to AA with all the time. I shouldn't say that," Paul immediately corrected himself. "He's probably a decent guy. It's just great. I can't blame anyone who goes after Amy, and with Amy's background, I can't blame her for going after him (or her). All I know is the prospect of her natural unfaithfulness never felt very good to consider, and it was inevitable. In a way, I'm relieved that it finally happened. Now I can go on, but I'm not sure with what. I know it was crazy to have wanted a kid with her, but boy, it was sweet, Phil, just thinking about it."

"Paul, I don't think I need to tell you how relieved I am that you and Amy are finished. I always worried what kind of a life you would have, never knowing if she'd show up or not. At least for now, and I won't say forever, Amy is addicted to everything. It's like in the Eagles song 'Life in the Fast Lane' … 'Everything, all the time.' Brother, that would literally *kill* even tough ol' you over time. No, I know it's rough. I know how much you loved her and still do. And I know Amy still loves you, too, probably more than she ever loved anyone, but is it enough? No. As long as she has this addictive personality, she's a walking, talking life-destroyer, and I'm glad she won't be in a position to destroy my brother's life anymore. Y'know, Paul, I was watching Dr. Charles Stanley the other day, and he had a set of five rules to follow, to deal with *any* problem. I used it on a financial situation Carla and I were facing, and it works outstandingly well. Number one: Look to the Lord. Don't look at the problem—that's what the devil wants you to do, so you'll feel bad, be emotionally distraught, and deal terribly with the problem. Number two: Trust in the Lord. Know the Lord loves you and will help you, and will do what He says He will do. Number three: Get with the Word. Read the Bible. The answers are there, for *everything*, as you know. Number four: *Obey* the Word. That's what you haven't been doing and you know it, as good as everything felt. And number five: Pray. Communicate with God. You might try those, Paul."

"Would you repeat those more slowly, Phil? I want to write them down." Paul took out his time book to write in, and Phil repeated the steps. "Thanks; they look good. It will be a real challenge to look to the Lord rather than Amy, but I'll do it. And I have a new Bible to read. Amy got me this Dake annotated reference Bible. The print is small, but I can still read it without glasses. I already read Revelation with the notes on the side. I learned a lot. And Phil, Amy wrote the most awesome inscription to me in the front, about how I had brought good into her life. I don't know if I can remember it all, exactly. But I've read it enough times that I've probably memorized it. She wrote something like, 'Paul Barnes, I feel as though you are a special gift given to me from God. You have brought good into my life. I am so grateful to have someone so loving and caring. You have such a special place in my heart. God works miracles. He has for the both of us. Remember, always put God first, and we will come out on top together as *one*. Paul Barnes, I love you. Amy.' Isn't that great, Phil?"

"Yes, it is, Paul," Phil said, admiring her sentiment and believing Amy's thoughts had been sincere *at the time*. Phil always liked Amy, and never judged her. Phil never judged anybody. He was very happy to leave that job to the Lord. It was more work than he wanted. He looked at Amy as a beautiful tigress, an animal that really couldn't help the way it was, but was dangerous by virtue of the reactions she was issued to use. There was no evil intent, but one swipe and she'd tear your heart out.

"Have you seen the Bear Man lately, Pauly?" Phil asked for two reasons: one, to get his brother's mind off Amy, and two, because Phil and Paul were always concerned for their close friend who was more like another brother. The last times Phil and Paul had seen Barry in Ellisville, he had seemed despondent and distant.

"No, Phil, I haven't." Paul realized with his brother's question that he had unintentionally neglected Barry's problems while attempting to deal with his own. "He doesn't call me like he used to, and I must admit, I've not been able to concentrate on anything but Amy these last few months. It was like the world disappeared except for her."

"I saw him in Ellisville a couple of weeks ago, and he looked terrible. He's let himself go. We didn't get a chance to talk much, but he said sometimes, he wishes he'd just die. I told him to call Ned Lingle. A week ago, I called Ned, and he said Barry had called him. He told Barry we *all* have felt like that, and that he should trust God, that He has a plan for him, even though things seemed rough now. He said he didn't think it got through to Barry. Barry told me about a year ago that he thought he screwed up everything he touched. He said his marriage and family were about gone. He said his mom hates him. He said he never got a chance to become a dentist, his childhood dream. He said he didn't do anything in CP management, although they loved him. He told me his father, Bill, told him, 'When someone hands you a ball, you run with it.' Paul, with a very dejected and sad expression on his face, Barry told me, 'Phil, I not only didn't run with it ... I fumbled it.'"

Phil's attempt to change his brother's focus was only instantly temporal. "That's really too bad. Poor Bear. Well, I better go ... where, I'm not sure ... Just need to go somewhere. Thanks again for listening, brother. Love you."

"No thanks necessary, Paul. With all the teasing you had to put up with years ago, it's the least I can do," Phil said, trying unsuccessfully to sneak humor into the situation. "Carla and I are planning to have Barry, Susan, and the kids over for some beer and brats on Sunday. Why don't you come over? I'm sure the Bear misses us as much as we miss him, and the kids miss you. It will be good for all of us. You've got regular days off again."

"That sounds real good, brother." Paul managed a tired smile.

"You okay, brother?" Phil looked with sincerity into his brother's eyes as he downed the last swig of beer.

That small question from his brother was worth more than the Taj Mahal to Paul. Yes, he *was* okay. He would be able to go on with whatever. He had never really planned a serious future with Amy because that potential could have changed in a nanosecond. Even at the time he bought the ring and asked her to marry him, he felt like it was somehow playacting, although it felt great to act like that with her.

"Yes, I'm okay, and you know, it feels pretty good already, the prospect of not sinning."

"Well, don't get too down on yourself about the sinning," Phil continued to comfort his emotionally wounded brother. "Remember, we all sin in some form or another. When we think we don't is when it's the greatest sin. Then we become Scribes and Pharisees, not Jesus' favorite folks. And keep in mind what Ned Lingle said about how he thinks God views our sinning. I don't know if there is scriptural reference for this, but Ned says he thinks God grades on 'degree of difficulty.' Leaving Amy alone would have to be *extremely* difficult."

Paul smiled and shook his head. The two hugged, said their good-byes, and drove off in their separate vehicles. Phil drove home, and Paul drove to another little sports bar, the Unicorn. How much he loved his older brother, he thought. Phil was always the stable one, the firstborn. From somewhere and for some reason, Paul thought of the only time he had ever wanted to blast Phil. When Paul was sixteen, he had smarted off to Rose after a senseless argument with her, which always ended in a losing effort anyway. He had told her to "eat it." Phil, who had walked in the door just in time to hear the remark, had responded by shoving Paul, who accidentally fell backward over a footstool in the living room. Paul, who was as big as Phil, jumped up and drew back with his fist.

But looking at his older brother, he had seen both fearlessness and disgust in Phil's eyes, and something else … Disappointment. And Paul knew Phil was *right*, and he was ashamed he had ever said that to his mother. He looked at his brother, who conversely had not drawn back to fight, but was just standing there. "I'm sorry, Mom," Paul had said, and Paul remembered so clearly Phillip smiling, nodding, and winking at him. Then Phil had just turned and walked off like it was a nonevent. It was Phil's junior version of Batman. It was also love, no more, no less, and Paul knew his brother's love, like God's, was constant, when the world's or Amy's was not.

On the way to the Unicorn, Paul was punching through the radio stations when "Just My Imagination" by the Temptations came on. Paul smiled, and mumbled, "It figures." He knew he would not be hearing that song too much. He didn't listen to oldies as a rule, and did recently only because Amy liked them. He'd already heard "Layla" 1,499,000 times, and although he liked it, he was tired of oldies in general. He knew "Just My Imagination" wouldn't be a constant reminder of the sweet memories he and Amy created with that tune in the background. But Paul left the stereo on that station, and when the part, "Someday we'll marry, and raise a family ... in a cozy little home in the country with two children, maybe three," he began to feel his eyes tear up as he sang along. No, this isn't going to be easy, he thought. "But it was just my imagination," he sang to himself, and he managed a semi-smile. Yes, it was.

As Paul drove into the Unicorn parking lot, which was within walking distance to his apartment in case he "loaded up" too much, he happened to look up at the stars. There was the Big Dipper, with its handle pointing to Arcturus. He knew he would never again be able to look at Arcturus or even the Big Dipper and not think of Amy. And, unlike "Just My Imagination," Arcturus just might be around on a nightly basis. Paul had looked up at the beauty of the stars often while working the night hours of railroading, and had loved looking at them since he was a child. He, Phil, and Barry used to sleep out in their backyards and look at the stars in wonder. In an instant, Paul got the strangest feeling that Amy was looking at Arcturus at the same time. Over the years, Paul would look up at Arcturus and often wonder just that.

He would always love Amy. He knew that. Not only did he love her for the extraordinarily intense physical sensation he felt being with her, and all the sweet things she did and said, but he also loved her because she really *tried* with him. Having one and only one male at a time was totally foreign to Amy. She had never felt the need to be special to anyone. But she had tried very hard with Paul, and he loved her for it. "Falling in and out of love with you," Paul thought as he recalled Vince Gill's words from Pure Prairie League's "Amie." This hadn't been an affair or a relationship. This had been Paul's first and only *romance*.

Amy was no more able to give up Paul than he was her. Over the next few months she called him incessantly, but he never returned her calls, even though she left a myriad of messages on his answering machine. Paul would check his messages and Amy would be on there several times, carrying on a one-way conversation with him as though they were still together, as though she couldn't deal with the reality that the best man she'd ever known and loved was gone. A horrendous void now existed in her, as though more than half of her was nonexistent. She was semi-going with Lance when she wasn't with someone else. She too wondered if Paul ever looked at Arcturus and thought of her. Sometimes she would walk in Ellisville Park by herself in the late evening and look at the Big Dipper, whose handle pointed to *their star ... hers and Paul's*, and imagine Paul was next to her. She played "Just My Imagination" over and over, and imagined Paul in her arms. She envisioned his big arms surrounding her as they danced slowly, sensually, and lovingly to "This couldn't be a dream, it's far too real ..." Amy was in parallel pain with Paul, and she couldn't give him up, even though she held the unfamiliarly wise attitude that she was no good for him. She knew that to love him from a distance was the best plan. She couldn't change, and relatively soon after the breakup, was back to her old ways of sleeping with whomever, whenever, now leaving Lance in pain. As it says in the Bible, "Like a dog returneth to its vomit, a fool returneth to his [or her] folly." Yes, we do.

Paul began going with a woman a little older than Amy a few months later. She was Paul's intellectual equal, and he cared about her a lot, but he just didn't love her. But the woman helped Paul get over Amy, at least as much as possible. In many ways, Amy unintentionally ruined Paul for other women. Over the years, he would always subconsciously search for the same intensity he'd had with her, the same *electromagnetic connection*. But there would never be one. Being with other women just reassured Paul that much more that there would never be another Amy. The subconscious comparison was always there. Sometimes Paul would miss Amy so much that he would imagine that he was able to touch her all over her body with his body at the same time, a physical impossibility and a thought he never had about any other woman. And the thought was not necessarily sexual. He "felt" her that much.

Over the next few months Paul attempted to rationalize the hope and unrealistic potential of being with Amy again, with a positive, though illogical, lingering thought that she could change. He would call his understanding brother and run thoughts past him. Phil, at the very least, did not want to give his brother hope of finding the Holy Grail at an unholy site, and at times resorted to verbal brutality.

"Hey, Phil, Amy was on my answering machine *again* today. She always comes back to me," Paul would say, expecting some positive reinforcement from his brother.

"Like a dog comes back to the same tree?" Phil would say.

Paul would have many future discussions with Phil, who reminded him that Amy was never his intellectual equal, and although that was not everything in relationships, it was to be considered. "What were you going to do when you tired of each other physically, Pauly?" Phil asked. "Talk about the stock market? The crisis in the Middle East? And wouldn't it have been great to constantly wait for Amy, never knowing if she was going to show up? And what friend could you trust her with? Not too many men could resist her, Paul. She nailed a lot of good family men who no one would have believed would have strayed. No, you didn't need that, Pauly. And there is a pretty good age difference, too, Paul."

In addition to seeing John Hagee that day in Amy's apartment, Paul had received a call from Crystal Matthias in Kansas City, his fine female friend from college. Crystal was amazingly devout in an era when everyone else, including Paul, was basically decadent. She had tried, albeit unsuccessfully, to convert Paul to Jesus while at college, but she did manage, unbeknownst to either of them, to sow some seeds. And eventually, along with Phil and Barry's input, and certain excellent TV preachers, the seeds began to grow and thrive within Paul. His gradual leanings to the Lord, which invoked a negative response to his and Amy's sexual acts, prompted him to write Crystal about Amy.

Crystal was so distraught over her lifelong friend's choices that she called him. She hadn't commented much at the time of the phone call, the conversation being mostly catching up on all the years. But later, she sent Paul some extremely pertinent scripture, which she had often done in the past. The scripture references were what God wanted out of male-female relationships. None of what Paul and Amy were doing aligned with what God wanted for His children. "Paul, where are your spiritual eyes?" Crystal asked.

Paul applied the five steps Phil gave him from Dr. Charles Stanley's sermon, and his loss of Amy, although extremely painful at first, lessened enormously. A wonderful, unexpected by-product of Dr. Stanley's approach was that Paul developed a greater love for the Lord. He was at peace, and prayed constantly for Amy and her children.

Paul began to read scripture a lot. As he slowly refocused his spiritual eyes, he was able to look at Amy much more clearly. He was assessing facts, not being judgmental. One time he was reading about the seven churches in Revelation, and when he came to Jezebel, who was seducing the saints in the church of Thyatira, he thought, *That's Amy*, and sighed. Revelation says that as a result of her sins, Jezebel's children would die, and Paul thought of the welfare of Jason and Megan. He prayed for the three of them forever, hoping for the best, and most of all, hoping God would replace Amy's current malevolent spirit with the Holy Spirit.

Paul had talked with Amy about the Lord quite often. Amy was interested, but Paul felt she didn't "feel" it, although she went through the motions. Paul thought often about how Amy had told him she thought God put him in her life. Now he tended to think Amy probably said it superficially, without conviction. It was the right thing to say at the time. He had been desperate to believe it. What Paul didn't realize was that Amy really *did* feel that God had put him in her life. And Amy also felt the Holy Spirit guiding her and telling her "good" and "not good," as did most God-fearing people. She just chose not to listen when "not good" was the directive. Like many of us, she chose to ignore it and do what her flesh wanted, rather than her spirit.

When Phillip was first on the road, he too wanted to talk to Amy about the Lord. He too was amazed when he met her, like all the rest who were initially struck by her extraordinary beauty. But her beauty was of no consequence in Phil's mind after he learned how depraved she was. Phil's natural genuine love for people moved him to want to save their souls. He got his chance to talk with Amy one time when the two were alone in May's.

"Do you ever think about heaven, Amy?" Phil asked.

"Sure," she had replied.

"And what kind of behavior do you suppose gets you there?" Phil posed the question.

"I dunno. I thought we were saved by grace," Amy replied, remembering what the nice lady had told her while she was in prison.

Phil thought, I wonder where she heard that? But it was right on. Phil was so glad he was not given the job of judgment. But he knew Amy could go to the well, or bed, as it were, once too often. "Mr. Goodbar" might find her. Amy just didn't get it. She did not understand sinful consequences. She'd blink her fascinating bluish-purple lasers and think immediately about something else.

When Evander Holyfield whipped Mike Tyson, he was wearing a robe with Philippians 4:13 embroidered on it: "I can do all things through Christ which strengtheneth me." That verse, and the verse "With God, all things are possible" were becoming part of Paul's view of everything. God can do anything, the only catalysts being the Lord's own decision and timetable. Like Amy used to say, "God *is* awesome." Paul thought, If Jesus can get seven devils out of Mary Magdalene, he can get them out of Amy. He also thought, very nonhypocritically, that he could probably use the same exorcising. Maybe God could heal them both before he combined them as man and wife, if ever. Paul could feel, somehow in his very being, that he needed to clean up his own heart. Then the Lord would answer his prayers for Amy, Jason, and Megan. If he were loyal to God, God would be loyal to him.

Paul joined a church and actually sang in the choir. It corresponded nicely with his new yard job position, which had Sunday and Monday as days off. Crystal had suggested to him in the letter that he fellowship with Christians, something Paul had never done intentionally, except for Phil and Barry. He wanted to do something for God and felt that singing in the choir was a way to accomplish this. The reciprocity was wonderful. Paul would leave church with the music they sang still in his head, and the choir people were wonderfully spiritual and blessed.

Paul could feel the power when they prayed together. He would ask the choir to pray for Amy when prayer requests were solicited.

Often over the years, Paul thought of the beautiful Amy, and how much they had shared and felt in only a few months. The electromagnetics between them had been nuclear detonations. The joy she gave him was without comparison. And Paul, as is so often the case when we look back, nailed down exactly what he found so overwhelming with Amy. It was her beautiful, considerate, innocent inner being ... the *real* Amy. Very few, if any, had seen this. No one got past the physical with Amy, so that's how she responded. But Amy's inner being was *pure*, yes, pure and sweet ... like our beings are pure and sweet thanks to our Savior's blood. She *was* the sweet, wonderful, happy cleaning lady on the front of the card she'd made for Paul, just wanting to help and please and maybe clean up her life. No one else saw that, not even Phil. But Paul knew it was the *real* Amy, the one who'd accepted the ring from him. The physical was merely Amy's coping process with the world. Paul reflected often on that beautiful, dizzying time over the years, and would smile happily and say to himself, "What a *great* romance!"

Paul would never go on the road again. Even though the money was superior "out there," his brush with paradise/hell was enough to keep him happily in Kansas City. He was really enjoying his new approach to life, and singing in the choir.

Paul was again working a Quindaro job, which felt like home. Besides working with his buddy Pat, he saw all his old Quindaro acquaintances, including Jethro. One day, Jethro was peeling an apple with his twenty-year-old pocketknife, which didn't have much blade left, or "bwade weft," as Jethro pointed out. It was because of Jethro's incessant sharpening. Jethro looked up with his milky blue eyes at no one in particular, and formed a temporal visual, followed by a brainless smile.

"Ol' Bwue tweed a toon. I wooked up in na twee an' saw dey was no toon in nat twee. An' I tawt, dat dawg is smawt! He knew dey *would* soon be a toon in nat twee." Paul couldn't help but smile.

About two years later, Phil, who had stayed on the road, as did Barry, told Paul that Amy had disappeared. No one had seen her at the usual railroad haunts. She had said to Phil every time she'd seen him, "Tell your brother hi," and like the loyal and honest brother Phil was, he reluctantly passed the greeting along to Paul. Phil was always relieved at Paul's never-changing reaction each time. It was to not look directly at his brother and give an "air wave" with his right hand. Inwardly, though, Paul still ached for Amy.

The news of her disappearance was cause for great concern for Paul. He had always thought Amy had been playing an extremely dangerous game with her horrendous lifestyle of end-to-end, so to speak, sexual adventures. After years and literally hundreds of sexual contacts, the odds of a *Looking for Mr. Goodbar* calamity were extremely good. The truth was, Amy had come very close to dying on several occasions in San Antonio, but the killers she had been intimate with just didn't feel like killing on that occasion. No one would ever know it, but Jason's father had snuffed a couple of people himself, in drug deals gone awry. Yes, Amy had been extremely fortunate. Her angels were always working overtime. But her disappearance had another effect on Paul, besides anxiety.

Over the years, with Amy only as far away as Ellisville, Paul had enjoyed encapsulated fantasies about her. No matter who he was dating, in the back of his mind, he always thought he and Amy would again have what they'd had. And with her so close, only 147 miles away, that had always been a possibility. He had loved it when Phil had told him of Amy's communications over the last months, even though he never responded to her himself. Phil had always told Amy, "Paul says hi," and it wasn't a lie, if you thought about Paul's nonchalant hand wave. Amy loved it. It was a minor chord between them.

But now, with her disappearance, it was at last, finally, *over*. Paul thought Judy might know something about Amy, but didn't want to contact her for several reasons. But the main reason was that it was time to move on.

# CHAPTER 31
## RAIL CHANGES

In the early eighties, recession took a bite out of many businesses, including the Central Pacific. Many engineers were "cut back" to firemen, some with twenty years' seniority. Phil and Barry stayed on the road as firemen. But during that decade, there were changes in the railroad industry that changed railroading forever. The firemen position would be abolished ... No more firemen. The cabooses became, for the most part, historical relics, occasionally seen in small town parks across the nation. Railroads kept a very small fleet of cabooses for certain local jobs that involved lengthy shoves of several miles, or shoves that necessitated crossing public crossings. The railroads called them "shoving platforms" and locked the cabooses so the railroaders couldn't get inside. They just rode on the steps or platform, still more comfortable than riding the side ladder of a railcar for extreme distances. And some short lines still operated with a few cabooses, but for the most part, the era of the caboose was history. And in a way, so was the romance of railroading.

Groove Whitfield was playing his guitar in the dormitory at Ellisville one time, and cranked out a bluesy number called "We Cut Off the Caboose":

Dah-da-a-h, dah-dah
Woke up this mornin'. Dah-da-a-h, dah-dah
Got ready for work. Dah-da-a-h, dah-dah
The telephone rang, and they said,

Stay home, you jerk,
'Cause we cut off the caboose. Da-da-da-da-da-da-dah
'Cause we cut off the caboose. Da-da-dah, da-da-dah
Hang loose, Mother Goose 'cause
We cut off that freakin' caboose.
Da-da-da-da-da-da-da-da-da-da-de-da-do-dah-dah-dah
Dah-da-a-h, dah-dah
Talked to an official. Dah-da-a-h, dah-dah
He said don't be square. Dah-da-a-h-dah-dah
Don't walk to the rear end.
That caboose just ain't there,
'Cause we cut off the caboose. Da-da-da-da-da-dah
'Cause we cut off the caboose. Da-da-dah, da-da-dah
It just ain't no use, 'cause,
We cut off that freakin' caboose.

The rails had loved the song, but unfortunately, it was all too true. Phil always enjoyed the times when he was deadheaded on a caboose, like with his close friend McGee Brown. It was such a change from the head end, where the locomotives were uncompromisingly noisy. The turbochargers were always screaming in your ears, a higher pitch for higher throttle settings. And the air pressure exhausting from the brake valves further destroyed ear tissue. More than one engineer had lost the better part of his hearing as a result of these severe noises. To converse, the locomotive cab occupants often had to scream at each other. But unlike the extremely noisy head end, when a train began to move, the caboose merely quietly advanced slowly forward. Phil was amazed that people could actually hear each other talk without yelling on those rare occasions when he would deadhead on a caboose. Those cabooses equipped with cupolas were tailor-made for not only train viewing (hotboxes, anything dragging or hanging, shifted lading, and so on), but also panoramic scenery viewing. It was hard to believe folks were paid for viewing the beautiful countryside. A train just didn't seem like a train without a caboose.

However, as much as the loss of the caboose cost many jobs, it also substantially decreased the number of injuries and resultant claims, thereby greatly increasing the railroad's net profits. The greatest amount of ink-drainage from the profit margin was caused by injuries and ensuing lawsuits. The caboose was, in many ways, an accident waiting to happen. Many a railroader had been injured or killed on a caboose. There were accidents where cabooses were rear-ended by other trains. Other caboose accidents were caused by sun kinks, where the sun superheated the rail enough to cause expansion, and there was nowhere for the rail to go but sideways. As a result, many cabooses were derailed, finally coming to rest on their sides, sometimes resulting in the death of a conductor or rear brakeman. Rear brakemen and conductors often became human ping-pong balls in a shaken box when they experienced the normal "rough handling," as it was called. Many caboose occupants were injured during horrendous train handling exhibitions like Beauregard Banks's bunching clinic at Topeka.

The caboose was replaced by a telemetry device, known not so affectionately by the railroaders as FRED. The *R-E-D* name stood for "rear end device." And although some would say the *F* stood for "flashing," which the device did, the railroaders knew different. The *F* stood for the adjective one can imagine the railroaders used to describe any device that was responsible for replacing the head brakeman and rear brakeman. So the firemen, the head brakeman, and the rear brakeman were cut off, and "Fred" was here to stay. Fred didn't require salary, railroad retirement payments, or medical and dental insurance. And Fred didn't lay off sick or fall asleep on caboose cushions.

As a result of the cabooses being phased out, the conductor now sat on the lead locomotive right beside the engineer. In the old days, there was always a competition of sorts, about who had the ultimate responsibility for the train. The rule book said that the conductor and engineer were jointly responsible for the train's safety. Technically, the conductors *were* in charge of the train. But some engineers felt that since they operated the train, they should be in charge. One engineer told his conductor in the caboose era, "How can you be in charge if you're the last one to arrive?" Engineers also had a higher rate of pay than conductors, a sore point for some conductors.

But now in the mid-eighties, railroading was in an evolution process. Some would say *devolution,* a word brought to the forefront of the time by the group Devo. Train size was increasing, in some cases to two miles. This was coupled with the greatly lessened crew size from five to two. What used to be a railroad crew made up of an engineer, fireman, and head brakeman on the lead locomotive, and rear brakeman and conductor on the caboose, became only an engineer and conductor on the lead locomotive with no caboose, and Fred. Of course, each of the two remaining positions had added duties to compensate for the loss of the other three. Like Arlo Guthrie sang in the early seventies in "The City of New Orleans," "This train's got the disappearin' railroad blues." It was the "disappearin' *railroader* blues," also.

Switches on leads were now thrown electronically, from a switch tower. Some switches were even solar powered and radio controlled. Yard jobs took a beating. Gradually, run-through traffic became the preferred operation. Yards were used to swap blocks of cars, rather than switch, and although humping operations remained of necessity in some yards, other yards became totally run-through. Costs were cut, and streamlining was the norm. When Phil, Paul, and Barry had initially hired out, the number of workers in the railroad yard used to remind them of ants on an anthill, they were so numerous. Now, with so many jobs cut off, and the lessened crew size, there might be two or three locomotives moving at different parts of the terminal, where twenty-five or thirty locomotives operated in the late sixties and early seventies. Yardmaster towers and shanties were destroyed, entire diesel shops were razed, and even executive offices were wrecker-balled to the ground.

On local jobs, an extra brakeman was usually added to the crew, making the job a little easier, but like in all business, the name of the game was cost cutting. Job satisfaction had little or nothing to do with the bottom line. In the eighties, management made everyone "cut in," a term taken from coupling air hoses, meaning to cut in the air. In other words, "Let's get down, and *stay* down, to business." The "quit" became a thing of the past, and all jobs worked no fewer than eight hours.

The steel rails were also being replaced. It was a process that had gone on for twenty years, and was continuing. What used to be almost universally jointed rail was being replaced with continuous welded rail. It was also called ribbon rail, and to see it lying beside the main line in quarter-mile lengths, it did, indeed, look like a long ribbon. That steel could lie on the ground with curves just like a ribbon, or garden hose, seemed absurd. But it did. It reduced, tremendously, the potential for derailment. It also reduced the need for so many section workers. In the old days, a section was a certain segment of track, some said originally seven miles. Track workers used to hire out and retire providing maintenance to the same section. Of course, as time passed, section length increased, but nothing like when ribbon rail was introduced.

These section workers could whip their weight in wildcats. It may have been the hardest work on the planet. To see two section workers driving a spike into a creosote-covered, oak railroad tie with spike mauls was poetry in motion. If one wasn't paying attention, he could "gong" the other quite severely. As tough as these guys were, it probably wouldn't have bothered them. The veterans never missed the spike head anyway. But there were dozens of newly invented track machines hitting the market at this time that *would* gong them. They put thousands and thousands of section workers out of a job. John Henry may have whipped the steam drill's mechanical ass one day, but progress was whipping the railroaders' collective asses.

The ribbon rail also stopped the rhythmic clickety-clack that could put sleepy passengers gently in La La Land in a heartbeat during the fifties. It was now gone, since the rhythmic sound was caused by the joints in the jointed rail. The railroads had long since run off the passenger trains, because they clogged the rails and generated very low revenue. Those who may remember the incomparable passenger-train era know that Amtrak, although still enjoyable, is a poor substitute. Good-bye, caboose; good-bye, clickety-clack; good-bye, railroaders.

Along with the "do more with less" approach to railroading, the reduced worker population looked different in the eighties. There were many more women and minorities making up the workforce. Personnel officers like Tom Moffat and Barry had done their jobs well. But there were pitfalls. Essentially, nature took its course when women and men worked together. Not only did the railroads, by virtue of the work, require husbands to stay away from home for extended periods of time, but nowadays there were also females amongst the troops during these extended periods. Some of them were quite attractive, although that was not necessarily a requirement for a railroader to "slip off the curb." Without having to have a PhD in sociology, anyone could see the obvious outcome. And nature *did* take its course.

Yard urination had long been a "standing tradition" on the railroad, as Paul once said. Railroaders could not take time to find a bathroom. It was unheard of. Normally, they did at least try to find a car, or bridge, or weeds, to cover themselves as much as possible. Even engineers whose locomotives were equipped with toilets would just go outside the back door of their locomotives and pee off the side, when they had the chance. The toilets on the locomotives were never cleaned sufficiently. The bums probably used them more than the railroaders. One of the engineers, Gene Edwards, reported the smell to the Federal Railroad Administration. The FRA had told him to take a picture next time he was assigned a locomotive with an unclean toilet. Gene asked, "How do you take a picture of a smell?" But with women in the yards, this pee-anywhere behavior was changing. There were many unintended exposures at first, because of the "standing tradition." With guys now getting busted by the female switchmen, the male railroad population developed discretion. But this public pissing cessation was nothing compared with the soap opera atmosphere developing at the same time.

One young, not-too-bright-but-nice switchman, Danny Yeager, was climbing up the steps of a GP-9 yard switcher, or "Jeep," as they were called. These locomotives got their names the same way the military Jeeps got theirs, from "GP," or "general purpose." They were built by the Electro-Motive Division of General Motors. Although there were many kinds of locomotives, General Motors and General Electric had the lion's share in the field, with a few old ALCOs in use by shortlines. At the same time young Yeager was climbing up one side of the Jeep steps, Debbie Voss was climbing up the other side. Yeager, who was twenty-four and already had two children by two different women, said it was "instant karma." He fell for Debbie, and she fell for him.

Debbie was an ex-hairdresser and very attractive. Most of the male railroaders acted silly when Debbie was in the vicinity. Yeager left his second wife for her, and within three months, she was with somebody else. Danny was suicidal for a while, but made it through. There were a lot of similar instances.

No, there were changes everywhere. In the past, changes on the railroad took twenty years to come into being. Then it was every ten years. Then it was every five years. Then the changes came yearly. In the eighties, railroaders never knew what to expect when they got to work. Huge mergers were definitely a part of the changes during this period, too. In Kansas City, the Central Pacific used to interchange with thirteen Class I railroads when Phil, Paul, and Barry first hired out. By the year 2000, the nation was serviced by six large railroads and hundreds of shortlines. Many of the large Class I's had merged. Something about losing railroads didn't sound healthy for the country in the long term.

One day the CP trainmen and enginemen came to work and found a computer terminal staring them in the face. The CP had an IT (information technology) jock on the premises to assist the railroaders in their new computer directives. If the transportation and operating people had taken a severe hit employee-wise from electronic and mechanical technology, the clerical ranks had been bombed by the computer. Now the trainmen and engineers had to tie up on a computer, as well as log in, when they came to work. Hugh Vanderveen said, "If I'd-a wanted to be a &*^%$%^&&n accountant, I'd-a gone to school for it." But they all eventually learned the process. They had to, or quit.

# CHAPTER 32
## RESTRICTED SPEED: BE ON
## LOOKOUT FOR MORE BROKEN RAIL

Once Fran married Don White and began to systematically pick at Barry, finding constant fault with him, she never let up. On those miraculously rare times Barry would actually be off for a holiday at family get-togethers, Fran would zero in on him. "Barry, you could never have made it as anything but a railroad worker." Instead of celebrating the fact that Barry held a time-honored, traditional—some would even say romantic—job, which made substantial money, Fran would belittle Barry in front of Susan and the children. She never made one complimentary comment to or about Barry, *ever*. It was always a discredit. Evidently Barry thought, with insufficient logic, that because he lacked a father, he might have an even more approving and proud mother. But now he had the exact opposite. Erin and Graham, hearing nothing but negatives about their father, were as wounded as Barry, but they wouldn't find out until later in life. Fran would have bitten her tongue off before ever saying to them, "Listen to your father. He always has good ideas. He's a good man."

When she tired of discounting everything Barry was, Fran would act like he wasn't there. It was almost as if Fran were jealous, like *her* marriages ended in failure, so why should Barry have a good marriage and family? Barry just tried to mentally shrug it all off. He thought his mother was basically mentally sick, and further mentally shot from having to deal with the extremely evil White on a daily basis. Barry thought she was lucky to be able to put one foot in front of the other. Externally, Fran appeared superficially fine, always flashing the giant Loretta Young smile underneath the Lucille Ball eyes. But inwardly she was a therapist's nightmare. Barry understood somewhat, but it still hurt him tremendously. He remembered a great-grandmother from his childhood. She evidently had Alzheimer's, although it was not called that at the time. She wasn't packing a full sea bag either. But Barry remembered her as being really sweet, so he had a hard time associating Fran's unrelenting viciousness with insanity. Over a period of several years, this mean, discrediting, and disregard began to have a deep effect on Barry. Barry began to withdraw and die slowly, inwardly.

Susan, who looked at Fran as the mother she hadn't had since she was sixteen, saw her viciousness toward Barry, but chose to see it Fran's way. Actually, it was more important now for Susan to have a mother figure again than to exhibit any loyalty toward Barry. Barry would have liked for either of them to have just loved him as before. Was that so hard to do? He wanted desperately for the two women he loved most dearly, besides Rose and Erin, to just be nice to him. But it wasn't happening. He had tried to talk to his mother about it, but was always met with blank Lucille Ball blinks and stares. Then Fran hated him even more for questioning her behavior. Barry wasn't looking for sympathy from Fran, only empathy and understanding. Fran sadistically enjoyed intentionally never giving Barry understanding or caring. Couldn't she just be nice?

Barry would attempt logic from a dozen different angles in hopes of making Fran "see." He would ask her, "Would Grandma have said this to you, or acted like this toward you?" More death stares. And again, Fran would perceive these times as "impudence" from Barry, and enjoy cutting his emotionally distraught throat that much more. Barry's perseverance in these futile attempts to evoke love from a now loveless Fran always set him up for more tearing down. Even Rose, Phil, and Paul began to notice Fran's absurdly inappropriate behavior toward Barry, although Fran tried to hide it from them. Rose even called Fran, mentioning her strange actions in regard to Barry. Fran promptly changed the subject.

The eventual knockout punch for Barry was Susan joining Fran in the same destructive onslaught. How could his mother, whom he had perceived as a little boy as so wonderful, and the beautiful, caring wife he was sure "God had saved back for him" do this? What had he done? Was it the lusting that Barry never had physically realized? Barry was destroyed. He loved them both so much, and he literally did not know what to do. How was this possible? How could this happen? Neither would talk to him about it. He just kept working and bringing home the money, as always. Like Phil, Barry worked all the time, never laying off. Susan wanted Barry to get a vasectomy, which Barry considered and probably would have done, but because he worked so much, he just never scheduled it. As a result, Susan cut him off, physically as well as mentally. Barry got nothing anymore from Susan. There were absolutely no Scrabble games, no Moose Surprises, no nothing ... nothing but disinterest. Susan was always aloof, treating Barry like someone she had to put up with for now. She would chime in with Fran on the "Barry blasting," with Erin and Graham still recipients of collective collateral damage. This killed Barry, and he thought it surely killed his credibility with his dear children. The kids were puzzled and confused. Eventually, in addition to withdrawing, Barry became despondent, complacent, and overwhelmed by life in general. He existed for many months in that state. He tried to ask Susan if he'd done anything, and she wouldn't give him the time of day. Again, it was like his wife and his mother were looking at him through a horrible, evil smokescreen or something. As everyone knows, people you don't care about cannot hurt you emotionally. People you love can destroy you, *if* you let them, and easygoing Barry seemed compliant with that.

There was a young woman in Ellisville, Sherry Smith, who always flirted with Barry. They had spoken a few times. She was a doll, but Barry was always true-blue to Susan. It was one of the main reasons he'd left CP management. There were just too many opportunities to "foul up" on Susan, and it was very important for Barry not to do so. He really believed in that, and thought adultery was the most degrading thing one spouse could do to another. But now, he didn't know where he stood. He expected Susan to leave him at any time, and he thought his own mother was orchestrating it. One day in Ellisville, Barry went to May's to have a beer. It felt very good going down. He had just gotten into town and wouldn't be getting out till the next afternoon, even if they did deadhead. On this particular afternoon, Barry had about six beers. It was his one remaining connection with "feel-good." As he was about to get up and walk back to the dorm, in walked Sherry. Barry always filed Sherry's beauty in his subconscious random access memory whenever he noticed her around Ellisville. It was that electrochemical thing. But Barry normally never had a second thought about her, doggedly determined to honor his vows to Susan. But today, he noticed Sherry. He *really* noticed Sherry. She was immediately saved in his hard drive.

"What's wrong, Barry?" Sherry asked, easily discerning that he wasn't his usual relaxed, pleasant self.

"There's just some strange, personal stuff goin' on in my life, Sherry, that's all. I'm not really sure what to make of it," Barry said, shaking his head and surprising himself with his candidness. It was beer candidness. He would have reached out to just about anybody who cared enough to ask.

"You need to talk to somebody, Barry?" Sherry said very sweetly, and genuinely concerned.

Barry normally would have excused himself politely at this point, but the beer barrier wouldn't have it … That and the lack of any of his loved ones being close. "Yeah, Sherry, that may be just what I need."

"Come on over to my apartment. It's quiet there, and you can crash there if you need to." If Sherry was planning a seduction, Barry didn't see it. He just thought she was being nice and decent, something he hadn't experienced from his wife in years. They left May's and went to Sherry's car. When they arrived at her apartment, Sherry asked Barry if he'd like a drink.

"Have you got any rum and Coke?" Barry and Paul shared the same taste for rum. Maybe it was something about those defensive football players.

"Sure," Sherry said as she reached in her cabinet for the Meyer's, and mixed him a quick one. She mixed herself one, too. "So what is it, Barry? I've never noticed you being like this."

"My wife and my mother have been acting like I'm the Boston Strangler for months. Y'know, it's actually been years now. Time flies when you're having fun. I really do not know what I could have done, but they seem to enjoy hating me, laughing at me, and generally discrediting everything I do. I *do* feel like an underachiever, but I've always brought home the money. And I've always loved and respected them both. I just don't understand it," Barry said with a long sigh. "I wish it didn't bother me so much."

Sherry had chosen to sit in a chair in case Barry wanted to relax and lie down on the couch while they talked. She knew Barry was telling the truth, because she'd tried to flirt with him for years, and Barry wouldn't flirt. Compassionately, she got up, walked slowly and caringly across the room, and sat next to Barry. Putting her drink on the table, she began to rub his temples. "Maybe they're the ones who aren't right, Barry," she said.

"That feels so good, Sherry, I cannot tell you," Barry said honestly, not having had any female touch him with tenderness in what felt like decades. He leaned his head back and closed his eyes.

After the temple rubbing had gone on for about ten minutes, Barry asked, "Aren't you getting tired, Sherry?"

"Barry, I could rub you forever." Now, Sherry was no dirty leg. She was not a railroad rag. She was a sweet local girl who had married the wrong guy and had been divorced for some time. She had worked for years, and then had gone back to school, taking courses from Kansas State University. She was halfway through toward a business degree. Her husband had been a no-account scrounge, thinking himself a ladies' man and even infecting her with gonorrhea, the last straw for Sherry. Sherry had always admired Barry. He was tall, very strong, good-looking, and, very important to her, did not partake of the ladies available. She liked the fact that Barry was faithful to his wife, and wished that she could find someone like him.

Barry had had just enough beer, and was just tired enough of being treated badly by his loved ones, and was feeling his body respond just enough to the affectionate rubs of Sherry, as well as her great looks, to do something very out of character. He gently pulled Sherry across his lap and kissed her. It was a great kiss. It was very sweet. He really needed it. She really needed it. When someone has been cut emotionally adrift by his or her loved ones for an extended period, he or she will respond to about any port in a storm. And this port was beautiful and caring. Sherry responded perfectly. She herself hadn't felt male consideration for a long time. The sweet kissing continued, and gradually evolved into a long, wonderful, loving encounter. Barry and Sherry both finally fell asleep, each temporarily fulfilled.

Barry awoke at 6:15 a.m. and realized what he had done, by degrees, as reality overwhelmed hangover. As Jim Stafford sang, "The morning after the night before comes back in bits and pieces." He hadn't been really drunk, but had somehow put everything out of his pained mind but the sweetness of Sherry. He temporarily hadn't had to think about his wife's and mother's hatred. Then, the enormity of the act finally fell on Barry like a large building that had been instantly demolished by strategically placed charges. He had just committed adultery, a heinous violation of one of God's Commandments. He felt emotionally and spiritually like he was *dead*. In all the years he and Susan had been married, he was never even close to another woman. The dance in Pocatello had been it. He had now done the very thing that was the main reason he left management. He never wanted to do this to Susan, and now, he had done it. Other people did this. He did not.

Then, a buried memory that had been lying in wait for just the right time surfaced. Like a syphilis spirochete finally damaging the brain with paresis after years of dormancy, Barry recalled the words of the crusty old yard foreman, Chance Armstrong: "Talk to me in twenty years, kid." He'd pondered the point at the time, and now Barry knew exactly what the old switchman had meant. There would be a time. And Barry's time had just happened. It went with the territory. Again, as Barry had surmised during his time in Central Pacific management, people are fallible, but much credit went to the situationally dividing work. It separates people constantly. Then it takes you out. It was like one of Harold Barnes's two left jabs, a head fake, and a home-run right cross.

Barry wrote a note to Sherry, who was still sleeping soundly, and signed it "Blessings, Barry." Then he went to the dorm, read his Bible, and went back to sleep until he was called. Barry's life the last few years, up to and including this last indiscretion, could be described very simply: "Kick a dog … Dog bites … Shoot the dog." And because Barry was always immune to such behavior, and abhorred it now, he figured he *deserved* every negative thing that he got from here on. However life wanted to beat him now, he had to take his stripes. He had 'em comin'.

When he returned to Kansas City, as fortune would have it, Susan did not answer the phone when he called from the CP depot. She normally did. When he got home, he found a note that said, "Barry, we have only been 'existing' for years. I have met someone whom I love. I didn't intend this, but it happened. I know you have tried to be a good husband and father." The word *tried* hit Barry right between the eyes. The insinuation was, I have judged you as *not* being a good husband and father. The note continued, "I'll let you see Erin and Graham, of course, anytime. We'll work out the particulars later." The note from hell was signed simply, "Susan."

"Thanks for the horrendous gut shot, Suz," Barry muttered to himself as he read the note. But he instantly surmised that he deserved it. He deserved to be shot. It had to have been over already, or he wouldn't have done what he'd done this last trip. He felt sick at his stomach. The Big Bear was goin' down. Paul and Phil were both at work. Because of the railroad work, the three were rarely together anymore. He needed to talk to someone really badly. He called Rose.

"Rose?"

"Hey, Barry. How's-a my bigga Bear?" Rose said in her usual high-strung, raspy, upbeat voice.

"Well, I don't think I'm doin' too good, Rose."

"Whassa matta, Honey Bear?" Rose asked, using one of her nicknames for Barry since childhood. Actually Susan had first heard the nickname from Rose and liked it. Rose had also called Barry Sugar Bear when he was young with her own two boys. Susan had long ceased ever using any name when addressing Barry.

"I got a note here. Susan is leaving me for someone else."

"Oh, Barry, no! It can't-a be, son." Rose's voice sounded deeply concerned, and more excited.

"I've felt it for a long time. Things have been rough between us. I've been gone so much."

"You been-a gone-a makin' a livin'-a, son!" Rose spoke with forcefulness, defending Barry and displaying the motherly loyalty she felt for Barry that Fran totally lacked.

"I think my mom has helped her to hate me, Rose. I don't understand."

"That White-a clown-a she's-a married-a to, Bear … He's-a no good. You' mama ain't-a been-a the same. She's-a notta the same-a woman. I don't-a know what's-a matta there. You wanna come over here, Bear?"

"No thanks, Rose. I just wanted to talk to someone. Thank God you've always been there for me."

"Always-a will-a, son. Always-a will-a. Now remember, if you-a need-a to come-a over here to stay or anything-a, I betta I can-a find-a some pasta or-a somethin'."

"That's not fair, Rose," Barry said, attempting to be upbeat and realizing what a wonderful woman Rose was. And Barry loved Rose's pasta. "Thanks anyway. I've gotta get my rest. I'll probably get back out in eight hours." Barry always wondered how such a little woman could have such a great love for so many people.

"Okay, but remember-a, Bear, if I can-a do-a anything, letta me know. Im-a so sorry. You come-a by now, when-a you can."

"I know, Rose. Thanks for the ear. I love you."

"I love-a you too-a, son. Bye-bye now."

Barry really loved Rose. He knew his life was better because she had been in it. But it didn't make him *feel* any better. He thought of the new, nice feelings for Sherry in Ellisville, and how she always seemed to care about him. Immediately, he thought how Susan used to feel the same way, and he put Sherry out of his mind. Barry was served his marital pink slip, his divorce papers, a couple of days later. He and Susan were divorced a month later ... just like that. All those years of marriage, and two beautiful children, "just like that." What in the crap happened?

Phil and Paul were stunned. Of all people, Barry and Susan, the eight-by-ten glossies, the perfect couple. "That's why I try to make it a point *not* to fall in love," Paul told Barry. "I got whacked by Amy, but it wasn't a whole lifetime with kids. I don't know what the answer is, that's for sure."

Phil had told Barry he thought his own marriage was on shaky ground. "Carla and I don't do anything together anymore, and I mean *anything*! When I am home, we just pass in the hallway. When I think of how much I needed her ..." Phil was not aware of his remark being in the past tense. "I don't know what the answer is either, Barry. Well, actually, I do. The answer is Jesus. But unfortunately, Jesus takes a backseat to everything in modern American family life. The fault is ours."

In the ensuing months, Barry suffered more mental trauma. Even though Susan had told Barry he could see Erin and Graham, who were now confused young teenagers and really needed their father, she had changed her mind once the courts set the exorbitant child support. "That will keep me from laying off for sure," Barry had said, trying unsuccessfully to be humorous. But he couldn't be humorous about not seeing his beloved babies. He, like Phil and Paul, loved his children more than they would ever know. Like Phil, he understood God when it said in the Bible, "Children are gifts from God." Amen. But now that Susan had her tax-free money coming in monthly, she saw no reason to let Barry see the kids. She found out the system in the form of the Division of Family Services would allow her to take the exorbitant child support and not police visitation. So she took Barry's gifts from God. She wanted her new husband to be Erin and Graham's new father. Fran drove a few extra death spikes into Barry's heart by supporting Susan's insane "substitute dad" approach. Fran adopted an equally insane "substitute son" approach. Fran, who had received a substantial heritage from her folks, even bought New Son a boat, a boat dock, and just about anything he wanted. Now she not only never spoke positively about Barry in front of Erin or Graham, but also began to talk as though Barry was a mistake as their father. When his name was mentioned, she and Susan would roll their eyes and smile in front of Erin and Graham, like anything associated with Barry was a joke. Barry was now the pariah, the family member who embarrassed the rest. He was to be shunned. Every future holiday would have Barry by himself missing his beloved children, and yes, even missing Fran and Susan, since Barry hadn't learned to hate those who hated him. Fran would laugh and tell jokes at these holiday gatherings without the slightest concern for her emotionally dying son, and made certain sure she hugged and encouraged New Son constantly. She was purely a demon, a creature not worthy of breath who never should have been a mother, and Barry was in trouble for sure. As it says in the Bible, "And a man's enemies will be those of his own household." Barry would mutter to himself, "What a slow, horrible death," thinking of the doomed caterpillars on Grandpa and Grandma McAlister's tomato plants that were being eaten alive from the inside out by the wasp larvae. Barry now knew what it felt like.

Phil had reminded Barry of Jesus' statement that should make all of us feel better in times of perceived or actual unfairness directed at us from any source: "Marvel not that the world hateth you. It hated me before you." Obviously, if we're being treated unfairly, we're in the best company: that of Jesus. And I doubt if any of us are actually being nailed to a cross. No doubt, there are endless emotional and physical crosses for us all to bear. Phil watched Barry's expression remain unchanged as he reminded Barry of Jesus' wonderful scripture. He knew Barry was "in the zone" mentally, and that "No Admittance" was flashing red in Barry's psyche.

Years before, Paul, when first dealing with wild Ramona, had remarked that he thought it was the SOBs that were behind all the problems. According to Paul, this stood for "Secret Order of Bitches." Paul would rest his case with Susan and Fran. When Barry told Paul of Susan not allowing him to see his kids, Paul said to him, "Congratulations, Barry. You have been initiated, and you are now a charter member of DAWGS—Dads All Will Get Screwed. I've been a card-carrying member for years."

But at the time, referring to Ramona, Barry cautioned Paul about bitterness, and how it always turned inward. Paul actually didn't feel this strongly, nor was he anti-woman. Look at Rose. There were some wonderful women out there. He just hadn't met one for him. And he knew *his* litter box wasn't the cleanest. He just couldn't resist some attempt at humor. Sometimes the feeble attempt was in itself funnier than the quip. It seemed to help. Humor smoothed rough edges in life. And there was definitely some truth to the DAWGS reference. But both Barry and Phil tended to think the problem with Susan and Fran was one of a spiritual nature. In Ephesians 6:12, we're told, "We wrestle not against flesh and blood ..." That's pretty straightforward, referring to who the enemy *really* is. We're just the conduits for doing good or evil. And Susan and Fran were extremely evil-conducting conduits.

One day, Phil was behind the throttle on his way to Ellisville, and talking with the head brakeman while running the train. The brakeman, Gary Samuels, remarked, "I hope there's a magazine between the mattress and box springs. I'm going to need some intellectual stimulation."

"I know," Phil replied. "I always check, too. It sure helps me sleep." But Phil, who always felt the "tug" of the spirit, questioned out loud, "I wonder what God thinks about it."

"God's probably happy we aren't going out on our wives," Gary offered. "Has anyone ever had to pay their hand alimony?"

"I don't know," Phil said seriously. "I know psychologists and sociologists all tell us to wear ourselves out. If it feels good, do it. But everything I've read in the Bible seems totally against it. It *is* a work of the flesh, even though no one else's flesh is present. It's like substitute fornication. I guess if you were thinking of your wife, it would be okay."

"Yeah, but who'd be dumb enough to do that?" Gary responded honestly. "When I first hired out ... Did you ever meet old Cuppy Garza?"

"No, I've heard about him. I think he was retired before I got down here," Phil said.

"Well, Old Cuppy told me when I first came out on the road, 'Son,' he said, 'remember this: a railroader's right hand is his best friend.'"

"I know, Gary. But it can also be your worst enemy. One trip I knew I probably wasn't going to get together with Carla as usual, and the call of the wild was present. I'm half Italian, you know. The desire is almost *always* present. That stuff flows in buckets in Italians. So I made sure I got enough releases to get it off my mind. As luck would have it, Carla had called my mom to watch the kids, and met me at the door wearing a beautiful new negligee, and holding a bottle of champagne. It was horrible. I wasn't in the mood. In fact, I was sore. She felt rejected, understandably. I mean, what are the odds? Carla usually *never* feels like it anymore, so I just relieve myself. I don't want to go out on her. But I don't want to walk around looking and feeling like a bull elk either. The horns gotta be trimmed once in a while. It's just this miserable work situation. But still I can't see God wanting us to do it without 'da womens.' It's a piss-poor substitute. It *is* an abuse."

Gary, who was working through his second marriage, understood. "You may be right, Phil. But my hand never has a headache, and I don't think my hand will go out on me either. At least I hope it won't."

"It's not me who's right ... It's God."

As the train sped down the tracks, Phil and Gary were silent, but both were thinking about the lack of wifely companionship and self-sustained releases. Phil recalled a buddy of his with whom he played base team basketball overseas, while in Turkey. This guy would take a snapshot of his wife and set it down beside the pillow of the whores he nailed. Phil wondered what God thought about that deal, and again was glad judgment was left to the Lord.

Unbeknownst to Phil, Carla had had another reason for meeting him at the door in a negligee. Carla, who had not consciously been attracted to another man since first meeting Phil that night at the party in Topeka, had found herself flirting the last few months with the local grocery store manager. He was a nice-looking guy, John Avery, who had always noticed the lovely Italian woman coming to the store with her two daughters, and sometimes by herself. John was divorced, and although he wouldn't have considered himself "on the make," he fantasized about Carla a lot. Carla was still quite curvy and beautiful. Because Phil's absenteeism from home had subconsciously left a massive hole in Carla's life, she had struck up quite a conversation with John one day while the girls were in school. Both of them enjoyed it immensely. Both of them were lonely. As time passed, these meetings grew more and more enjoyable, and began leading to luncheon dates.

It bothered Carla to be attracted to another man. Before it went any further with Avery, she wanted to try something. So she met Phil at the door with the champagne when he came in from that trip. She wanted to rekindle what they had, before she let anything more serious occur with Avery. After what Carla thought was rejection from Phil, when in essence it was only bad timing, she made it a point to see Avery every day Phil was out of town. Eventually, she even began working part-time at the store. And this led to the obvious outcome. One time Phil returned home to find a note that read, "Phil, I'm leaving you. We haven't had a life together for a long time. You have been a good husband and father when you were here. You just haven't been here very much these last few years, and we lost each other. Sorry. I will always love you." Unlike Susan's note to Barry, Carla's note had respect and compassion. But then again, you're still just as dead from friendly fire. "Huh-huh! Another one bites the dust, huh-huh!" as Freddie Mercury shouted from Queen.

Phil was mega-stunned. He knew he and Carla had grown apart, but he was still doing what he was supposed to be doing. He was making money for them the only way he had trained to do it. Was her life that bad? He just sat down on the floor, cross-legged, put his head in his hands, and felt like he was on another planet. Several weeks later he would cry for hours, but for now the shock of the note just left him numb. He had never believed this day would come.

He learned from talking with Carla later about the particulars of the divorce that a guy named John Avery was involved. She didn't tell Phil where he worked. Phil had no idea who he was. Phil, Paul, and Barry all grew up with guys who would snuff Avery for really very little. But Phil, the eternal Christian, knew everything he did was on "God's DVD," and the thought to do bodily harm vanished as quickly as it had entered his mind, like Paul thinking about Lance Alward. In the Book of Revelation, verse 20:12, it says, "... and the books were opened; and another book was opened, which is the Book of Life: and the dead were judged out of those things which were written in the books, *according to their works.*" Food for thought: we are not only being monitored, but there is a record available. If we, being God's children, can get a lifetime of information on a mini-chip, it isn't much of a stretch to see the potential for the obvious, that God has our lives in a file for future reference, maybe for us.

Divorce was going to kill Phil, but Carla assured him she would never keep Angela and Margo from him, and unlike Susan, she kept her word. Phil thought to himself, But what about you? You're keeping *you* from me. Six months after the divorce, Carla married Avery. He proved to be a decent stepfather to the girls, but a substitute for Phil with them he was not. They would always hold their mother in disdain somewhere in their hearts for divorcing their father. Phil would continue to work as a hoghead, now paying some horrendous child support to Carla and Avery, who didn't even have to claim it as income. And Phil was taxed on it. The ex-spouse could use the child support for transportation and housing as decreed by the state law and the Division of Child Support Enforcement. So with Phil's added tax-free gratuity to them every month of $800, the same as Barry's monthly stipend to Susan, Carla and Avery bought a bigger house and a nicer car. It worked out. God bless America. Phil would have liked to have his salary with nothing taken out, and for someone to pay him $800 tax-free extra money every month for about ten years. It *could* work. Thank God, heaven is forever!

When he saw them, Phil got lots of emotional support from Paul and Barry, although Barry was about "half there." Now all three were in the same divorced-dad status. Harold and Rose still loved Carla, and vice versa. But unlike Fran, Rose had told Carla, "You been-a like-a daughter to me, Carla … the one I never had-a. Shoot-a … you *been-a* my daughter! But my son-a, he is-a *my* son-a. Now you are just-a the mother of-a my gran-a-kids. I will always love-a you. You know-a that. But you ain't-a my daughter no more." Rose was extremely bright, but kept the word *ain't* in her vocabulary. It was her connection with the earlier Italian immigrants like her father, when they first learned to "speaka de English." Phil actually didn't want his parents "dissing" Carla. He would always love her for the good wife she had been to him and the good mother she was to the kids. He blamed the railroad as the ultimate culprit. If he and Barry could have had jobs to allow them to be home just a bit more, maybe things would have been different for them both. A woman and man are married to be together. Still, Phil appreciated tremendously that his mom took up for him. Rose didn't know any other way to be. Rose was as loyal as a mother as Fran was disloyal.

Back at the railroad, Groove had written another song. He was considered a "Jesus freak" by his fellow railroaders. For some baby boom railroaders, the path to Jesus was by way of drugs. It was not an uncommon path for the 1940s-born sixties generation. It was all a search. One time Phil, who was always a little more controlled than most, asked one of the so-called Jesus freaks why he had to experiment with drugs in the first place: wasn't that a heck of a way to find the Lord? The switchman's answer was to tell Phil he hadn't intended to let the drugs get to him, and wasn't Jesus happy to get us any way he could? It made sense to Phil, and he was ashamed for semi-judging the switchman.

But the Jesus freaks had trimmed their beards, or shaved them off completely over the years, and cut their hair shorter. And they were all great guys. Groove had cleaned up also, but he'd left the earring, a remnant of the late sixties and early seventies, to remind himself and others where they'd come from, lest they forget. But Jesus seemed to be occupying more of Groove's songs of late, like his latest contribution, "Ups & Downs." It was a song with which most railroaders, truckers, factory workers, and anyone who experienced the daily meat grinder could easily identify.

## Ups & Downs

Up on coffee,
Down on beer.
What excitement,
What a career.

But it's what gets me
Through the year.
Up on coffee,
Down on beer.

Up on hope and
Down on life.
Lost my job and
Lost my wife.

It's these ups and downs
That I fear.
Up on coffee.
Down on beer.

Chorus

Ups and downs are all we see
When we are here.
Sometimes it seems
That all I see are downs.

But I get some relief
From my caffeine and beer,
And muddle through with
All the other clowns.

Up on country,
Down on town.
I don't like buildings
All around.

I like to see them
In my rearview mirror.
Up on coffee.
Down on beer.

Chorus

Up on heaven,
Down on hell.
Jesus is comin'...
I know it well.

I can't wait till
He gets here.
Won't need coffee,
Won't need beer.

Up forever! Jesus is here!

# CHAPTER 33
## GOD'S GIRL

One Sunday, Paul was sitting on the couch in his apartment watching a Kansas City Chiefs game. It was October 12, 1991. The Chiefs were winning, but their archrivals, the Raiders, were threatening. Paul felt subconscious security from a rivalry that dated back to the sixties. It was nice when some things didn't change.

There was a knock on the door, and then the doorbell rang. At the same time, Paul heard shuffling and what sounded like children's voices. Must be Girl Scout cookie time, Paul thought as he went to answer the door. Do they sell cookies on Sunday? he wondered. They *do* sell some good ones.

When he opened the door, he almost fell over. There, standing in front of him, statuesque and lovely as ever, was Amy Johnson. Her hair was longer, and there were maybe five extra pounds, but she was still *very* stunning. She had an eleven-year-old girl and a twelve-year-old boy with her, and she was shaking uncontrollably, crying tears of joy. "Hey!" Paul yelled with astonishment and an overwhelming happiness he hadn't felt in seven years. They all four instantly hugged. Then they stepped back and just looked at each other in sweet amazement. Then Amy began to speak excitedly.

"Paul, after you and I broke up, I, well, you know, I went back to the way I was. Then one day, a trucker came into town and stopped for lunch at May's. He looked over at me and smiled, and I guess I, well, you know." Amy was talking excitedly and loudly, with lots of emotion.

"You went with him," Paul helped her, too glad to see her to bother scrutinizing the senseless choice. "Yes, Phil told me you had disappeared."

"So anyway," Amy caught her breath for another round, "we went all over the United States and everything. I had to call Judy to get checked out of my apartment and have her handle things and sell my stuff and send me money, and … well … oh, this is Megan," she said, cupping the back of her daughter's head in her right hand. "And this is Jason," she said as she put her left hand around her son's neck. "Aren't they beautiful?"

"Of course… Look who their mama is," Paul said with enormous delight, still not stable from the initial shock of seeing the love of his life at his door. "Amy, come in, you guys, and let's all sit down." Paul took their coats, turned off the Chiefs without thinking about them, and sat down next to Amy on the couch, wondering if he was dreaming. The children each sat politely and quietly, in different chairs.

"So listen, Paul," Amy went on. "Something made me call Mom to see how my kids were doing. She was so glad to hear from me, she started crying. She had quit drinking, divorced the rat, and pulled the kids out of foster care to live with her. But Paul, she told me Megan had cancer … *Cancer, Paul!*" Amy was barely able to catch her breath. "So I left this trucker and went home to San Antonio. Paul, I prayed to God for Him to heal Megan. They said she was *terminal*, Paul, and *look* at her! They said it was a *miracle*! Anyway, I made this pact with God. You know how I liked *Little House on the Prairie*? Well, I'd heard that Michael Landon made a deal with God, that if God would let his daughter who was terminal live, he would always do good stuff, you know. Well, his daughter *did* live, and Michael *did* do good stuff. Well, I made a deal with God that I would give myself *totally* to Him if He'd let Megan live, and look at her, Paul!"

"She's perfect. And so is he," Paul said about Jason, smiling at them both.

"So listen, Paul, they said her chances were zero, but she *is* perfect. The next few months were like I was on a different planet, Paul. Mom loves me again, and is so sorry for what she did. She's a wonderful grandmother. The kids love their nana. And Paul, God began showing me the evil I did. Each horrible act, one by one, God made me contend with, and repent of, until there were no more left. I saw every sick thing

I had ever done. It was like I was watching another person. It was so weird. Paul, this took *weeks*. I know He's forgiven me. I have not had crack, coke, liquor, pills, grass, or anything since then. That was *five years ago*. I haven't even had sex, Paul, at least when someone else was present." Paul knew what she meant.

"Paul, I'm *really* different. I can't explain it, but I am. God is awesome."

Paul could see it in her bluish-purple eyes. Amy had always had a devilish look in her eyes, attractive and seductive, that said, "I'll do anything, anytime, anywhere." That look was gone and had been replaced with an absolutely loving, tranquil quality. It was the look of, well, peace, and maybe even more ... *wisdom*. And to Paul, Amy's eyes reflecting godly love were even more beautiful than they were before, and they weren't red from overindulgence now. They looked like flawless, bluish-purple sapphires.

"I never realized how really screwed up I was, Paul. I just existed. I'm a new person, Paul ... a *new* person in Christ, and Paul, you know what? The new Amy loves you *even more* than the old Amy!" she bawled, tears now streaming down her face.

Paul, too, was now crying, as were the kids, who were so close to their mother, and happy and confused at the same time to see her so emotionally keyed. Paul was beginning to believe in every happy ending he had ever seen, and thought to himself, Only in the movies.

They all seemed to be aware of a chosen pathway for the four of them. There was a strange "liking" that was evident with all involved. Acceptance between Amy and Paul and Amy and the children was obvious, but there was a bizarre acceptance, almost like predestiny, that Paul and the children felt toward each other ... that was something else. They seemed to sense Paul's subconscious and natural desire to be their "daddy," and they liked it ... like he was *supposed* to be their daddy. And they *needed* a daddy. Paul had already thought about them for years, always reliving when he and Amy sang "Just My Imagination" and the part about the children in the song. Over the years, he had prayed often for them and their mother, and never stopped. He felt a wonderful "need" in both Megan's and Jason's hugs, and he knew he could easily supply that need, always feeling he was *supposed* to be their father. The electromagnetics were in overdrive this afternoon.

Amy had even taken college courses over the last five years, and had almost completed a counseling degree. She had been on a new medication that had replaced Ritalin, to control her ADHD, and the "noise" had finally stopped, allowing her to concentrate. Amy had always told Paul she wanted to help others, another of their mutual wishes.

"Paul," Amy said, tearfully, lovingly, and seriously, "we're *all* ready to become Barneses, if you'll still have us. Will you?" Amy still possessed the confidence and boldness that resulted from the off-the-scale closeness she and Paul had shared years before, but at this particular moment, *everything* she had dreamed about rested on Paul's answer. As soon as she had aligned with God and Megan was cured, she had a singleness of thought, after her own children, and it was about Paul. She thought constantly of them being together, without any thought of the possibility that it would not occur. Amy had never stopped praying for Paul, either, over the years, and knew no one else could ever replace him in her heart. After Megan was miraculously healed, all three, Megan, Jason, and Paul, were Amy's "loved ones." Now she had just asked the only man she had ever *really* loved, properly, beautifully, if he still wanted her ... if he would marry her. Her bluish-purple lasers were wide open with purity, expectation, and hope, just waiting for Paul to literally make her dreams come true.

Paul thought the question was totally unnecessary from his beautiful bride-to-be. She was all he had ever dreamed about ever since he'd first fallen in love with her. In the years since, no one else was ever even close. The hardest thing he had ever done in his life was leave Amy, and actually, he never mentally or emotionally had. He knew he could never let another female in his heart, because it was already occupied. So for Amy to ask him this question was like asking a man dying of thirst in the desert if he'd like a drink of water.

"You better know it!" Paul grabbed Amy and held her so tightly that she felt like his own body. Amy, too, had a hold on Paul any Worldwide Wrestling Federation participant would have been proud to learn. They just hugged and hugged, sobbing with pure joy and affection, in a dynamic embrace, bound together, as was the case with the two of them from their beginning. Megan and Jason, too, were still sobbing gently with joy. Paul reached a big hand toward them and motioned them over to him and their mom. All four continued the hugging. It was wonderful!

Finally, the Paul and Amy Electromagnetics Pregame Show with two young, highly touted draft picks began winding down. "Anybody hungry?" Paul asked, still feeling like this was a beautiful daydream.

"We're starved," all three said in unison.

"Good, let's go fill up." The four of them, the happy future family, all rushed down to Paul's truck, which had the small bench seat in the back. There, Megan and Jason would be quite comfortable while their mother held hands with their new dad in the front seat.

"Paul," Amy said with a beautiful, patented Amy smile, her bluish-purple eyes showing just a slight hint of the former impishness. "I was checked, and I can still have children, honey." She grinned. "As soon as we're married, let's begin work on Roman Carlos or Alison Rose."

Paul just smiled a huge smile, looking ahead at the road. He loved Rosalinda so much, and his nieces and nephew, but thought after he and Amy parted that another offspring on this earth wouldn't be happening for him. He turned to Amy. Paul hadn't missed it, and had correctly taken Amy's cryptic message of "As soon as we're married" to mean he wasn't going to be involved with any of the explosive Paul and Amy Electromagnetic Reviews until they were actually man and wife, joined before God. Paul loved it. Amy was the real deal. She was now indeed "God's girl."

"Let's work on them both," Paul answered happily, sensing the most wonderful, totally content feeling he could ever remember. Amy just smiled and put her hand up behind Paul's wide, muscular neck, and leaned over and kissed his cheek. "Paul ... God *is* awesome." The four of them drove off, talking and laughing, secure in the beautiful future that only a short time ago, none of them had. Life was, at times, *really* wonderful!

Paul thought of his brother, Phil, and Barry. How absurd, he thought. He had been the screw-up. They were the constants, the pillars. They had been his wonderful, unwavering mentors all through life, his older brothers, and he had been the unstable, good-time boy. And now, he was the one with the family, and they were separate and apart from their families. Yes, life was really wonderful sometimes ... and totally absurd at other times.

# CHAPTER 34
## PICNIC

Paul and Amy were in the process of last-minute preparation for the Fourth of July picnic they had planned for some time. Guests had already begun to arrive, the first being Harold and Rose. At first, they had been extremely leery of having Amy as a daughter-in-law, since after Paul and Amy's breakup, both Paul and Phil had discussed Amy's horrendous past with them. They viewed the breakup as Paul dodging a hellish bullet. They were monumentally relieved that Paul had not ultimately been saddled with Amy. They could not imagine how anyone with such a history could be anything but bad news for their son.

But after Paul and Amy were married, Rose and Amy hit it off like mother and daughter, because the new, improved Amy was a clone of Rose ... loving, caring, strong, selfless, putting others first, and most important, godly. After Amy had surprised Paul with the children that afternoon several years ago, Paul couldn't wait to introduce them to his folks. So the very next day after Amy showed up on Paul's doorstep with the children, the four of them went over to Harold and Rose's to tell them of their marriage plans. Jason and Megan had gone into the living room to watch TV, where Rose had fixed them some Italian sausage, Italian bread and fontina cheese, and Cokes. The adults had stayed in the dining room. Before anyone could bring up a subject, Amy began her story to Harold and Rose. Her honesty was overwhelming. Thank God she did not go into lurid detail, but she did end the explanation by saying, "But I'm *not* like that now, and *never* will be again." She said this with stern conviction, more than just from the vocal cords or even the heart. She spoke it from her spirit. Rose and Harold were both impressed. They were chosen to be wonderful parents for Amy, and wonderful grandparents for Jason and Megan. Jason and Megan loved Rose and Harold instantly, and vice versa. They were blessed with wonderful grandparents as quickly as they were blessed with a wonderful dad. Paul observed the love gathering just as he knew it would be, because God was at the base of it all. He ordered this. He ordained this.

That was five years ago. It was now 1996, and the Paul and Amy Electromagnetic Review had placed Alison Rose Barnes and Roman Carlos Barnes on the earth, to the great satisfaction of Rose and Harold. Alison and Roman were incredibly beautiful, intelligent, musical, and athletic, just like Paul and Amy imagined their offspring would be years before. This was such a special Fourth of July, because it marked the twelfth anniversary of the first time Paul and Amy met. And the fireworks were still exploding. Halleluiah!

A horn honked in rapid succession, signaling Phillip's arrival. He had a pickup full of beer, soft drinks, and brats. As he pulled up to meet his brother in the driveway with the rest of the clan inside, he asked Paul, "Is Barry comin'?"

"Dunno, Philsy," Paul said, and he shrugged. "He said he'd try. The extra board has evidently been turning like a top lately, and he didn't know if he'd get back in time. Then he'd have to get back out in eight hours. Everybody wants off on the Fourth. I talked with him Tuesday. He seemed distant, as usual."

"Yeah, I don't know about the Bear anymore. I think Fran and Susan have just about killed him, literally," Phil said, extremely disgusted. "He's never rebounded. All these years Fran won't talk to him and has encouraged his kids to look down on him, just like Susan has. It's just pure evil. And Bear Man won't talk to me about it."

"Why do you suppose this has happened? Mom can hardly stomach talking to Fran. She became such a flake anyway. How could a woman that wonderful make such a dramatic change in behavior?" Paul said, equally disgusted and feeling the hurt in his gut for Barry that Phil did. "I think it's that demon Fran married, Don White. He's a real treasure.

And you know, Philsy, Barry has never come out of it from his divorce either, like you did. I think he still loves Susan."

"I know, Paul. It's sad. I used the very same five rules I gave you for dealing with the loss of Amy years ago, that Charles Stanley preached about: Look to the Lord, trust in the Lord, get with the Word, obey the Word, and pray. It still wasn't easy, but it was much *easier*. You can't waste time wondering why. I gave the five rules to Barry, too. Whether he used them or not, I don't know. You just have to trust God. But also, the difference in my case is that Mom would die before she would have anything more to do with Carla after she left me, other than exchange the normal banter about the kids. Mom still cares for Carla, but as soon as she left me, that was it for Mom. Mom prays for her, but she stands by me. Fran has not only turned on Barry, her *only* kid, but has showered Susan and New Dad with hundreds of thousands of dollars over the years. Fran evidently received a pretty good inheritance from her parents when they sold their farm in Iowa. And she's encouraged Erin and Graham to look at their father as a jerk. Fran's son is now Susan's husband ... Talk about the gut shot that was heard 'round the world. Is that nuts or what? I think Fran has lost it. She was like a second mother to us growing up, but she makes me literally puke now. What could be more painful? Another difference is that Carla lets me see the kids. Susan has destroyed Barry, keeping him from his beloved bambinos. But Barry just keeps on going, like a big Irish Energizer Bunny. I don't think there's much energy left in the big bunny anymore. I don't know how he does it. I mean, can you imagine Mom or Dad turning on us?"

"No, thank God. You know as well as I do that the thought could never occur to me that those two would ever be so horribly cruel to us," Paul added. "But then again, Fran was a decent mom to Barry when he was growing up. She must be really screwed up between the ears. What a horribly hateful woman. Barry told me one time, making time and a half on the holidays gave him a pain in the gulu, because it meant he was working to keep that clown Susan married in cigars and beer. And the clown wound up with his family on those holidays. I guess he's turned into quite the squirrel, according to Erin and Graham. They do pretty well. Susan got a job at the mall, and he's a salesman. Barry gives them $800 a month. Erin's off child support now, but Graham still has a while, and Barry's divorce wasn't child-specific. So the amount is the same, even though Erin's off of it. There's all that, plus the big bucks Fran gives them. Do you know Fran paid for Susan and New Dude's honeymoon? I also heard she bought them a beautiful house to use as rental property, and who knows what else."

"You must be jivin' me. Fran did all that? Why didn't she just shoot him? I hope Barry can hold out. Fran can't be mentally right. It has to be some form of dementia. I know she's played the 'buy everything for the grandkids' game. She thinks this counteracts the discrediting of Barry with them. It doesn't even sound right to repeat. But remember what Uncle Phil used to tell us, Pauly? God, He's-a takin-a notes. I think the Bible somewhere allows for remarriage, but in Matthew 19:9, Jesus says, 'But I say unto you, whosoever shall put away his wife, except it be for fornication, and shall marry another, committeth adultery; and whoso marrieth her which is put away, doth commit adultery.' There's no confusion there. You never hear preachers or priests touch that one, or they'd lose half their memberships, and as a result, half their tithes. But Uncle Phil is definitely right ... God *is* taking notes."

"I've tried to tell Barry that, Phil, and that God tells us not to be weary in well-doing, and that he *is* doing well, but he's wearing down. He lost his dad in the early eighties. He lost his mom to the devil years ago. And Susan followed suit. I've told him to blame the devil. The devil's purposes are 'to kill, to steal, and to destroy.' I don't want Barry destroyed anymore. And although sometimes it may not seem that way to him, his kids *do* need him."

"I know, too, that he feels like an unsuccessful drone at the railroad. I always figured the railroad chose me. I didn't choose the railroad. Heck, I don't think this is necessarily what I wanted to do either," Phil commented.

"I still don't know what I want to do, Phil." Paul laughed at the thought.

Phil, Paul, and Barry, over the years, had all developed a middle-aged paunch. None were in the Olympian category of Paunch Phillips's anatomical wonder, but all were naturally heavier. Paul had the least tummy extension, because of his occupation as a conductor and often being on the ground walking. Since the rear and head brakemen had been cut off, all the switch-lining, car-riding, and brake-tying duties were left solely to the conductor. Paul had somewhat of a workout at work. Plus, Paul and his buddy Pat Anderson had worked out together for years to help defray the weight their beer consumption would have put on them otherwise. So Paul had remained a rather still-muscular 235 pounds.

Phil and Barry hadn't fared as well being stuck behind the throttle for years. While they were married, Carla had seen to it that Phil had all he could stand to eat. Again, Phil and other railroaders called their lunches "nose bags," like farmers used to tie on horses. Phil felt like he ate like a horse. Phil would eat the great lunches from Carla, and then when the crew went to beans, Phil would go with them and order additional food. This cumulative process had netted him an average weight of about 250 pounds, like his father, Harold. Phil still looked good, though, because of his large frame, and the extra weight was proportioned all over.

Barry was by far the largest of the three. He was the proverbial "mountain of a man." In fact, he looked like a mountain man. Because of his depression, he had taken to eating too much and drinking copious amounts of beer, both unintentional attempts to search for any kind of "feel-good" attainable. This behavior, coupled with the normal lack of exercise that plagues most railroad engineers, had left Barry with a weight of 310 pounds. With his 6-foot 4-inch height and his naturally large frame, a genetic gift from both Fran and Bill, Barry still didn't look that bad. Phil and Paul would look at him and think, *That guy could snap anybody's neck in a heartbeat, if he wanted.* Yes, Barry was "the Bear" for sure, but he was an ant when it came to his own mother and his ex-wife, and they'd stepped on him every chance they could. And in recent months, he'd turned into a stoic zombie.

"Well, I brought a load of golden elixir over, and some Johnsonville brats, and beaucoup fireworks. We need to become festive. Smells like you guys already got the grill going. The beer won't bother Amy, will it?"

"Not at all. She's like Mom. She only has a little Chianti wine now and then. She just lost her desire to drink anything alcoholic. She's still a Coke freak, but it's the liquid kind. Let's get those brats on the grill, and give me a brew, brother."

The newly dumped white rock gravel crunched under Barry's blue S-10 as he approached Paul and Amy's place. The white road, combined with the green pastures, cropped short by the neighbor's Holsteins, and the blue sky made Paul and Amy's white picket fence–surrounded place look like a little piece of heaven on earth. They made it, Barry thought as he turned into the driveway, and smiled. As Barry put his truck in park, he was aware of the summer's first *zur-ees* by the cicadas in the trees. A strange sadness began to pour over Barry, eclipsing even the generally depressed mood that now typified his personality. He subconsciously felt something was about to end.

"Hey, Bear Man," Paul yelled. "Why don't you get yourself a bigger truck? You can afford one now." Paul, as usual, was attempting humor, referring to Barry's large size in the small truck. "How 'bout a brewski, brother?" Barry liked his S-10, because the gas savings meant more money for his kids. He had taken the back off his seat, so his back was against the back of the cab. It wasn't a bad fit now, even with Barry's king-sized body. Although it did look absurd, seeing big Barry get out of the little truck.

The day was perfect and the mood did become festive ... for all but Barry. Paul and Phil were always glad to have their "other" brother around. Harold and Rose were glad to see their "other" son. Amy and Barry had also been friends from the railroad, so this time together was wonderful, all except for one thing.

Barry had been really putting the beer away, even before he came over. He had not marked off, and had planned to lay off sick, which he never did as a rule. But since he was now working the engineer's extra board again, he was expected to cover the jobs where everyone else had laid off for the holiday. The CP really did not like anyone laying off on extra boards that were designed to cover the jobs of employees laying off. You marked up on the extra board to work ... all the time. But Barry had mentioned earlier to Paul that he was really sick of work. Barry had no life other than railroading. He wasn't the type to delve into the dirty legs at Ellisville, and the isolation inherent in the work never allowed him the opportunity to meet another decent woman other than Sherry. The incident with Sherry years before had embarrassed Barry, because it was so unlike him. And even though he really did like her, he'd avoided her from then on. His thoughts at the time were, I used to love and trust Susan, too, and look what happened to that. Eventually, Sherry married someone else, perhaps a missed boat for Barry and Sherry both, but Barry would never know.

Barry had listened to and enjoyed the great song by the group Extreme in the early nineties, "Hole Hearted." One of the lines in the chorus is "There's a hole in my heart that can only be filled by you." Barry had four holes in his heart. And as wonderful and supportive as Harold, Rose, Phil, and Paul always were, it wasn't enough to replace the loss of Susan, Erin, Graham, and Fran. Barry had lost a monumental amount of mental, emotional, and spiritual blood from these holes. And he was still bleeding profusely. There wasn't much left in him.

Had Graham and Erin realized that every corpuscle in Barry's large body constantly ached for them, his precious children? Barry knew the answer was "probably not." And Barry, ever the quiet giant, always looking for the best, realized it was probably a good thing that children, in general, were easily occupied. It lessened their pain. Erin and Graham had reached young adulthood almost by default. Although they were exceptionally gifted, they both had dropped out of high school, and eventually got GEDs. It just wasn't right. How could the kids be that gifted and not do anything? It was more worldly destruction for Barry. He blamed himself, but it wasn't even remotely his fault. Susan had just quit mothering them, her own life being much more important. Barry often imagined, *If I could just have been with them a little bit ... guided them, maybe they could have found the handle.* Barry didn't want them worrying about their dad. Did Fran and Susan realize the years of pain they had heaped on Erin and Graham with their insensitive, insane hatred for Barry? Again, the answer was "probably not." The devil does some fine work on this planet.

Phil could identify somewhat with Barry, but since he'd seen Angela and Margo almost as much as when he and Carla were married, the separation wasn't nearly as bad. Carla hadn't wanted to hurt Phil the way Susan wanted to hurt Barry. And Susan knew she could hurt him the most by keeping him from his babies. As a result, Angela and Margo were much better served, and were less neurotic than Erin and Graham. And, although Barry felt otherwise, Erin and Graham had missed and loved their father very much over the years. But on this Fourth of July in 1996, Barry's mood had degenerated from relatively benign to almost psychotic. "I'm tired, Paul, really tired of it all. It never changes. I'm just *so* tired of it." Barry's voice wavered from genuine depression. He sounded as if he were almost ready to cry, but was fighting the urge.

Quiet, easygoing Barry had mentioned to Phil and Paul years before that at one time, he actually thought about killing Susan's new husband, Dave. Phil and Paul had referred to Dave as "Dave the Dude," from the Damon Runyon character, or "New Dude, New Dad," or "New Son," since he'd simply replaced Barry in the McAlister family. Like a cuckoo offspring replaces the other baby birds after it kicks them out of the nest to their deaths below, New Dude took over, totally. Barry's uncharacteristic murderous thought had been fleeting, like the immediate response to someone who deliberately cuts you off in traffic. It quickly goes away, unless the road rage gremlin gets you. It had occurred hundreds of thousands of times before in life, no doubt: "If I can't have her, neither can you." (Boom!) It had all seemed so unfair to Barry. This guy had stolen his wife, his kids, *and* his mother, of all things, essentially what Barry had considered his *whole life*. Over the years, both Paul and Phil had attempted to console Barry with the biblical standpoint that it's all "just for a season." They told him there was a much better life that lasted for eternity. They also told Barry all evil comes from the devil. If we retaliate, then the devil gets us all. No matter what cards we were dealt here on earth, they were nothing compared with eternity in paradise. Sometimes it had actually helped, and helped a lot, for Barry to hear these words from his buddies.

Phil and Paul also reminded Barry of a couple of Harold's nonscriptural jewels, "The strength of steel is the test of its temper" and "You can tell the strength of a man by the strength of his enemies." Barry agreed with both statements, and they also helped. But the persistence of evil had triumphed. Fran reminded Phil of the hideous excuse for a mother portrayed so perfectly by Mary Tyler Moore in *Ordinary People*. It had been brutal to watch Fran's unceasing viciousness.

But tonight, the beer was successfully anesthetizing Barry to the point of building a barrier between him and the Holy Spirit, who always made the choices between right and wrong clear. There were lots of barriers lately. Alcohol-based choices are not good choices. Right and wrong were beginning to mix together in his clouded mind, and he was tired, so tired of the hatred coming at him. He just wanted it to stop.

The comforting words spoken by his good friends over the years, and at present, did not settle in his psyche at this moment. His countenance took on the look of the chubby recruit in *Full Metal Jacket,* played so brilliantly by Vincent D'Onofrio, right before he blew away the gung-ho DI, also brilliantly played by Lee Ermey. Another salvo of the cicada chorus began singing in the trees ... *Zur-ee, zur-ee, zur-ee.*

"I think I'll be headin' out, you guys," Barry mumbled almost imperceptibly to Phil and Paul.

"Why don't you just lay off sick and crash here tonight?" Paul said immediately, although he knew it was already a moot point. When the three boys were younger, quite often they drove with a "load on," and always drove respectably and carefully. But this night, there was a difference. Phil and Paul had seen Barry—quiet, normally steadfast Barry—seem rattled to the point of total despair. Amy had invited Erin and Graham, but they were at the lake with friends.

"Did you say good-bye to Mom and Dad, and Amy and the kids?" Phil quickly asked, thinking if Barry went to say good-bye to Rose, she'd make him stay. Rose could always control Barry like that, as she could Harold, Phil, and Paul, and now her grandchildren. Rose could do this because she was strong, insistent, and *right*.

"Yes," Barry lied to his lifelong *gumbas*. "See you," he said, barely audibly. "You guys will always be the best." There was something ominously final about the way Barry said, "You guys will always be the best," like "no matter what happens, and something may." The cicadas had begun a loud, steady chorus: *zur-ee, zur-ee, zur-ee.*

Phil and Paul watched in dismay as the blue S-10 backed slowly out of the blacktopped driveway, and crunched as the rear tires hit the new, white crushed limestone that had been dumped and graded on the country road. The S-10 pulled forward, stopping after a few yards. Because light waves travel faster than sound waves, Phil and Paul saw the flash in the S-10 cab a nanosecond before they heard the report from the .357 Magnum. Their hearts cried out together in inconceivable anguish. The S-10 had rolled forward a few feet and jerked still when the engine died. Barry's foot had lost the strength to keep the clutch pedal depressed as he, also, died.

Neither Phil nor Paul could remember getting to the truck. They were there immediately, witnessing a scene they never dreamed they'd have to observe. There was nothing beyond this. Nothing could be said. Behind the house, Harold, Rose, Amy, and the grandchildren were happily setting off a myriad of different fireworks. They had supposed the extra-loud report coming from the front was a large aerial bomb their uncles or father had gotten for the Fourth of July. They came around from the back, all smiling and laughing, Harold and Rose with jacketed ice teas.

"Mom! Amy! Keep the kids up there!" Paul shouted, half insane, the hopelessness in his quivering voice evident.

"What's the problem, Paul?" Harold yelled with his right hand cupped on the right side of his mouth, a subconscious attempt to make the sound carry farther.

"Keep 'em up there, Pop!" Paul yelled again. "Have 'em go back around in back!" Harold began trotting toward the S-10. Phil had been cradling Barry's blown-out head in his arms, totally speechless and feeling nothing, not even Barry's last blood on earth, trickling over his fingers. Phil would never be the same.

When Harold got to the truck, he had already associated the loud report with the horrible outcome, and all he could say was "Oh, no." And he repeated it over and over and over: "Oh no, oh no, oh no."

"The Three Musketeers," or "Mouseketeers," as Harold used to tease them when they were boys, would never ride again. An entire lifetime of Barry soared through Harold's mind as he looked upon the unnecessarily wasted life. He remembered when the boys, ages eleven, eleven, and ten, had attempted to paint the house one night after he and Rose went to bed. They were wired from a good time at the drive-in, too many Cokes, and a full moon. They wanted to help, and surprise Harold, so they got paint buckets and brushes and painted the Barnes's house during the night. Of course there was more paint on them than the house. But it did save Harold a lot of work. All he had to do was touch up. Harold had dubbed them Larry, Moe, and Curly after the house-painting episode. No one was sure it wasn't all a horrible nightmare at this point.

Rose, who left Amy in back with the young people, was quickly on her way to the S-10. She was already in tears, having guessed what had occurred, like Harold, having simultaneously associated the loud report and Phil and Paul at Barry's truck. When Paul had yelled for them to keep the kids up there, she knew for sure. Rose was running with her hands pressed to her face. She had tried unsuccessfully, many times, to break through the horrible barrier that Fran had built between herself and Barry. She had even gone as far one time, after talking with Barry and feeling his hopelessness, as driving over to talk to Fran and tell her she was killing her own son. Fran's reaction, of course, was to blink the Lucille Ball eyes at Rose and refrain from comment.

Rose stopped twenty feet from the S-10. Normally frantic, she now displayed an eerily calm, mission-bound demeanor. She slowly and deliberately turned around and walked back up the driveway, and got into her and Harold's Accord. She drove out of the driveway without looking at or talking to anyone. She drove directly to Fran's house, where Fran was sitting across the table with her third husband, Don White, the controlling, despot-like retired foreman from the local auto assembly plant. They were soused, as usual, making goo-goo eyes at each other and engaging in mindless, inane small talk before what usually degenerated into either a sloppy, awkward, unfulfilling sexual encounter, involving White's hands, or a slapstick boxing match, which Fran usually lost. It sure beat spending the holidays with your only son and his family.

Rose knocked and entered at the same time, not waiting for permission, quickly walking up to the absurdly amorous duo. "I hope-a I will notta say-a or do-a anything I will-a regret-ta," Rose said in an uncharacteristically calm but firm voice. There were still tears in her eyes. Don had not yet met Rose, since Rose and Fran were no longer close. He was trying to make sense of what was happening, since he'd swilled more Jack Daniels than Fran at this point. He usually did. He blinked a couple of times and pulled off his glasses, clumsily wiping them with the same handkerchief he'd used for his runny nose.

"You should-a be-a very happy this-a July Fourth, Fran. You'll-a always have-a somp-a-ting to celebrate the rest-a of-a you'-a life on this-a date."

"What's that, Rose?" Fran asked with booze-assisted indifference.

"*The death-a of-a your-a only son!*" Rose yelled, finally unable to contain herself, and slamming her powerful little fist down on the dining room table. As she did, Fran's glass tipped over toward her on the table, spilling the Jack and Coke in her lap. Fran, in a reflex action, pushed back from the table and fell over backward in her chair.

"Now look here, lady," Don said as he stood up at the table. In an instant, Rose, diminutive Rose, jumped up and hit aging Don White right in his bulbous, booze-soaked, runny nose. A trickle of blood appeared. Out came the utility handkerchief.

"Don't-a you *ever* stand up at-a me like-a that again, boy!" Rose said with her hands on her hips, leering at Don White the way a nineteen-year-old Mike Tyson leered at his opponents before tearing their heads off.

"Sit down, Don," Fran slowly said, quietly crying now. The bad news finally soaked through. She was still in her backward position in her chair, like a sixties astronaut waiting for liftoff. Her tearful eyes were closed, and she was visualizing Barry as a little guy. What a wonderful son he had been. All the while Fran had decided to hate Barry, she had never given any thought to the insanity of her behavior. It was "right" to her. No logic was ever involved. Over the years, those who knew the situation and tried to talk to Fran about it had been met with Lucille Ball wide-eyed blank stares and the proverbial unspoken comment. No one got through. Fran was never going to be convinced otherwise. Now it was all over. No more hatred was necessary. Fran, Susan, and the devil had now won.

Rose calmed down and took a step backward, not bothering to attempt to help Fran up. "I don't-a know what's-a been-a wrong with-a you, Fran. But I hope-a one-a thing, and one-a thing only, and that is, that you will-a live *every day-a* of-a the rest-a of-a you'-a life-a with the knowledge that-a you-a, this-a abusive-a drunk, and that-a sickening gold-a digger of an ex-daughter-in-a-law have-a *killed* your only child."

As Rose turned to walk away, Don White pulled off his glasses and wiped a slight bloodstain on one of the lenses with his less-than-antiseptic hanky. Fran just stayed in her horizontal sitting position in her chair with her eyes closed, never wanting to move again.

Rose drove over to St. Aloysius for confession.

# CHAPTER 35
## FINISHED TRIP

Barry's had not been the last dead body Phil had to deal with until Ralph Dunne. Two years after Barry's death, Harold was mowing the grass with the riding lawn mower. It stopped running, still with half a tank of gas, and Harold was pushing it up to the garage to work on it. He felt severe pains in his chest and called for Rose to call 911, which she did. Immediately after, she called Phil. Paul was at work at Central Pacific, where Rose also called. Phil arrived just as the emergency techs were loading Harold into the ambulance on a stretcher. Harold reached up his hand to Phil, smiling, and grabbing him by his big forearm, he calmly said, "Don't worry, son. I'll be all right." It was the last Batman action Harold would be able to perform. He died on the way to the hospital. As fortunes or misfortunes would have it, Uncle Phil died of a heart attack also, two months after Harold.

For Rose, it was a devastating one-two knockout punch from life, strike three if you counted Barry's untimely death. After losing her faithful, life-partner husband and her much beloved brother within two months, and her "other" son two years before, she had all but given up on life. She and Harold had been a matched set, and Uncle Phil had looked after her since she was a baby. He had been a loving big brother. Rose couldn't have hidden the smile if she'd tried, every time she'd hear him passing on his wisdom to the boys, beginning with, "I gonna tella you somp-a-ting." She had always put her hands on her hips, shook her pretty head, and made a *tsk-tsk-tsk* sound with her tongue on the roof of her mouth as she smiled at her brother's old-country wisdom. Rose loved so strongly that with Harold, Uncle Phil, and Barry leaving the earth, she too vacated ... mentally. Phil, Paul, Amy, and all the grandkids helped all they could. But now, all Rose wanted to do was go to Mass, light candles, say novenas, hang on to her rosary, and mourn.

With Harold's, Uncle Phil's, and Barry's deaths so close together, Phil was sure death was by far hardest on the living. He remembered when Barry had lost his father in the early eighties. At the time, Barry had told Phil, who couldn't totally identify until it happened to him, "Phil, the worst part of living is losing those you love. The world is never the same. It is literally a *different* world ... not as bright as before." To Phil, the world *did* presently look quite gray. He had never been able to clear his mind of the bloody scene of Barry's blown-out head in his hands. Death *was* horrible for those who remained alive.

Now Ralph Dunne shared the same fate as Harold, Uncle Phil, and Barry. And his family would have to learn to cope. Is that what life was when we got older: a systematic sequence of losing one's family and friends, and then merely enduring the time before our own deaths, coping after a fashion? It looked that way. Phil now had twenty-five years at the railroad. What had this last twenty-five years meant? Nothing? He thought about the happier days with Carla, the undisputed love of his life, and the kids, the wonderful kids she had given him. His wonderful father, uncle, and his lifelong friend were still part of the mix at the time. It was unstated security, an Eden of happiness, not fit for entry by any foul spirit. It had been wonderful. Now, slowly, and painfully, it was all unraveling, *disappearing.*

Fran was spending her remaining days in Sunshine Suites, a local old folks' home, with no one to come see her, ever. Susan was no longer interested in Fran because Fran's money was all used up ... by Susan. And with Barry's death, the Sinister Sisterhood had no more reason to propagate any further the deliciously malevolent intent of life destruction it once created and finally fulfilled. So Susan, who also underwent a strange life personality change, simply didn't care about Fran anymore. Why would she? All Fran was, minus the money, was the mother of her hated ex-husband. Erin and Graham never thought of visiting Fran, holding her responsible for their father's death.

White had died of liver failure years before, and with him went his strange, manipulative control over Fran. With him gone, Fran was able to focus a bit with a somewhat clearer mind, which was definitely detrimental. She now cried every day, sometimes to the point of hysteria, for which she was thankfully prescribed a high dosage of Valium by a mobile psychiatrist, an "auto-shrink," who monitored the Sunshine Suites inhabitants and other assisted-care facilities. The reason for Fran's incessant crying was that Rose's hope/curse became reality. Fran thought about nothing but Barry the entire time she was awake. She would have dreams where he would be alive, and then awaken to the reality of his death. She would think of when he was an exceptionally intelligent, happy little toddler. She imagined his smile and laughter as a little guy, and the way he tried to pronounce words, like saying "pugs" for "figs" in California. How she enjoyed watching Barry increase in his substantial learning abilities, and how gentle and vulnerable he was. Then reality would strike like a medieval mace, and she would realize she had pulled the trigger on her own son. And this day-in, day-out awareness lasted years. What life Barry *did* have, away from the railroad, Fran had successfully demolished. She took his kids, she took his wife, she took his life. Her life was now one long, endless, hideous horror show rerun. With White's evil, Manson-esque hold on Fran, she had been quite comfortable with her unwavering and illogical hatred for Barry. But with White dead, she was subjected daily to her own loneliness, with plenty of time for reflection. And now she genuinely hated herself for her psychotic treatment of her only child every second of every day. Now *she* wished she would die.

Rose could never bring herself to call Fran after Barry's death, because Barry had been like her own son. She held Fran responsible for killing "her" son. Phil and Paul held her responsible for killing "their" brother. Fran's pain was immeasurable. If Barry had been around, he'd have hated to see it. There were three reasons Fran's remorsefulness was so severe: One, she believed she had actually killed her own son, one of the most heinous crimes that could ever be committed; two, she could never bring Barry back, because it was too late; and three, a monstrous fear had settled within her flesh like leprosy. It dawned on her between Valiums that we were all God's children, and that God, very probably, will treat us the way we have treated our own children. After all, wasn't

He the author of the Golden Rule and the idea of sowing and reaping? Didn't He say our children are gifts from Him? Fran was feeling the incalculable pain and confusion she had forced her own son to feel. Odd, how that works out. She would die an old, nasty, miserable, neurotic, sometimes-suicidal mess, with nothing to show for her life but a dead son, and nothing to take to the grave but regret.

Phil had wondered often if Barry had made it to heaven, thereby allowing him to see Barry again, since that's where Phil planned on residing for eternity. He knew he would see his father and his uncle Phil there. Barry was as good a person as Phil had ever known, as close to Christ-like as Phil had ever seen another human. Yet taking one's own life was considered a no-no in the Catholic Church ... actually a no-no in any church congregation. But the Catholics were more severe about it. Phil even remembered a discussion Harold and Rose had had about someone in the parish who had committed suicide when Phil was a young boy. Phil seemed to remember the deceased was not buried in the same cemetery with the rest of the deceased parishioners, because he had committed suicide.

"Why isn't he good enough to be buried with the rest?" he recollected Harold as saying.

"Because he's-a notta supposed to-a make it to-a heaven-a, Hal," Rose said matter-of-factly, "unless-a he received-a absolution, and he didn't, evidently."

"Well, you know more about these things than I do, honey, but I thought the only thing that would keep you out of heaven was blaspheming the Holy Spirit."

"How much-a more blas-a-phemous-a can-a you getta, if you take away the dwelling-a place-a of-a the Holy Spirit, the human-a body?" Rose had reasoned.

That conversation had pretty much kept suicide far from Phil's mind all his life, no matter how tough things got. He wasn't sure if Rose was right or not. He'd heard of some awfully wonderful, caring people, just like Barry, who'd pulled their own plugs. He just had to feel that God is a loving God of second chances. Although Phil never had been suicidal, he loved the Lord enough, and trusted the Lord enough, to know that the scripture that said, "To be absent from the body is to be present with the Lord" was sounding quite good to him now. Life just wasn't the same without Carla and the kids as a family, Harold as his strong, stable father, Uncle Phil as his godfather and lifelong mentor, and Barry as his lifelong buddy. He *was,* however, aware that his blessed children still needed him, as did his mother, especially now. And he knew how important his existence was to his brother, and his terrific nieces and nephews. He would have to be strong.

Phil really hated good-byes. To him, if there was to be a continuing relationship, good-bye was unnecessary. His service buddies misinterpreted it when Phil didn't show up for farewell parties or didn't shake hands and wish them well. They didn't understand. They thought he didn't care. They didn't know the severe separation anxiety Phil was feeling inside. His approach was to just not deal with the personal loss by ignoring it. When it became time to part with service buddies, Phil always managed a quick exit. He sometimes even subconsciously dynamited the friendship ahead of time, because he knew the stable, familiar environment provided by the friend would soon be over. Phil hated endings, especially the ultimate kind. One minute, someone is positively impacting your life ... the next, never again. And death was the ultimate separation, at least temporarily, in this third dimension.

Then it occurred from nowhere, suddenly and hopefully to Phil, that *he* was "Uncle Phil" for Rosalinda, Erin, Graham, Jason, Megan, Roman, and Alison. What a great responsibility, Phil thought pensively and positively. The baton is passed, but will I have the wisdom to pass on that *my* uncle Phil had? And will they listen as Paul, Barry, and I did? Uncle Phil had truly "godfathered" him literally, till the day he died, and now Phil would do the same for his nieces and nephews. Then Phil realized Uncle Phil had experienced the losses of family and friends over the years, and had dealt with it. We all had to. As the Falstaff beer commercial of the seventies said, "We're all in this together." Life is always transitional. Then Phil discovered the gem: He thought, Maybe I can do something for God with whatever life I have left. Counseling the kids in a godly manner is probably doing something for God, for starters. Life began to provide some meaning for Phil again as he regained his spiritual focus. It usually does when we think about God or others.

And then Phil's mood soared as he realized, vividly, that he had already discovered the "best of the best" of realities: not only would he see all of his deceased loved ones again, but he would be with them forever and ever and ever. The temporary grayness of their temporary loss would be light forever with them and the Lord. What a wonderful thought! Then Phil immediately thought of how the *most important* aspect of one's death was whether or not they were Christian. If they were Christian, and their remaining relatives were Christian, then all was very well. As Paul says in 1 Thessalonians 4:13–14, "But I would not have you to be ignorant, brethren, concerning them which are asleep, that ye sorrow not, even as others, which have no hope. For if we believe that Jesus died and rose again, even so them also which sleep in Jesus, will God bring with Him." God looks at death as "sleep." How wonderful! What exceptionally pleasant, comforting words, Phil thought. The only thing separating us from our loved ones in Christ was a few short years. The grayness was already turning to light for Phil.

Phil wondered what it would be like to see his pop, Harold, in heaven, or his Uncle Phil. I know they made it, Phil thought decidedly. They were both such good men, such great role models, often referring to the Lord and the Bible. They are now present with the Lord. And what about Barry? Would he see Barry again? Did Barry make it? Was a lifelong Christian like Barry, deprived of seeing his beloved children, whose remaining parent turned severely against him, to be held accountable for not seeing the big picture? He would have always been with his children in heaven for eternity, no matter what kind of meanness was perpetrated on him on earth. He needed to stay around to ensure Erin and Graham were Christian to allow that to happen. Phil would learn biblically comforting words too late to tell Barry. Psalm 27:10 says, "When my father and my mother forsake me, then the Lord will take me up." And one cannot have a better parent than the Lord. He definitely trumps your birth parents, good or bad. Barry needed to look at the spiritual, rather than the physical, like Dr. Stanley's first of five steps in dealing with a problem. Barry had constantly looked at the problem until it finally took him out. He didn't look to the Lord. When Phil read Psalm 27:10, he wished he could have told Barry while he was still breathing. Then again, Barry had not been receptive for years. Still, Phil hoped he would see Barry again in heaven. What would it be like there?

As Phil pondered his memories, and life in general, he wondered how someone as lost, depraved, and devil-accommodating as Amy could now be an absolute angel. She definitely was the modern version of Mary Magdalene. Conversely, he wondered how women as wonderful and caring as Fran and Susan could metamorphose into such demons. He wondered how his brother could have been such a maniac, and was now singing in the choir. Phil's pondering didn't take long. He knew it wasn't luck or the lack thereof. It was God or the lack thereof. The Holy Spirit now thrived within Paul and Amy Barnes.

And Phil also remembered Chance Armstrong's philosophy. He'd had a conversation with Paul about it once. Paul had said to Phil, "You know, Philsy, maybe Armstrong had something with his 'Treat a whore like a queen and a queen like a whore.' Look at you and Barry. You both treated your wives very well, like queens, and they both disrespected you and left you."

"But you treated Amy very well too," Phil quickly responded, "and look how well that turned out."

"Think about it, Phil," Paul quietly replied.

Carla and Susan would both be divorced again, Carla in four years and Susan in three. Carla would never again marry and would become close with Phil again, with both of them mutually desirous of a good life for their kids and grandkids. In their hearts, both Carla and Phil knew it was the life situation that had separated them in the first place. And soon after being married to Avery, Carla had quickly learned he was not the man Phil was. But Susan would drift through a series of men, disgusting Erin and Graham. All these men naturally hated Erin and Graham, which didn't bother Susan a bit as long as she was "getting off" once in a while, not unlike her insane ex-mother-in-law. Her countenance, too, had degenerated from one of peaceful beauty when first married to Barry to her current image of an old, dried-up, smoking snake.

Phil imagined his and his loved ones' lives of ups and downs, like Groove's song, as one long railroad turn that never had a return trip. He remembered his uncle Phil saying, "Phillip, c'mere. I gonna tella you sompa-ting: it's-a long-a road-a, that-a has-a no turns." Phil reflected on his twenty-five-year railroad career: the thousands of times he worked that were never the same, the slow orders, the sidings, the derailments, the work in all kinds of weather, the endless days and nights, the odd hours, and a bumper sticker he'd seen while in New York City, "We're all here, because we're not all there." Phil thought about the railroad exactly the same way. All the time he wanted to be with Carla, Angela, and Margo, he was "here," at the railroad. He wasn't "there" with them. And Phil was all too aware of the double meaning of the bumper sticker, referring to one's mental state.

Phil thought back on his perfect, whirlwind high school years and all that had transpired since. How simple life was then ... with tons of teasing and laughter. He remembered dating a very pretty girl, Kathy, and how she was more than a little aloof. Back in those days, the front bench seat of the cars of that era was an automatic "date-o-meter." If the girl sat next to you, it was going to be a great night. If she sat in the middle, the night was up for grabs, literally and figuratively. If she sat next to the car door, it was going to be a tough night. This farthest-away body language of the time was also known as "polishing the chrome," given the girl's proximity to the outside chrome of the car door. Kathy was buffing chrome on this night in the front seat with Phil. As luck would have it, Barry and Paul pulled up next to them at a stoplight. Barry was driving and pulled out a handkerchief, laughing, and waved it at Phil. Phil couldn't help but laugh also. Then the reality hit quickly that he could no longer discuss good times with Barry.

In speed-of-light imagery, Phil imagined his life as comparable *to* the railroad, always moving, changing. He saw it as a lengthy series of maximum authorized speeds and a few, but still unfortunate, derailments. The max speeds were fulfillment of life, together with his family and friends, and the quickness of life ... progressing smoothly, satisfyingly, in an "all is well" idyllic progression. During these times, life passed hellishly fast, with literal decades zipping by. The derailments were definitely the deaths of those he loved and his divorce from Carla, and anything that altered his life negatively. Like derailments, everyone knew deaths had to happen sometime, but also like derailments, it was always a shock when they occurred. Derailments stop trains, but only temporarily. Death stops humans, but only dimensionally. Life goes on eternally.

Phil guessed a huge part of life could be summed up by the inherent desire to feel good. All behavior could be lumped into achieving that end, from crying about a wet diaper, to sleeping, to eating, to sex, to happy hour, to church, to security, and so on. Even work was geared toward feeling good about a nice dwelling, a full belly, and a secure future. People were famous because they caused feel-good sensory feelings for others, through acting, sports, music, or comedy. After thirty-plus years of observing human endeavor, including his own, Phil saw feeling good as the motivating factor for everything. The bad rail occurred sometimes in the journey. Phil witnessed that if immediate "feel-good" was desired, the percentages were poor, like gambling versus a nest egg, or happy hour versus exercising, or sleeping in versus church, or a one-night stand versus waiting for a fine wife for life. He had heard many fine preachers point out that if the reward of feeling good was sought immediately, the devil was usually in the details. If the reward was a result of long-term planning and frugality, the "feel-good" was extremely substantial, and God was usually in the details. Phil understood, but he hated to watch some of the journeys taken by his fellow railroaders. Instant gratification was usually the norm. "I want 'feel-good' and I want it now!" That only worked functionally well with dinner, like Paunch Phillips's fried chicken and beer ... or getting rid of it later. And even too much of food feel-good could kill you in the long term.

Looking back, Phil hoped his life would represent that he had been able to positively affect the lives of those he'd known in some way. Whether it was a humorous comment or an understanding ear or just caring for these folks, he hoped he'd made a positive impact. He hoped he had provided "feel-good" to many others over the years of his life. No one gets outta here without some regrets, Phil thought. But the fewer, the better. Maybe that was the secret to success. It certainly wasn't the inane and indulgent, "He who dies with the most toys, wins." How about, "He who dies with the least regrets, wins." And *definitely*, "He who dies in the Lord, wins."

The rule book for life, well, that was easy: God's Word, the Bible. God gave us the proper running orders. We just needed to follow His track warrants to be safe ... much easier said than done. Rebelling against them as we all do meant derailments and death. Following them meant ribbon rail rides and life. No guarantees, though, either way. It truly does rain on the just and the unjust. The constant parade of different trains and different jobs structured the lives of the railroaders.

And the railroaders, themselves ... well, they *were* life. Railroaders constantly progressed through their own lives, with each other. Most railroaders spent much more time at the railroad than with their families. Like it or not, the railroad *was* their family. Their home families were precious, and why they worked, but the railroad *was* life. The rails were life itself, a wonderful cross section of human endeavor. Watching and working with them for years was like having different cable channels to watch over a lifetime. It was a lifelong reality show. They were all individually, exceptionally unique, from the wisdom of Alex Hollander, to the simplistic insights of Jethro. Phil realized how much he cared about all the railroaders he knew, and how much their lives meant to him. After working thousands of jobs with his fellow railroaders, there were thousands of incidents and stories. After all the years of working together, their lives intertwined like bittersweet vines. And as long as they were breathing, the railroaders perpetuated these great stories.

And the literal rails, the steel ribbons, what at one time equaled two million miles of track, and now was less than 140,000 ... well, Phil could imagine they represented the rails of heaven and hell. And all the railroaders spent their time exactly in between the rails while performing designated train operations from a locomotive or caboose. But while on the ground, they were *never* to be caught in between the rails, like Ralph Dunne. We are all in between the rails, Phil thought pensively, in any endeavor we may face. At any given moment, we were offered the keys of heaven or hell, in any situation. Phil had watched that occur, noting all the exemplary *and* bizarre behaviors of his family, friends, and people in general over the years. We could be Christ-like or devil-like. There was always a choice. When the temptation train came steaming down the rails, we better be ready to jump to the "right" side and not be caught between the rails, gorging ourselves in ungodly pleasures until it's too late, like so many Quindaro yard rats.

Phil felt very strongly that it could easily have been him who had ended Ralph Dunne's life. Even though Mel Landers hadn't really done anything incorrectly, he was still at the controls when Ralph died. Mel had experienced every engineer's worst nightmare. Phil knew he could still get a pretty good retirement if he left the railroad now, rather than wait another five years. It wouldn't be as much, but he felt he had to leave *now*. He thought he'd give Trainmaster Simon more than just a witness statement when he finally tied up for the night. It had been a good living … a very good living.

The Peggy Lee song "Is That All There Is?" crossed his mind. But immediately, Phil thought about eternity in paradise, and he knew the answer to that song's rhetorical question: "No." He knew it was impossible to be able to understand the incredible beauty, peace, and happiness that awaited us in heaven if we chose Jesus, realizing the Lamb's blood was for us all. All we had to do was claim it. He knew our five senses and our pitiful logic were not enough, and never would be, to properly conceive of the delights of heaven. It *was* purely and simply, a faith trip. But meanwhile, Phil knew he would have to occupy the precarious position we all occupied while on earth. He would, until he stopped breathing, be faced with choices … choices of pro-Christ or anti-Christ. What would Jesus do? Phil's youngest, Margo, had given him a WWJD bracelet when she was a child, explaining to her dad what the letters meant. Phil prized it and still had it.

Phil thought if people would just look around at the world, they would see much evidence of the Lord's plan. Why was there an animal in all climates inhabited by humans that was just perfect for assisting the humans in their endeavors? The horse, the perfect animal for a human rider, couldn't have been designed for anything else. The form and weight distribution is too perfect. Horses helped humans by the billions explore, conquer, and settle many new lands, and assisted in farming and building. The camel in the arid desert regions just happens to not need water for a long time, and is perfect for carrying a human. The elephants in India and Africa, the sled dogs in the Far North, not to mention all the food animals and plants provided for humans, in all the areas of the world they inhabit. All this … just chance? And what about all the wonderful pets? It was just an accident that we love them, right? And why do we love the looks of plants? Because we're dominant? How 'bout because a Supreme Creator created this world for us. *Everything* is for us.

What "told" a gecko lizard to look like the bark of a tree so it wouldn't be eaten? What "made" a South American orchid plant grow flowers that look like a female wasp, so that when the male wasp of the species attempts to mate with the flower, the orchid is pollinated? It is the same intelligence we use when we decide, "It's a little chilly today. I think I'll wear a jacket." It took us a few seconds to make the decision. It took the gecko and the orchid a few million years. But what is time to God? Both are evidences of intelligence. Both are problem solving. One type is internal. One type is external.

Why are butterflies beautiful to us? We don't eat them. Why are sunsets, sunrises, fall foliage, the night sky, birds, and scenery beautiful to us? Why are we made to enjoy the beauty of the world? Why are snowflakes uniquely six-sided, and intricately perfect, and why do we have the ability to acknowledge this? Why does honeysuckle smell good? It just happened like that? Yeah, right. The examples of God's love for us are endless.

One time Ned Lingle, who was so on fire for the Lord ever since returning safely from Vietnam, had discussed with Phil, Paul, and Barry how there were obvious lessons in nature. Ned had told them of the many death/rebirth occurrences he had noticed … always new beginnings. "First, there is the obvious: day and night. Everything goes to sleep and begins again the next day. Then there are the seasons: summer, fall, winter, and spring. Trees go from lush and beautiful, to dazzling in the fall, to gray and drab, only to emerge again with beautiful shade-giving leaves after being reborn in the springtime. Storm clouds gather, turning from gray to charcoal to black and sometimes even dark green, wreak havoc, and then the day returns to beauty, peace, and calm, sometimes with a beautiful rainbow."

Ned had further told them all that he thought death was like a metamorphosis: "Caterpillars devour, consume, devour, just like we do, and then they 'sleep,' just like the Bible says we do, when we refer to it as 'dying.' Butterflies, after sleeping, awake as these beautiful, symmetrical, peaceful, benign, perfect wonders, just as we will be." Ned had once again made sense.

Everyone loved Ned because he was not pretentious, like some preachers who enjoyed insinuating they had never sinned. The Bible says, "Such were some of you." Ned, even after he'd become a very devout man of God, used to say, "When I was a young man, I spent all my money on booze and women, and wasted the rest." No pretenses there, uh-uh.

And Phil knew the secret to life: it was the Parable of the Talents, Matthew 25:14–30, the King James version:

For the Kingdom of Heaven is as a man traveling into a far country, who called his own servants, and delivered unto them, his goods. And unto one, he gave five talents, to another, two, and to another, one; to everyman according to his several ability; and straightway, took his journey. Then, he that had received the five talents, went, and traded with the same, and made them other five talents. And likewise, he that had received two, he also gained other two. But he that received one, went and digged in the earth, and hid his lord's money.

After a long period of time, the lord of those servants cometh, and reckoneth with them. And so he that had received five talents, came and brought other five talents, saying "Lord, thou deliveredst unto me five talents; Behold, I have gained beside them, five talents more."

His lord said unto him, "Well done, thou good, and faithful servant: Thou hast been faithful over a few things. I will make thee ruler over many things: Enter thou into the joy of the Lord."

He also, that had received two talents came, and said, "Lord, thou deliveredst unto me two talents; Behold, I have gained two other talents beside them."

His lord said unto him, "Well done, good and faithful servant. Thou hast been faithful over a few things. I will make thee ruler over many things: Enter thou into the joy of the Lord.

Then, he which had received the one talent came, and said, "Lord, I knew thee that thou art a hard man, reaping where thou hast not sown, and gathering where thou hast not strawed: And, I was afraid, and went and hid thy talent in the earth: Lo, there thou hast that is thine."

His Lord answered, and said unto him, "Thou wicked and slothful servant. Thou knewest that I reap where I sowed not, and gather where I have not strawed. Thou oughtest therefore to have put my money to the exchangers, and then at my coming, I should have received mine own, with usury. Take, therefore, the talent from him, and give it unto him which hath ten talents.

For unto everyone that hath, shall be given, and he shall have abundance, but from him that hath not, shall be taken away, even that which he hath. And cast ye the unprofitable servant into outer darkness. There shall be weeping and gnashing of teeth."

We are *charged* to share the Gospel of Christ. If we don't, it's "outer darkness" time. It didn't sound too good to Phil ... "a weeping and gnashing of teeth." Phil feared nothing on the earth, not man, not beast. He did fear for the health of his bambinos and *familia*. But he feared the Lord, greatly. He knew that no matter what cards were dealt him, or anyone else, that we were supposed to share our love of the Lord and the joys of the Lord, the promise of heaven, and the sacrifice and blood of Jesus, with as many as we could. Why would we want others to go to hell? It's forever. Given the choice, and we are, Phil desperately wanted to spend eternity in heaven and help others to do the same. The things of this world were just temporal, both the beauty and the horror. Mortal life is also temporal. There will be the deaths of those we love, and our own some day. But heaven is eternal. That's the awesome Great News! And all the pain and agony and suffering is worth it. It's just for a season.

When Ned Lingle was in Vietnam, he received a letter from his fiancée telling him she was no longer in love with him and was going to marry someone else. Ned had taped her picture inside his helmet, so she could "be with him" until he returned. He would look at it dozens of times daily and smile, hoping God would keep him alive and in one piece for her. It was what kept him going. The letter broke his heart and spirit. All he'd thought about for months was returning to her arms. Two days later his two best friends were sniped while on patrol. One was killed immediately, and the other died within hours, long enough for Ned to speak to him. The soldier had told Ned how much he'd enjoyed meeting him and how inspirational he was. When his buddy died, Ned walked away from all the other soldiers. He began to whimper, which led to outright uncontrollable crying. He just cried and cried, and finally, looking upward, screamed out to God, "Why does it have to be like this?"

Ned received an answer. It wasn't a voice, as we hear it. It wasn't like an imagined or telepathic voice. But it was a stated, *knowing* voice that definitely and clearly said, "It's like a woman in travail of birth." Ned knew immediately the significance of the statement. There is pain and suffering in conception, but the child is *so* worth it. We experience pain and suffering here, but when we get *there*, it is *so* worth it. It was then that Ned got down on his knees, prayed, and vowed to serve the Lord the rest of his days.

The Reverend Billy Graham was once asked by an obviously unbelieving, famous, high-salaried female news correspondent what he hoped his Lord would say to him when they finally met. The Reverend Graham didn't even hesitate. He said immediately, "I hope He says, 'Well done, thou good and faithful servant,' just as in the Parable of the Talents." Amen. Dr. Graham and many other wonderful pastors and evangelists on the scene today, inspired by our God, have much and have given much. We all have that wonderful opportunity, each in our own individually unique ways, to glorify God and share with others the Gospel of Christ.

Phil remembered as a freshman at the University of Missouri, the geology professor who used the Empire State Building in an analogy, since at the time it was the tallest building in the world. He said, "If you let the Empire State Building represent geologic time, then putting a razor blade on top of it would represent recorded history." In other words, six thousand years of recorded history was represented as the thickness of a "razor blade of time," compared with the five billion years estimated time the earth had been around, represented by the height of the Empire State Building. Phil had thought then, And our minuscule life spans on earth are only a minute part of that razor blade thickness ... maybe seventy, eighty years at the most, of those six thousand years. The Bible says our lives here on earth are as a vapor. Phil had decided right then that he wanted to be around as long as that Empire State Building would be, stacked end to end with an infinitesimal amount of others just like it, going vertically out of sight, skyward, and continuing forever. Imagine living for more than billions and billions of years ... in heaven, for eternity ... never dying!

Life is not the opposite of death. Birth is the opposite of death. Life goes on forever. Thermodynamic laws would tell you that. We're matter and energy. We cannot be created or destroyed. We're just going to change form. The body is "ashes to ashes, dust to dust." But the energy that is "us" is *going somewhere, forever.* We have a choice where we want to spend somewhere forever. To Phil, it wasn't too tough a decision.

Phil had seen many cussing, nasty, dirty, adulterous railroaders find the Lord over the years. It was "beautiful to watch," as one sportscaster used to say. If Phil had one wish, he would wish for all the members of his family, his friends, and especially, all the railroaders he'd ever known, to accept Jesus and thereby accept paradise in heaven for eternity. Phil knew that after what they'd put up with all their lives, they definitely deserved it. Accept the gift, that's all. It's that simple. You don't have to dance for it, although you'll want to. You don't have to sing for it, although you'll want to. You can't work for it, although you'll want to. It's free for the taking.

But Phil knew for the time being that until our Lord called, it would be constant spiritual warfare. And he knew he would cherish forever the good people and things God had put in his life, though they were temporal, like everything in this present world. Entropy and time were sure bets. He knew also, fortunately, that the bad things, too, were temporal. And he knew that, until Jesus finally came, we *all* would be … In Between the Rails.